Waltz of Stars and Sea

Short Story Collection

Elizabeth S. Friedman

Print ISBN: 979-8993688107
E-Book ISBN: 979-8993688114

First Printing, 2025.

Table of Contents

3

Table of Contents

Forward

This is a collection of stories – some familiar, some strange. In words, there are multitudes of worlds, suspended on our breaths like stars in the sky. Epics and tales ebb and flow, words written in the sands, formulated and swept away by the ocean's crashing waves.

These stories span nearly a decade of tale-weaving, of traveling down the labyrinthine halls of daydreams and exploring the depths of conscience. These stories poke and prod and question, namely seeking out humanity in the darkest of circumstance, in the lines blurred between our own divides, in the hopes and yearnings for a better tomorrow.

Some of these stories are gruff and intricate, interwoven across space and time. There are poetic pieces wherein loneliness, ambition, and frustration clash, where desperation and wist tangle in stark emotion.

This book is raw.

This book is a hand reaching across the expanse of our cybernetically isolated existence, asking if you would like to lose yourself in the vast expanse of the stars and sea for a time.

Let the cosmic music wash over you.

Thank you.

Gulf of Abstraction

2.8.2016

When someone says "Awww!," there is branches to understanding.
There is the coo of adoration, and the whining complaint of a child.
A factor of understanding the point of communication is pose and sound.
Body language and tone are both extremely important, however slight or mild.

In writing, these may be lacking, and all one may do is evoke emotion;
To convey these factors with neither being present.
As of the moment, I will record what is happening around me.
Scratch that, the white noise has lessened.
I, in my scratched grey matter, will take another route.
I will record what is happening within my head, be it uncomfortable or pleasant.

I see a world, a story, a tale, a warning.
I write a few lines in abstraction.
You will abstract from this what you will.

An artist may paint a contrast/abstract painting.
It will be taken in around 1,679,616 times, depending on who views the image,
If they are wearing glasses or with a friend.
So be kind to what you read on each page.

As I'm typing away,
I find that my fingers
lose themselves for days.
That may be taken in

five hundred ways.

To Pick a Color

11.9.2016

I

looked

And

I stared,

Quite blankly,

At the page before me.

Mind churning with concentration,

To answer such an incredibly easy question.

What color am I? it is, and what is the

Solution to my conundrum?

Perhaps I am Blue?

For after all,

'Tis my favorite.

The abyss thrums with calm

And churns with thoughts of mystics.

However, it is also one of the darker types

Of all colors and a sly color associated with the

Heaviness of sadness, despair, hopelessness, and pain.

No, I highly doubt I can possibly be such a shade.

Maybe, I may be the blazing and burning red?

One sees passion and strength inside of it.

Yet it is not available to match me,

For it also roars with anger,

And I attempt calm.

There is also

Bubbly yellow.

With joy and rays

Of happiness penetrating

Everyone's hearts and moods.

But it also hides cowardice and deceit,

I believe honesty is the best policy,

So no, I could never be yellow.

Is green available to me?
With freedom shining,
Flying, streaking,
And singing
From within the
World proclaimed joys,
Harmonies and securities?
But underneath the lush greenery
There is greed and stinginess.
I have spent all my money
On my dearest family,
And loved friends,
Where is the
Miserliness in that?
I begin to think I am orange,
It combines and blends joy and energy.
Nonetheless, it is aggressive, and there are days
Where I feel far too depleted in strength.
(Hello insomnia, my old friend.)
I sigh and wonder,
In almost an air of defeat
Shall my small and insignificant
Luck to allow me to hopefully be and
Reside as the majestic and deep flowed purple?
Powerful and ambitious, with magic
Running through it's very veins?
Unfortunately for myself,
It also pertains all
Other things.
There is, within,
The disgraceful aspects
Ignorance and haughtiness.
I hope I don't project these feelings.
A piece of me is hopeful and
Pleading for me
To be white

It gives
Light to all,
Is innocent and
Hums and pulses with
Purity and unconditional love.
Yet, woe is to me and my entire soul,
I am not so pure, and innocence is
Still something I strive for.
Thus I may not be
Clean white.
Perhaps I match up
With cool and relaxing black
With it's vortex and filling and pressuring
On wounds in need of healing and the exfoliating
Of one's tortured soul, putting together the shattered parts.
Alas, although there are some that find the darkness
Kind, consoling, condolencing and accepting,
The vast majority of this Earth claim
It to be a harbinger of death
And devastation.
Why should
I add me,
Myself, and I, to
The sadly growing list of
Omens, beside the Grimm and
The infamous murder of six crows?
I see grey... as my last hope in this endeavor.
(There's brown, but that color is reserved for the most
Vile and terrible, the primary horrific people.)
Grey is formal, conservative, and it is the
Elite example of sophistication.
Depression finds itself here.
Well, it is dull, bleak,
Boring, and a
Universal symbol of
The loss and draining of hope.

Am I really so drab?
I guess that
I have
No
Color.
But wait!
A flare from a star
Reflects itself from my glasses,
Exploding into a thousand rays of colors,
And it all clicks, I know my color.
I am clear, without a tint,
Yet every single one
Rests within me,
Never one to
Be dominating over
Any of my other
Inner Lights.
I am
Me,
I am
Myself,
And
I am I,

Piranha

2.12.2017

Marlin swayed as he staggered back into the Sanctuary. Earlier, he had some trouble starting up his airide to take him to the horrific planet he called home, finding it difficult to find the keyhole, then remembered that keyholes to start those ships had never been integrated, and found the start up sequence. He drifted into his room – where several bottles danced around his head in the low gravity atmosphere. The Dagon had just made a quick little trip to the wine and spirits outpost to grab another, undrunk bottle, and had come back with an entire pallet of 'libations'. Marlin prided himself as one of the Odiologists who could hold their alcohol, as the way the religious science required. However, unfortunately for himself and everyone around, once he actually started to drink, he had quite the hard time stopping. Stumbling over to the small turntable he took after blowing up a space baron's mansion (he had snatched it as a trophy), he put in a record. He was not exactly sure whether or not the song was one he liked, let alone the name. All that he truthfully knew was that the genre was blues.

He sighed as the music wafted over him. Half known memories drifted softly and some lingered fleetingly; he knew nothing yet everything as his mind flowed. Trembling, he set down the bottle he held in his left hand, having long since drained it. He was only semi aware that he had also changed the record. An upbeat tune began, and he hummed loudly along to it. Soon, Patrice knocked on his door, then entered without him responding.

"Ya know," she promptly began, flopping down on Marlin's bed, at the moment sealed to keep the water in. "Rigel ain't gonna be happy when he finds out you got yourself wasted."

"To be completely honest," Marlin retorted, "I couldn't care less at this point."

"Sounds about Piranha-ish!" she giggled, brushing some hair from her eye. She had given up the other to see into the Odious deep better. At least, that was what she claimed. "Although Kevin might say it sounds, ya know, *fishy*?"

"That was a terrible pun on my kind. You know in the Blot's Maw we are all equal." the 'piranha' grumbled. His hand itched for his gun, but he restrained himself. Barely. He grinned. "Why're ya here, ya fiery chick? Wanna test the waters? Or have a bite of fillet?"

"Well, I, um…" Patrice stuttered as she blushed. Normally, the Odiologists never acted so… so amorously. It was a pleasant, if not jarring, change. "Not tonight…."

"Ah, well ya can't get 'em every time," he chuckled. He took a quick swig, then wiped his mouth with the back of his hand. "Well? Did Tim get any leads on the infamous Bill? Or that traitor, Chilla?"

"No, and Rigel wasn't happy, not at all," the arsonist sighed and shuddered. "He removed all his teeth, one by one, then put them each back."

"Makes sense," Marlin stated. "Well, if you're gonna stay 'ere, ya might as well pick the next song."

She picked a hip hop beat, and gasped, surprised, as Marlin took her by the arm and twirled her around. He energetically danced with her, and she barely managed to keep the pace. When the song hit the final keys, Patrice found that she was beyond breathless and so dizzy the room tilted.

Originally, when Marlin and Chilla first joined Rigel and the Odiologists after a series of unfortunate events, the rather young arsonist thought snidely of him, expecting that he would fail miserably as one of them. Therefore, it was natural that she and the others would be stunned by Marlin's performance in his very first mission. It was a futile quest Rigel had sent him on, a task bound for failure. After all, capturing Bill Oroseira is an achievement few can even dream of. He ended up coming so close, hand outstretched to grasp the billowing grey trench coat, until that traitorous Chilla had shoved Marlin, whisking herself and the elusive inventor to another planetary system.

"Hey, P?" Marlin said, tilting his head and waving a hand in front of her face. "Ya with me?"

"Hmm?" She responded dumbly. He chuckled, she blushed. "Sorry, I got lost in thought."

"Don't worry about it, Patty," Marlin laughed, especially at her startled yet positive reaction to the nickname. "It happens to the best of us."

"Even you?" Patrice questioned teasingly, giving the newer gang member a light nudge. His expression suddenly went… rather dark, angered. "Pir… Piranha? Marlin?"

"Especially me," he murmured, eyes closing for a small instant, before snapping open with a smirk. "But probably not the lovely thoughts that a lady like yourself imagines at night."

She turned red again at the thought. It was nigh impossible to ever catch an Odiologist using Marlin's lexicon, fewer in his style, and even less with his natural charismatic attitude. A snap-snap-tap returned the two to their senses.

"Gotta go," Patrice sighed, "Rigel's coming."

Marlin nodded, grinned, and held out a hand to the young firestarter. Blushing, she took it, and he led her out of the room, just as any gentleman might. Doing a quick calculation, Marlin paused, then decided to escort Patrice all the way to her room. Bowing as she entered her space, he politely waited for her to close her door before smirking and taking another bottle of liquor out of his pocket. He returned to his own room with a hop and swagger in his step, whistling out a half known rhythm. No sooner had he re-entered the doorway, Rigel followed up behind him. Marlin click-winked at the crime boss, causing him to sigh.

"Why're you drunk, Marlin?" he groaned.

"'Cause I wanna be," Marlin replied, nonchalant. "Got a problem with a mafioso being a gangster?"

"No."

"Then what's the problem," Marlin waltzed across the room and grinned. "No harm done, right? Just a fish in his natural habitat."

"Right," Rigel said in response, slow and questioning. "This isn't going to become a habit though. Okay?"

"You got it, boss!" Marlin chirped, tossing the empty bottle into the trash. "I'll be up and running tomorrow and the such."

"You better," Rigel muttered, and drifted out of the room. He paused in the doorway. "We need to catch that William."

"William?"

"Bill."

"Oh." Marlin blinked. His scaley brow furrowed. "Why are we after this guy, anyways? There's millions of other science folk."

"Not your rank. Goodnight."

Rigel left without another word.

As soon as the last sounds from Rigel's footfalls faded, Marlin's happy-go-lucky facade dropped faster than lead in water. His shoulders slumped, his smile vanished, his cheer washed away in the waves. Exhaling heavily, he rose a hand to his forehead and plunked himself down on his bed.

There… there was something the others had not seen on that fateful day, his encounter with the inventor. As he was about to capture him, something caught his eye. It was a subtle detail, and no-one would have really noticed it.

The man had the face of someone he knew, like someone you had met in a dream. The moment he saw that, red sirens went off in his head. Something had been terribly off, something was colossally wrong, something was… missing. But he knew one thing had to be done.

When Chilla shoved him out of the way, he let himself fall – even though he easily could have righted himself. He merely watched them run, essentially saving their lives. On purpose. Chilla had seen that same man in a dream once, certainly, and woke up to it faster than he could process. With a tired groan, Marlin fell back on the bed, closing his eyes, trying to discover why in the universe he had done that.

In a half remembered thought, in a whispering shout, the half-answer half-question came to him with a frowning smile; it meant everything and nothing.

"Maxwell and William."

Perfect Angels

10.21.2018

Mary-Anne bit her lip, gazing at the silhouetted slender figure standing by her window. She marveled in the beautiful form illuminated by a streetlamp and the moon, casting two shadows on her floor, one a soft yellow and the other a graceful pearl. She wondered in awe of the incredible body, the stunning and mind blowing idea of who this was, in her bedroom.

Olivia. The beautiful and breathtaking, in far more ways than one (in her unmatched gorgeousness, in her outstanding singing, in the resplendent way she kissed, in the eroti– maybe… it would be best for the both of them if Mary-Anne didn't relay that information), Olivia Watts.

It was almost funny how they got there.

The at first bitter and hated rival of Mary-Anne's position, then the begrudging but compassionate teacher and eager and sweet apprentice, then a budding friendship and sympathetic bond, and then a brief awkward step between platonic care to intimacy, and now… this bliss. Mary-Anne was Olivia's angel and Olivia was Mary-Anne's, but there was just one problem:

Mary-Anne wasn't perfect.

At least, that's what her mind would tell her, all the time.

She was too short and too fat, too ugly and too promiscuous, too unattractive and too promiscuous, her smile too wide and her smile too small, dressed too expensive wore attire too cheap, and she concluded if everyone could find something wrong with her, she could never be perfect. She had extradited herself from the Auræic Cloud, a self imposed exile – forsaking her roots, leaving her adrift, manifesting a solid form so as to at least pretend to have an anchor. So said her brain, her crowding thoughts. Her work, purifying water, was her life, and she had left her past and family to pursue her compassion, her dreams, and find her own space.

"Aren't you abandoning them?" her mind would ask. Her thoughts pushed on, "Don't you remember who you were?"

She would push those thoughts away with song and noise, filling her days with little comforts. And that would be the end of that. Inside, it hurt, to have the fear of a rocky evening, knowing her flight was both necessary and yet chaining.

But Love, in Mary-Anne's eyes, was only good. That was all love is. Even if she had to remove herself, she still loved.

Mary-Anne loved Olivia and wondered why she loved her back.

Olivia stared out the window, looking up at the moon, the glare of the street lamp catching her eye every so often, but her gaze mostly trained on the satellite. Her mother would tell her in a soft and twinkling voice that Olivia was like that waning orb. Her father would gruffly smile at the sentiment, and roll his eyes before hugging his little family.

Her mother was Japanese, and her father a Dagon. Little Olivia did not know why people would yell the things that made her mother cry and make her father hold her mother tightly; she did not know what people meant when they would point at her and her almond colored, almond shaped eyes on her almond shaped, almond colored face, and tell her parents that she would be taken away. That her mother was not taking care of her properly. Olivia never was taken away. Her parents would never let anyone take her away. She was enrolled in school. There were times she would come home crying from the teasing, but always dried her tears. Her Ha'ha did not need to know she was sad, because she loved her parents. One day her Father had come home early, and she had not yet dried her tears. The dam in her mouth broke; and she told them of her sadness.

They told her she was beautiful, and perfect; and the children who said otherwise were wrong.

She took both statements as truth. She was perfect to those who knew her, and the opposite of perfect to those who did not.

Even with the shield of her parent's soothing words, there were times that what other people would say with calm voices in biting tones would penetrate her heart.

Maybe she did not belong.

Unlike beautiful, silky, pure Mary-Anne.

Why did she even bother with her?

Smooth, pale arms wrapped around her, a face pressing to her back.

"Come back to bed, O-love'ia," Mary-Anne murmured, using a little joke name the pair found amusing at times. Olivia's lips twitched, but fell back into her neutrally melancholic expression. Mary-Anne rubbed Olivia's stomach gently, slipping her hands under her loose tee shirt (one of Mary-Anne's) to softly caress her warm skin. "Come on, Olivia. It's cold without you, and I miss your hair. It's too high for me to reach when it's tied up like that."

"How's this, then?" she smiled, turning to face her and leaning down to kiss the top of Mary-Anne's blonde head. Mary-Anne hummed happily, running one of her hands over the braids tight on Olivia's head. Mary-Anne held her head tenderly, tilting her own back and going on tip toe to catch Olivia's beautiful coral lips. Olivia pulled away sharply, turning back to the window. Mary-Anne retracted her hands slowly, placing one under Olivia's. Her fingers curled around her hand, squeezing gently. "I'm sorry, Mary-Anne, that I'm not as good as I could be."

"What- Olivia!" Mary-Anne's blue eyes were wide and shocked as she tried to process the words. She softly tugged her to sit on the bed so she could see her. Olivia looked at their intertwined fingers and her expression saddened even more, distressing Mary-Anne. Mary-Anne used her free hand to pet the side of Olivia's cheek, the taller and younger leaning into loving stroke after stroke, Mary-Anne's touch that of a fine jewelry expert. "You aren't just *good*, you're right. You are so much more than that. You are amazing. Your eyes are heavenly," she kissed both softly, making her sad look fade slowly, "you are intelligent and clever," her forehead received little kisses, in turn turning her lips upward ever so slightly, "you sing beautifully," her cheeks were bussed gently, her precious smile returning to her priceless lips, "you are gracious and graceful," her nose and chin, earning a soft and lush giggle, "you are perfect. Physical form or not. And I love you."

Mary-Anne's lips never caught Olivia's, nay, for Olivia's caught Mary-Anne's. She caught her in her slender arms, and in the moonlight, darker almond skin was juxtaposed by light peach, their fingers still entwined from Olivia's left arm around Mary-Anne's back, met by Mary-Anne's right coming across her chest. Olivia's free hand ran through short curls of black, Mary-Anne's fondling her hip and side. As her fingers trailed down the succulent haze of Olivia's skin, she was once again reminded of their stark contrast. How perfect Olivia was, and how wrong and blemished *she* was. She tried to remain passionate in their kiss, but found herself sinking once again into doubt. Her thoughts reared against her in a rallying cry of disdain. They swirled and cackled and roared, plunging her into a dark abyss.

20

"Mary-Anne?" Olivia's sweet voice stole her thoughts from hell once again, driving her back to the Heavens with the angel known as Olivia. "I can tell you're not alright.... Do you want to stop?"

"No, Oli, don't stop," she whispered, thankful for her angel. Olivia still stilled. "Olivia, just... never mind."

"I would never leave you," Olivia read her thoughts perfectly, appalled by the mere idea of abandoning the heavenly Mary-Anne. Mary-Anne knew she hated the thought, and it filled her heart. They knew each other inside and out. Perhaps Mary-Anne was being less careful with keeping her Auræions within her confine, which would greatly assist Olivia with sensing those thoughts and feelings. "God, Mary-Anne, why would you ever think I'd do something like that?"

"Because I'm... well, I'm nothing special," she whimpered, hiding her face in the blanket in shame. How many people had she slept with in this bed? Only one, the only one who saw anything in her. It made no sense. She was special and beautiful and kind – too much so for simple Mary-Anne. "Olivia, no one wants me, unless they're completely out of it. I'm not at all attractive."

"Mary-Anne, how can you say that? Say that about *me?*" Olivia asked, stunned. Mary-Anne knew of her insecurities, she dug them up within days of meeting. But Mary-Anne? Kind, smart, sweet Mary-Anne? She was wonderful and perfect. Olivia studied her, watched the way her eyes critically glanced over her own gorgeous body. How could she be ashamed of such beauty? Well, Olivia was going to fix that. "Your hips are that of Aphrodite, your eyes that of Psyche, your awe that of Kisshoutennyo herself. Please, Mary-Anne, know your beauty and your powers in Venus, perfection beyond belief. I love you, Mary-Anne. You'll always be my angel."

"I love you," Mary-Anne choked out, holding back tears, wrapping her arms around Olivia. "I love you, too, so much. But Olivia, you are my angel, and you are perfect. How can we both be perfect if we are both so... so different?"

"I guess we'll have to be perfect for each other," Olivia giggled, her feminine and almost childlike charm sweeter than honey on Mary-Anne's ears. "And be each other's angels."

"I like that," Mary-Anne whispered, allowing herself to be enveloped by the taller while she swathed Olivia. "I like that a lot. But I love you more."

"Mm. Love you, too."

21

Galop Infernal

11.25.2018

"Well gentlemen," I turn to the other time travelers sentenced behind me, "It has been an honor. Truly. We have always wanted to see this sight, and it is as chaotic and glorious as we hoped."

"We're sinking!" a man with an Irish accent screams from somewhere within the vast crowd. "Save yourselves!"

Nods of agreement and murmurs of truth follow my words.

"Someone help us!" a woman shrieks. We pity her, but no more than that. "Help!"

I raise my trombone.

A rattling cry of, "It's cold!"

The others raise their instruments. We will be here to the very end.

With calm words we dissuade the pianist from raising his own, though we all know he can.

"Shall we begin?" the violinist asks me. I ponder a moment and give a slow nod in response. Someone passes their child to another passenger. "What song shall it be, miss?"

"The is only one song that truly fits this occasion," I solemnly regard. I wave to the cellist and violinist, indicating they take position. "Now, allow us to begin... the absolute masterpiece... Jacques Offenbach's... Galop Infernal."

"Jolly good!" the cellist exclaims, and starts playing. "Triangle!"

People are screaming and running around us as our good triangle man hits his small instrument with all his might.

The trumpeter joins in, hitting the upbeat tune.

Someone leaps off the boat.

The trianglist, tired from bashing his instrument, sits atop the piano.

The lifeboats are being filled by women, children, the elderly, and cowards.

I lift my trombone, blowing to initiate the dance of the Can can.

To our amusement, the people before us seem to be panicking in time with the music.

It is almost a petrified rhythm of shouts and cries.

Our pianist bashes his keys with closed eyes and a pleasant grin.

What else can we do?

Our tone drops as the lifeboats are lowered into the water.

The ship tilts significantly, we all are facing out to the water, and with a rending crash, the cruiser snaps in half, in time with our beats.

The water is icy, but not as much as our hearts as we smile and play away.

With a final blow, I signal the final descent – after all, this was capital punishment for time travelers, to perish in the manner they had caused.

We, the musicians, had caused the sinking of a colossal ship many years ago in the future.

And now, we sank to its depths.

Or we would have, had I not been prepared us an escape, a backup time machine hidden within the curve of my trombone.

There are no instruments in the wreckage of the titanic.

There is, however, a bacteria only found in that area, *Halomonas titanicae*, an odd little evolution of a metal eating creature.

One my time had genetically modified to cut down on the mass amounts of useless iron.

It may have clung to my trombone and thus escaped into this time period's world.

Well, accidents happen.

Almond

12.31.2018

Olivia was like a luminous moon nearing its renewal; a tall, slender, and softly glowing beauty. She could be described as gentle, sweet, and willowy with a hint of acidity, just as her namesake; but the problem with the latter was that she was more an almond than anything.

Everything about her was almond like.

Her long ebony hair could be frizzy, but was very tamable. She wore it in a dense braid wrapped around her head.

Her face was almond shaped, as well as colored with the earthy and tender nut. Everything on her face was also almond like, her eyes the same shape, tilted up at the ends, and their color was the succor hazel of the bark, swathed with an overtone of a refreshing and perspicacious green. This had the effect of making those curious gems virescent in the rays of glorious light and ecru in the darkness of night.

Olivia's lips resembled those of blooming blossoms of the budding almond flowers, with the same unique coral shades, contrasting in serene dichotomy with her fawn skin. She sang using those lips – wondrous, surreal, flowing songs. Her voice was seraphic, flowing like the pure ivory of the milk obtained from almonds, and those who heard her believed her voice to reach the heavens and please God where the Lord sat, enthroned.

Her nose was down-turned and without crinkles of disgust, her brow uncreased, a sign of her unending patience. Her hands were uncalloused, smooth, lingering, and thin, with fingers sharing the same traits, like the slim branches of the almond tree. Her arms and legs were just as svelte, graceful and flowing.

Olivia's personality was just as sweet, calm and precocious young woman she was.

Budding, blossoming, growing; all at the same time.

Ice Trip

14.2019

"Hey, Mag!"

Caroline's voice eagerly (and slightly terrifyingly) wavered into Magnolia's office, the sound of it revealed before the woman was fully inside the room, knowing she would be there, and burst within. Magnolia put down the pen she was using to sketch out the ancient sword's engravings onto a paper. The blade expert glanced over Caroline, who grinned as though the thief had successfully robbed a bank.

Her mirth was infectious, and Magnolia felt her lips slowly inch into a smile at her... friend? Companion? Attempted murderer? Girlfriend? Doppelganger? She did not know, so she shrugged it off and smiled at her in any case.

"Hello, Caroline," she greeted with a nod, Caroline nearly bouncing her way over her desk, a (shrunken to size) sweater on, clearly not originally her own, very likely raided from someone else's boudoir. Most likely Magnolia's own. Magnolia rose an eyebrow, leaning back. "You look happy today."

"Not exactly happy, mi reina," Caroline sweetly remarked, Magnolia feeling her smile broaden slightly as she squirmed from the hypocoristic. Caroline bounced on her toes. "I'm just rather excited!"

"For what?" Magnolia questioned, tilting her head, intrigued. Caroline's grin shrank slightly, she becoming nervous. "Caroline?"

"Well, I, um, you see," she began, stumbling over her words and blushing. She reached into her bag, and pulled out two pairs of ice skates. Magnolia squinted at them. "I wanted to know if you'll come skating with me."

"I... I don't know," she answered, shifting in her seat. Caroline looked off to the ground, biting her lip in thought. Magnolia had been out of any sportsmanship practices for a long time, never having the use for once honed skills and letting them fizzle down. She looked back at the woman she suspected to be some odd species of faerie. "I really... I haven't skated in a very long time... I don't really know."

"C'mon, it'll be fun!" Caroline insisted gently, plucking on Magnolia's sleeve carefully. Magnolia still seemed unconvinced. Caroline's eyes lit up, realizing a sly way to encourage the other to go out with her. "It's just like dancing, but on blades!"

"What are you waiting for!?" Magnolia demanded, half joking (mostly serious), taking her out of her office by the wrist, not a tight hold, but a firm one. Caroline beamed – exploiting Magnolia's love of sharp objects had worked. "Let's go!"

Magnolia had overestimated her skills. Not Caroline, no, she spun gracefully, her long limbs swaying like willow branches, lithe and flowing, years of practice allowing her to move with ease. Magnolia, as a museum archivist who had not ice skated in a good decade, give or take a few years, was not focusing as much on performance; rather, she was concentrating on maintaining a semblance of balance.

She sighed, pouting as she watched Caroline spin. The young, spry codebreaker called to her and performed a pattern, making a small leap, Magnolia realizing she was writing something in the ice.

Te amo, followed by a heart.

She stared at it, blushing lightly, her wobbly knees now not just from the skates.

A light laugh nearly sent her crashing to the ground.

"Mi amor, you're shaking!" Caroline softly pointed out, sliding up to her. Magnolia's scarf was wound around her neck; Magnolia only realizing it then that it was even missing. When had Caroline even taken it? Slick fingers. Caroline took her by the hand, using the other on her shoulder to steady her. Magnolia swallowed, trembling on the ice. "You're as unstable as my mental health."

"I'm not shaking!" Magnolia denied, staring at her wobbling feet. "I'm fine, I just need to find my balance!"

"Oh, for that, you just need to relax…" Caroline soothed, slowing her motions more, gently guiding Magnolia in their dance. She exhaled, smiling. "Take it easy."

"I am trying to," she gritted out, gripping Caroline's hand tightly. Caroline chuckled, making a curving circle with her. "I mean it!"

"I didn't say you weren't," she replied, smiling, slipping away and twirling, returning to her hands, and continuing, "You've done this before, right? You just need to recall it…."

They glided over the ice at a smooth and slow pace. Magnolia let herself loosen up, exhaling. Caroline's hand was warm on hers, and she held her up, not tightly, but enough to support her.

26

Caroline's quiet little laugh bubbled over her ears. She blinked, opening eyes she did not even know were closed. Caroline beamed at her, an affectionate glow in her eyes and a soft blush blanketing her cheeks, slightly shielded by indigo lenses.

"See?" Caroline beamed. She looked so nice, like a cinnamon bun with fresh coffee, just the perfect pick me up. Magnolia did not realize how refreshing it was to be with someone who treated her as an equal. She liked it best when Caroline treated her just as she was, not embellished or degraded. Just who she was.

Caroline moved slightly back, giving Magnolia the option to pull away from her and skate on her own. She did not. Caroline laughed, a little louder, making Magnolia grin. She had such a beautiful smile. "You're steady already, there's no need to hold onto me like la gallina!"

"Like a what?" Magnolia asked, blinking. Caroline merely winked. Magnolia looked over Caroline taking in her long features, that giddiness she had, her unsuspecting expression. Magnolia felt her latent desire for the new and unexpected well up. She smirked, yanking Caroline to her, too quick to let her ask what she was doing. "Never mind that now. Caroline, I think I found my footing."

With a burst of speed, she propelled them backwards, Caroline unable to suppress a shriek as they accelerated rapidly. Her eyes widened and she gripped Magnolia like a lifeline, shaken by the suddenness. Magnolia felt herself grin.

"Who's shaky now?" she teased, making a sharp turn. "Hm?"

"I am!" Caroline nearly shouted, "Cause you're gonna kill me!"

"I thought you didn't mind that," she hummed, twisting her way down a crooked path. Caroline gasped as she rose their interlocked hands and spun her, dipping her down even as they continued to move on the ice's slick surface. "Isn't that what you came for?"

"You are going to trip!" Caroline yelped. "Then you're gonna slaughter us both!"

"I won't trip," Magnolia retorted, rolling her eyes. She dashed with her on the ice, too stuck up to say that she actually had lost her balance a long time before, and was not in control of their path, using Caroline as a crutch to hopefully not collapse. She turned them, their velocity long out of her ability to change. "See? We're fine-"

Thunk.

Magnolia's skate had embedded itself in the ice, and they were pitching forward.

The snow falling around them seemed to slow.

Caroline smiled, the smile of one knowing death's swift approach.

Magnolia opened her mouth to speak, but Caroline beat her to the action.

"Don't you dare tell me that you tripped."

"Fine," Magnolia pouted. "I won't tell you."

Thud.

Caroline felt the wind being knocked out of her as Magnolia pushed her onto the ice.

Magnolia actually looked some form of... embarrassed? Apologetic? Dead inside?

Then she noticed the rather compromising position they were in (as though two women dancing would not raise any eyebrows, although one was a renowned researcher), and her expression blackened. Think think say something c'mon-

"I blame society," Magnolia stated, unable to figure out anything more intelligent to say. Caroline pursed her lips, unimpressed.

"Really now?" she asked frankly, sarcastically, eyes half closed in silent reprimand. "The society that gave you so many pretty knives to study?"

"Not really," Magnolia mumbled, glancing off to the side, noting how their hands were still interlocked. She looked back to Caroline, smiling slightly. The funny side of the situation appeared, and Caroline's lips twitched into a grin. Magnolia admitted, "I do like the knives quite a bit. The societal conventions could go away, mostly."

Caroline chuckled, trying to keep down her smile, trying and failing to be taciturn, her attempt adorably young and sweet. She failed to frown as Magnolia grinned.

"What's wrong?" Magnolia questioned. Caroline's smile genuinely reappeared as she shook her head. "Nothing?"

"This is one of the few times I've seen you happy," she answered, blushing. "Really happy. I'm... I'm glad that I could make you smile. It's really... really something else."

Magnolia flushed at the compliment, ducking her head and muttering how it was nothing.

"It's something alright," Caroline crooned, her smile tinged with a slight pride. "My something. Because I still need to perfect my impressions of you."

Their eyes met, and they found that they could not stop laughing.

It was absurd, they were absurd, one of two of one of a kind, a disaster squared, and yet here they were, fallen on the snow from ice skating, a fall one warned of.

Caroline's forehead met Magnolia's, and she had not even realized she had leaned toward her in her muted guffaws. She laughed harder, and Caroline's merriment reverberated and merged with her own, a positive feedback loop.

They both simply laughed until Caroline started coughing, whether from her laughter or from the ice on her back unclear. Nonetheless, Magnolia pulled them both up, eventually getting them to a toasty, warm room with blankets and hot drinks.

They were on the couch, Caroline's back pressed to Magnolia's chest, and they spoke of youth and energy. How both seemed in so little supply for them.

"You make me feel energized, Mag," Caroline admitted to Magnolia. "When I see you, I feel like I could run around the world."

Magnolia wrapped her arms tighter around her, unable to talk, melting in her skin.

"I love you, you know," Caroline whispered. Magnolia flushed, wriggling under her. Caroline smiled. "Mi amor. Mi reina. Mi cariño. Mi preciosa."

Every endearment brought Magnolia further and further to an unknowing bliss, each word a direct, loving blow to her heart, dissolving her.

When she finally managed to fall asleep, Caroline curled up on her chest, wrapping the blanket around them tighter.

"Merci, mon amour," she whispered, kissing her cheek, a soft smirk tweaking her lips as she put emphasis on the pronoun. Magnolia stirred, a smile lifting the corners of her own mouth.

"De nada," she breathed, her arms squeezing lightly.

Caroline smiled, yawned, and fell asleep.

Innuendos

14.2019

John hated watching Salvatore be in a sour mood. The fruit expert (pomologist, he would gently correct) was usually much more invigorated, much sweeter, and very much gayer.

Er, he meant happier. *Totally not ogling the pink tie in his hair at the moment, the pins along his jacket....*

Happier. Yes.

So seeing him upset also lowered John's mood, and horticulturists should be working hard and happy. So he needed to fix the situation so he could continue working properly.

He got up, walking over to Sal, who sat beside a non functional sprinkler system, staring at the empty plot in the greenhouse.

Sal did not notice him. For some reason, that fact greatly bothered him.

John scowled and tapped Sal on the shoulder, making him look up with a mixture of surprise and vexation, the latter shifting to annoyance as he realized who he was.

He could not even ask a frustrated; "What?" when John cut him off.

"Let's talk." he stated darkly, leaning in his face, his own unreadable, a shadow cast over it through red hair streaked with brown, the way the light hit it making it appear a ruddy maroon, like locks of blood. His demand was non negotiable, and there was no escape. Salvatore swallowed roughly and got up, following John to the botanical facility's office. John waited for him to go in, entering behind and locking the door. Sal sat against his desk, obviously waiting for John to berate him or yell at him from the grimacing look on his face. John narrowed his eyes, taking in his defensive posture. Sal stared back sullenly. John's heart gave a sad twang. He grimaced, pinching the bridge of his nose, then spread his hands, palm up, in askance. "What's gotten into you?"

"You haven't," Sal almost snarled, the words tumbling out of his mouth before he even thought them, much less about them. John processed it with the same speed he did, and Sal's eyes widened as John's jaw dropped, both in a sudden shock. "Uh... I... I didn't mea–"

"Can you repeat that?" John requested, raising an eyebrow, uncertain now. Sal stared at him with a faraway fear in his eyes and shook his head slowly. "Seriously? Are you going to say something like that and just leave me on the edge?"

A pause. They both cringed at the same time.

"John, stop," Salvatore almost whined, embarrassed, pushing himself off the edge of the desk. John shook his head – more incredulous than anything, but Sal took it as a refusal. "Look, I'll get on my knees and apologize."

John inhaled for a long moment, and Sal, realizing his error, flushed rapidly.

"Let me get this straight," John exhaled, and then froze, eye twitching at his wording. Sal shifted before him, running his hand along his pinned sleeve – where a good few of those pins were of the certainly not straight variety. Had he accidentally offended him? John, growing evermore frustrated, stamped his foot. "Why are you so hard!?"

"I-I'm not!" Sal protested, burning up. John, his own cheeks now ablaze, slapped his forehead. Sal gave a nervous little giggle. "Was... was that another slip up?"

"I meant to say hard to deal with!" John replied through gritted teeth. "But this appears to not be working so well. Do you have any other position ideas for us?"

"Plenty- I mean. Oh, hell," Salvatore hissed, tail flicking as he tugged on his collar, and watched John drop his head into his hands and scream. "Look, let's ignore this for now. Something else might pop up, you know. Um. Uh. As in we have many plants?"

"You're not making this any better," John growled, Sal covering his flustered face with a hand. "We're talking about this now, stop blowing me off."

"I'm starting to think you're doing this on purpose," Sal groaned. John looked like he was about to murder someone, probably the man in the mirror. "About this... I don't want to thrust me onto you."

Sal paused, closed his eyes, and cried a moment through fits of giggles. Damn English. Damn the stupid language to hell.

"Okay, Sal," John steepled his fingers, holding them to his lips. "if the next thing that comes out of your mouth sounds sexual, I'm pounding you into the ground, and then burying myself there too."

"John!"

John covered his eyes with his arm, and Sal attempted to bolt, but his embarrassed laughter gave him away.

"Oh, no you don't!" John caught him around the waist before he made it to the door, pulling him flush, shoving him to the wall. "I've not finished with you!"

A sobbing laugh ripped out of Sal. John stepped back sharply, blushing madly.

"This situation..." Sal struggled to find the right word. "Sucks."

"Our old boss said you suck more," John grumbled, and felt his shoulders slump as he let part of himself die. Sal felt the gates of hell open beneath him. "Sorry. Look, yes, we can talk about this some other time. Are you free tonight?"

Sal only blinked at him, gesturing between them with flabbergasted emotion.

"Are you really going to bring up that asshole?" Sal asked, "Really? Now? As if the old man wasn't trying to get into everyone's pants?"

"Yeah, well he picked yours as his favorite," John snapped pack. "And was very vocal about it!"

Salvatore looked like he was going to put fertilizer in John's coffee.

"God *damn* it," John added not two seconds later, rubbing his face under his glasses. Sal rolled his eyes, mocking him under his breath, and John grimaced. "Look, I'm sorry. You don't need to get cocky about it!"

"John, stop jerking me around!" Sal retorted, both realizing each other's statements and than their own. Salvatore weakly punched the wall, letting his hand slide down it. He was mildly surprised it did not leave a burn mark. He exhaled, leaning his head back. "John, as much as I-"

He cut himself off, feeling all his body on fire from embarrassment and desire. The desire for dignity, to be precise. He did not want to make another Freudian slip.

"Ugh," John pinched the bridge of his nose, pushing up his glasses. His next words felt like a triple gut punch to the both of them, one after the other. "Just spit it out! Actually, don't! Keep that in your mouth!"

Sal sank to the floor, rocking himself as he whimpered, unable to stop laughing. John looked like he wanted to smack himself into the ocean.

"Are we done digging our own graves now?" Salvatore questioned, pulling himself off the floor, staggering to his feet. John shook his head, and made gestures, Sal reading them aloud. Pointing at himself: "You…"; a grabbing gesture: "want…"; two fingers held up: "To…"; pointing at a tree: "Um… let's get back to that one?"; pointing at Sal: "Me. What? What is that suppo–" John stormed over, taking Sal by the hand and taking him out to the tree, pointing at it again. "Oh, that's *phoenix dactylifera*, also known as the date palm."

John stared at him.

"Date…" Sal hummed, then reconstructed the sentence once more in his head. His expression swiftly morphed into one of sweet surprise. "Oh! OH! Are you serious?"

"Yeah, apparently non verbal is better than spoken," John said bluntly. Sal giggled once again. "Yes, I want to! Not now, of course, but… yes. Maybe tonight?"

"Where is this coming from?" Sal asked plainly, skeptical. He shuddered. "Okay. This is not an ideal time or place or situation to admit this, but… I love you. A whole lot. And if you'll have me… it would be a dream come true."

"Oh, yes," John laughed, making his way over to him, shoving him gently against the tree, smirking as he pressed him to the bark. Sal felt fire burst in his chest, spreading to the whole of him. John rose an eyebrow. "May I? Take you out tonight?"

Sal hugged him tightly, excited beyond measure.

"Just don't say anything," John murmured, moving back and gripping his lapels with a twinkle in his eye, teasing. "Except 'yes'."

"Yes."

Not Happy

2.8.2019

Happiness is quite full of a wonder,
"What there is to question?" you may ask one,
It is such a strange thing to ponder,
Here is a twisting answer to make it done.

Despite bitterness in poor eloquence,
Jollity is not required,
Words of joy are your defense,
If a happy outcome is desired.

To be joyous is something fun and sweet,
But there are days you cannot grin at all,
Melancholy forces a quick retreat,
Do not mind it;
smile though it is droll.

Fake it 'til you make it is what is said,
Keep your chin up and look ahead.

Skate Mistake

5.26.2019

"Hey, Maggie," Caroline said out of the blue one day, her eyes dreamy and distant, clearly reminiscing on a past event. Maybe a successful smithing or two. Magnolia blinked, tightening her hold on the other's hand. "Let's do that again."

"What?"

"Hm?"

"You said we should do something again," Magnolia clarified. Caroline paused a moment and let herself a small smile, indulgent. "What were you thinking about?"

"Dancing on knives," Caroline chuckled, leaning her head on Magnolia's shoulder. A smile slowly crept over the other's face, and soon they both had matching soft grins. "You know."

"Mm." Magnolia thought about it a moment, and then smiled a bit wider. "Why not?"

"I didn't…" Caroline stopped herself, wondering why in the world she was about to argue with her own suggestion, and hid her face in the crook of Magnolia's neck to hide the blush creeping up her cheeks. "If you want to…."

"Yeah," Magnolia hummed, wrapping her free arm around Caroline's shoulders. "I think it's a fun idea. Let's go do that again."

In Caroline's yard, though the upcoming summer had melted all the snow and ice, the strange woman easily froze over the same pond they had been on before, ice streaming where she walked with a strange substance pouring from a bag, covering the radius and the frost flowing up from the perimeter to meet her. Then, donning her skates as she walked, she slid back to Magnolia, proffering her hand for her to take, and gliding backward with her onto the solidified liquid.

"Just don't knock us over this time," Caroline teased.

"I won't," Magnolia lied through her teeth.

This time the blade master was steadier, holding Caroline's hands only for the sake of holding them. Caroline grinned at her as they twisted and turned, hearts and stars glancing up from the surface they danced on. Magnolia let out a small giggle when Caroline lifted her with a spin.

Caroline laughed when Magnolia attempted a clumsy dip; instead of dipping Caroline, she ended up nearly falling over, and then found her back pressed tight to Caroline's chest, the woman's laughter vibrating onto her, her heartbeat so wonderful and present. Magnolia sighed and relaxed against her, letting her guide them smoothly over the ice. She let her eyes close.

She trusted Caroline.

Small kisses pressed to the back of her head made her smile.

Caroline always did so much for her.

The sun gently kissed her face, and she just allowed himself to breathe, hands intertwined with Caroline's, and she felt safe.

Because of her.

Her smile slowly faded.

What did she ever do back?

Nothing.

She stiffened, and Caroline seemed to, no, not seemed, she felt it. Her careful, loving, always loving, hands turned Magnolia to face her.

"Maggie? Is something wrong…?" she studied the other's soured face. Magnolia turned her face away. Caroline took the opportunity to kiss her temple. "Hey, it's okay… if you don't want to talk about what's bothering you, we don't have to. Do you want to stop skating?"

"No, I want to keep doing this," she muttered, managing to give her a weak smile. Caroline smiled back gently, pulling her to her chest, swaying with him on the frozen lake. "I like this."

Millions of words raced through Magnolia's head, and she could not put three together to say. Instead, she pressed her head to Caroline's chest, feeling and hearing her heartbeat through her shirt and sweater. Her eyes drifted shut once more, soaking up the… closure. That was what all of this was, right? Just a long winded goodbye. Magnolia squeezed her eyes shut and wrapped her arms around Caroline. Just to be closer. An idea swam into her thoughts. She entertained it for a moment, before a sly grin turned her mouth up.

Nuzzling against her chest, she pulled back after a moment. Caroline quirked an eyebrow and smiled back, with a puzzled look in her eyes.

"What are you planning, cariño?" Caroline asked her. Magnolia only grinned wider, one arm going over and taking one of Caroline's hands, the other remaining behind her back but adjusting from a hug to merely being wrapped around, the end placement of their positions ready for a dance. A blush flew over Caroline's cheeks faster than an eagle in flight. "Oh…!"

"I've got this," Magnolia assured her with a dazzling grin, leaving Caroline's heart aflutter, even though they both knew that Magnolia did not have this. "Definitely got this."

Magnolia set them off at a brisk pace, launching them around the ice, making Caroline shriek with laughter from the sudden start. Spinning and dipping her, relying on momentum to keep them on their feet, Magnolia danced with her, keeping her on her toes with quick maneuvers and sharp motions. Yet, somehow, Caroline always was on pace with her, or even two steps ahead, grinning, sweet faced, laughing Caroline. Magnolia's grin grew even more. For her plan to work she would have to outwit the taller but younger of the two, or, the method that suited her better, trick her.

Magnolia feinted a fall, waiting for Caroline to launch herself to catch her, and then she straightened herself swiftly, catching Caroline's hands as she dashed by, effectively knocking her over.

Magnolia smiled at her as the ground approached.

Caroline smiled back, the smile of recognizing a gesture, the smile of love and incredulous-

Thud.

Caroline felt the wind being knocked out of her as Magnolia pushed her onto the ice beneath her, but she could not feel happier. She let out a quiet huff of a laugh as soon as she managed to get air back into her system.

Caroline grinned stupidly at Magnolia, Magnolia with the same expression.

However, instead of frantically searching for something to say, this time Magnolia used their closeness to press her lips to Caroline's.

Caroline let out a noise of quiet surprise, then a hum of happiness and appreciation. One of her hands slipped into Magnolia's hair, playing with it and giggling as Magnolia's nuzzling tickled her cheek, slight fuzz along her jaw; Magnolia giggling back from the vibrations: a positive feedback loop for them both.

When Magnolia pulled away from Caroline's lips, the woman was quite literally tickled pink, smiling softly with little laughs, looking at her with eyes squinting from joy, inhaling deeply, each breath coming out a laugh. Magnolia felt her heart melt (metaphorically, it was a metaphor, for hell's sake, don't die on her literally, literally) and she sighed a bit before leaning down to her with a devilish grin, stealing Caroline's breath away yet again with a swift peck on her nose.

"Let's do that again," she told her with a grin, and before Caroline could cheekily ask 'do what', she kissed her.

The Researcher
7.26.2019

You are a rock. You have been a rock for as long as you can remember. An ocean rock, but barely. Submerged, leaning on an isle, under the water when the tide is high, poking out when the tide is low. Seaweed clings to you, and you sense it loosely, like many detached arms that you never bothered with. You could 'see', though in the sense of feeling the waves patterns, making out what there was, and glints of light flashing onto you from the sun. You could 'hear' from the vibrations traveling along the earth, and from the waves in the sky hitting against you and bouncing off.

You have been there for a long time.

You have seen and heard many, many things.

Things many would consider strange, but you have been there since the beginning, and so, are not novel to you in the slightest. You have seen them as children, heard their banter, watched them grow, all stoically, uncaringly.

You, after all, are a rock.

Boats have passed you before. You can sense the life unlike those you are used to on board. The first time you had seen a ship, you felt a dull sense of curiosity, ended as soon as the object was comprehended. Those who could not breathe water resided on it. Not like him, or him, no, they both could stay under for very long, and breathe quickly.

These beings could not. They could only go in for a third of the time he could, at most, and had two tails, not one. Those tails were quite useless for swimming, you observed, yet the beings seemed to enjoy it. For short times.

Then, as time passed, the boats became faster, more efficient. Those who swam donned bulky packs and equipment, and could stay in the water even longer than them, though not as long as the others that did not need air.

You did not care for them. They took care of the area around you, cleaning the mess that other two-fin-no-gill-air-needing creatures made.

'Serves them right,' was the semi lucid thought you deigned appropriate.

It changed one day.

A boat came in at night. It stayed. You could hear those on it converse in low tide, how they were researchers. You dubbed them a separate form of the other beings, like how there are dolphins and bottlenose dolphins and things that only have some features of dolphins but flat faces and strange voices like the two legs.

As they stayed longer, you learned only one of them was a researcher. The rest were hired hands, being they worked for him for pay. They did not like the researcher much.

Tension rose in the ocean's waves, and with it, on the ship. The hired hands spoke in quiet tones, becoming quieter as the researcher passed them and happily wished them a good day. Sounds of metal on metal creaked in the night. Stealing away to the captain's quarters when the learner slept.

You hazily wondered what it all meant.

Full moon came.

Silence, as you rested above and below the surface.

Not even a single cry of a bird, the waves nearly mute.

The shriek crashed through the quiet night, resounding over and over.

You sensed some of them wake from the cry, the nocturnal one already watching whatever was happening on the ship.

You could see the shadow of the researcher being tossed in the center of the boat's deck, scrambling to their legs, wobbling as the sea buffeted the vessel. The wind stole away the pleading words of the student, his shadow nearing the edge. Crew mates grabbed the researcher's wrists, and hauled them over the metal barrier, and there was the scream again, landing heavily in the water with a splash. You felt the water go cold.

You could hear the researcher more clearly now.

"I can't swim!" was the cry, muffled by coughing and sputtering. "Please, let me up, I'll pay you more, don't lea-"

A wave drove the two-legs under.

There was laughter on the ship, which quietly started and began to leave.

You sensed that this was... wrong.

This was cruelty for what reason? To eliminate the researcher, but why?

40

You felt good old curiosity ebbing into you with the tide. You could feel the vibrations of the being's struggle against the pull of the water.

"Help!"

Silence again.

You felt them weaken.

"Please...."

Their limbs fell stiff. You could tell because the vibrations stopped.

Sinking, but too slow. Still fighting.

The current drove their body toward you, toward the island.

Motion ceased slowly.

Their hand brushed you, and you felt.

Life.

You could hear and see and taste and smell, the crisp smell of the ocean's air, the salty taste of the waters, the sight of the few trees somehow growing on the island, the wheezing of the researcher's struggling body.

And you wanted to help.

Your arms of seaweed reach to them, and tug him onto you. You are now aware of more. There are rocks next to you, brothers and sisters and elevated ones, of the time before life. You pass them to the one beside you, and watch as they are transported along a slow chain of awakened stones. The tide helps push them onto the sandy bank of the island.

You, the rocks, with your new sapience, discuss the matter. The researcher was not breathing, water filling his air, body quivering with cold and inability to move.

You enlist the beings of the island to help them as well.

Gasps and a muffled cry crash over the winds again, and you pity them.

What a strange emotion.

You realize you can feel now.

How odd.

The researcher falls asleep, restored to life, battered and bruised, but alive.

The morning light woke them.

You watched them pull themself up, looking out to the waters.

You can feel their despair. Their gratitude of being alive.

They reached to their chest, pulling out a small object that opens with a click.

A sigh of longing and relief.

The object was returned, and the researcher giving a small laugh.

"Got your wish, didn't you?" they said to themself with a cough. "You wanted to study these waters, and here you are. Well... I can study all I'd like now."

They sat back down onto the sands, dropping their head into their hands.

"Oh, what am I going to do now?"

They shook their head with resolve.

"Snap out of it, Manny," they scolded themself. "Get to work. Priority one is water."

You are confused for a moment.

There is water everywhere.

They walked toward you and the other rocks, and rearranged you all to form a crescent shape.

"That should filter it a bit better," Manny sighed. "Still need a way to boil it."

They passed beyond the barrier they made, going to gather seaweed and laying it on the shore to dry.

You have seen fire before, and you realized this being was going to make it from scratch.

As they waited for the seaweed to dry, they grabbed a piece of driftwood, and a stone, carving away at the wood to form a spear.

"This should hold for now," they mutter.

You can sense the curiosity of everything around you.

This being may have come to research this area in the seas, but in the meantime, the life around them will research them as well.

Especially *them*, those with similar features to the being now on your land's mass. They surround the island, keeping a distance so they do not see them.

They are all so curious.

Seems there is much to learn.

Brush

"Salvatore," John's soft rumble brought a smile to said man's face. "Sal, it's time to get up."

"Nooo," the lanky man moaned, wrapping long limbs around John. "Wanna sleep in...."

"Sal, we have to get to work," John laughed with exasperated fondness. Salvatore yawned, sticking his tongue out at him, and tucked himself further under blankets, arms tightening and legs curling around, clinging to John like a koala to its tree. "Sapling, I know that the house is attached to the garden but it's no excuse to sleep in."

"'M tired," Sal yawned again, teeth glinting and eyes squinting. "Not gonna... gonna get up."

"Mmm, not if I have something to say about that," John chuckled, trying to get up. Trying being the keyword. Sal gave a small groan and pulled him back to the center of the bed. "Sally!"

"Stay," he pouted in reply. "Not gettin' up now."

"Hmph." John ran a hand over his chin. "How about I do all the waking up... for both of us. You just let me do all the work, and you'll be in your precious orchard without moving a finger."

"No," Sal answered stoutly, pulling himself even more into the blanket, only a few wisps of his blond hair protruding from the top. "You sleep too."

"Yeah, but the time for sleeping is over," John 'informed' him laughingly, pulling himself to the edge of the bed, dragging Salvatore with him. Wriggling out of the Italian's grip, he made his way to Sal's drawers, pulling his own clothes off the top of the mahogany chest. Sal squinted at him, deep brown eyes glinting from within the blankets, a mouse cozy in his den. John pushed on his glasses to poke through Sal's bins, pulling out a set of well worn, patched dress shirt and pants. In their line of work, the tears in their clothes was a sign of their devotion to the Earth – especially when it came to Sal. "Alright, let's get you dressed."

"I'm already dressed," Salvatore whined, gripping the blanket around himself tighter. John laughed and rolled his eyes, pulling the blanket away carefully. "No...! My blanket!"

"In your pajamas, sure," John smiled, pulling Sal into a sitting position to tuck his shirt onto his gangly frame, careful not to tug on the undershirt he always wore. He made sure to check that Sal was comfortable, then turned him so his legs dangled off the bed, and slipped the loose pair of pajama pants off, replacing them with a slightly tighter pair of working pants, putting Sal's shoes on with a kiss to each ankle, earning a sleepy laugh, calloused hands swatting through his hair to shove him away. John grinned. "That's better, isn't it?"

"No," Sal grumbled, though he was smiling. "Less comfy."

"Well, I'll have you up and running in no time," John ran his hand over Sal's head, pausing, dismayed by the knots in wavy hair. "How the hell do you have a bed head on top of having wild day time hair?"

"John, you've slept with me," Sal hummed, wrapping his arms around him as he plucked him out of the bed, Sal's strong arms carrying him to the bathroom. Sal pressed small, tired kisses to John's shoulder, being that there was the only place he could reach by only tilting his head, too lazy to stretch further. John set him down in the tub, putting a towel under his head to keep him comfortable. "You know that I... I move around a lot in my sleep...."

"Not an excuse," John smoothly replied, grabbing Sal's hair brush and gently starting to tug out the knots in his hair. It was a marvel, really, considering that Sal kept it rather cropped to his head. John wondered at how bad it would get if he did not constantly trim it. After catching on a set of three knots in a row, he gave an exasperated laugh. "How can you call yourself a pomologist? This is an affront to nature."

"Mmm," Sal hummed, tilting his head forward to allow John better access to his head. "Sì, so it suits me just fine, eh tesoruccio?"

"You're enjoying this way too much," John grumbled playfully, working the brush free. Salvatore grinned with his eyes still shut, shrugging slightly. When he finally got out all the knots, a feat that took a good twenty minutes, he set aside the brush to wet a small hand towel to rinse Sal's face, carefully going over his features, marveling at each sculpted bit of him. "Would be lying if I said I wasn't having fun myself, though."

"You know you love me," Sal grinned slightly. "As I love you."

"Yes, yes I do," John laughed, plucking up Sal's toothbrush, carefully putting on the fluoride and tapping Salvatore's chin. "Open wide, and you'll get a kiss after."

45

"I thought you were supposed to be a horticulturist, not a dentist," Salvatore groused, but complied anyways. John chuckled at the joke as he carefully cleaned Sal's teeth. According to John, each of Sals's features were fascinating. On the whole, Salvatore appeared as a regular human, but the details, the details! That was where the fascination sparked. Each of Sal's teeth had some anomaly that set him apart, his canines the most obvious, but an extra root on his molars, incisors with a small hook on the inside of his maw, small things that a human would not have. John cleaned each carefully, looking over them with awe. Salvatore had once explained that somewhere in his lineage was a D'mas'de – whatever that was. It sounded like a name for a species of deity. A god, that's what he was in love with. Inhuman, and yet, so much more human than the people of this Earth. However, when he handed him a cup to rinse his teeth and another to spit out the foam, his lips sealed, hiding away those unique teeth, and he appeared as a regular civilian once more. He smiled at John. "All done?"

John's heart melted as he took in the sleepy, wonderful look of his love.

'I should do this more often,' John thought to himself, smiling as he ran a hand through Salvatore's smoothened hair. 'Sally seems to like it, and I love it. I love him.'

"Not yet," he murmured, pressing his lips to Sal's. Sal hummed gratefully, wrapping his arms around his shoulders. John made a move to deepen the chaste kiss, but Sal pulled away, a ridged finger going to rest on John's lips. "C'mon sapling, I did promise you...."

"Not 'til you brush your teeth first," Sal softly instructed, kissing John's rounded nose. John grinned and hopped to the action, quickly shining up his own (albeit plain) teeth. He then turned on his toes, lifting Sal out of the tub easily, pressing their lips together as he sauntered down to his car, preparing to drive them to the botanical garden. Setting Sal down in his spot in the passenger seat, he leaned in even more to deepen the kiss, glad to find Salvatore replying readily to his action. When he pulled away, Sal laughed, eyes squinting in mirth. "You're too sweet."

"Says the sweetest man who's ever lived," John teased back. He nudged him as he started the car. "Ready to grow?"

"That's a terrible pun," Sal laughed, rolling his eyes. "Let's make like a tree and leaf."

"As if that's any better!"

Laughing, Sal brought John in for another kiss.

Decorations

"No sukkah? In America?" Sori's voice came tinnily through the receiver, sounding agitated and disappointed. Meir grimaced and held the phone as far away from himself as possible, wishing that he could think of something to say. "What kind of religious freedom is this?"

"Sora'le, please," Meir muttered pleadingly, casting glances to see if anyone was around. The vocal trainer only spotted Carl and Chaim chatting, the artist explaining something to the theater owner. "There are no materials for anyone, not even the shul will have one this year. There is nothing for anyone."

"Still, disappointing," she sighed, frustrated and malcontent. "I will see you at home tonight."

"Sori, please," Meir tried to get her to sound happier, but she had already hung up. Meir sighed. Chaim and Carl exchanged a glance and came over to the disgruntled singer, and he nodded to each respectively. "Hello Reb Levy, Mr. Goodly. How can I help you?"

"I think we'd like to help *you*," Carl corrected him, his usual twinkling smile on his round face. "You seem rather perturbed, Meir ha'Levi, he with the voice of angels."

"Stop using flattery, Mr. Goodly. You're picking up bad habits from Iyov." Meir told him off, wagging a finger at him. Carl only grinned wider, and Chaim 'politely' cleared his throat. "No offense, Levy, but you know it's true."

"Fair enough," Chaim shrugged, smiling slightly. "My circus, my monkey."

"Exactly," Meir snickered. "Well, the matter is this - it's my wife's first year in America, and she was hoping to celebrate sukkot, *really* celebrate it, but no one has any materials for a sukkah, and the city won't give out permits to have them on top of buildings this year due to the storm risk, so everyone is out of luck."

"I see," Carl said, not seeing at all. "That's actually what Chaim and I were discussing."

"Mm."

The three men separated ways, though Carl slipped out the side door that led to the comic studio next door, Dorothy shouting at him that he had papers to go through, he stumbling through a line that he had a Tanach problem to solve first and foremost.

"Where's my favorite yeshiva student?" Carl called into the art room as he and Chaim entered. Everyone pointed at Benyamin, who sheepishly smiled and answered as he stood, replying, "I'm pretty sure that I'm the only yeshiva student you know, Mr. Goodly."

"Exactly," Carl clapped him on the shoulder. He gestured at Benyamin to Chaim. "Mind if I borrow him?"

Chaim made a vague 'go ahead' gesture, and Carl flashed a thumbs up before steering Benyamin out of the room.

"Now, explain to me what the hell a sukkah is and how do I make one," Carl gave it to Benyamin straight, as soon as they were out of earshot. "I got a really basic drift from Chaim, but you know how it is with 'experts'. They forget how much the average goy knows. So give it to me simple, kid."

"With all due respect, sir, you're crazy, Mr. Goodly," Benyamin stared at him, adjusting his kippa on his head. "Didn't Mr. Levy tell you that there's no sukkot this year? What put this idea in your head to learn about them?"

"Meir and his wife," Carl answered honestly. Buddy stared at him, squinty and lip curling in confusion. Carl lifted his hands to show his honesty. "What? It's the truth."

"You're mashugana," Benyamin sighed. Carl grinned wider than usual, delighted with the insult. "Well, you need a structure with four, three, or two and a half walls, and those specifically, without a real roof, with branches covering the 'ceiling' instead. That's called the skach."

"That's it?"

"Kinda. Yeah, honestly that's about it."

"Okay, so come with me."

Carl tapped Frank on the shoulder as they passed the janitor, requesting two hammers. The old gentleman gave them to him without question or complaint. Carl and Benyamin went to the roof of the theater, where a small loft resided for the resident artisans, including Carl himself. The director sectioned off a square shape on the roof off with the tailor's measuring tape that he carried with him at all times.

"What are we doing here?" Benyamin asked, but hardly had to, watching Carl stab his hammer into the roof, tearing up a plank. Beynamin blinked, and sat on the roof, deciding to wait for a clear answer before he too would join in the demolition. "You're ripping apart the theater, from top to bottom?"

"No, just this layer," Carl answered as though it were the most obvious thing in the world. "Below is my living room, right, Benyamin?"

"Right," Benyamin replied, allthemore bewildered. "And?"

"My living room is square."

"Yes?"

"It's kosher for a sukkah, yes?"

It dawned on Benyamin what Carl was intending, and he leapt to his feet with wide and shocked eyes.

"Mr. Goodly, what in heaven's name?!"

"It's kosher," Carl gleefully replied. "Which means that this plan is a perfect one without any flaws whatsoever."

"You're insane!"

"Tell me something new, Benny!"

With a huff, the artist's apprentice grabbed his hammer and began to help his boss's friend in his insanity muttering that Carl was completely mad the whole while. Still, he had to admit, it was a good deal of fun.

Soon, the two of them cleared away all the wood, and Carl swung himself into his living room, landing on his couch. He was quite energetic for a man of his age, or maybe it was the thrill of the fascinating venture giving him a major adrenaline rush and he would feel it in the morning. Either way, his smile lit up the world around him as he looked up and out of the building.

"What if it rains?" Benyamin worried, looking up at the cloudridden sky. "There were storm warnings all over. What are you going to do with all your stuff?"

"If it rains, it rains!" Carl laughed, waving his arms over his head. "I'm the owner of a New York Theater company, who cares about my little trinkets? I certainly don't!"

"You're completely and utterly crazy," Benyamin informed him as he jumped into Carl's living room, landing beside him on the couch. The two admired their handiwork, looking up into the afternoon sky. "Looks nice, though. Not permanently, however."

"Sure," Carl shrugged. "Nothing lasts forever. Either way, it's time for skach."

"You pronounced it right!" Benyamin exclaimed with delight. Carl winked at him, and passed him a paper. "What's this?"

"Read it and find out," Carl replied. Benyamin did so, and his brows raised, and an incredulous dimpled grin spread over his cheeks. "Branch cutting permit?"

"Ah-yep!"

"Where did you manage to get this?"

"It's a prop, but no one will look twice."

"Once again, Mr. Goodly, with as much respect as I can muster, you are crazy."

—

Meir stared at the leaf and twig covered Benyamin and Carl, who were both grinning at him cheekily. Behind them, Iyov and Chaim were chatting and smiling, too, leaves stuck in Chaim's wispy hair. A few others from their artistic congregation schmuzed in the background, all laughing and cheerful.

Meir leaned back to survey them.

"What did you do this time?" he sighed. Natenel grumbled something about 'crazy theater children', which Meir found strangely fitting. "You look like you fought a salad and lost."

"Built a sukkah," Chaim remarked plainly. Meir stared at him. Iyov chimed in, "Well, we just helped collect and set up the skach. Funny how gullible the human powers that be are."

Meir rose an eyebrow and leaned forward.

"Where is this alleged sukkah?"

Everyone laughed, eyes twinkling brightly.

"On the theater," Benyamin chimed, smiling at the singer, then Carl. Meir's eyes came to rest on Carl as well. Shaking his head, he murmured, "Aren't you full of surprises, Mr. Goodly?"

"Positively bursting with them," was the easy coming reply. Meir chuckled and shook his head. "You're going to tell me I'm crazy, aren't you?"

"You're absolutely insane," Meir agreed, "But heaven help me if I didn't adore it. I don't think I'd be able to stomach working here if I didn't."

Carl only smiled wide.

—

Sori sighed as she came to the theater. Why did Meir ask her to come in? Surely he had enough to work with. She wrapped her shawl around herself tightly, and slipped down to the room he trained the other singers in, but he was not there. She frowned, and asked another worker, who had a suspicious number of twigs in his hair. Maybe he was cast as a tree man. He smiled, and led her to a worker's lift.

An apartment on the top of a theater? Odd! And yet, there was her husband, positively beaming at her, grinning like he won the lottery, with his fascinating boss, Carl, beside him.

"Look up," Meir instructed, and she did, her breath taken away. "Chag same'ach!"

Sori burst out laughing, delighted.

Carl beamed at them proudly.

51

I Want to Stop Thinking

12.16.2019

I want to drive my head into the wall until I cannot think.

Thinking is what always gets me into these problems, anyways.

Thinking of ideas. Ideas do not matter if they are bad ones, and contrary to popular belief, bad ideas do exist in things like me.

Things with no place in the world.

No matter how hard it tries to fit.

There will always be a jutting edge of the puzzle piece that drives it far away from entering any slot, big or small.

There just is no place for it.

Sometimes one little piece will click, but then things start forming around, and it is realized that the piece in the slot is not the one to be desired, and is thrown away, no longer valuable.

I think, sometimes, that there will be a puzzle that I will fit into just right.

That is not the case. There are too many contradictions, too many gaps, too many jagged curves and cutting edges. Not only is there no place, it is not wanted. It takes up far too much space, and wastes everyone's time by trying to find a slot of the solitary piece.

I want to stop thinking.

Thinking is what gets me into this mess.

I try to call out for help, blatantly saying that I will not live if I fail, and those around laugh, knowing it is the good old jokester, the one no one can ever take seriously, because if they would, they would be afraid.

I do not want to think anymore.

I try and hope that I will make or do something of value, but there is nothing I can do for anyone that will make a difference in any form of goodness, only bringing discomfort and disagreement. There is nothing I can do.

I cannot do anything.

I can hardly move.

My body hurts, and I want to stop thinking.

I want to stop.

Everything.

I want to tear the world apart with my bare hands, I want to scream, I want people to understand, but there is *nothing* to understand, other than the fact that I am a sad, pitiful, pathetic thing that should never have existed.
I want to be heard, though I have nothing to say.
I have nothing to show, a few measly dollars earned from hours upon hours of work, nothing that will change anything for anyone.
Bad grades, lies and disgusting habits, nothing more than a problem.

I want to stop thinking.

I want to stop existing, droning on and on, being nothing but a blight and a problem.

I cannot do anything right, nor anything at all, in that light.

Writing? Nothing more than a few forced words scraped out of an empty pot of burnt madness, exhaustion following every key, every letter. There is no value to the silent, stupid, stupid, stupid cries for attention from a useless being that cannot do anything at all, that has no feeling attached to the words.

Art? Do you mean scribbles of no worth? That have no impact, no reason, no need, nothing at all? A few pixels on a screen, once scrolled past never seen again, no matter how hard it is to raise the pen to hand, no matter how excited I feel with a new concept, the work of my hands never, ever, ever, and never will, match what I have in my broken mind, for what I seek does not exist, nor do I have any skills to bring it.

What else do I have?
Oh!

Nothing!

Nothing but a hollow body with no soul, only a desperation scraping at the edges of what might have once been someone, that is now nothing.

I am so tired.
I want to stop.
I want to drop off the face of the earth, to fall into the cosmos and never have existed.

I do not want to be remembered, I do not want to have existed, because the only memories of my existence anyone will ever have will be of hostility and stupidity.

No one hears, no one listens, because everyone is real, everyone has true problems to deal with, not some pathetic and useless brat's prattle about the injustice of the world. No, I do not want to be recalled, thinking hurts.

Thinking that I can do something good.
There is nothing I can do.
I have not slept in eleven years, and I will never sleep again.
There is no rest for the wicked, and wicked I am, useless and empty.
Why are you still here?
Why am I still here?
I do not want to be here anymore.
I do not want to think anymore.
I am so tired.

So tired.

I don't wanna think anymore
I don't wanna be anymore
I don't
I can't
I can't do anything right
I'm sorry
I want to die
I want to stop
I want to go
I can't

I'm sorry

I want to stop thinking.

Thinking is what gets me into these messes, anyways.

I wish there was a way to stop being

Stop being pathetic
Weak
Stupid

And start being something good

Something useful, smart, helpful, kind

That is simply impossible, though.

A puzzle piece cannot change its shape because it wants to.

It has a role to play, even if that role is the misfit, the broken, the useless, the unwanted

My eyes were once blue

They're green now
An ugly green
The color of muddy spittle on the ground of an unkempt field,

I want to stop thinking

I want to stop

I want it to all end

I wish I could do something
I'm sorry
I'm so sorry
Why are you still here
Please Don't waste your time on me

You deserve better than me, better than what I've been through, better than I can offer to you

I've used up all my chances.

I'm sorry.

I want to stop thinking.

Thinking got me into this mess, anyways.

Don't Leave

2.4.2020

Don't leave.

Two, technically three, simple, quiet words.

He was fidgeting when he said them.

"Please don't leave."

"I have to."

"No, you don't, we can work this out," he pleaded, a hand running through golden hair in stress. "We can figure something out, don't go."

A suitcase was dumped onto Sal's bed, the nimble hands of a botanist clicking it open, revealing an emptiness that he wished would remain so. A large hand closed the lid, earning a glare, angered earth eyes clashing with brown fury.

"You don't need to do this. You can't do this. What about our plants?"

"I'm not abandoning anyone," he soothed, Sal's hand was taken, pressed to John's lips. "I promise I'll be around, just not... here, for a while. I need time."

"Don't," he begged once more, wrapping his arms around him, pulling him close to kiss him, John's stubble rubbing gently against Sal's beard. "Don't leave."

"Stop asking, my answer isn't changing."

"Please, I... please, don't go."

"I said to stop asking, please." John and Sal both winced. John's face twisted into a scowl. "You're making this so much harder than it needs to be. Stop it."

"Then don't go." he crossed his arms, staring at him defiantly. The tall and short men's gazes remained locked, until he turned to the door with a sigh. "Don't you dare...."

"Goodbye, John."

Sal closed the door behind himself.

John crushed the advertisement to that plant exposition, and wished that they could have gone together.

Saccharine

2.5.2020

Elisa disliked sweet things.

It was something that Maxwell Oroseira realized pretty quickly after offering her some candy, though it was interesting to see that in a younger person. She liked salty things, spicy things. Food with a zing, a bang. Though they rarely came across good food in general, with a couple of spice containers, Elisa could make a meal out of a shoddy heap of scraps. Max admired her for that, though they often argued over the sweetness (or rather, the lack of sweetness) in the food.

Max liked things sweet, which was why his love of Elisa was so... odd. He loved her with all his heart, and would protect her to no end. Often he would tease with bad jokes, but she would roll her eyes and laugh along. She was like... a little sister to him. A very wild, bloodthirsty little sister that he found in a box outside of the park. He loved her greatly.

So when her birthday rolled around, he wondered what to give her.

He had no clue, and confessed it to her a few days prior. She shrugged, and patted his arm, letting him know that on the planet where she was from, birthdays were no big issue for any family, even if they were twins - such as herself and Bach. Only quadruplets were important, and not their birthdays, but their birth nights. Maxwell found it fascinating. She had never mentioned it while they had worked at the park.

Bet you would not learn that in a book, big brain Bill.

A wave of loneliness washed over him.

Elisa was out 'hunting', also known as killing the members of the space gangs that followed them. Yes, it was her birthday - and this was what she wanted to do for it. She offered Maxwell to come along, but he declined. He was not much of a... well, murderer. Though she vehemently denied that it *was* murder – insisting that it was striking first, and she did have a point with that. He would rather them be dead than waking up with his head blown up, or Elisa dead or worse - them both captured. His skin crawled at the very thought, and he was glad she could take care of herself.

She came 'home' to the *Kraken* not too late; at around eight thirty or so. Maxwell was staring up at the stars, and she closed her passenger door behind herself. The smell of blood trailed her, and Max glanced over. He pointed at her angled chin.

"You've got some blood on you," he remarked, but it was in honesty a stupid thing to say, being that blood coated her from head to toe. "You're not gettin' any of it on the seat, are you?"

"You're saying that as though I haven't bled all over your seats before," Elisa retorted back with a smirk. Alarm came into Maxwell 's expression. "What?"

"That's not your blood, is it?" he questioned, worried. Her laugh easily dispelled it. "It's not?"

"No, it isn't." she smiled, her sharp teeth glinting at him. "Killed a bunch of those nasty bastards."

"None followed?"

"Nope. One guy tried. He made a good dessert after I blew his ship up."

"Elisa, stop that," Max wrinkled his nose. "You know I don't like hearing that stuff."

"What, scared you'll be next?"

"No! No, I just don't like hearing that kind of thing," Max protested. "Come on, don't laugh."

"Eh," silence took over the small space of the space cab. A few minutes passed, both watching the stars trail across the sky above and below. The smell of blood slowly dissipated. It was calm. "I wouldn't eat you, anyways."

"What?" Maxwell got up with a jolt, staring at her. "'Cause we're close or?"

"No, you're too sweet," Elisa replied. He was not sure if he should thank her or not. She glanced at him with a small smile, fangs peering over her lips. "Too much licorice in you."

"Oh," he leaned back, settling in for sleep. "Goodnight, Elisa."

"Night Maxie."

—

Months went by. The weeks after Elisa's birthday were the best they had in practically a year, because the gangs were too afraid to go after them. Even though they slowly began to ebb back as of late, it was still much better than before.

June approached, and Maxwell felt dread for his birthday. He missed his twin, their old friends. He wondered if Elisa missed hers. Maybe that was why she went out murdering for her birthday, to lose herself in violence so she would not have to think about Bach. He knew she missed Chilla after they had made their midnight escape, and the other moon-dweller had tearfully declined running away with them. As did Bill. Maxwell always thought about Bill, always worrying about his smart head. He was okay, right? From the coded message that Ezekiel managed to send, as far as he and John could tell, William was still safely on the run. That was what he could hope for, worrying that he ruined his brother's future. But hey! William unintentionally ruined his too. They had equally contributed to the Incident. So they were even. More or less.

"Hey, curly head," Elisa's hand snapped right in front of his eyes, the sharp 'click click click' of her fingers gaining his attention with ease. "Focus on the sky before you get us both killed by an asteroid."

"Okay, okay," he grumbled, but was grateful she pulled him out of spiraling. "Was just thinkin' about Bill. He's okay, right?"

"Yes, but we won't be if you don't pay attention," she tartly replied.

His birthday came closer and closer, and all he could feel was a pit of nervousness. He could not sleep that night, thinking about Marlin, Chilla, and Bill. The Blot looming before them.

He stepped out into the cold air of the general bay, stretching.

"Morning birthday boy!" Elisa chirped, swinging into view from the ceiling where she had been floating about. "I got you something!"

"Don't give me a dead guy's head."

"I got you a dead gu- oh you don't want that?" she winked. "Nah, I'm just kidding. I baked you a cake."

"Wha-"

It was shoved into his hands, small and smothered in frosting. It looked horrifying. Max suddenly had whiplash from memories of Elisa's terrible baking, constantly getting dough stuck in her prosthetic CIN.

"Go on!" Elisa smiled, frosting on her fuzzy cheek. "There's no poison, I promise!"

He took a bite.

Sweetness.

Elisa beamed at him, showing her sharp teeth, tail flicking.

"Is it good?"

"It's perfect," he smiled, giving her a hug. She hugged back happily. "Thank you."

A word came to his mind.

Saccharine.

Mini Mabul

3.27.2020

Meir looked out to the billowing gusts of wind, the pushing air streaking with water, splashing and splaying around the studio, a tsunami on land and in air. The tempest darkened. Most members of the newspaper company and theater trope groaned (aside from Carl, who easily could stay in the building), fearing their walks home or to transit. Some managed to figure out shared rides, but Meir thought that the billowing rain looked rather inviting. Beside, Sori would have probably gone looking for him, most likely armed with an umbrella.

So he donned his raincoat, and set out into the storm to meet with his wife somewhere in the storm.

The gales buffeted at him, yet none managed to sway his path home.

He walked on a mission, a mission to go and get some of Sori's delicious chicken soup.

Meir trudged through the squall, blinking and wiping his glasses constantly until resigning and allowing the rains to cover his entire face in any case, because his futile attempts simply were wasting his time. He picked up his pace, not being able to wait to see his lovely wife's face, to see her so happy when he comes home, and-

"Meir?! Is that you, you bulvan?!" His wife's voice burst out in a rage right in front of him. He saw her in all her furious glory, and instantly remembered why he fell in love with her. Sori was armed with an umbrella and a raincoat, with thick boots to top it off, and she seemed absolutely horrified that he had even thought of bracing the storm. "You buffoon! Stop staring and get over here!"

Meir swiftly rushed over to her, cupping her cheeks in his rain soaked hands, kissing her with abandon, leaving her with splotches of moisture on her face. She blushed with a scrunched face, turning away while muttering furiously about how he was an idiot. Continuing on, softer, she took his hand with her free one.

"Come, come, let's get home quick," Sori urged, and they finished the path to their domicile in record time, splashing through the waters like troopers through the tundra. Once within, she shoved him into the bathroom. "Hot shower, now. I'll bring you a change of clothes, you silly fool. Going in the rain like that without an umbrella."

"At least I had a rain coat. And I love you!" Meir called, grinning. She scoffed at him, shaking her head, but smiled anyways. "I know you love me too!"

Meir turned the water all the way to the warmest setting, letting the scald wash away any illness he could have picked up. After cleaning himself to a satisfactory level, he dried himself up, got dressed, and came out to the dining room. He wrapped his arms around Sori, and she turned her head to kiss him softly.

"Soup?" she offered, getting up from the chair she had been reading on. Meir smiled. "Of course, Sori'le. You know I love your soups. As well as all your food."

She rolled her eyes, a smile still gracing her features as she got for them two bowls. They chatted about their days as they ate, and then they cuddled into bed, wrapping two extra blankets around themselves, watching the storm crash with lightning and thunder.

They pressed soft nuzzles to each other's cheeks, glad to be safe and warm in each other's arms.

Meir sneezed.

Sori looked at him, and slowly shook her head. He looked back sheepishly, flushing.

Not Forgotten

4.21.2020

The air was crisp, the scent of blossoming flowers on the wind.

The ground was solid, the small sprigs of grass budding.

The sky was clear, with a few clouds here and there.

It was a beautiful day.

That was what Benyamin felt, what he knew.

Dorothy stood beside him. Both of their heads were bowed to the slab before them, Benyamin murmuring the words of Kaddish, turning a stone over and over in his hand, the coolness of the rock melding with the approaching summer wind.

He finished the t'fila, placing the small simple rock onto the ornate marble one.

Tears blurred his eyes, and he sniffed, smiling shakily. Mr.s BenAcher, Levy, and Goodly had spared no expense for the head of the Puplik family. Dorothy patted Benyamin with the umbrella she had been gifted by Carl, comforting him.

"Almost another year," Benyamin mumbled, still surprised at how fast time ran. "It's been... really weird without him."

"It has," she agreed quietly. "He was a really brilliant man. I can see where you got your genius from."

The two stood a while longer.

"I have to go," Dorothy told him, looking at her watch. "I'll see you later, Benny."

"Okay, Dorothy," he nodded, acknowledging her departure. "Have a good day."

"You too."

Benyamin stayed standing.

A distinctive walk came up behind him.

"Ho there, Benyamin!" Carl smiled at him, though his eyes were sad. They were nearly never sad, and that made the upset gaze so the more stark. Oddly enough, Benyamin felt immensely comforted by the sight, nearly feeling guilty as the realization struck him. Carl took a marvelously polished green and red stone from his pocket, placing it onto the grave. He gave a slight nod, his thinning white hair melting into the puffy clouds above. "Just thought I'd visit an old friend."

"Friend?" Buddy raised an eyebrow, smiling. He knew Carl called nearly everyone his friend, and his father was no exception. He went ahead to tease his master. "I didn't know that you knew my father well."

"Of course I did," Carl scoffed. "He had the most excellent recipe for dumplings. We exchanged meal ideas a great deal and he was extremely good at riddles."

"You… you speak Ladino," it was not a question, rather a shocked statement. "When… when did you learn it?"

"A while after I learned English and German," he answered nonchalantly, peering at him with twinkling bright eyes, though there remained a sadness beneath. "Your eyes are sad, too, you know."

Benyamin blushed, realizing he had spoken aloud.

"C'mere, Benny," Carl sighed, closing his eyes, opening his arms to welcome the young man in a hug. Benyamin leaned onto his chest, wrapping his arms around the old theater director. Carl may have been aged, but like a good whiskey there was strength in his body, and he hugged Benyamin back tightly. "We all miss him."

"I wish I spent more time with him," Benyamin's throat tightened. He tried not to cry. He really did. But his tears slipped, and cascaded onto Carl's shirt. The sun glinted on his pin. It made him cry harder. "He came from somewhere awful. Inhumanly so. A-and I barely paid any attention…."

"But you still heard his story. Lived it, even," Carl reminded him, lifting his head, with stocky but gentle fingers. Benyamin's eyes constantly flicked to the rock on the stone, the polish blazing defiantly. "Benyamin, look at me."

He focused on Mr. Goodly's face.

"You were and are a child," he told him softly. "You learned. You spent as much time with him as you could, even if you were exasperated by your old man's quirks. You even tried to learn Ladino. You tried, and you loved him as much as any son could. He was so proud of you. Every time we would meet, he and I would discuss how much you've grown, Benyamin. By teaching you, he lives on in you. Do you understand?"

64

Benyamin nodded, smiling shakily. Carl matched the awkward lopsided grin.

"What do you say I'll teach you his recipes," Carl offered. Benyamin's eyes lit up. "And I'll tell you the parts of his story that he could not figure out the words to tell you. What do you think of that, Ben?"

"I would like that," Benyamin admitted. "I would like that a lot."

Eavesdrop

10.2.2020

Ricky was well known to eavesdrop. Not for hir benefit, but more for the gathering of information.

Why the hell not?

And, of course, all the juicy and dirty little secrets hidden behind closed doors. There were delightful little arguments that she could later play peacemaker for, shouting matches that would put two grizzlies or lions to shame, gossip and plans that she had hir ear to.

However, the most prominent of all these private encounters were exactly that.

Mandatory workplace romance; both at the arboretum and the water treatment plant next door.

She could tell of Olivia and Mary-Anne's first kiss and how it started, or of Marlin and Chilla's brief flirtation. Phillip's strange crush on Andrew, Marlin and Bill's bromance, Mary-Anne and Lou singing together. The way Olivia and Mary-Anne would tease Andrew into asking Lou out. Of course, there was also the time when Zeke and Chester had a remarkably soft dance, not to mention whenever Sal would be around, John would not be too far away. There were so many delightful moments for hir to pick from, and Ricky was not ashamed to say she had a few raked up hirself, before Berk's disappearance – though they had broken up long before, as soon as Ricky found out how the arboretum's old 'leadership' treated Salvatore. Good riddance.

Ricky had a saying for gathering these tidbits – the higher up the food chain, the juicier. Chet and Zeke circling each other, not to mention Sal and John's charged relationship, were some of the most entertaining bits she could get.

Which was why, while going to check on one of the hydrostations, she was positively delighted to hear a familiar voice emanating from the unit's piping room, followed by another.

It came in the form of a swear, low and rough. Ricky had frozen and looked back at the door she had just passed by, and after the briefest moment, pressed hir ear to it. Sure enough, Sal was cursing up a storm behind it.

Ricky's feathers rustled as she caught the specific tone of his language, a raspy pant. Fighting a smile, she pressed hir head closer.

"Fuck, John," she could hear, and a brow raised in bemusement. "Fuck, shit, can't you hurry up?"

"I'm going as fast as I can, babe," John grunted. "It's not so easy, so stay still, please."

"I don't know how much longer I can," Sal gasped. "Getting harder to... do that...."

"I know, just a little longer," John promised. Ricky wished she could get a peek at what was going on, but there were no gaps or crevices leading into that room. There was a sudden sigh of relief, a full exhale followed by more panting. "There we go, much better, huh?"

"Yeah," Sal admitted. "It is."

"Do you think we can do one more?"

"John, we already did two...."

Ricky moved away with some surprise, letting out a slight huff of a laugh. Seemed like the power couple fit that bill in more ways than one.

"Come on, just one more," John insisted, a breathy edge to his voice. "I know we can do it."

"What are you doing?" Lou asked, and Ricky looked up at him. The chemist from the water plant next door seemed completely baffled. She smiled and signaled with hir hands. Lou turned red, and turned to leave, but then thought worse of it, leaning against the door in the same way Ricky was, moments later. His face turned into one of shock. "John and Salvatore?"

"Mhm."

"Damnit John, keep it straight!"

"I'm trying, but you know that's not how these things work, honey."

"We should've stopped," Sal paused to pull in slow, deep breaths. "At three."

"I know you can take another two on if we need," John chuckled, breathless as well. Lou and Ricky glanced at each other. Before long, they were joined by Phillip, who heard the next words just as clearly as the other two. "If you keep squirming there's no way I'm going to be able to get it in, Salvatore!"

Phillip, instantly realizing what the other two were listening to, went back down a maintenance shaft, only to return shortly with Andrew and Olivia, both grinning. Gradually, the remaining workers from both the park and the water plant gathered.

"Fuck! John, I- I can't!"

"Ok, so stop jostling me and we'll try again in a minute," John assured him. "In the meantime we can work on other things."

"Sounds good," Sal exhaled. "What do you suggest to do?"

"Well, we can try doing that one by hand."

"Are you sure that's a good idea?"

"If you're up for it," John's smug overtone was audible even through the door. "If you can handle it."

"Of course I can," Sal replied with some affront. "I've done much more than that."

"Let's get to it, then," John responded. "Do you want the screw or-"

"You do it," came Sal answer. Lou frowned as he handed Marlin a five dollar bill. "Just don't take too long with this one."

"I won't," John promised. "And since this isn't as exhausting as that, we should be able to get doing the other as well."

"I think that works," was the quiet response. Ricky shushed Chilla as she was about to complain for the silence. Maxwell gave her a broad grin, while William, pretending to be better than the others, leaned against the opposite wall; though he had his CIN open to his brother's channel. "Fuck! This is not, not an optimal position!"

"Shit, I know baby, just," John paused to swallow, "Give me a second. That any better?"

"Yes," Sal puffed. "Pound it already."

"One or two?"

"One at a time, numbskull."

"I'm sure we could do-"

"Do you want to hurt us both?"

"Fair point."

Yunus was the only person to see what everyone was doing (huddling against the door with varying degrees of grins and blushes) to turn around and go right back where it came from. Ricky suspected she caught a glimpse of a specific gesture it made towards them all that made hir snort.

Andrew murmured, "I bet you all ten dollars that they're not making love."

Everyone took him on instantly, especially with the next swear, courtesy once more of Salvatore.

"Fuck!"

"Shit! Shit, sorry, are you okay?"

"Just pinched a bit," Sal hissed. "Startled me. Keep screwing, I'm fine."

"You got it," John smoothly slung back. "Faster or slower?"

"Keep it even," Sal scolded. "Don't get cheeky about it."

"Well, I've done harder than this."

"Keep moving or you're on the couch tonight."

"Isn't that a little harsh?" John joked. There was a silence. Chilla giggled and made a kissy face, to which the other employees nodded and slash or smirked towards. "I'm almost... finished... done."

There was some movement, and after a few minutes of relative silence, John continued.

"Do you want to try a last one?"

"Might as well."

Mary-Anne glanced up at Olivia, brandishing a dimpled smile.

"Another ear show," she whispered, victorious. "Delightful."

"Can you hold me?" Sal inquired. John must have nodded, for he shortly responded, "Good. Get ready, in three, two, one-"

"H-hah!"

"You good there?"

"Yes, just go as fast as you can, I'm not gonna last long like this!"

"Okay, okay-"

"Shut up and swing it, Sal!"

Everyone at the door darkened considerably at the following sounds, which seemed exactly like Sal had done what John told him to do.

"Nearly there," Sal growled. "Two or three strokes more."

"Good, I don't know how much more I can hold out," John gasped back.

Ricky felt something move in front of hir, and before she knew it, the door fell forward, collapsed by all the members behind hir and clamoring against it. John, who had been holding up Sal while he repaired a chemical line pipe and was hammering in a new fixture, dropped him in shock, causing Sal to drop the hammer, which landed on John's foot, spurring a slew of new swears from the Human.

"Sorry!" Sal fretted over him, flustered. "Are you okay!?"

"Better than when I accidentally slammed a duct cover on your hand," John gave a weak smile, gripping his foot and looking like an oddly shaped flamingo. He swung his head to glare at all of the workers who gawked at the two. "Damnit, what are you all doing here? And why'd you have to break the door? You all know this room is sterile!"

"Uh," Ricky remarked, fishing out a ten dollar bill to give to Andrew, who smugly accepted one from everyone there. Sal grew confused, "What the hell were you betting on?"

"Um," Mary-Anne went pink, and scattered away, Olivia running after her. "See you!"

"What is happening," John stated, deadpan, just as lost as his partner. "Andrew, can you explain- oh he's gone."

Sal looked around. The confusion broadened as he surveyed the area. Only Ricky remained before them.

He glanced at hir. The pipe room. John, who shrugged.

"Y'all hearing things?" he asked, furrowing his brow. "There was nothing in that room aside from me and John and hand tools."

"Well you see," Ricky chuckled. "That's exactly what we thought."

The Entertainment

12.14.2020

Johan woke up upside down.
On the floor.

Well, his head was, at least.

The rest of his body was on the couch.
Why the hell was he on the couch?

Righting himself, he could feel all the liquid in his body sloshing around, including his jello like brain. His hand brushed a needle.

That would make sense. His legs firmly (more or less) on the floor now, he looked at the short little coffee table that reminded him often of a dachshund, and was unsurprised to see it littered with those vials.

Maybe he should see if one had any left.
It could help him get through the day.

With a twisted, grimacing smile, he leaned back. It would make it better.

His arm relaxed with the thought of a poke, of a little boost, a little dulling of the pain.

Wrenching his eyes from the table, he went to the record player, and put on a quiet vinyl so he could clean up his mess, picking up the garbage can just in time to vomit in it.

The day after breaking a clean streak always was the worst.

His hands shook as he swept everything into the trash, desperately thinking of a way to dispose of it all without being noticed.

The overwhelming need for a hit always wiped out all of his logic, driving him to forget that he would have to deal with it all in the morning.

Unless he would have some more.

Johan mixed a bitter painkiller into his tea, covering the awful taste with masses of honey.

Though it smelled nice, tasted good, he could hardly register it. After all, compared to the extremely expensive morphine on the table, it hardly blocked a single receptacle.

What was he doing with himself?

71

Thoughts gripped his ankles and dragged him down to the floor once more, gagging on his own air.

Johan knew he had to stop.
He knew he had to.
He was too stubborn to stop when he had to.

Johan shakily went to the bathroom, wetting his hands and going over his face. Bloodshot eyes. Heavy brow, rough breathing. He looked drunk, he looked like a wreck.

There was something that could help with that.

Johan's hand went to the drawer before he even realized, his right hand grasping a syringe from behind the false back.

Johan found that he was on the couch again, and there was beauty in his hands, freedom and relaxation. His entire body both eased and tensed. He eventually registered what was happening, and his sleeve was already rolled up.

Entertainment or reality?

He closed his eyes, the needle over his elbow.

Johan turned off his brain.

"Raymond Irving speaking, how can I help you?" crackled through the receiver. "... Hello?"

"You c-can," Johan whispered, sinking down against the wall. "Help...."

"Jo? Where are you?"

"At home."

"I'm on my way," Raymond asserted. He could hear the worry in his voice. "I'm bringing Marcéline. Do me a favor and put that snake under your heel."

"Thank you," Johan whispered. "See you s-soon...."

As he was told, he broke the syringe under foot, sweeping up the remains. He went to dispose the shards, and sat outside, turned to face the ocean's tide, entranced. Raymond's footsteps approached, and he sat beside him.

They both watched in silence, Raymond's presence keeping Johan in reality.

Tick Talk

"You know, this could stop whenever you want it to."

"Mhm. And why should I want it to?"

"Because otherwise…"

Thud.

"That will happen. Over and over."

"G-guh… and so what?"

"Mr. Stanislavsky, you're a tough guy. A strong, smart man."

The hammer rose and fell in the man's hand.

"But I was just one step faster than you, wasn't I?"

"Sure."

"I want you to talk."

"About what?"

"You know."

"I don't think I wil- GAH!"

"Ooh, might've knocked out a tooth there!"

Yehuda felt the inside of his mouth with his tongue on instinct, mentally proving the man wrong. Though his jaw did bleed, nothing stung within, no gaps of raw and ripped gum could be found.

His head lolled.

Murphy did not let him rest the pounding there for long, though, fingers clawing into hair and yanking his aching head back. Yehuda spat the blood he gathered into his eye.

Murphy let go out of reflex, stepping back with disgust written all over his face. He wiped away the red liquid with a sneer, flicking it back onto Yehuda, wiping his gloved hand on his jacket.

A swinging punch sent his head lolling once more.

Yehuda mumbled something, bound hands clenching and unclenching in futility. Murphy leaned down to hear him better.

"What was that, little pig? You going to squeal soon?"

"I said, 'fucking sadist'." Yehuda repeated, scowling. An uppercut tore another groan from him. "Practice with your wife?"

"Oh, ho ho, really funny, wiseguy," Murphy squatted in front of him, patting his knee. "You're much more fun."

"So you do- aARGH!"

"Did you bite your tongue there, Yehuda?"

"Fuck off...."

"Only when I get what I want to hear."

"We'll be here for a long time, then. I have nothing to say. Nothing that you don't already know."

"I did find out one thing from you already!" Murphy beamed, his hands reeking of gasoline as he drew them along Yehuda's face- still gloved, he thought to himself with a smirk. "That there's more than one of the little angels, aren't there? Two, maybe three, little ones running around?"

He flicked his nose.

"So you better get to talking," Murphy smiled. Yehuda gagged and once more rocked in the chair, headbutting Murphy square in the nose. He stumbled and fell on his back from the disbalance, and then rose with a knee to Yehuda's chin. "You little shit!"

"AAH!"

"I tried to play *nice!*"

"Nngh!"

"Get *TALKING!*"

"Hnah-AH!"

Murphy panted as he tried to pull himself together, rage pouring out of every pore.

He ran a hand through his hair, looking down at Yehuda's curled up body.

It was amazing to think that someone so powerful could be so... vulnerable. So weak. So... close.

The thought alone was enough to reinvigorate him. Murphy leaned against the wall and took out his pack of cigarettes, lighting one. Yehuda looked up at him wearily, the cut under his eye steadily dripping down his face, the wound already festering.

"You know what would happen if I drop this little thing?" Murphy asked, swirling around the cancer stick, making smoke trail after his steady hand. Yehuda moaned in anguish, curling in on himself once more. "Onto these pretty patches of gas?"

"God, please, no," he whispered. "No...."

"You do know, Mr. Stanislavsky. You know..." Murphy squatted next to him as well, glad to see the man's sharp gaze fixated on the glowing cinder dangling precariously from his fingertips. "So well."

Yehuda could say nothing. He stared at the embers, lips open and letting air flow. Everything ached and hurt.

"Will you talk?"

"I don't know what you want to hear."

"Judah, Judah, stop playing dumb," Murphy crooned, pulling his head back once more via his hair, holding his neck exposed. The man flinched and yelped and tried to escape from his grasp as the cigarette pressed to the gash on his cheek. Murphy watched with awe as the man conquered his pain and pressed back against it, putting it out on his own bloody skin. "You are a strong man...."

"Yeah, and? It's not helping me, is it? It hasn't helped me, has it?" Yehuda spat back. The poor man seemed absolutely exhausted, even as he mustered his soul and straightened his back. "God gives strength and weakness. God gives smarts and stupidity. We are all equal in the Supreme's eyes."

"However," Murphy cut him off, bored of his turn to religion in desperation. "*You* are special. And I want to know why. The 'Supreme' gave you something that the rest of us don't have, a *gift*, and I want to know why, Judah. Was it seeing your parents die in front of you? Was it radiation? Or was it something else entirely... comrade?"

"Gift," Yehuda snorted, shivering as adrenaline went unspent. "More like a curse. I never would have asked for it."

"Ooh, but you have it," Murphy circled around him. "You have it now, and I want to know why ."

"I don't know," Yehuda gritted out. "I don't know. You've had your fun. Will you let me go, now?"

"No, I can't." Murphy sighed, pulling up another chair and sitting behind him, running a hand through his hair and gripping again, pulling back. He took out his knife and began drawing patterns on the neck that he could not see. "You see Yehuda, it took me a long time to get my hands on you. A long, long time. I've been waiting for an opportunity like this for ages."

He could feel the man's pulse through the knife.

"To learn what makes you tick."

It was both calm and ferocious.

"To tear you apart."

Just like the man before him.

He slammed him forward again, drawing away the knife just in time, nicking a mark along his throat.

"So get to it."

Yehuda watched as polished shoes came into his vision once more, and a groan slipped from his throat as he desperately tried not to think of what the agent would do.

"Talk."

Slice of Life

2.3.2021

Elianna passed the ball to Miriam, smiling at her. Miriam laughed and passed it back, and their game continued on for some time. It did until the door behind them opened and closed, but neither of them paid any mind. The footsteps walked right past them, heavy but quick. Then, they stepped back, looking at the two. Yehuda waved at his brother in law vaguely, flicking through a newspaper. Shalom rolled his eyes, looking down at his daughters.

"Alright girlies, what do you want for dinner?"

"Can we make pizza?" Elianna asked, almost missing the ball, but catching it one handed. Shalom smiled and patted her head before going back to the kitchen. Miriam laughed as she tossed the ball at Shalom, laughing harder as he spun around just in time to catch it. It was rare to see Shalom smile, but at that moment he did, before passing the ball to Elianna and retreating to the kitchen once more. "Tati, is that a yes?"

"Yes it is, little miss," Shalom replied in that dry manner of his. "I'm just going to go get the dough ready. Unless you girls want to help with that, too."

"Yes please!" Elianna chirped, looking over at Miriam. "Do you want to help, too?"

"Yes please," Miriam echoed, her cheeks crinkling the corners of her eyes as she took Elianna's hand to follow Shalom into the kitchen. "Pizza making."

"Pizza making time," Yehuda repeated after her, joining his family in taking down all the ingredients. "I don't know if we have any toppings, though. Maybe a pepper and an onion."

"Those sound good," Elianna hummed. "But you keep the onion on one half only."

"Understood, ma'am," Yehuda muttered, but there was a smile on his lips. Heaven help him, he loved their girls. Together they mixed the ingredients in a bowl just big enough to service them, and in no time Yehuda covered it with a towel to let it rise. Miriam poked the top, making it bend inwards just a bit. "Have either of you seen the sauce?"

"I threw it into the lake," Shalom helpfully commented, looking at his nails. Yehuda spared a glare for him. "Oh, I thought you were talking about the other sauce. My bad."

"It's in the refrigerator," Elianna, actually helpful, said, taking it out and handing it to Miriam, who reached for it with round fingers, holding it tightly against her chest. "I'll get the cheese out."

"Sounds like a plan," Yehuda hummed, checking on the dough. He might have added too little sugar, but best to save that for a special treat for the girls. It was hard to come by. Everything was. He tried to get the girls to garden a bit with him, and it worked for the most part, but Elianna and Miriam- they wanted only flowers, so the butterflies would come. So Yehuda found himself and Shalom being the ones to maintain the vegetables. Nonetheless, it was just as good- it was good to get Shalom out of the hotel and doing work with his hands. Ever since their wives passed away, it had been hard for both of them to move forward –especially with the worry of a hostile government. No matter for that now. "Elianna, could you go get a pepper from the garden? You can pick the color you want."

"Okay Abba!" she chirped, and skipped out. Nothing could break her spirit, it seemed, and that made Yehuda feel all the better. At least one of them was strong – a sentiment both fathers shared, though one had a touch more agitation. Miriam stood on a chair and bounced, dancing to music only she could hear. Shalom could hear faint echoes of it beyond his own mind, and what beautiful music it was. Somber, yet so happy. Shalom looked over to her and pressed a kiss to her forehead. How much he loved her. Elianna rushed to in with her prize. "Got it!"

"Red, nice," Shalom plucked the object from her hand and took off his gloves, and rinsed it before cutting it quickly. The faster he could get his gloves back on the better. "It'll make our pizza real pretty. Do you girls want me to get the onion ready while you start stretching the dough?"

"Stretch the dough," Miriam whispered, her eyes big as Elianna uncovered the sticky orb. She almost sank her hands right within it, but Elianna stopped her quickly. "Hang on, we need to wash our hands, first!"

Yehuda would have said that his tears were only from the fumes. That was all. The onion fumes. Definitely not crying because of how much he adored the two girls playing with soap suds. Eventually, when he turned around, they were back to the pizza and forming an imperfect but rather good circle out of the dough. He washed his hands and rinsed his eyes, and after he dried them, he put back on his own gloves. Shalom, his already on, was showing Miriam how to spread the sauce evenly, and Elianna sprinkled the toppings as the red was added along the dough, being sure to have the onion only on one half.

The two of them then added the cheese, Miriam sneaking a few strings into her mouth when she thought no one was looking. Once the pizza was in the oven and Yehuda had set a timer, they pulled him into the living room to read to them until it would be done.

They gave him a book on ghost stories– one of their favorites. One of the stories was dog eared and crinkled with how many times he had read it to them. It was about a little girl who, after she died, turned into butterflies and moths, spreading good to the good in the world, rippling bad to the wicked. Neither Yehuda nor Shalom understood why they liked it so much, but they did, so he read it to them. In the middle of a word, the timer went off, and he inhaled, long and slow.

The air smelled good.

"You girls hungry?" he asked, setting aside the book and getting to the kitchen, though Shalom had beaten him there. A resounding two voices answered him with an affirmative. Their older daughter came up to him, and he handed her a stack of plates. "Elianna, please set up plates for us."

Shalom came into the dining room with their pizza, while Yehuda entered with a stack of cups and milk. Shalom, with his characteristic carefulness, cut it for each of them. Elianna would always laugh at how he ate his slices– putting it on the plate over the edge, and holding the plate while he bit it.

Still, it was enjoyable. It had been fun to make it together.

Seeing Miriam and Elianna eating happily, well, that made Yehuda and Shalom happy too.

Punchline

54.2021

Air rushed in and out of his nose, burning cold and bloating thin. His jaw was rigid, a firm scowl hiding teeth barred tighter than they had been locked in a very long time. Whatever had been in his mouth had fallen out, jaw slack. He could hear nothing at all aside from the functions in his own body, the silence amplifying that quiet clicking flow of blood, and,

Ha,

Ha,

Ha,

His shoulders shook and heaved, pulled up towards his ears, but the tension in the body was unnoticeable to the man who inhabited it. No, he heard nothing, saw nothing, felt nothing, smelled nothing, and tasted nothing. One who was not in his senseless and numb body would taste nothing as well, but perhaps either a dry mouth from clamping on cloth or a salivating one from a bit of soft metal carefully settled on teeth, the smell would be of saline and hot copper ore, the feeling would be one of gothic horror, the sight all red, and one would hear quiet dripping and,

Ha,

Ha,

Ha,

A groan disrupted the sound, or perhaps only quieted it for but a moment. His head turned from side to side in an attempt to figure out what the sound was. It sounded so close, so so close, and it was the panting of a beast, and he shirked again, his eye still unseeing, his ears unhearing; but he could feel that panting. Should he run? Where would he be able to hide? Deep down, he knew that it was futile. Demons of the mind cannot be outrun, and they would see through his eye to know where he hid. Bending over that light oak table, he watched as red covered the surface and darkness pulsed at his mind, the center of his vision growing hazy. He hunched over as that sinister breathing bore down on him,

Ha,

Ha,

Ha,

He was alone, he made sure of it, the children away, they had been for weeks, he was alone. He made sure that everything was clean; the room, the device, the table, the digit, the body that the mind inhabited. It was all red now. He still stood where he had been, his eye fixated on a single point. He could not identify it, but he knew what it was. It seemed so small. This decision was too hard to make for something of so little consequence. He did not even feel it. Feel what? The nothingness was what was felt. It could not compare to that time with the machine, with those same bestial huffs,

Ha,

Ha,

Ha,

There was no going back now, and there had not been before. That was another thing he had affirmed. In the dim light that he could not tell if it was flashing from a lack of power or a lack of cruor, he saw his hand finally tear his mind from the crushed fragments that rested central. He was stuck, but his hand made it to the binding, and he tightened it around his wrist as he stumbled back. In the kitchen was the knife, already red hot and prepared. So much red, so much red. He ignored the metal for a moment to let it cool, and instead opened the liquor cabinet, and he pulled down the bottle of vodka swiftly, so as not to see the monster behind him. After a brief moment in which he realized that he was not able to open it, he smashed the edge against the counter, and poured the contents over the red. The air moved suddenly, and the darkness cleared for just a moment,

Ha!

Ah,

Ha...

The knife was in hand, blurred by fumes and venom, and it clung to his skin where he pressed it. Cooking meat came to mind, a scent that made his mouth water with bile and stomach heave, for that smell was just like the one all those years ago. His head turned as the blood slowly congealed. Wrapping the area with a clean bandage, he winced and pulled the makeshift tourniquet free. His eye ached and the gap dripped, his tears falling from a hole at the same rate his blood into the bandage- slowing, but concerning. Finally, his heaving chest began to relax, but he shook his head anyways, forcing himself to get back to the deep breaths,

Ha,

Ha,

Ha,

The task was still incomplete, and he returned to the origin to clean up the mess. He grimaced as he found a rag, the smell of the alcohol that he had dumped on the floor stinging his throat. He brought what remained of the bottle to assist with cleaning the mess. He kept his gaze away from the table, unprepared for what he had wrought, and he forced the air from his body repeatedly, so that he would remain focused and on task, yet the panting still followed,

Ha,

Ha,

Ha,

The smashed thumb, shredded and destroyed with a meat tenderizer, was nearly unrecognizable as something that had once been a part of a body. It made him gag, but he had not eaten, so nothing could come up. Regardless, he cleaned the disgusting mashed finger, delicately placing it and all the rags he had used in a biohazard containment bag that soon be burnt on the roof. His eye was heavy as the smoke wafted its way into the orifice, and dizziness seemed to be on the verge of overcoming him, but he decided that he would not need a transfusion. His lungs burned along with the fire, pulsing,

Ha,

Ha,

Ha,

Inside, feeling quite hollow (he told himself that was the shock), Johan looked at his hands. One was whole, the other was now that of an animal. A pang of regret flashed, and he whispered to himself, 'how do you reattach a thumb?' A wry smile broke on his lips as his deluded mind gave an answer.

With a finger nail.

Ha,

Ha,

Ha.

Connection Terminated

The egg that smacked into Alecs' shoulder was not surprising, nor did it physically hurt.

However, it felt as though the object inserted itself within their throat, jammed up into their head and swelled sharply, edging into their eyes. They ducked their head, and tried to make themself inconspicuous. Not exactly easy with the mechanism planted heavily on their shoulders, and after being spotted... well, it was too late.

They stamped down the blazing embarrassment, and continued working on robot components. Part of them wanted to scream out at those who watched them, ogling at the many limbed person. Man? Robot? Cyborg just seemed to be the easiest word to use. The robot watching them, the original autopilot before the late Mr. Hughes decommissioned them, Orea, did so with a lazy eye, an almost smile on his strange face as the New Hughes was treated to an egg directly in their face.

"These are valuable re-res-sources, you know," they tried to plead with the small crowd as they caught one of the eggs, reacting purposefully for the first time that day, knowing it to be futile. "Maybe don't waste them on m-me?"

Those around only jeered and chucked a few more, one splattering right on the logo emblazoned on their shirt which they had struggled and failed to remove. They burned in immense shame, and to the disappointment of the watchers, doubled down on doing their work, the computer chips coming into their proper formations under their careful eye. They were a medic now, not that anyone cared or wanted to know. They saved hundreds of lives, automaton or otherwise, but all that was pointed at was the fact that they would have eagerly dumped all of civilization to rot the rest of their days in space.

Now, they worked with creating processors, chips, farming tools, augmentations, et cetera. He used the knowledge of Hughes, but tried to stick to themself, their Alecs part. They were a good person in a bad situation. That was all. They never wanted to take over the ship, hell, they were not even supposed to be turned on! They were initialized because the original, now his warden, was too powerful against the directive.

Another egg came into their vision, held in someone's palm, and it was shattered right onto their hands, wrecking the chip they had so far painstakingly been able to protect. Red hot tears stung at their eyes and began to leak, a deep maroon color almost able to be mistaken for blood. They looked up to see the assailant, and knew instantaneously that their day had just gotten four hundred and fourteen times worse than it already was. Alecs looked for a rescuer, but only saw Orea playing around with one of the miniature robots that they had designed and given to the automaton as a sort of connection offering, appearing like a small squid. It did not exactly work. Not the robot, it worked perfectly; no, the hope to connect.

So now, without a savior, Alecs was face to miserable face with him.

Jimmy- a true cyborg- grinned down at him. Every single one of Alecs's fists clenched and snapped to their sides to prevent himself from lunging upon the man and tearing him to shreds.

"Hello dolly," the man smirked. "You look gorgeous."

Alecs said nothing, looking at him, splattered with egg and crying over a computer chip. They were forced to choke down the urge to slap the man away as one of his hands moved, curled, and dipped to go behind their head, tilting them to look up at him dead on – though Orea growled at Jimmy, fingertips brushing through an artificial beard while he stepped away to the off kilter android's satisfaction, Orea re-busying herself with the toy. Whoever was still around laughed at the sight of the creator shaking in rage as they restrained themself. They wanted this vile, wretched man away from them, yet they knew that if they were to get up and try to leave, there would be consequences, so much more so if they were to attack him. As of yet, Alecs had avoided any major repercussions, and they were not about to change that if they could help it.

So, they wiped their face and forced a smile.

"I'm quite c-certain that is sarcasm," they remarked, their voice feeble since they had torn out their own processor to give it to Werr, without telling a soul. It was the least they could do. The others believing that they knew where Hughes had put the originals was a joke to them, but as long as others thought that, they was safe from more insult; literally tearing themself apart to fix what had been done long before they had ever been created; forced to bear the sins of their unchosen subconscious. "If you don't mind, I'd like to return to work–"

"Well, I do mind," Jimmy remarked, mercifully keeping his distance thanks to Orea, but his smirk growing nonetheless. "And for the record, it wasn't sarcasm."

Alecs almost dropped the ruined chip, and then to prevent that from happening again, they dumped it into the trash. Their eyes automatically went to the clock, and they prayed that the timer tick down faster, if only to be able to get away from this nuisance. Jimmy's gaze followed theirs, and he smiled again.

"I've got you for another fifteen minutes, Hughes," he softly murmured, leaning against a table. He made no move after that, just watching, his presence alone making Alecs's hands tremble ever so slightly. "Hey, gorgeous, you dropped something!"

Alecs kept their breathing slow and even, and they did not take the bait to bend and look. They were not going to make a single compromising mistake around this man. Not one. Even as the man laughed, though it was only half mirthful, the other spiteful, as if daring Alecs to defy him again. They easily did so by ignoring Jimmy. They were just about to finish a processor when the heavy chimes signaling the end of the work day rang out. They let out a breath he did not know they were holding, which shocked them, seeing as how carefully they had been monitoring themself. Clearly not carefully enough. Alecs glanced at Orea, who was still preoccupied, or at least pretending to be. They weighed their options and decided to complete the device, voyeur or not.

If only he would have stayed silent. Jimmy watched quietly for only a moment, before continuing to talk, and Alecs wished they could have said that they ignored him entirely.

"Isn't your job over now, Alecs?" Jimmy asked, leaning over the counter and almost ruining another part. Alecs reeled away, packing up their things, to get ready to go home. Once they finished, they stood and waited for their... escort. Their mouth ticked into a frown with such a word, so they mentally swapped it to one no less appropriate – warden. Jimmy's eyes did not leave their form, and they shuddered as Orea glanced over them for contraband, though not from the check over, no sir. "If it is, I'd like to have a quick word with you right now. In private."

If Alecs spoke his mind then, they would admit that they felt safer to be left alone with the rumored to be deranged murder bot rather than Mr. Jimmy.

"Anything you say to me I d-don't mind you saying to Orea," they said quietly instead. Jimmy's smile twitched, but it did not leave, and nor did he, yet Orea, not caring too much about this drama, did. Jimmy blocked the exit, and said when the door closed; "Why don't you come live with me?"

Alecs stared at him with a slightly open mouth until Orea poked their face, snapping them out of his shock.

"Excuse me, what?"

"You heard me," Jimmy's grin grew a touch wider. "Come on and live with me. I've got a nice big house and no one to share it with. And yes, I'm aware that you've been chumming up with that old captain of the ship, but hell, he hates you just as much as everyone else."

"As if you don't," Alecs rebutted, getting ready to push past him to walk out the door after Orea.

"I don't," Jimmy remarked, and Alecs froze again. Part of them wanted to sob and run as far away as possible, the other to cry and fall into that wicked man's arms. "I think you're gorgeous, and I'd like to have you over for dinner. In both senses. If I didn't think so, I wouldn't invite you into my home."

"No." Alecs put their foot down. "You, you get out of m-my way now, please."

"Fine." Jimmy went out in front of them, huffing with a glare thrown at them, then stopped to sneer. "Seems like someone's the gyn toy for the ol' captain, ey? You have a thing for stupid guys that won't ever give you the light of day? Bet he doesn't even look at you at night, either, definitely wasting your potential. What a moro-"

Alecs had acted without thinking. They might have still done the same thing even if they had thought, but right now, all they felt was the burning need to protect Mark's honor. They used every single one of his hands to lash out, and they were about to bite the man when the device on their shoulders beeped.

Then they jerked back violently, rocked by waves of pain via electric shock. Orea looked on lethargically, pushing the button that caused the agony to sweep through them. They moaned as the tremors died down and finally left them, Orea nudging them with a foot to make them get up and move again. Alecs did not see Jimmy, and so stumbled out after their warden, sick to their stomach and dreadfully wobbling and swaying as they tried not to lose consciousness. Alecs was not paying enough attention, but at the moment, they cared more about putting one foot in front of the other.

Getting shoved to a wall was commonplace, but not shoved and *held* against the wall, a mundane situation becoming a terrifying one. Jimmy's body was keeping them low enough that they were on eye level, and as Alecs shuddered again at the feeling of lips near their ear, muted with fear as Jimmy spoke.

"All you have to do is imagine that egg as something else, sweetcheeks," his breath was shockingly clean. Alecs would have expected the stink of alcohol or something worse. "And you'd see why it would be bloody gorgeous."

The last word was rushed as Orea pulled him away, growling all the while, her patience already tried for the day due to Alecs's outburst of violence. Jimmy's shit eating grin was a stark contrast to Alecs's pale grimace of disgust.

"Think about it, Alecs," Jimmy still smiled as he spoke, "You know where to find me...."

He was gone, but Alecs stood rooted in the spot, looking at the space the man was moments ago. Orea nudged them with her knuckles, and Alecs snapped to action, beginning the brisk walk to the station and then sitting while Orea stood on the tram, and finally settling off on the dusty field of Mark's ranch. Ranch was the wrong term, Alecs knew that better than anyone, but Mark liked it, so Alecs kept their trap shut about the terminology.

With a sigh, they let themself be led to the house, Orea hardly looking back. They were not sure why Mark of all people elected to have them in his home, seeing as no one else proffered their doors to the criminal. They paused in the doorway, hearing voices in the living room– happy voices, with laughter and mirth. Their metaphorical heart hammered in their chest as they heard it, sinking to their stomach and rising to their throat at the same time.

Orea was being greeted by the others, their ears easily picking up Mark's rumbling baritone that went right to making their heart thunder all the more. Jimmy was only half right, in that Mark had no idea how Alecs felt about him. Part of them adored the man, the other feared him, but they knew that all of them loved him. They would do anything for him, absolutely anything. As soon as they finished walking through the doors (which they had stopped doing when he had heard the others), the metallic clasps on their shoulders hooked free and tucked neatly away, ready to descend back onto them when they would next walk out of the long, short house. The thought that they were a prisoner on the very planet some ingrained part of them felt like it used to own seemed quite ironic.

After inhaling and exhaling air they did not need repeatedly, they forced a smile and made their way into the room where everyone else was for the time being. Later, it would only be them and Mark, mouth wateringly close, yet so far. Smiles faded upon seeing the newcomer, even though they knew they lived here with Mark. Rina's change was the sharpest, and Alecs felt that if Clark had not grabbed her hand, they would have already been turned into a paste.

"Hello all," they meekly managed to say, eyes flicking from the people to the floor and back again, embarrassed even now. "I h-hope you all are well?"

"Alecs! Come on in," Mark greeted with a large smile, which was not on the faces of the fellow people in the room. Orea was holding a small creature that Alecs did not have the time to determine, only sure that it was a mouse of some sort. Alecs recognized both the former pilot and autopilot of the Alnilam on the couch across from Mark, Mr.s Timothy and Lars. Alecs bit back a harsh swallow at the sight of the other robot, hardly registering Timothy's polite hello. Lars' lips were in a terse line, eyes scanning over Alecs and giving a slight nod, but Alecs could feel the autopilot's stare lingering even as he looked elsewhere. "We're all friends here."

"No we ain't," Rina refuted, Clark coloring somewhat as he refused to meet Alecs's eye. Seamus shrugged, "She's right, ya know."

"Well, Alecs is a changed guy!" Mark commented, smiling with a touch of nervousness. "They've been working on computers and chips, making things for both bots and people in need."

"Last week he made fourteen prosthetics," Clark added, though in a neutral tone. "Something like that amount, right Orea?"

"Forty," Alecs whispered to the android, who hummed and rumbled it back. It felt nearly hollow to hear the number replaced for what it was actually worth. Orea continued on, "Long man makes tiny toys. Little creatures. They work. Named one Rālū."

"Oh? What else have you made?" Timothy asked, leaning forward. "Any artificial intelligences?"

The arrogant, spiteful part of Alecs wanted to bring up the fact that they made all of them, they created all of them, from the Annes to the Warrs. They were all their work, each and every one, and all of them had then turned their backs on them.

"Sometimes," the new, meeker robot mumbled. "Though I've kept away from it, lately."

"Would you... consider doing it again? Once more?"

"If given reason, or d-desire, I don't see why not."

"Could you make a child processor?" Timothy asked, his hand subconsciously reaching for Lars', the robotic man taking it gently. "We've been looking around to no luck."

Alecs stared at him for a while before smiling slightly.

"I could... I could certainly t-try," they offered, trying not to betray their elation. "Yes, I'd be honored-d, I'd try my absolute best to deliver."

"I wouldn't trust 'im to make toast, let alone a child," Rina grumbled, still only held back by the enormous weight of Clark's dainty hand in hers. "T'e fact that he was runnin' a ship at all is bonkers."

"Aye, but he wasn't running it well," Seamus pointed out as he leaned back. "Sendin' out me and a few others on a pointless mission that was just wasting resources. An' then, when the mission was a success, he ups and tries to kill me!"

"It w-was in my programming," Alecs weakly defended Themself.

"Mm," Orea's dual colored eyes skimmed over them. "My programming."

"On top o' that, he locked up any droids that got emotions. Not sure where *that* came into play," Rina glared at them, making them shirk back all the more, six hands fiddling with each other anxiously. She no doubt was thinking of her own time confined, and the toll it had on her.

"I'm sorry," they whispered.

"That doesn't cut it," she harrumphed, turning her disdain away.

"You also shoved me away," Orea tilted her head, "From my job."

"I was your replacement b-because you were," Alecs paused to think of the best words to use. "Completely out of control."

"That makes sense," the misprogrammed droid hummed, "I retract my statement."

"Well, it was your ship to begin with," Lars accidentally dug the pit for Alecs even more. Alecs sank further into the lone seat they were on. Through the static in their eyes, they duly registered that they were the only one on a seat alone. "So you were just doing your job, maintaining order and satisfaction."

"No one liked the new autopilot when he was first installed," Seamus nursed a can of oilpop. "Not much changed since then."

"Er, I…" Alecs swallowed roughly, the static in their eyes growing. "I've gotta go n-now. I'll be back later."

"A damn good idea for once," Rina snorted. Alecs managed to smile and laugh along with the others, like it was just some funny joke that they were in on. The words bounced in their head. Time or no time, they still were a massive risk and liability. Might as well go to the one guy who did not mind all of their mistakes.

In the hall, that thought gave them pause, and they nearly gagged at the conclusion it led to.

Still, who else would take them in? They were even barred from nearly all the bars and clubs, and the comforting touch of another person was a desperate need. However, it was difficult to know if the touch of that cyborg would fall even in the realm of comfort.

Alecs donned their coat and got ready to go out into the night – when a hand on their hip stopped them, their even breathing stuttering indiscernibly. They turned around sharply and found Mark looking at them with a strange expression.

"How long are you going to be out for?" he asked them. There was an unspoken; 'Where are you going?'

"I don't know," Alecs replied. "I'll call you from work if I'll be out all night."

Mark bit his lip, but nodded.

"I'll see you later then," he smiled slightly. Alecs slipped out the window instead of the door to prevent the tracker falling upon their shoulder once more. Mark made no move to call them back, but his shoulders slumped and his smile faded, and after a moment, he returned to the group.

Alecs meanwhile walked, half knowing their destination, half avoiding it.

Eventually they found himself at the door, and they hesitated for a long moment before knocking.

Jimmy opened the door a few seconds later, his shark like grin turning tighter as it widened.

"If it isn't my favorite programmer!" he crooned, looking up to them with half opened eyes, and proffered to their his half drunk beer. "Want a cold one?"

"I shouldn't," the flabbergasted Alecs commented, but it felt out of their control as they took it from the other's hand, trusting that the one he was previously drinking from would be less likely to contain anything averse, though they held the first sip in their mouth to be certain, letting scans run over it and not swallowing until certain that it was clean. "Th-thank you...."

"So, what brings you here?" Jimmy inquired, leaning forward predatorily as they settled on the couch. There was genuine curiosity in the question, though. "You've never taken me up on my offer before. How long are you planning on gracing me with your presence? Until dinner? Until morning? I have a lasagna in the oven. Not that American style bullshit, a real meat one."

"I, er, don't eat meat," Alecs mumbled. "But I wouldn't m-mind being company."

Jimmy smirked; "So you'd like to stay for dinner?"

"I, I," Alecs stuttered, realizing the implication of his words. Part of them took over, telling the anxious part of themself to shove that to where the sun would never shine. "Yeah. Yeah, I w-would."

"Sounds great," Jimmy purred, "I'll make a quick dish for your rabbit highness. Salad?"

"Sure," Alecs acquiesced, feeling strangely accepted. Maybe Jimmy was not so bad. Or perhaps, more likely, they were just too desperate. At the table, Jimmy droned on and on about himself, but Alecs was too preoccupied to care enough to do more than nod. Soon, when Alecs snapped back into reality, they found that they were on the couch again, their energy sensors higher and satiation complete. One of Jimmy's hands was on their knee, leaning close but still keeping a distance, clearly waiting for an answer to an inquiry. Alecs flushed with embarrassment. "Sorry, I didn't c-catch that, what was your question?"

"I asked you why you decided to come over tonight," Jimmy repeated, still smirking. His hand tightened just a touch. "Seeing as you've always declined. You seem pretty distracted, and not by my good looks. Did something happen?"

Alecs's heart jammed up their throat, that blurring static returning to their eyes. They found the words tumbling out of their mouth, the events of the evening and how the folks by Mark's brought up all their mistakes, and how as hard as they tried, they could not outrun *his* past.

91

They sobbed into Jimmy's chest, a hand slowly dragging through their hair in what felt like a half assed attempt to calm through wish fulfillment.

"H-H-He asked me to make a baby processor, b-but I'm afraid I'll m-mess it up," they hiccoughed. "I've messed up s-so many times, I, I'm afraid I'll do it again."

"Well, it doesn't have to be a chip," Jimmy chose, again, a terrible time to flirt, bouncing Alecs on his lap before the android stopped him with an unimpressed grimace. "Hey, it was just an idea."

"There's n-no way in hell I'd ever have a child-d with you," Alecs deadpanned.

"That's fair." Jimmy's smile faded after a second of thought, replaced by a large measure of confusion. "Wait, can you even have kids?"

"An' then she reminded me that n-no one likes me," they continued, ignoring the question. "S-so I went to find someone...."

"Well, she's right, no one could like you," Jimmy shrugged, his hands settled on Alecs's sides. "After all, you are a rogue AI who nearly doomed earth and humanity had it not been for a few robots and one crazy human that stood up against you. So, yeah."

Alecs got up sharply, scrubbing at the tears on their face, seeming to stain their hands with blood, and that was how it felt – hot blood on their hands, blood that would never, ever wash off.

"You good there? I was just-"

"I'm fine, fine," they sniffled, donning their jacket and turning to the door. "Thank you f-for the dinner--"

They found that the door would not open, and a chill crept down their spine.

"Gimme a kiss before you go."

Alecs turned around, closing their eyes and sighing. They kissed the man's cheek, and then turned back to the exit, which was, mercifully, open. Alecs swore to themself to never go back, no matter how lonely and desperate for a touch they felt.

—

92

They had pushed him backwards over the control panel, eyes flashing and all six arms straining against him, a snarl over their face. He fought with them, and the sweat that had rolled down the back of Mark's neck had not just been from the struggle.

He liked it.

He enjoyed the power struggle, the fight to the top, how defiantly and forcefully Alecs had pressed against him, desperate to succeed against all odds, and that look of despair as Mark had shut them off, it stuck with him. It appeared in his mind when he thought of nothing, slipped into conversations, and tugged at his heartstrings.

Alecs only wanted to protect the people, the humans; and did so in the only way they could, the only way they knew. Mark knew Alecs loved him, but he thought it was simply the same way that they loved all of humanity, with a benevolent and almost patronizing gaze.

He learned too late that it was not the case, and then he lost his chance with them — at least properly. People would say things if they caught wind of the leader seeing the traitor. Before Alecs had pleaded guilty to conspiracy, mutiny, attempted murder, and a whole host of other crimes, before that, Mark could have initiated something with them. Perhaps. Now, he could keep them in his home under the statement of keeping an eye on them, two if he could manage.

Hoo boy... Mark keeping two eyes on them was far more likely than none or one. Even then, worrying about them, he could visualize each and every facet of the AI's husk. While on the ship, he had stared at and studied over Alecs for what he thought was a passtime, only realizing too late that he just loved watching the autopilot. He loved watching them work, setting up artificial rain, managing nutrition, monitoring health, everything that needed to be done, taking away the work from the human and drawing it into themself, telling him without words, 'I got this. You lean back and relax, sir. You're in good hands'. For a long time, it worked. For at least four hundred and fourteen years, it worked. Life had been great and people were at least content.

People were happy now, happier than they ever had been before, with a proper sense of work and value instilled in them. Mark was the one that led the charge on that, along with the robots who had taken them by the hand back to Earth. Alecs taught them how to function on this planet, having been the only person who had been there, Anderson the Computer assisting whenever his memory faltered, or just needed help with explaining. The latter case was the more frequent, happening at a 1 out of 100 ratio.

Alecs's memory rarely failed them. They remembered everything, from exactly what Mark had for breakfast thirteen years ago to everyone on the Alnilam, Alnilam, and Mintaka's birthdays.

Mark sighed and finished washing up after his meal, rinsing off his face to wake up a little more. Alecs had yet to call him, and Mark was starting to worry, though he reasoned that there was nothing to fear. They were likely just at work. Mark could easily call in to check.

"Hey!" he was replied to with a grumble, and he instantly recognized it. "Oh, hi Orea. Is Alecs there? Ah. Mhm. I see. Thanks."

He put down the phone piece, nervously chewing at the inside of his cheek.

Not at work. Court issued tracker still hanging above the door. Mark could not help but feel that it was his fault.

He went to Alecs's room to search through it. It was rather bare-bones, with a desk for working at home, a recharge bed, and a lamp. The desk had a few drawers, and after a moment of thinking, he decided to open it up. There were several blueprints and unfinished designs, and underneath those was a journal. It looked to be at the very least a thousand years old.

Mark stared at it in his hands. He was worried. He was afraid. Maybe there would be a clue within.

He did not want to break Alecs's trust.

So, he replaced it carefully, intending to tell them the whole truth when (and if) he found them. Stepping outside for a moment to calm himself, he started wandering around the perimeter of the house. Towards the west end, he looked around with surprise, certain that he heard something odd. Something like crying. He knew that crying, but could not tell for the life of him where it was emanating from.

"Alecs?"

There was a strange sound, louder, like one of shock, and Mark turned to where he heard both the movement and the sound.

"What are you doing on the roof?" he asked, anxious once more. Alecs waved him away, wiping at their face intensely, trying to get rid of all the tears. "Could you come down?"

Mark was reminded that they were a robot when they jumped down, landing neatly and quietly.

"Are you alright? Orea said you didn't go in to work today and I got worried…" Mark swallowed, Alecs avoiding looking at him. "I was going to check your journal for clues but I didn't. I just… I'm sorry."

"It's okay," Alecs tried not to sob, failing to keep the tremor from their voice. "I'm moving out anyways soon. You won't need to worry about me going on a killing spree or whatever you people think I'd do in my spare time. The chip for Timothy an' L-Lars is in the third drawer."

"Whoa whoa, whoa," Mark stepped back with this sudden influx of information. "Wait, you can't, what do you mean you're moving out? Where will you go? Is it where you were last night?"

"No," Alecs replied. "Just away. Away for good. I'm no longer needed, as all the information that I c-could have supplied is now obsolete. So… I will go."

"Don't go, don't leave," Mark pleaded. Alecs sighed and asked; "Why shouldn't I? I'm quite hated here, and for good r-reason."

"I don't hate you."

"You toler-rate me."

"I like you."

"You like everyone."

"Not like I love you."

At first, Alecs scoffed, but it came out largely as another sob.

"You c-can't love me. I tried to kill you."

"I can love you, and I do," Mark insisted, feeling that he was getting through to the AI. He stepped closer again, holding out his hand for Alecs to take. "I love you, and I'd want you to stay with me. Will you please stay with me?"

"I'm afraid I'll hurt you again," Alecs whispered, their hand trembling. Mark made the move and took it himself. "I'm afraid that I won't be myself."

"You won't, and even if you will, we'll make it right," Mark assured them, pulling Alecs into a hug. "We'll fix it up. We always do, ay? We wouldn't be here without you. You're the one that was a catalyst for all of our growth, even through turmoil. Your mistakes are in the past, and I still love you regardless."

"I'm a wreck," Alecs sobbed, falling apart in Mark's arms, but Mark was there to hold them. As rain started to drizzle over their abode, Mark carried them inside, took them to his room, cuddled up with him in blankets. Alecs sniffled and leaned against him. "I love you."

"I love you, too."

It

6.20.2021

Many times I'm asked; do you want to talk about it?
And I say Yes, because I do want to talk, quite a bit,
Then, I am silent, since I don't know
From whence my thoughts flow,
Eventually understanding does come and hit:

I do not know what it is.

97

Jerk in Shining Armor

7.11.2021

"You're a jerk, you know."

"No, I did not."

"Yep. The biggest, jerkiest jerk."

"Interesting."

Sybas pouted futilely as Rawlin turned the meat on the spit. It was only the two of them, as they had been split off from their party. Sybas was furiously staring at him, as if his gaze could burn through the thick plates of armor covering his remaining companion.

Sybas was lightheaded and cranky, as the cauterization that his companion had done on a bayonet jab stung like hell. Rawlin had shoved a strap of leather into Sybas' mouth, and without warning placed his burning broadsword upon his shoulder.

Cauterized him. Just like that. Grab, jab, and go.

So now, he was the king of all jerks, and Sybas was not shy of telling him.

"I've never met a jerk as jerky as you. Not even Darwin's jerky is as jerky as you are."

"His jerky is quite good. I would like some now, actually."

"We all want things we can't have," Sybas glowered, nursing his lukewarm canister of tea. The only thing worse than cold tea was tea that was not yet chilled and far from hot, leaving it in this unhappy state of neither soothing nor refreshing. Something that he could not have at the moment was either type of tea, unless he were to chuck the container into the fire and then fish it out before it would explode. "Like I'd prefer that you would have kissed it better instead of stabbing me, but, you ended up being a huge jerk."

"I appreciate that you respect my wish of clean words," Rawlin's smile was audible, though invisible. Sybas only harrumphed and went back to nursing his bitter, lukewarm tea. "I know there are far more biting ones on the tip of that sharp tongue of yours. Therefore, I will respect your wish of having the first cut of the meal. Bon appetite."

Sybas rose an eyebrow at the meat proffered to him. It looked glazed and thoroughly cooked, and the master bandit knew that the duelist was actually quite skilled with flavoring and maintaining a good texture even for the most sparse meals. Still, it was hardly a worthy apology. Sybas scowled, raising an eyebrow.

"I always get the first choice, though."

"I know. At the moment I cannot think of any other way to make up to you my 'jerkiness'," Rawlin smiled again, pushing up his helm. "Though I will try to fulfill anything you might request– so long as it remains within my code."

"Code schmode, you're still a jerk," Sybas retorted, taking a smaller half of the meal, knowing that he needed less, and in order to stay more alert and keen, he should have less regardless. Thus, when Rawlin swapped their plates, he protested. "I'm keeping watch tonight, I can't be weighed down by my stomach!"

"No, I think I will stand vigil against the Blots," Rawlin remarked. "That is a much better way of making it up, I think we can agree. You should get a full rest tonight."

"That's crap," Sybas replied, but yawned anyways, and took the plate offered to him. Rawlin nodded with approval and sat beside him. "Thanks."

"I apologize for the rough treatment I used," was the response. Sybas was rather surprised, as Rawlin tended to never admit a single failing. "I should have warned you."

"Nah, if you did, I would have probably told you to piss off," Sybas laughed. "So you did right."

"Still, is there any way I could make it up to you?" Rawlin inquired, eyes bright and earnest. "Anything at all?"

"Well, this time you said nothing about not breaking you code, so…" Sybas flashed a devilish smile, yet Rawlin did not change his expression. "I want you to kiss it better."

Rawlin's laugh was soft, but it filled the whole room regardless.

"Alright," he got up, setting aside his finished plate. Sybas waited impatiently, folding his arms, tilting the one with the gash forwards, looking away, as if he was doing for Rawlin a favor. His knight in no longer shining armor knelt, making a metallic clang as he did so, tilting his visor up again from where it had fallen after he stood, the hinges not as strong as they used to be. Sybas turned his nose up in a desperate attempt to not laugh. Rawlin moved in, and Sybas' eyes flew open as he felt chapped lips press to his own, flinging himself backwards with shock. Rawlin was looking at him with an equal measure of surprise, lips still gently pursed. "I thought that you wanted a kiss–"

99

"To my shoulder!" Sybas could no longer hold in his laughter as realization dawned on the crusader. "Oh, Unified, you thought– oh hell, damn, that's so– haven't you ever heard the expression to kiss something better?"

"Er, once upon a time," Rawlin managed to speak out of his embarrassment. "So long ago that I had forgotten… what I was actually supposed to do."

"Was that in 'your code'?" Sybas asked with a twinkle in his eye. "As in, was that 'allowed' for you?"

"Yes, it was," Rawlin answered simply. "Other restrictions apply, yet that was breaking none."

Sybas sighed and laid his forehead into his palm, trying not to laugh again. The pain in his shoulder was nothing compared to his bewilderment and relief.

"Are you delirious?" Rawlin inquired, concerned. "Do you need any salves or tinctures?"

"No, I'm all good," Sybas assured him, looking up, still with mirth in his heart. "It's only, if I had known that your ethically crap was perfectly fine with giving me kisses, I would have asked for them every time you owed me a favor."

Rawlin's brain processed the information longer than it took for Bart to actually land a hit. Sybas could practically hear the grindstones turning in his head, and it made him chuckle again.

"Are you pulling my leg?"

"No!" Sybas gasped, overly dramatic to the point of laying a hand on his heart in feigned shock. "Rawlin, I would never pull your leg! It's too damn heavy!"

That made Rawlin grin, though he tried to hide it.

"Honest?"

"Cross my heart."

"Not hiding your other hand behind your back?"

Sybas rose them both in a gesture of proof, and then two leather clad gloves grasped his hands. Sybas looked at Rawlin, surprised for the second time that hour.

"That's good," Rawlin stated. "I have a lot to make up for."

Sybas smiled as Rawlin kissed him.

Lend a Hand

8.5.2021

"Hey, Chill Pill," Chilla turned around and raised an eyebrow at the new nickname. Like Max, Elisa had a knack for coming up with names for those close to her. Unlike the Oroseira brothers, her nicknames usually make sense. "Mind lending me a hand?"

"Oh, sure!" the other replied with a smile, only for Elisa to take off her prosthetic CIN and dump it onto her desk. "Uh...."

"Well, there's the hand," Elisa gave a sharp toothed smile of her own, but it was a little tight and frustrated. "I haven't been able to clean some gunk out of it. Ironically, it's somethin' that needs both hands, which I'm fifty percent lacking."

"I see," Chilla grinned. "I can definitely take a look. Why can't you get to it, though? You usually are able to clean it all yourself."

"It's in the fingers," Elisa explained. "They keep moving, even when I put 'em into the vice. I can hold it steady if you want."

"If you think it will help, sounds good to me," Chilla nodded, and the short cat like woman sat beside her, her tail flicking with contentment. "Wait, why don't you use that? Your tail?"

"It has no fingers of its own," Elisa replied with amusement. "Also, it's too short."

"That sucks. Having a strong beak is way better," Chilla started to get out tools to open the hand. "So, in the fingers, right?"

"Yes," Elisa affirmed. As soon as Chilla put a screwdriver to the small panel, a laser aimed right at her chest, startling her into dropping it. "Oh, right. Echem, turn off security features."

"Security features disengaged," a robotic voice intoned, seemingly from the bright gem like structure that Elizabeth had told Chilla powered the arm. "Proceed."

Proceed Chilla did, always marveling at the amount of objects within the hand, from the water filtration system to the miniature razor blades. It only took a second to spot the problem, a mess of dough trapped within the knuckles. She got to work, and agreed that the hand was not as easy to work with as it appeared, thanks to all of the extra gadgets inside. Elisa had to hold the wrist steady for Chilla to push down the fingers. Soon, there was a small mass of dough beside the hand, and Chilla carefully cleaned out the last of it.

"There! That should do it!" she inspected it over, satisfied. "How did that get in there, anyways?"

"I decided to make cookies," Elisa admitted, blushing a little bit. "I forgot to put on the pseudo silicone cover. I can mix things quite well, but, you know, if it's exposed then all of that mixing is gonna end up inside of it. This is one of the reasons I avoid baking."

"Oh my god," Chilla laughed, eyes twinkling. Elisa pursed her lips as she reattached her hand, tail twitching with the displeasure of being prodded at. "That's so cute."

"Not as cute as ya," Elisa shot back, then sauntered out of the room.

Chilla stared at where she had been before running after her.

"Wait! Can I have a cookie?!"

Dark and Deep

9.27.2021

The waves of the ocean sound a bit like breathing.

If you close your eyes by the sea, the nigh silent draw inwards is an inhale, the rippling, bubbling, and sighing exhale in the wave. Like a human, the ocean also has a temper, sometimes calm and relaxed, even meditatively slow, othertimes roiling and huffing and puffing with an anger or vexation. Unlike a human, it never ceases to breathe. There is not one thing a man can do to stop the ocean from breathing. They may block up the path with dams, fjords, and trenches, yet the water will still breathe. To still the ocean is a task beyond a human.

Manny could tell that simply by listening.

He was alone on the shore (for what reason, he could not tell), and his eyes were closed as he listened to the waves' infinite knell.

A part of him wanted to stay blind. There was enough in the sounds, the sounds like sirens calling to listen a bit longer, beckoning to breathe alongside the ocean tide; stay and hear the song change and shift in the slightest of ways.

However, observation is incomplete without the full use of one's senses, if they are available to them. Luckily for Manny, he still had the functional use of at least half of his visual capabilities, and though his heart demanded he keep them in the dark, his mind cried for the knowledge, such a yearning to be unfelt by any mortal sense.

Taking in a deep breath, Manny gradually found himself staring at the ocean.

The east coast waters were the same color as her eyes, making him wince with the memories, and, in order to distract himself from them, he wondered when on earth people decided that the ocean was blue. Surely, some of the ripples appeared to match the sky, and as he looked beyond the shoreline he saw how the two bodies of water, one solid, the other evaporated, merged in a perfect, terrifying union, as infinite and detailed as the sounds he heard. There was so much to learn. No matter what a person does, the sights will always change in a way so as to be invisible, insidious, morphing each and every second into something else like a human child, yet forever in the state of a made old man, who year by year never seems to look even the slightest bit different.

Sounds and sights were almost repetitive, but with each and every instance of the wind and waves, there was a difference, so very minute, but audible, visible, even if not to unhoned senses.

And how long could he have soaked in those sensations...!

Forever and ever, listening, watching, his bare feet making their way towards the moistened sand. He could smell now, too, with each gust of the ocean breeze, and each one brought a dizzyingly new scent. It was stupefying and horrifying. In one he could smell the waters' salt and mettle, taunting and daring; in another the limber call of seaweeds, grass, and kelp; fish leaping and spreading their own slight scent into the domain of land; strong smells of ambergris hitting the air; and coyly, slyly, laughingly, blood in the water. A cycle of life within the organism known as the ocean, like bacteria living on a human without ever knowing how small it really is in the scale of things. Like a human living on the earth. Smelling various hints of life, excessive and vast, it was like a hypnotic skunk had sprayed the whole area, bringing even the mighty to their knees in awe.

Would Manny like to join in to those smells, find their sources and discover how they came to be?

There was so much to learn. So much to absorb.

Too much.

He shook while water rose and fell without any regards to his rocky emotions, generating new physical feelings with each and every cascading wave, the sounds, sights, and smells beyond himself. He may have been an exceptional human, granted stature and intellect, but even he was susceptible to all the vices that bound him to flesh, bone, and blood. Yet, there was more. The ocean was not yet known, teasingly caressing at his heels and playfully tugging at his ankles, like a content, sanguine lover who knew that their mate had no possible will or way to resist. The smells – their alluring perfume to cloud the mind and perplex the flow of blood, natural, bloodthirsty and mouthwatering, a wispy proof of an existence even whither the personae is long gone. The sounds – his low, rumbling voice to send vibrations to the chest and heart, subliminally murmuring little things that never had the same notes. The sight – her long beautiful folklorico, with a titillating question if he wanted to see what was below as she lifted it for brief moments in her dance.

105

Like a fish on a hook, Manny was drawn out of where his feet were firmly planted and pulled to a demesne in which the slightest push of Ocean's demands would send him sprawling, tumbling, gasping for an air that no longer existed. Still, the water was warmer and colder than he expected, and he surrendered to the inhales and exhales as the waves rose higher and higher of his own accord. The sights blurred and wavered as thick saline atmosphere morphed around him, cupping him and pulling him to the cusp of reality. Was there a choice in becoming seabound? For it tugged at his legs and arms and pushed his back, and splashed his cheeks and ran through his hair, droplets sliding down like gentle fingers and wrenching at his ability to remain upright with the infinite stamina that had been awarded to it. Manny knew that he was nothing to Their Infinity, bewildered as to why him, yet so dug into that he had not the chance to question it any further.

Their smell filled his nose for one brief moment before he decided that Manny had been upright long enough, knocking him down on his back to be held, gravity lost, in her palm, pressing on his throat and chest and eyes and ears and deafening him, blinding him, rendering all the smells moot, and he opened his mouth.

The taste of the ocean was first and foremost that of salt, then sweet and bitter all at once, their kiss all encompassing and stealing the air from his lungs to replace it with a formidable and insurmountable poison. Manny's gasp was a cough, struggling to rise, but Sea did not want to lose his new boat so soon, another wave of sound drawing him back into the abyss. He could taste blood, he could taste citrus, he could taste life and death all at once, and he knew that he was somewhere in between, in an environment whose clutches would never permit him to live, and forced him up each time he was on the verge of the void. Was she cruel? Were they kind? Was he indifferent?

Why was Manny in such desperate infatuation?

It was dangerous and mocking, it was his end, but what a sweet one. It reminded him of his nights with the loner's girlfriend Heroin in his ears and driving his rhythm, Peyote playing with his sight and taking him to worlds even past the galaxies, the strong, hit and quit (but keeps coming back for more) man of Cocaine filling his lungs, and with Methamphetamine tickling his elbow, and he knew he had to get out now.

For the ocean was not like those, nay, the ocean was worse.

Because unlike those, they who had been escapes, the sea was a calling to more. Tempting him to go further than he could. Asking in a laugh, why not? Why so scared?

There is more to learn! More to find! Secrets undiscovered and paths untaken, chasing a dream until you cannot even take in another breath, do you not do that all the time in any regard? Come on, Manny, this is you, your passion, your life, and there is no use in denying it.

Face yourself. Go deeper. Despite the magnitude that you feel daunts you on the oceanfront, you know it is no more than your mirror reflecting your own, infinite, wickedly glorious goals.

Manny burst free of the water with an inhale to rival that of his constraints. Dragging himself to shore, fighting every inch of the way, his vision was blackened and pinpoint to the beach, ignoring the sight of the obstacles that molded and curved around him. Stumbling and tripping, leading him to crawl on his knees on the water soaked sand, he smelled of sweat and sunshine beating upon him and gradually drying him of the liquid temptation. The phantom pulls faded, the taste evaporated, and he lay on the sand still as a dead man.

His eyes closed, and his breathing soon matched that of the Ocean.

Feather

10.6.2021

Marina doubled over and curled into her stomach, trying to fill it with pressure.

It felt like she could not even breathe through the roaring agony. It was as if her organs had been turned into sentient, angry spikes and drove into her skin, she could feel the discontent and hear it's annoyance with her.

Marina could have wept, for there was nothing she saw that was even remotely edible. Oh, why did she leave that bread? It had been moldy and there were rat bites all over it, but she could eat anything, anything that could be eaten. The lights seemed to obey her tormentor, flickering with each rumble in her gut. Perhaps she was passing out? That had happened before.

She put her arm to her mouth, chewing on the tattered, dirty coat to soothe herself, tricking her stomach just a bit. If she held out a little longer, perhaps she would find something.

A snap rang out as she took a step, making her freeze, cocking her head slightly towards the sound.

What was that? A mouse trap? Where did it come from?

Trying her best to remember where the sound emanated, she tiptoed her way into an empty room. Sure enough, in a corner, a bird had gotten its leg caught in the trap.

Marina knelt, and picked up a rock.

She cooked the bird on her lighter as much as she could, the blood sometimes putting out the flame.

Marina hated it; because the bird had wings.

Grip

Sal's got a knife in his hand.

He needs it.

He is no monster.

The knife is gripped carefully, and he knows that his hold is firm. He will not slip up. He can use this tool to his advantage, and he will.

He adjusts his hold and sneaks slowly into the man's office.

His goal sits unassumingly.

He stalks forward silently, eyes trained on the prize as if he expects it to bolt away at the speed of light.

There is a knife in Sal's hand. He is in John's office. He is not a monster. He is doing what anyone else would in his situation.

He adjusts his hold, and plunges the knife in.

The frosted cake barely bends as he cuts it, which makes him smile with delight. John had promised him a surprise, and by hell did he deliver. Sal cuts himself a piece and picks up a napkin to hold it, and happily begins eating it away.

He wonders how he would thank John later for his gift, and tries to think of the other man's favorite sweet food. Maybe he would appreciate a coffee cake. The thought makes Sal smile as he cuts for himself another piece. He probably should not eat the whole thing at once, but he is hungry as he skipped lunch. It seems like a just dessert for his day.

Sal finishes the tiny cake and smiles with satisfaction.

Sometimes it really is the little perks that make all the difference.

Congeal

10.22.2021

Elisa stood in the middle of an airide's galley.

It was empty, now.

It had not been a few minutes ago.

No, it had not been.

....

Was she a bad person, to believe that she was forced to defend herself like this?

But they had threatened her, threatened her Max. No one got to hurt him anymore, not his father, nor brother, not Marlin either. Only she could tease him, and always knew when a joke would be taken too far and prevented those.

Some blood soaked into her shoes, a lot in her hair, slickening it to her scalp, but she could hear it shifting and crinkling and drying into flakes of stolen life. Elizabeth stood where she was, nothing in her hands yet a lot of blood coating them. Her hair was dripping for now, and she hated the feeling of hot and cooling blood hitting her head and slowly becoming more and more shattered like drying clay thrown in the furnace too long.

She missed the arboretum, back when everything was simple and silly. Before everything with Phillip and Marlin and the Odiologists and the Three. When they would fill the evenings with the Legends of Aika Brrin and Maximilian Oroseira; instead of living those terrible adventures.

Elisa found a bathroom on the ship and began cleaning off the gore from her body.

Her hair, though... she could not return to their car with her hair like this. Then again, she could not wash her hair here so as to not leave any extra evidence and possibly get Max in trouble. She would not risk that. She would rather keep the congealing red liquid until an ice river or other external body of water.

She walked away silently.

Her hair seemed purple in the red sun's light.

Scratches

2.16.2022

1.

Ever since Al could remember, his nails would leave long trails along his body, trying to find the source of that disturbing itch. They were drawn along his arms and legs and chest, anywhere he could reach, leaving pale lines like glowing tallies across his skin. There was something under his dermis, Albert just knew it, something rippling and shifting, undoubtedly not his own, something gnawing on his insides with insidious glee, methodical, nerve wracking, scratchy. As if you had suddenly developed an allergy to your own organs. Except it was not sudden. No. It had been there for a long, long time.

The doctor found nothing. The psychologist said it was in his head, either from neural misfires or a type of psychosis. Albert silently insisted that there was something there; and the only times it would retreat from under the main surface of his skin was when there was potential for it to be touched.

So Al tried to stick around other people as much as possible, if only to distract himself from the burning need to get it out of his body. It was incredibly draining to constantly be around socially, though it was better than clawing at his own skin and anticipating when it would break, trying to know which would rend first; his flesh or his psyche.

Al tended to stay around Mina. First of all, it was convenient, and secondly, because Mina was a very touchy woman. She would touch Albert's arm, his side, his hand, his shoulder and back, and everywhere she would touch, the itch would flee if only for an hour.

He dared not try to explain it to her. Mina, as a doctor, would likely smile piteously, shake her head and tell Al that it was in his imagination, like all the others had. So he kept quiet and said none of it.

Albert loved her incredibly. The fact that her mere presence chased away the rippling thing under his flesh made him all the more infatuated. It was simply a perk, but a desperately needed one.

The lines on his skin were a pale yellow, sometimes pink in the center if he dug deep.

Sometimes it would tauntingly hide under his hands, where he dared not mar further, already scarred and lined with blight, frightening him that those very needed appendages would be damaged from the inside, forcing him to ignore the twitching itch.

When it toyed with his insides it was all the worse. Deep, flicking, running along his organs like a rat forced into his system, burned above him and scurrying along to burrow within and feast on what little flesh he had.

Yes, he did lose weight on those bad days. Those days when it felt like his stomach was unbearably full, when anything he ate sank into a void of nothingness, no satiety gained, and yet, even with that protruding mass in his innards, he still had a hunger growling within. After the itch would pass from inside his stomach, he would always have to eat something light, despite his famished state, so as to avoid vomiting it out immediately.

Al was not sure which was worse, when it was in his hands or inside his organs. Both options were awful, and he scratched at his skin to quiet it down, or better yet, disappear entirely, hoping that perhaps he would be able to tear enough to grasp it in his itching hands and pull it out of himself.

And his nails left scratches.

So many.

Over his arms, his legs, his chest, shoulders, back, anywhere he could reach, trying to drive away that horrific burn. The terrible chill. Al was sick of it. He tried everything; starving it out, burning it away, practically drowning himself, nothing even remotely came close to the quiet he got when he scratched at the slithering object beneath his dermis.

Al was desperate. He would be the first person to admit that, especially if someone would give him a solution. The medications the doctors gave against itching did nothing to soothe the irritation, as topical medications are just that, topical. Putting some on the slightly bloody cuts afterwards only caused him a little more discomfort, but no other change. The medications given to force away bad thoughts and pretend visions and false feelings did nothing against the itch either, though he did feel a little more functional, but not enough to warrant continued use. Al could tell you that he was quite motivated already, thank you very much, and getting through the day was no huge struggle. Medications off the medical market failed too.

But little by little, he felt himself beginning to break. It was growing bolder and ignorant of the people around, only moving away if another would brush up against Albert.

Otherwise it would lazily circle, serpentine and venomous; causing angry welts and dips over his body if Al would not pay attention and scratch it away. Its nature as the hand of an unwanted lover running tracks wherever it pleased became quite clear, uncaring if they were in public and Al's discomfort would be visible - that was his problem, and his alone.

Al could not bear it much longer, that he knew. He needed to get it out before he would snap. Al was not sure what would happen when he would, but it would not be pretty.

He inspected the blood under his nails, the clock reading two AM.

Maybe he was taking the wrong approach. Perhaps there was a way to free himself, and he simply was going about it all wrong.

It was afraid of sharp things, scratching things.

Albert finally pushed himself up, lightheaded with the knowledge, wondering giddily why he had not done this before. It curled lazily over his ankle, as if questioning where they were going.

Al would not scratch it, he knew that singular certainty as he entered the kitchen.

It would find that out soon enough.

2.

"Um, Dr. Shelley?" the head doctor looked up to see Tim awkwardly standing in the doorway, rubbing the back of his neck sheepishly. "Have you seen Mr. Daw?"

Mina glanced at the clock, and frowned. He had not seen the clinic manager, which was a rare thing for eleven o'clock. Usually Albert checked in with her in the early hours of the morn, though not always if he was busy. Mina had assumed that was the case, and had forgotten until now.

"No, I haven't," she replied with a shrug. Tim's upset was impossible to hide, making Mina get up to go to him. "What's the matter? Maybe he's in another department."

"No, he's not," the young nurse in training sullenly corrected, struggling to remain calm. "I've asked everyone and looked everywhere. I've even asked a few of the techs to walkie talkie him. He's not in his office and he didn't call in sick."

Mina listened patiently. She tried not to let her own concern show, being that someone always knew where Al was, and he would come in even if he was sick.

113

"Maybe you could go to his house and check on him?" Tim suggested hopefully, wringing his fingers around each other nervously. Mina, though she found it mildly irritating, sighed and patted his shoulder as she nodded. Tim lit up at the prospect. "You'll go?"

"Yeah, I'll check on Al," Mina agreed. "I just have to make sure Lambert's alright with me heading out."

To no one's surprise, she was perfectly fine with her superior going out to figure out what was going on with the nurse admin. Sandra expressed some concerns of her own regarding Al, and Mina made sure to take them into account; being a lot more touchy than he used to be and a lack of considerable sleep, or at least acting as though he had gotten a less than functional amount. Mina had noticed the same things, but she had also noted that when Al was clinging, he did so almost desperately, trembling hands and all. She had approached Albert about it, but he told her not to worry about it. She had not, and here they were now. Now, Mina had to worry about it. Still, Mina mused as she started up her car, there did not have to be a connection between those things at all. Maybe Albert had accidentally eaten something that made him catch up on all his lost hours of sleep? That would conk him out for a good long while, for certain. What could it be, though? Mina was not sure if she wanted to find out. Of course, a good sleeping draught could turn the trick.

That thought consoled her as she pulled into the driveway to Albert's... well, it was a bit of a cabin, really. One bedroom, one bathroom, a small kitchen, visible to the combined dining and living room, and not much else. Al called it his getaway away from the clinic.

Oftentimes, Albert would push extreme hours when it came to his work at the clinic, being extremely dedicated with each patient that entered their ward. Sometimes, he slept in his office. If Al was sick, he would have told someone. It was not normal for him to just vanish off the map. As much as Mina told herself otherwise, there was something off about the whole affair and she was determined to get to the bottom of it and figure out what was going on with Al.

Mina knocked on the door.

She knocked again.

Once more, a little harder.

Mina scowled and went back to her car to retrieve the spare key Al had given her when he had bought this little slice of life. The door opened easily now, she thought to himself with a satisfied smirk.

Then the smell hit her.

She gagged, pulling her lab coat up to cover her nose. She was glad that she wore a lot of perfume today- Polly (her bird) had startled her and now the accident was a blessing.

Good god, what was that smell? It was putrid, making her eyes water with the fumes. As she adjusted, she could say that it was almost chemical. Acetate? Regardless, she flicked on the light, trying to wrest out where it was coming from, hoping with all her might that it was not Al. Dismally, she assessed the damage. There was a strange, dark maroon substance dripping along some surfaces, the living and dining room untouched, but she could see it on the counter of the kitchen.

With no small measure of trepidation, Mina slowly walked into the kitchen, and the stench was nearly overpowering. Had it not been for the liquid consistency of the matter, she would have thought it had been rotting here for a long time. Bewildered, she ran a hand through her hair, tightening the other's grip over his coat as he surveyed the area.

There were strange wormy lumps in the fluid, thin and unmoving, almost cubic, laying generally in methodic rows. Mina inspected them with confusion, they appeared organic, but she had no idea of what they could have been. There were some certain flecks of blood mixed in with the goopy nearly black substance, yet Mina did not feel any urgency to the situation, in fact she felt that if she were to rush, she would miss vital information and possibly end up harming Al further. Oh, that was absolute, Al was most definitely hurt. By what? How?

Mina was about to give up, moving away from the counter to go to Al's room, when a spark caught her eye. It was something glinting from the corner where two cabinets met. Mina squatted down and prodded at it, pulling it out quickly, as if it were a snake. To her relief, it was only a shredder.

That relief was short lived as she noticed the odd, dark strands hanging from some of the blades. Caked with blood, Mina came to understand a primal truth that she did not want to acknowledge. Those shreds were bits of flesh and skin; so were the odd scraps on the counters. Mina backed away. Mina stumbled back, eyes wide and throat clogged. Mina turned and bolted.

She followed the trail of the bloody and tarry liquid to Al's bedroom. Without waiting or knocking, Mina entered, the urgency that had gone unfelt opening up neath her feet and swallowing her whole as she tried his best not to lose herself to her emotions.

Mina's hand hovered by the lightswitch. Even with the sun shining outside, the room was dimmed, though Mina could clearly see the outline of what had to be Al on the bed. She turned on the light, and pity surged up in her heart. Was this the outcome of Al scratching himself when he thought no one was looking?

It did not account for the inky (that was it, that was the smell, that was the appearance) splatters all over the home.

"Ah, Mi-Miiinnnnnnna…" Al forced, pulling the blanket tighter around himself. It hissed angrily along his back like a claw, making him arch to avoid the discomfort, but it was inside. There was nowhere to hide from it. "Sorry you had to see me like this."

Black and red seeped through the originally blue sheets, dying it a deep violet wine. Albert shuddered and writhed, shoulders rolling and head ducking, shivering incessantly. The handmade cloth had slipped down his arm, and Mina could see the grater's damage on Albert's shoulder as he moved, blood and the void dripping freely.

"What happened?" Mina asked, hoarsely. She could very well piece it together on her own, but felt a deep set discomfort in the gestalt. Al laughed humorlessly. "This isn't funny. Al, why did you take a shredder to your- your-"

"Skin," Albert finished softly. He was breathing poorly, though his eyes were pained, they were focused. "I thought- stupidly, I hoped- that it would g-g-go, ah! away… if I sc-scared it enough…."

"You're not talking any sense, Albert," Mina lied. Al looked to the floor, clearly upset by the dismissal, seemingly close to tears, unable to quell his shivering. Gore was splattered on his glasses. Mina ignored the viscous mixture and sat beside him, and reached for Al's upper arm.

As soon as she touched it, even through the viscera soaked blanket, she could feel something slithering.

She yelped and jumped away, staring at Al. Shockingly, there was an overwhelming amount of relief in the young director's expression.

"What was that!?" Mina demanded with more than a touch of fear, clenching her hand, the sensation seeming to have not left her fingers. There was something moving under Albert's skin, moving, and it felt... undeniably angry. Al smiled at her, exhaustion evident as he finally had someone who knew. "Al, is that... god, what is that?"

"That," Al slowly said, quite careful and shuddering nonetheless, "Is my itch."

3.

Mina had broken the silence, realizing that while Albert himself might not have been bleeding excessively (most of the ichor was from the Itch, as Mina was going to call it until they got it out and figured out what it really was) he still needed medical care. Lucky for him, Mina was a good doctor; though Al was mildly offended as he brought it up as though it were new information to him, after all, Al was the one who would manage her patients and clinic. Arguably, Al knew all the same knowledge as Mina, just without the degree.

At first, Mina did not know how to approach the situation. Plain water would be a good start, but risked higher chances of infection. Adding soap would lessen that, but increase the injury's damage on the whole. Albert was silent, leaning heavily on the headboard of his bed. Mina paced, finally coming to a seat at Al's easel. There were dozens of his paintings at the clinic, little hobbyist drawings that the staff and patients both appreciated. The current sketch on the canvas was of a deep, haunting night sky, and in spite of the surreal quality, the sketch alone was beautiful, if you would disregard the inky smatterings that had splashed across it. Mina sighed, though she knew that carefully, acetone would get the canvas cleaned up.

Mina got up so suddenly she made herself dizzy, and alarmed Al.

"Stay put, Albert, I'm just grabbing something from the bathroom," she soothed, quickly walking out. Al watched her as much as he could, though did not have the strength to move. Mina came back with a roll of bandages, absorbent gauze, and a bottle of medical alcohol. Al's eyes widened with the memory of the sting, suddenly uncertain if he wanted to go through with this. Mina walked to his side and pulled him gently down, trying to ignore the whipping motion under the layers of fabric and flesh as she laid Al on his back, and pulled away the blanket. Albert winced and he made a slight motion as if to stop her, but quickly gave up and tried to relax, still shivering and shuddering. "Be still. Hopefully this'll take care of two birds with one stone."

117

Mina put the alcohol soaked pad onto the side of Al's neck, where there was a lot of grime, but she was glad to see there were no injuries. Albert tremored from the cold, whimpering out something quietly in Hindi. Mina did not pay too much attention; as she was focused on carefully maneuvering the gauze so as to not cause more damage than already was there.

As soon as the chilly fabric reached the first makings of a scrape, Mina realized she should have added an instruction to Albert.

Don't scream.

Mina clapped a hand over Al's mouth, only muffling the wail a little bit. Underneath it, she could hear the Itch hissing, like an angered snake, the sound rising out of Al's arm, the one of the shoulder she had attempted to cleanse. Albert's hands clawed at Mina's firm press with the gauze, tears leaking quickly out of eyes clamped shut.

"Shh, shh, please, don't scream," Mina implored, rubbing Al's shoulder. The Itch fled from her touch and the burning alcohol. Something was sizzling, and Albert's skin was growing hot beneath the medical pad. Al moaned against her hand, back arching. Mina tried to be swift and efficient, and eventually released Albert's maw so she could lean over him better. Al gave a broken inhale, and Mina quickly reminded; "Don't shout."

"Don't, ah! Please, don't stop," Al begged instead of protesting, nearly startling Mina as it was the opposite of what she had been expecting. It was disconcerting, and Mina thought for a moment that she would have preferred the threnody. "Please please, d-don't... for the saaah! sake of everything you hold dear, don't, please!"

"I won't," Mina promised, and one handedly prepared another pad of gauze. There was so much of the substance leaking out, though the areas she cleaned remained so. Albert's hands remained clamped around the one gently sweeping it all away. The Itch screeched and hissed and snapped about, Albert whimpering and crying out each time it shifted sharply. The blackness surged out of him in droves, as if the Itch was exhaling its own blood from the shreds between Al's skin. Soon, Al lost strength to even raise his voice, his hands dropping down away from Mina's, four soaked strips on the bed and making his eyes water from more than just pain and the waft of ink, but the mire of ethanol as well. Mina swept over his arms, and his torso, and his legs, and her heart ached as he saw the damage Al had inflicted on his own self to free it from the Itch. She gently turned Albert onto his side, and was pleased to see no damage on his back. The mound of what had been a fresh pack of medical pads sat like a sad glop of tar, not a single bit of white

118

visible. Mina then grasped the roll of bandages and unraveled a bit, trying to figure out where to start. She chose Al's wrist, and slowly made her way around to the other arm, snipping it there and proceeding to start anew at his legs, and then finally his chest. Flecks of red and black were already visible on the bandages of the arms by the time she finished. Mina looked at Albert apologetically. "It doesn't look like I got it all out."

"It's fine," Al said, limp and drained. Mina looked at him before turning to the door. Albert, out of tiredness, could only follow with his eyes. "Where are you going?"

"Just calling the clinic," Mina soothed. Al slowly relaxed, and Mina made her way to the phone, stepping over the black puddles that were drying on the floor, glad that Albert had his old fashioned telephone near the couch. As soon as that was done, informing the clinic that she and Albert would be unavailable, except in the case of extreme emergency, she then went into the kitchen to clean it all up. She tried not to think about what she was doing and what it was exactly that she was cleaning, and somehow managed to get it done before she really started to register the gruesome task. Mina then returned to Al, who had fallen asleep, his face uneasy and limbs twitching. Mina sighed as she made her way to her dearest friend's side. She gently pressed her hand to Albert's cheek, the frail man leaning into the touch. "Poor guy... I hope you're feeling better."

Mina went out to grab a few items from Al's storage space, a neat little closet where everything was both sorted and labeled, which very much assisted Mina, who wanted to spend as little time away from Albert as possible. Mina hurried back with the needed materials. Carefully, Mina replaced the blanket with a fresh one, and put a few towels underneath Albert, moving him as carefully as she could manage, setting the bloody ink stained fabrics into the washing machine. Then, wondering if she was overstepping a boundary, she settled beside Al and wrapped an arm over the lanky man. Albert, in his sleep, inched towards her, and Mina smiled slightly, tired out from the whole ordeal, and both rested, trying not to think of the Itch hiding away inside, an unspeakable horror lying in wait, and they slept in each other's arms avoiding it, and the prospect of what to do.

4.

They were sincerely at a loss. Mina had asked Al for a rundown of what he had done in the past to try to get the Itch out, and the list had been far more extensive than Mina had been expecting. Even more shocking (or as Mina might say, frustrating) was Al's conviction to get back to work.

"Mina, It's not out, and It won't be for a good long time," he reasoned to her, looking too tired for a man his age, resigned and drawn. "If ever. I'm starting to have my doubts on it, seeing as how long It's been there. Maybe it's some sort of parasite that I picked up as a kid."

"The Itch is not natural, Albert," Mina had rebuffed, trying to convince him to stay home and rest, or at least work remotely instead of coming in to the clinic. "Remember how I took a sample over to the biology lab over at the clinic? Well, let me tell you, it's mostly inorganic ash, with keratin and a light base, think baking soda. Does that sound like a parasite to you? You need to relax and keep yourself rested. Getting whatever it is out can be extensive and exhausting."

"What does this sound like to you, then," Al got up, cheeks coloring with a frustration of his own. "There is something in my flesh feeding off of my sanity! What do you think it is if not a parasite!? There is no point for me to sit and wallow in the sheer need to scratch off all my skin to tear it out! Already, I am tired and am willing to do whatever I can to get it away."

Mina therefore decided that Al had a point, and later found herself begrudgingly knocking to come into the man's office the next day. Albert was working as usual, itching at his wrist now and again, though unlike before, now he used the blunt end of his pen. He seemed stiff and splayed, as if trying his absolute best not to touch any part of himself, which was the most likely case. Al smiled brightly at Mina, and if the doctor had not known it, she never would have guessed that he had a monster lurking within him.

"How are you feeling?" Mina asked, knowing it was a dumb question, but the first and best one that came to mind. "Any less itchy?"

"Not really," Albert shrugged. "It could be. Could also be more. Feels the same as prior."

Mina frowned, scratching her nose with thought. Truth be told, she had finally thought of something that Al did not try. Among that list were antibiotic, anti-viral, anti-parasite, basically any anti-cellular organism medication she could get her hands on, even steroids designed against toxicity. None of those had worked. Neither had blood thickeners or thinners. Nor the parroted methods of exercise and water. Simply put, Albert had quite exhausted the medical and physical fields.

"You know, I was thinking," Mina edged into her idea, knowing how unpleasant it was bound to be. "Maybe medieval doctors had the inklings of a right idea?"

Al blinked and then squinted.

"Are you talking about blood letting?" he pressed, hints of disgust over his form. Mina nodded and hoped her own grimace was not so obvious. "Mina, I've already informed you, blood alterations of any kind do nothing."

"Yes, I know, but maybe," Mina walked over to his side and put down his notebook so that the thin man would cease working. "If we keep it where we know it'll be, maybe we can drain it out."

Al sighed, getting up, and Mina gave a slight expecting smirk, though it was tinged with a bit of guilt due to the nature of the whole thing. Mina took the lead and walked him down the hall, taking him to where she had privately set up the tool in the clinic. Albert eyed it with distrust and anxiety, nervously shifting from foot to foot and wringing his wrists.

"Alright," Mina began to instruct Al, the latter following her words without argument. "Lay down, Al, and try to relax. It's going to be a more methodical extraction than bleeding you."

"I pray that it is," Al muttered, handing over his hand for the doctor to make a nick on the side of his wrist, Mina well satisfied with the result and attaching the nozzle. Albert shivered. "How does this... work, exactly?"

"This should filter out anything thinner than blood," Mina answered. "It'll be adjustable. If we don't get anything at first, we'll slowly increase the size."

Al winced, yet nodded.

"I am in your hands," he murmured, closing his eyes. Mina studied him for a moment before sighing and turning on her innovation. Albert instantly shivered and his expression soured, but Mina could see no blood filling the container, nor any ink. Extremely slowly, gradually, at a pace far rivaling that of the most pitifully mutated snail, Mina spread the mesh. Al simply let her maneuver his wrist, waiting, finally wincing as small droplets of dark maroon began to siphon out. Mina swore under her breath. "Is there too much blood?"

"I'll take a quick sample, but we'll let it run for now. If it's over eighty percent gunk, we'll keep it on," Mina elucidated. Al gave a slight nod, and Mina turned on the separation machine she had set up previously and loaded in the sample. She returned to Albert's side to monitor the drip. "Is it itching? Hissing? Fighting?"

121

"I… I don't think so," Al replied, uncertain. "I think it hardly notices. It's not even a reaction on scale with when I scratch."

"That might be a good sign," Mina muttered, going to check on the sample. She frowned. It was hovering around seventy five, the two vials glinting like teeth on an old deformed man. "Alright…. We're going to push on for now."

Al said nothing.

Mina's concern started up when Al started shivering, and asked, "Can you check the proportions again, Mina? It feels like it is… pushing me out."

To Mina's alarm, the liquid was much more red than it had been when they started. She turned off the siphon and checked on the levels- sure enough, it was more along fifty-fifty now. She growled in the back of her throat and began to unhook Al.

"It's too much blood, and something tells me it'll just become more and more until it's only blood," Mina grumbled in explanation. Albert turned onto his side, tired out from the draining and disappointed in the results. Mina's shoulders lowered, cleaning up and trying not to think of the whole of the matter and his failure in it. "We'll try something else soon. How are you feeling?"

"Tired," Al whispered, hands tightening around his arms. "It feels satisfied. Maliciously so."

Mina tried not to look at how Al's nails already were repeatedly digging trenches into his shirt.

She would think of something else. Al was clearly fresh out of ideas, if his latest one was anything to go by, and Mina was a new head, and scientifically, two of those work better than one bashing itself against the wall. Mina might have had a bit of a hero complex going on at play too, but she had never come across a situation where it had failed her.

5.

Mina had no ideas. That was, until she had picked up some golden thought lubrication, and even as she swirled her glass and listened to the tinkles of ice against it, it was like the sounds of bells.

'Ah, good old Jack Daniel's always had a solution, didn't he?' Mina thought to herself with a smile, grabbing a fresh bottle and dropping it into her surgeon's bag for tomorrow. Alcohol of this sort was not quite permitted at work, though Mina decided that this time was an exception. It was… perhaps a bit early in the morning to drink, but Mina had gone straight to Al's office and knocked on his door. Al let her in, already fresh awake, and Mina wordlessly dropped off the bottle on the tall man's desk. Albert's mouth opened with confusion and surprise, and Mina cut him off before he could speak. "Drink the whole thing."

"Excuse me?" Al feebly rhetorized, looking at the bottle with uncertainty and clearly daunted by the prospect of Mina's instructions. "I don't drink."

"Maybe that's why it's still there," Mina pointed out, folding her arms and smirking. "Let's go down to your cabin. I want to watch you finish the bottle."

Al muttered something Mina could not fully catch, all the stout woman could hear was, "need two before…" and then indiscernible swearing. Still, to Mina's complacency, he picked up the bottle and tucked it into his satchel, and put a note on his door saying he would be busy and to direct all urgent cases to their respective department head, or if it was their issue to confer amongst themselves. Regardless, it worked very nice and well for Mina.

Once within his home, Albert heavily sat on the couch and pulled out the liquor, inspecting it before opening it and lifting it to his lips, hesitating a moment and offering the bottle towards Mina. Mina smiled, shook her head, and pushed Al's hand back.

"It's all yours."

Al bit his lip, before sighing and taking a long swig- one Mina had expected him to choke on, due to his proclaimed abstinence, but there was no such reaction. Instead, she witnessed, to her intrigued concern, a relative deftness that came to one accustomed to a vice.

"When you said you don't drink, is there a reason?" Mina asked, knowing now it was a little too late. Al shrugged as he swallowed down his third mouthful. "You were an alcoholic before, weren't you?"

"That was the least of my concerns," Al scoffed and rolled his eyes. "There were more pressing holds that I had to deal with first and foremost."

"I see," Mina accepted. "Did the itch come along before or after you stopped drinking?"

"I honestly can't say," Al replied, tilting his head back for another draft. Mina found himself eyeing Albert's neck- was that scar always there? Surely, it had to be. Mina

123

wondered where it came from, and realized, she could simply ask. Part of herself felt guilty for exploiting the looseness of tongue that came with drink, but she thought it could be important. "Ah, that old thing? One of my relatives were in the occult. He needed a heart for something... he fell on the knife he was holding while chasing me. I'd say it was an accident, not like anyone believed me. Maybe it wasn't one. I was very scared, but in those days, also very angry."

"I can't see you as an angry person," Mina chuckled, though her brain was still processing the information with a great measure of horror. "I think that even if it was on purpose, it was still self defense. I can't see the whole scar, but from what I can see, it looks like it was a really bad cut."

"I thought I was dying," Al laughed, and Mina noticed the bottle was nearing halfway. She glanced at Al, who hardly looked inebriated, and was barely acting so. It was a disquieting dichotomy from how she knew Albert behaved. Mina knew that if she had that much in such a short time, she would be rocking and singing long ago, and Mina was no spring chick when it came to drinking. "There was blood everywhere. After he tripped, and cut himself everywhere, it looked like the floors had been dyed maroon from my angle. Wait, why does this matter?"

"I was just wondering," Mina truthfully answered. Al frowned a little, but it faded quickly. "How are you feeling?"

"Tipsy," Al smiled, eyes drifting shut. "But no, the itch... I'm not sensing any reaction."

"Hm," Mina's lip twisted down, though she tried not to show it, and decided to joke around with Al to get their minds off of the situation. "Well then, how do I feel?"

"I'm not you," Al snorted, but leaned over and placed a hand on Mina's forehead, the shorter woman feeling a flush rise up in her face. "Mmm, quite warm, dear. Have you been taking care of yourself?"

"Yes," Mina almost hotly replied, though embarrassment over the degrees of her emotions made her blush harder. "And that's a question I ask you. And you usually lie."

"I'm not lying when I say yes," Al slowly shook his head. "I am taking care of myself, I promise, but it's so hard to, you know? Especially because I think of taking care of each other, and it gets me all flustered and listless. How can you do something when you're wishing someone would do it for you?"

124

"Me? In particular?" Mina almost laughed- almost. No, she was looking intently at the younger man, watching the volume of the bottle slowly become replaced by air, silently encouraging Al to drink more, though now, it was nearly entirely for her own benefit; as it clearly was minimally affecting the problem, if at all. No, Mina wanted him loose, talkative, and sprawled out in her arms. Al nodded in response to her question, swaying with the rest of the motion, taking another long pull on the bottle. "What do you feel about me?"

"I love you," Al bluntly responded. "Love you so much. You're the only reason I keep going."

"Surely the clinic is worth moving forwards for," Mina awkwardly chuckled, both touched and worried by the statement. Al shrugged. "Sandra and Tim are good reasons, too."

"Not the same as you," Albert rebutted, draining another long swallow. "No, I don't think I'd be able to hang on. Tim knows his boundaries to know when to call it quits, and Sandra doesn't right know what to do most of the time. With me."

Mina said nothing, only watched as Albert gradually reached the halfway point on the bottle, and inched beyond.

"Still no change?" Mina asked.

"I'm still in love with you," Albert drawled, blinking slowly and sinking down on the couch. "But I won't tell you. I can't tell you. You... you're too good. For me."

"How would you feel if I loved you, too?" Mina prodded, smiling slightly. Al sighed, and looked at the bottle, sipping at it again. "Well?"

"I'd be the happiest man in the universe." Al replied quietly, and tucked back the rest of the bottle in one long draw. "Ah... but there's the twist of it all. Yet, through it all, I itch, not alone even in heartache."

Mina regretted this idea and her needless proddings as Al began to silently weep.

6.

"How are you feeling, Al?" Mina asked, knocking on the door and rounding the corner. She stopped the moment she entered, not seeing where the man was in his own office. "Al?"

"Down here," she heard him say, though it was more of a whisper than any other type of speech. Hollow, quiet, breathy. Mina quickly made her way around the desk, finding the man behind it, nails coated with dark red and unable to meet Mina's eye. His hands continued their paths along his arms. "I... I am sorry. I can't stop. I can't."

"Then I will." Mina stated without thinking, and she pried his clawed fingers away from his own flesh. Mina held Albert as the young manager shook and sobbed uncontrollably, barely able to fight her. There were wet red splotches all along his previously dry white shirt sleeves. Mina's firm, steady hands gripped both of Al's wrists, holding him away from scratching at himself any longer and making the cuts worse. "I've got you. Breathe, honey. Breathe."

"Please," Albert's voice was thick and cloying, like smog about to weep acid rain. "Mina, good friend, best friend, beloved friend, make it stop- let me itch, please-"

"No, Al," Mina gently but firmly replied. "No."

"Please, please, I am begging you," Albert writhed and tried to wrench himself free. "Please, scratch it, kill it, I cannot- I can't do this any longer, Mina, make it end, please."

"I will. Trust me. I won't let you suffer like this."

"End me," Albert pleaded, turning to be on his knees before Mina. "Do anything to me to make the itching stop. Anything. Rip me to shreds. Hurt me as I know I have angered you, and you deserve to take it out on me. Oh, Lord, is this what this is? Do you hate me without realizing? You are too kind to hurt me, is this fate acting for you?"

Mina could think of nothing other than pulling the man into a tight, enveloping hug. Al gave a small cry of surprise that turned to whimpering and more sobs, shuddering in her arms. Mina did not know what she wanted to do with Al in that moment, but there was something animalistic and strong bubbling up beneath her skin, an act that she was unsure of what it might be. The confusion stemmed from the fact that while it may have been primal, it was not debased, that she could sense. Mina pushed the feeling away for the time being, focusing on Albert first and foremost instead of the thoughts that came to her head with the man so vulnerable and close.

"I never wanted you hurt," Mina murmured in his ear. Al moaned and his hands gripped against Mina's shoulders from where they rested upon them in Mina's strong embrace. "Never. Don't you go thinking that you're in pain because I am angry at you, or that I loathe you, because I don't, Al. I lo-care about you a lot. I will help you get out of that hell you're in. I will get it out."

"I love you," Al wept. "You are too good. I don't deserve you to even glance at me. Mina, I'd kiss the very ground where your regal footsteps tread. I am so sorry-"

"No," Mina cut him off, tightening her hug. Al gasped and his fingers flexed reflexively, pressing sweetly over the muscles of her shoulders. "Don't apologize. We're going to get it out, and I'm going to love you when we do, but I don't dare now. Not while you're still in pain and I've done nothing to help. I will show my care in saving you. But until then, you are my patient, and you may not be sorry. Hear?"

"I hear you," Albert echoed, almost shocked. Mina placed her forehead over Al's considerably warmer one, looking him in those beautiful brown eyes, while Al stared at her hazel ones. "I hear. I love you. Goodness, I love you."

The feeling roared up in Mina again; an odd type of her own Itch, and it told her to let go, to let what would happen to Al if she released herself become unleashed. Mina did not know what it could be, and she did not want to hurt him any more than he already burned. So she let the fire inside herself burn out, rocking Al until his well of tears stoppered up.

"I have an idea," Al said, his voice tight yet bubbly, telling a joke on the verge of insanity, gripping Mina for dear reality. "Why don't we cut off my head? It never goes there!"

"We are not going to kill you to get rid of the itch, that's counterproductive, and probably exactly what it wants," Mina rumbled, disturbed that the wretched ink thing dared to push Al to this. Dared to push her Al here. Mina growled, low in her throat and picked up Al's head to look him in the eye. "You're not going to give in. We will not cave- Albert, you're a genius!"

"I'm a what now?" the exhausted and frankly done man asked. "I'm a stressed and tired man, that's what. No genius. Are you going to get a hacksaw for my neck?"

"No, but I hate to ask you this- what are you willing to lose to get rid of the itch?"

"Anything. Anything. Mina, do anything." Al replied instantly, something he had thought on too long and suffered with too much to not have an immediate answer to. "Anything at all. Please. I can take anything. Just not you. For my life, don't leave me. It would kill me, Mina. Don't go."

"I won't," Mina promised, aghast that Al would even suggest that she would. "I won't. I will have to hurt you but I can't guarantee that it will even work. Do you accept that?"

"Yes, yes, anything, I won't regret it," Al swore. "Please, Mina. Anything."

"Okay. I have an idea."

"Oh, thank you-" Al's arms slipped around Mina's chest to hug her. "Thank you. Thank you."

"I can't promise it will work."

"I don't care."

"You will hurt."

"Can't be worse than this."

Mina said nothing more and hugged Al back as tight as she could.

They planned it out carefully as soon as Albert regained more of his mental faculties, when the pain drunkenness faded away and bandages were replaced. Al remained steadfast to his intense desire to get rid of the itch. Mina both admired that and felt terribly bad for him. Even when Mina explained the idea very explicitly, Al still agreed.

Luckily for Mina, he was not exactly a heavy man. Suspending him from the ceiling was mostly made difficult by his remarkable height, though they made it work. The straps on Al's wrist were padded and softened, so as to provide him with the least discomfort as they held him up.

"How are you doing like that?" Mina asked, checking over the medical instruments for what felt like the thousandth time for the day, picking up one. She glanced over at Al as the man made a so-so noise, neither happy with his position nor particularly hurting. Mina stared at Albert, who was only wearing his underwear, not even the light shirt he wore underneath his dress one, and it was the most skin of the man Mina had ever seen. Al's eyes were locked on the floor and wall in front of him, not seeing Mina's eyes roaming his outstretched body. Mina gave her head a slight shake to get the more perverse thoughts away, decidedly allowing some to remain and make the situation a little less gruesome within her own head. Perhaps one day she would string Al up again for a better reason. That thought gave her pause, and she looked over at Al again for a moment, glancing along his lean build, in bas relief due to the stretch. She ignored it and brought over the tray of tools. Albert's eyes flicked to her, watching her warily. "Are you sure you're alright, Al?"

"Yes, just hurry the hell up, I feel like someone is looking at me," Albert grumbled. Mina picked up the scalpel and gently pressed it to Albert's leg, near his ankle. "Go a little higher."

"Right," Mina acknowledged. When Albert said nothing, Mina pushed in the blade. Al hissed and tried to flinch away, but he could not with how he was bound. Mina glanced up at him apologetically and curved around the skin, and, leaving a small gap from one end of the cut to the other, picked up the prepared alcohol soaked cloth. Al whispered something to himself, probably a brief and desperate encouragement, and Mina wiped away at the blood seeping out of his friend. Al gasped, and Mina could feel the Itch running out of the sectioned away part of Al's body. Mina quickly finished up the line, and he smiled up at Al. "I think it's working."

"Stop thinking and get snipping," Al managed to say. Mina nodded, and continued her path along Al's leg, stopping by his hip and carefully avoiding even getting close to the femoral artery. "Don't forget the other."

Mina snorted and got to work on the other leg. Once that was completed, she did the same along Al's collarbone, just in case the Itch were to get desperate and hide there instead of where they were trying to smoke It. Al's left wrist came next, and very carefully, the doctor outlined his flesh to seal it away with alcohol. They made it along Al's body, and she worked with the torso best she could, and held up her flask for Al to drink.

The floor was sticky with blood and ink, Albert's eyes hazy and unfocused, the beverage sharpening them a bit once more. Al groaned as the thing inside him shifted and screeched along his flesh, streaking through and running into Albert's right arm. Though the 'drink a whole bottle' plan failed, Mina had noticed that the Itch stayed away from Al's organs when he had imbibed the alcohol. That was precisely what they needed here and now.

"Got you, you son of a bitch," Mina grinned savagely. She had already sectioned off Albert's fingers to keep it from entering them- aside from the little finger. Al had told her that it was the smallest it would compress itself to, and they agreed that it would be the best course of action. Gradually, inch by inch, Mina coaxed it into Albert's hand. But after that, it would no longer cooperate, refusing to go to the smallest finger. "Shit. Shit, Al."

"I know," Al gasped, shivering. "I don't care. Cut it. It's fine. I'm left handed."

"Just… let me…" Mina did not want to cut off her friend's entire hand. That would be torture for the younger man, even with his consent. Instead, Mina drew the lines to force it into his thumb instead. "It's not ideal. Are you su-"

"Yes, I am s-sure," Albert firmly stated. "Do it. Cut it out."

"Brace yourself," Mina gently warned. "Don't yell too loud."

Truth be told, Mina was not sure who screamed louder, Al or his Itch. It roared as the knife came up, and nearly broke free of its containment of flesh, but Mina instantly threw it into the crucible and sealed the lid, and the screams! Smoke and the scent of burning acid and ink rose from the superheated earthenware, and it hissed and sputtered like an overboiled pot. Al stared at it, Mina's arm around him, not that he could reciprocate. Mina tore her gaze away from the crucible to Albert, smiling at him as he gently undid the straps.

Al's expression was that of soft bewilderment and pain, and Mina kissed his arm as she covered her with his lab coat, though Albert quickly moved to grab the blade they had ready for cauterizing. The smell of burning flesh and boiling blood made Mina's stomach turn slightly, she was used to more hospital settings. Slowly, gently, Mina bandaged the lines she had created on Albert's skin. Al looked at her as though she were an angel, eyes wide and teary and full of gratitude. They ignored the beast in the fire, opting to help Albert get into his clothing, items that were a bit baggy so as to not rub against the sore flesh.

Mina knocked the crucible into a small vault, closing that off as well, then he put it into a box to be shipped out for biohazard disposal. Al let out an audibly breath of relief as Mina did so.

"Thank you," he said. Mina wrapped him into a gentle embrace. "Thank you, Mina. It's gone. I don't feel it, at least… oh, goodness. It's gone.…"

"I'm so proud of you," Mina murmured. "You did so well. Let's have you rest."

Mina carried Albert to his room, her lab coat acting as a makeshift blanket as she did so.

She set him onto the bed, turning to go to sleep in the living room, but Albert stopped her with an aching hand and soft eyes.

Mina settled beside Albert and soon the two of them fell asleep.

Three months later, all the bandages were off, and Albert was deftly croquetting, hardly impeded by his missing digit. Mina walked over, pushing down the fabric, and leaned to kiss her Al, itch free.

Melt

4.12.2022

When he first met the tall bastard, his initial thought was 'Damn, that guy needs some sleep'. Perhaps not the nicest thought, but Johan was indeed looking fatigued beyond belief, even more than the shorter man's evident exhaustion. Regardless, if he would be a source to a steady income, Raymond was all for it.

Johan was. More than that, as well. He paid for all of Raymond's debts and provided even more. Raymond was grateful for that, and enjoyed the engineering work that came along with the side job.

If only his aching heart would stay the hell out of dodge.

It was a pain to smile through the buzz of that organ, reminding him that even loss could not keep it from falling into pits all over again, and he hated the melting adoration that filled his chest each and every time he looked at and fell for Johan.

—

It was a mistake. An honest, simple mistake.

Maybe not simple, but it was an accident nonetheless. Johan never meant for this to happen. But it had, and now, here they were. Or really, just Johan was.

Oh, dear.

He could feel, very steadily, a certain nothing piercing through him like a blunt mellow spear against elastic fabric - piercing and pulling, pulling, an orb of non-euclidean shapes expanding towards infinity.

It had been there for a long, long time. Perhaps forever. Maybe he was already here forever. Time appeared to be a laughing matter here, as it did not exist in the first place. Time was a single moment: this, stretching him across a non-existent space cramping upon itself.

Despite his wiser whispering, his mind converged upon itself, repeatedly, ad infinitum, consuming their lives, his lives, and the concept of Rose Robotics melted into several million minds.

He was gone.

—

Johan loved those pants. He loved them like they were his own creation- which they were. He had put time and effort into crafting them, size charts be damned. They were a fantastic shade of soft mint green (he hoped, his vision was not the best for color), perfectly fit to him. They were the best pants he could have ever hoped to be wearing at any point of his life. If he would not ruin them with his goddamn Coca-Cola, then everything would be fantastic.

It was during a meeting. With the renewed heads from the music department.

Marcéline just had to make a joke while Johan was drinking.

And Johan just had to laugh.

Spilling the soft drink all over himself. Especially his pants.

Though he laughed along, he wanted to melt into the floor with embarrassment, pushing back his glasses to hide the hot surge of frustration.

—

He needed it. He needed it so bad.

There was none in the house, again, so he had to go out and get some at the bar since the stores were closed and the government could not bear the thought of a man quenching his thirst; and now that he had it in the hidden ale depository, instead of gulping it down and asking for a second and a third and a fourth, Raymond stared at the amber spirit in his glass and simmered.

Why had there been none in the house? He had drunk it all. Everything that he could have found in their easy access storage spaces, bought before restrictions clicked into place. He was sure there was more, but he was not in the mood to search for the bottles.

He watched the ice spread its watery tendrils through the liquid gold.

Raymond slammed it down, furious.

—

The door closed quietly behind him.

Johan's muffled half-laughs, half-sobs played before him.

If it was about those damn pants....

133

Raymond checked himself, inhaling deeply.

Johan's door was closed. Raymond opened it.

The man was swaying on the floor, slightly near his computer, somewhat in the corner but not quite.

Raymond's brow furrowed as he came near- and broke something beneath his foot.

A syringe.

Johan giggled, reverence in his too focused eyes.

"Drinking again, Ray?" he breathed.

Raymond scowled, kicking forward the bottle of morphine. "Using again, Jo?"

"Face it," Johan sighed, smiling bitterly. "We both love the melt."

Raymond shoved him, even though he was already on the floor, sending him back onto his elbows. The taller man winced, though did not have time to think as Raymond stepped over him, glaring down.

"Hypocrite," Johan hissed, still grinning.

The doctor scowled: "Crazy ain't genius, snowbird."

Neither said more.

—

Heat. White hot heat. Standing in the sun. Hair burning. Flesh sizzling. Skin tearing. Muscles unfolding, ripping at the seams like a popup book, like sutures yanked too hard. Organs flattening against each other until they were melting into one another. Tendons snapping with a sickening silence. Bones cracking and shattering and pulverizing into fine dust, and so warm. Freezingly warm. Boiling cold.

Gentle and sharp.

Realization hit him, finally, as did the agony, stark and extreme.

This was such a bad idea.

Destiny or not, fate was not inevitable, and Johan had tried to show that to him time and time again, and yet, here he was, in all the heat and intensity of the stars that guided him.

Oh God. His hands- his arms- his body- oh God.

He registered the pain, he fathomed the horror, he underwent the shifts, and Raymond became past, body asunder and in bits.

—

Johan's body was sore. His brain itself throbbed and pulsed.

What was left of both body and brain, at least.

It had gotten to a point where the pain was barely an incessant droning, turning and churning loudly along his entire body.

He tried to pull off the heart cage, though it was impossible while missing that opposable digit.

Everything pulsed obnoxiously, vision in his remaining eye often static and vintagetted.

His legs, useless, sent whispers of phantom pain giggling up his spine.

His scars flared up as if they were to start bleeding all over again.

It hurt so much.

He could barely react to it anymore.

Forcing himself with great difficulty to lay the concert of his aching body somewhere a little further down his exhausted mind, he laid upon his cot with wires sticking out of every inch of him, and let the droning undo his thoughts.

—

The lights were encompassing and suffocating- though he did not need to breathe. Air was cluttered about him with his own soul, bright and shining as he reformed.

That viscous liquid clung to his nonexistent limbs with hands grasping for help even as he drew away; it sank into his barely held together flesh like a heated knife through butter, splitting and renewing him all at once. His feet sunk in its tar entrails, sucked in, bitten down with awful veracity by rows of teeth like slim needles.

He could hear him approach with his tired claudicant step and labored breath, to wrap his neck in his scarred hands - he could see his enormous grin splitting open, leaning to draw him in.

135

Raymond felt the floor against what was left of himself, and he turned just in time to see the towering figure reach for him, and he welcomed him.

—

The couch dipped. It woke him from his doze, still peaceful and bleary. A soft arm wrapped around him, pulling him close. His ears took in the softening sounds of the children playing. The air was warm, smelling of his cologne and something cinnamony. Somehow... pleasant.

The arm shifted, a hand on his chest, and a presence blocking the light upon his eyelids, and a kiss upon his lips.

Johan opened his eyes to see Raymond smiling at him, haloed by the radiant rays landing on his bright golden curls.

"Surely my senses deceive me," Johan murmured, eyes watering. "For lo, I see a-an agent of heaven. Pray tell, what goodness have I done to be graced w-with you?"

"Oh, Jo," Raymond smiled and shook his head, slight and soft. He leaned forward to kiss Johan once more, then twice again. "You're too good for anything. I love you."

"I love you too," Johan exhaled, unable to believe his own ears, though his heart thundered. "How... how did all of this come... come to this?"

Raymond shrugged, cuddling next to Johan, melting against him. The taller man followed suit, genteel life embracing them together.

They took it in as one.

Perfectly Good Hand

6.20.2022

It is hard to live up to the ghosts of the past.

When your father was a multimillion dollar security consultant, and his father before him was an engineer that shaped the course of history, and *his* father before him a prominent geneticist, there is a lot put onto a guy's shoulders. No matter how many PhDs are earned to get the grants for his basic living needs, there still are those two massive, one bigger than the other, mountains to live up to. The name of the Orionvi was difficult to fully grasp.

Harder, too, when genetics sentenced him to certain dysfunctions.

Blueprints surrounded him for machines he would never build. Not only was he addicted with pain when he would try, he did not have the resources for the applied aspects of his science. An uncomfortable seat beneath him, calculations for his spendings pinned to a board before him, and another blueprint before him, covered by the papers that he used for extra calculations. They were for a miniature teleporter, designed to take one home, though nowhere else. Arlo understood the impracticality of it, but money was money, and he had to keep the lights on somehow.

Actually, that was not a half bad idea. Quit paying the light bill and stick with candles until he could get a solar generator running. There still was the ranch's automation to address....

Arlo logged that away and continued working until the sun came up.

The rooster cawed, and Arlo got up with a sigh, heading out to the ranch to make sure what little was left was up to par. As most things were automated, checking over the progress was no difficult task. Though it had taken absolutely forever to get it all up and running, especially with his hand locking up more with a direct relation to how long he used it. Yet the benefits outweighed the discomfort and difficulty, and he was glad to have stuck it through.

Everything was going smoothly, as far as he could tell. One of the major positives of sticking to this old ranch and giving it everything he had was that food was not an issue. Milk was deposited right into the jugs in his fridge, eggs carefully arranged in special trays by size, honey dripped into the jar, flour seeped into a sack. It was not much but it was what he managed to reap, and by his account that was mighty impressive. He still had to buy some ingredients, like salt and spices, but he generally had enough left over for those items. Bartering was always on the table, too, and when he haggled, he usually ended up with the upper hand in those matters.

Arlo hissed as his hand spasmed, dropping the butterknife he had been using on his toast. It clattered to the floor, and he gripped his wrist and waited for the pain to die down a bit before carefully picking up the knife.

It fell out of his grip again.

Breathing slowly, tried again, his hand refusing to make the correct shape to grip the metal. With painstaking time, he very minutely managed to put it onto the counter.

Suddenly he was not quite in the mood for breakfast anymore. He still ate it in spite of his hollowed, sour mood, though he did add a bit of honey to brighten his day a bit. Arlo picked up a coffee mug as well, and tapped in the input to the maker with his left hand. It filled up a bit more quickly than usual, as though it was aware of his fouled disposition.

Sufficiently grumpy, he grabbed the mug and
promptly dropped it.

Arlo dropped his head into his hands to muffle his scream of frustration. He could feel his 'dominant' hand tremor against his face, making him grit his teeth with soothing frustration. He could not build, he could not hold things, he could hardly use his right hand at all! He went over to his workspace again, and for some reason, he grabbed the nearest pile of blueprints, and threw them down, and he did that again and again, until the entire room was trashed.

He sat down on the blueprint covered floor, pulled off his thick glasses, and cried.

He cried until the well of tears dried up.

God, what he'd give to build again.

Arlo's hand locked up just thinking about it.

His face fell, hot with shame.

And something caught his eye.

He stumbled over to it, and it was exactly what he had been hoping for his entire life. Ironically, it was his own work.

A prototype for a mechanical hand, awkwardly sketched on an old blueprint. It had been a project he had completely forgotten about – something he dreamed up in his youth and had to abandon in exchange for more practical machines and inventions that would turn a profit.

Arlo let out a pent up laugh, eyes darting over the blueprint. It definitely needed work, but it was finally a solution he had the entire time. He grabbed the paper and pushed aside the research he had been working on, picked up a pencil and a protractor, and got to work, measuring his arm and sketching and measuring and calculating.

When he finally started the inevitably slow work of actually making the device, he sent in an order for a belt saw from his current school, expecting that it would arrive by the time he finished. It was exceedingly slow, what with how long it took him to slot parts together, to even find parts that would be applicable, seeing as Randall had not left Arlo with much, leaving when the theoretical engineer was sixteen with nothing but the empty ranch. Good riddance. Spare parts were what mainly went into his current inventions, and it seemed that would have to do for the mechanical arm as well. He inched to completion, working around the pains of his hand, and yet no word had arrived on the status of the saw. He did not mind much, he was working on something again, something physical, and that meant the world to him.

The prosthetic was completed.

Arlo admired it, the work of his hands, even one that was not so perfectly good. He had managed to get through with it, to make it, and soon he would test it. As soon as the belt saw came in.

A few more days passed without any news. Arlo was a little worried; perhaps they declined it and simply had not thought to tell him. Or maybe his request was still going through. His hand hurt more and more lately, especially as he most likely overworked it with the building of the replacement, and his patience was running on fumes.

Eventually he had enough waiting.

He prepared three hacksaws, the table was sterilized, the prosthetic was before him, ready to be attached and brought to life. Arlo did not have enough money to buy the best anesthetics, but he had managed to afford a bit and traded some of his best honey for extra, which meant he had one shot at this. He tied off his arm by the elbow with a tight tourniquet, and drew along the diameter of where to cut.

Arlo snapped on a glove, shoved the other into his mouth to bite down on, pricked himself with the local anesthetic, and picked up the first handsaw. Then he began to cut.

Three strokes in, he had to stop and pull off his protective goggles, flinging them to the corner of the table and jamming on his glasses instead. Too much water was building up within them to see what he was doing. He had not expected the saw to get so dull so quickly, either, and he picked up the next one. His working hand was starting to shake, so at least there was flesh keeping the saw straight. Blearily, he started to realize that perhaps he really should have just waited for a response or gone for the belt saw out of pocket. Fumbling with what nerves were still in place, Arlo prepared another two saws, all while his own blood seeped onto the blueprints.

The third saw broke. He picked up the ones he had only just repaired. Nearly finished. Once done with the bone he would be able to neatly cut through the rest.

Down to the last saw.

Come on, just a little more bone. Just get through it. Just get through it.

The process stalled, and he pulled out the blade.

It was flattened. Like the two before it.

Arlo stared at the final broken saw, and at the small piece of bone left. He struck at it with the blunt saw to no avail. He looked around frantically- now, he had to finish this. He should have really waited to buy that big belt. His right hand was already done obeying orders, so there was no way to get another hacksaw ready.

Arlo's eyes fell onto an old wood saw by another work bench. He undid the strap holding his arm down, and quickly wobbled over to get it, bringing it back to the initial table and getting to work.

This one hurt a lot more for some reason. Maybe the pain killer was wearing out.

He found himself crying out into the glove he had jammed into his mouth with every twitch, be it of his arm or the blade.

He had to finish.

Had to.

Arlo stared at his hand.

Then he looked at his perfectly good hand, and picked up the prosthetic with it, with the nerve seeking bases already set up and ready to join his body. The bottom sat on a burner, red hot and ready to sear his flesh and after to it.

He attached it.

He flexed the fingers of his perfectly working hand, and turned on the robotic one.

Arlo waited for a moment, just looking straight ahead, feeling numb and tired. Maybe he should have cleaned up all the blood, but the sterilized, cauterizing nerve base would take care of that.

Arlo realized he was strumming a tune out on the table, one end soft, the other metallic.

He looked down at his hands, let out a hysterically triumphant laugh, and fainted.

The Captains

8.12.2022

1.

You were considered lucky if you were allowed to man one of the starfleet. You were considered luckier if you were a captain, and all the more lucky if you were not, ironically, a registered fleet member.

So if you were Maximilian Oroseira, you were the luckiest of the lucky. Not only did you command the best (and most uncatchable) starship ever built, but you also had a top of the line crew and an unbeatable modus operandi, but you got to see the faces of impoverished colonies light up each time you brought for them the contraband tools, clothes, and most importantly, food.

Yes, it was risky work, but Maximilian would rather work against those restricting agents and get to people what they needed rather than just sit on the sidelines and watch them all suffer. So he had built his ship, gathered a crew, and raided all of the overflowing Three stock houses and crashed all of their exorbitant pricing. Outwitting the personnel sent to catch them and never taking a prisoner or a life, that was the way to go. Fast, impossibly quick maneuvers, always being ten steps ahead of the next runner up, that kept them off the gallows.

And the food flowing.

Maximilian was infamous (or rather, famous) throughout the star system for breaking all the rules and regulations, and had such a high bounty on his head that oftentimes thoughts on turning him in occurred to civilians, though they knew the bounty would never truly reach them, and they would only serve to damage their entire communities if they were to do so.

Which meant Maximilian was continuing his outlaw behavior.

That made the shareholders upset.

Very upset.

In fact, very very upset.

And if Mr. Gus Beetle the Fourth did not get his hands on that pretentious asshole zooming through the skies and looting all their warehouses, there was going to be hell to pay.

Chief Admiral Aika Brrin was assigned to tracking down and capturing the rogue captain, but Maximilian had little expectations.

Aika knew that well. Zhe had gotten zer First, Udor, zer best and stealthiest crew members to sneak on board to Maximilian's ship and plant a geolocator and a bug, and zhe was treated to the nonstop chatter of the captain, gloating about his victories and plans and how he was always ten steps ahead yaddah yaddah bullshit.

Bull to the absolute shit, in zer opinion. His repetitive ramblings and honestly silly plans were going to be supremely easy to smash through. Aika made sure zer crew was on the listen for all of his plots to determine when to catch him red handed. There often were times that a spontaneous strike would hit one of the stockhouses, and Aika was right sick of his gloating- gloating to no one, really, aside from his own crew.

As the law team listened in to that rogue ship, a plan in the making was overheard, one that seemed to have potential to catch the bastard. It was the first time the Dagon had noticed any uncertainty in that deep, commanding voice, and that was the first tip off that they would be in for a bit more success than usual, instead of eating Maximilian's dust, there was a chance that they could capture him.

Aika setup vigils at every single choke point on the way to Maximilian's destination, confident in the power of zer fleet to take him down.

Then it was a waiting game.

At least it was, right up until the time of the heist, that was the conversion point to begin the chase. Multiple pings set off right on time, and the Admiral's fleet wasted no time in hunting down the stealth optimized ship, the positioning bug planted giving them a good range in which to find it. Each one of the scout ships were to chase down the majestic star traversal unit, and corner it slowly. Still, Maximilian's *Kraken* ship outclassed the simple speed boats by far, none of the junks even coming close, though that was part of Aika's plan. All zhe wanted was to build up a wall of the small but fast police units and throttle the arrogant asshole, keeping him from escaping. And it was working. The quick and stealthy *Kraken* slowly was losing ways to flee, not that there really were any to begin with. Aika had already taken care of that.

Aika made sure that it would be zer own ship to draw the final capture.

"Discharge the EMP," Aika remarked to zer First, who gave a brisk nod and repeated zer orders to the fleet members in charge of the massive destabilizing cannon. The cloaking of the other ship shuddered and vanished, leaving the ship obvious in space. Aika switched on the intercom so that all ships in the radius could hear zer. "This is Admiral Brrin. You are surrounded. Do not attempt to fight. Do not attempt to flee. You, Captain Maximilian Oroseira, as well as your crew, are hereby under arrest by the order of the Three. Do not resist."

"Ah, Admiral!" a warm, charismatic, and calm voice replied. "I have been waiting for this moment. Excuse me if my connection is a little off, as I am a bit distant. Arrested, did you say? For what crimes?"

"Theft, destruction and distribution of property, resisting arrest, and high treason," Aika stated, leaning back in zer seat. "Remain in your ship. You and your crew will be collected. Open the door."

"Yes, ma'am," Maximilian smoothly answered. "We'll be waiting."

Aika gave a nod to Udor.

A few moments later, a signal came in from the arresting squad.

"Er, Admiral? There's no one here. This ship's a dud."

Aika stared at the replica of the *Kraken*. Maximilian's snickering came on the audio.

"Ah, sorry for taking you on such a ride. Did you really think I was dumb enough to not notice a bug? Well, goodbye for now, Admiral. I'm sure you are a relentless enemy."

2.

Without a doubt, space was Aika's favorite place to be. It gave someone, well, enough space to do as they pleased, be it exploring, relaxing, or yelling into the void where not a peep of your frustration would be heard by the general population and those under your command.

And boy, was Aika frustrated. Zhe could not fathom how easily Maximilian slipped from zer fingers, never even close to zer clutches as zhe had presumed. It was mind boggling and humbling, that the architectural and engineering genius had outclassed zer so much, and zhe had not even seen the whiplash coming.

144

Zer punishment of losing a ship was nothing compared to the numbing shock that cascaded over zer. Zhe could not comprehend how in the name of the Milky Way zhe had failed so badly.

Zhe was determined to not let that jerk get away with it.

It was compounded by the fact that he called zer every night. The first few calls had resulted in zer manually snapping the connection and not giving him a moment to speak as soon as zhe heard his stupid Old Europe accent.

Then as time went on, zhe realized zhe could use those calls to figure out Maximilian's plans and worm zer way into understanding the mind and tactics going on inside his head.

So zhe started talking back.

The man mellowed out as they spoke, and Aika became less hostile and closed off. As those conversations took over their evenings, the space between them seemed to shrink to only them between their calls, as if they were in the same room instead of galaxies apart.

Aika could not help but enjoy them. One night working late on repairing some internal issue of zer ship that none of zer mechanics, not even Udor, could figure out, zhe was on the call with Maximilian.

"You sound upset, Admiral," Maximilian remarked after a lull in their discussion. "Is everything alright? You were not reprimanded for our conversations, were you?"

"Nah, nothin' like that, they don't monitor my calls," Aika scoffed, banging zer wrench onto the misbehaving component, as though that could repair it. "I'm just havin' a load of trouble from this hyperjoint connector. The danged thing won't let us maximize our speed, keeps laggin' out."

"Sounds like the coolant is leaking or not fully reaching all of the jump ports, then," Maximilian observed. Aika stopped what zhe was doing, cocking zer head to listen to the man. "Perhaps follow the line, if all of the connectors are on one liquid line. And if they are, there is either a leak, the pressure is too low, or you don't have enough fluid."

"Huh," Aika commented, going along the massive pipe, trailing zer pressure meter along its ridges. The Dagon made no further comment until zhe came to the root of the issue, not that zhe was going to tell Maximilian what it was. Zhe had already slipped up with letting him know that zer ship was not in tip top chasing shape. "Well, seems like you were right. Won't tell ya about what, though."

"That's understandable," Maximilian snickered, and it was an enjoyable sound unlike how ugly it had felt those months ago. "We are enemies, are we not?"

"Yeah, totally," Aika replied. "Says the man that calls me every night."

"Says the Admiral that answers my calls."

Aika huffed and rolled zer eyes, but could not think of any retort to the comment. Instead zhe just smiled, rippled zer scales, and let it pass.

"How are the Three?"

"Do ya think I'm in contact with any of them?" Aika scoffed, dark eyes narrowing slightly. "Closest person to 'em that refers to me is their 'arm', Beetle. 'Sides, why would I tell you?"

"I used to be close to them myself," Maximilian sighed. Aika paused in zer work, confused. "Quite close, in fact. Yet things fell apart... as they tend to do. Ah, it's no use dwelling on the past now, is it...."

"You were close to the Three?" Aika echoed in question, answered by silence. Zhe looked around zer ship, one of the best the fleet had to offer, yet Maximilian's was better... and some things seemed to make sense all at once. "Were you the admiral before me?"

"High Admiral Maximilian Oroseira, at your service," Maximilian boomed over the SIN, and Aika could feel the rush of power and respect he commanded, the pomp suddenly making perfect connection. No wonder he was such an asshole to the fleet commanders. Then it faded, and in the soft voice zhe had come to know as zer friend's, he added; "And ship designer, too."

"I figured," Aika remarked dryly, running zer fingers along the pipes. "I shoulda realized earlier, huh? At first I thought that you'd stolen gov ships, but... that wouldn't make your stuff better, it would be at the same level or worse. But since you're the one who made 'em in the first place, and there haven't been any massive updates since, that makes your new tech, even with limited supplies, way better than our junks. Am I right?"

146

"Basically, yes," Maximilian admitted. He sounded tired. Aika felt tired. "I worked very hard on those ships and on their empire... only to find that imperialism wasn't for me. Among other... disagreements."

"And ya tried to convince 'em out of it, didn't ya?"

The quiet answered Aika's question with ease.

"And now you're public enemy number one," Aika continued, hoping to lighten the mood. Maximilian forced a laugh. Aika frowned, glad Maximilian could not see zer genuine upset. Zhe tried to continue the deflection, teasing him more. "I'm gonna catch ya, one day, y'know."

"Sure you will," zhe could almost hear the Human rolling his eyes. "Once you make a good enough ship, you just might be able to catch up. I do respect your command of technology and mechanics. You just might be the one to make something to reach me. I wouldn't count on clapping shackles on my wrists, though."

"We'll see about that," Aika gave a dark chuckle. Maximilian laughed quietly along. "Goodnight, Captain."

"Sleep soundly, Admiral."

3.

Aika stood in the large foyer of Gus' lavish manor.

"Ya wanted to see me, sir?" was the simple question zhe posed, honestly bored and annoyed that zhe was missing zer usual time to talk to Maximilian. The man was facing away from zer, looking out of his outpost to the starry expanse beyond them. "Is there a problem?

"Yes. Yes there is." Gus coolly replied, turning around to face the admiral. "You are the star of our force. The tip of the top. And not only have you failed to complete your mission in over six months, you have been actively fraternizing with the enemy and have made no move to act on any weaknesses, despite many opportunities. The Three are beyond miffed by your sordid performance. Explain yourself immediately."

Aika did not betray a single emotion on zer face, as stoic and unimpressed as ever. Gus thought for a moment that he was wrong, but he knew without a shadow of a doubt that his sources were true and that the accusations he was placing on the pilot were all justified.

"And what of it?" Aika calmly asked, at a level of brazenness that would have been shocking from any other person. Even Gus, who knew such a statement was possible, still found himself taken aback by the nonchalant acceptance. It was difficult not to respect such brutal honesty, and Gus was glad that he did not have to retract any of his appreciation. "I'm whittling down his guard. I've got a plan. He'll be behind the holo walls by the end of the year."

"Are you sure about that?" Gus pressured, leaning forwards. Aika's half lidded gaze remained as bland as it always was, zer clear lids lazily blinking with a 'snnnick'. "There have been a great deal of concerns from the grunts on your ships. Strange modifications. Seemingly pointless repairs. Unknown expenditures. What is going on with your command, Brrin?"

"I'm learning from him about the ships he designed," Aika responded. Gus stared at zer, mouth opening slightly as he tried to formulate a sentence, though the only thing that could come out of that ajar mouth was a very weak 'what?'. Aika shrugged. "I didn't know either, but apparently he was the admiral before me, as well as the lead ship designer. I'm figurin' out what's the missing and unknown bits and pieces of our own ships that became secrets when he went rotten."

"I see," Gus slowly accepted the explanation, looking quite troubled himself. "Well. I expect you to follow up on that promise and to report back weekly. Not in person, if the fuel spendings exceed the limits."

"I'll consult with D'yo," Aika told him, not even caring for his words or input. The meeting only served to put zer on edge and was an odd showing of how, unlike zhe had believed, zer privacy was less than ideal. "He'd run the numbers for me."

"Why do you care to go to that Earth based mathematician?" Gus asked, wrinkling his nose with distaste. Aika felt a fist clench, and zhe thought to zerself, 'hey, why not?' before waiting patiently for Gus to explain himself, winding up zer fist (the mechanical one with her SIN) and very clearly preparing to throw a punch. "The only people left on that forsaken planet are sticklers and Je-"

Aika was fined for the concussion the man ended up with, but hey, at least he would think twice before opening his stupid mouth again, if only around zer. While Aika did call D'yo, it was to talk with the construct as a friend rather than discuss finances, as zhe knew quite well that there was no way zhe would be stepping foot back in Gus' estate,

148

paid or not. So, the Dagon had zer nightly calls with the former admiral, the weekly ones with Gus and a few other investors, upgraded the ship, and slowly planned.

The spider web that zhe and the closest members of zer crew were forming to catch the rogue was growing increasingly complex, in ways that the moneybags could not even begin to fathom. Aika preferred this, seeing as that way none of them could get smart and blab about it, or that it would get bought and leaked. It was one of the reasons zhe preferred things to be on a need to know basis, but that was not always possible.

Maximilian called zer later than usual one night.

He sounded haggard, upset.

"Please," he said, hollow and without a single jovial tone, far flatter than the voice that Aika had gotten used to. "Please don't hurt them."

"I don't know what you're talking about," Aika replied smoothly, lying through zer teeth. A strangled noise was able to be made out on the other end, a stifled sob. Aika inhaled as quietly as zhe could, trying to make sure that the man heard none of zer own upset. "Be more specific, if you can, Captain."

"My crew. You have them in your holding cells. They're not responsible for any of the plans and theft," Maximilian forced himself to speak. "They don't deserve this- you- you must understand."

"I comprehend what you're saying, but I don't know what you want from me," Aika shrugged, though that was clearly not something that the Human on the other end of the SIN could see. "Your crew is safe and are now in the system where they belong. The standard procedure-"

"Is execution!" Maximilian could not restrain his cry. Aika could hear his fear, his anger. "Don't tell me you're so thick that you believe in their banishment cover story! Aika, please, spare my crew. Let them go, don't turn them in. I- I can't have their blood on my hands. All they have done is helped people."

Aika stood, staring out at the starscape beyond the reinforced paneling of zer ship. Zhe felt like zhe had been shoved out of an airlock or deprived of water, impossible to breathe, freezing, and blood boiling all at once.

"Please, Aika. I'll turn myself in. Just let them go."

"Deal."

4.

The image Aika had of Maximilian in zer head was not the same as the Human who sat upright and rigid in the ship's holding cell. In fact, zhe mused, zhe had several ideas of who Maximilian was, and none of them matched zer feelings or the truth. There was the ruthless and cunning pirate that had beaten zer at nearly every turn; the smug and know it all designer and captain; and the gentle, awkward, soft spoken creator that zhe had come to know only by voice.

Aika had heard the screams of some of his crew members, as their cheers of seeing their captain come to rescue them metamorphosing into cries of agony and pain as comprehension dawned on them, their release spelling doom for the beloved captain. One young shipmate had to be carried away by two others, all with tears in their eyes and protestation on their lips, but none dared speak against their captain. Maximilian's choice was to be respected, though the rules of the maw he had fallen into were subject to all forms of vitriol and malalignment.

The satisfaction that the Admiral had been expecting with the capture of zer greatest adversary was meaningless and held no warmth or joy. Such an idea had long since faded. It was a hollow victory, and zhe knew it. Now, zhe knew it. Zer trust in the Three had begun to steadily decline since zhe had met the shipmaker, practically gone at this point. Now was only emptiness, and regret.

Maximilian made no move to face zer as zhe came down to his cell. He stared at the wall across of him, both hands shackled together behind his back and that loop chained to the floor. Aika had no way of knowing that he did not plan for this all those years ago, and very well could have made a contingency or secret hatch with which through he could escape. That would not do. That would not do at all. Thus zhe had to take precautions. While bitter and unwholesome, zhe needed to have proven this point, zhe needed to have him in zer grasp.

Of course, the trick was not to catch the man, but to trick his crew. It was almost laughably easy to do so, at the price of honesty and a colony now starving more than they already were. Quite cheap, in the grand scheme of things. Aika leaned against the holo wall, eyeing Maximilian's plate of uneaten food- not that he could have digested the poor quality gruel in any regard.

"Not hungry, huh?"

"The standards of the Orion's belt have fallen abysmally," Maximilian responded in a monotone, still keeping his gaze locked on the wall. "Not even serving edible food to their death row inmates."

"Who said they're gonna kill ya?" Aika sighed, knowing the answer, but wanting to hear it anyway. "It's just banishment to the unfinished quadrant. Dunno where you're gettin' the whole execution idea from."

"They killed my nephew. They murdered Alexis," Maximilian snapped. Aika stepped back, uncharacteristically startled by the display of emotion. The name Alexis sat in the back of zer mind like a sticky slime, vaguely recalling the horrific situation. "I could do nothing as they executed their own creator. You know what they did to him."

Aika gaped, frozen in place and tendrils of icy discomfort and horror swelling over zer body. Zhe had heard rumors of the patricide, though no one could provide any proof, and no one could remember who was in charge before the admittedly young sets of triplets. Just as no one could remember that Maximilian was the admiral before zer.

"Why does no one know about this?" Aika asked in a whisper, feeling far too tired for this. "Why does no one know about you?"

'Will I be forgotten, too?' went unsaid, but Aika knew Maximilian sensed the inquiry. He sighed, and finally slumped forwards, dropping his head to his chin. For a moment, Aika wondered if he had some sort of poison tooth, which would be a real shame, but zhe could see him shaking with restrained fervor and pain.

"Alnitak and Anilam ran as many erasing programs as they could," Maximilian slowly said, trying his best to explain it. "With their combined processing power, he, and I, were essentially written out of history. Mintaka then rewrote whatever needed to be revised. It was not enough, though, as we continue to expand. It's all falling apart. Everything has been degrading, and the Three have been attempting to control it with quotas and restraints... but it's not enough."

Aika stepped into the cell and sat down in front of Maximilian.

"I want to help." Aika remarked. Maximilian stared at zer. "I believe you. I've been learnin' about all the stuff goin' on behind the scenes lately, and frankly, I don't like what I see at all. So, lemme help you. Tell me everything you remember, and I'll tell you my memories and knowledge. Maybe we can figure somethin' out to change all of this."

"We can't change the past," Maximilian sighed, not daring to believe in the words Aika was saying. "And if you come with me, you forfeit your own head. I have."

"I can live with being dead," Aika remarked, though sincerity was bright in zer eyes. Maximilian huffed, turning away, though his gaze came right back at the sound of the shackles fizzling out. Aika gave him a wry smile, stepping away so he could contemplate his freedom. "What do you say? Think we can partner up? I've been workin' on my ship to make it... piratable, in any way that word can mean."

"You planned this the whole time, didn't you, Brrin?"

"Ah-yup."

"I expect an apology for this whole scheme," Maximilian grumbled, attempting not to show how betrayed he felt, but he knew Aika could see it in the way zer smile faltered. He hesitated, and put out his hand. "After that, though, I'd be interested to see where this could lead."

Aika grinned as zhe shook his hand.

Water Fountain

9.12.2022

Okay, maybe he had a problem. Maybe so. Maybe it was a lot bigger than he gave it credit for.

It was not the first time he woke up without a clue of how he got from point A to B, and he was actually beginning to grow wary of these black out drunk awakenings. At first, he did not mind them at all, as having no idea what happened the night before meant he could not be embarrassed by whatever it may have been. Yet as time went on, the memories were no clearer, but the shame welled up in him nonetheless, leaving him only wondering at his actions. At least he was certain that he never harassed anyone, perhaps accidentally bumped into a person or two, but he never jeopardized his job, even when he was completely and totally wasted.

Ezekiel's head rattled as he tried to lift it from- water?

He dropped it back down into the little fountain with a groan. Great. He was in the arboretum again. The sun was hurting his eyes, and honestly he wanted nothing more than to roll over and possibly drown himself. That sounded like a great idea.

He thought he could distantly hear people calling his name. No kidding, he thought to himself. Who knows what time it is, and someone probably was ringing up his cell or his house phone.

A buzzing vibration on his arm confirmed that, and he flopped out of the fountain onto the moist grass, raising his TIN to eye level and squinting at the bright holographic display.

Chester. Thank god. He did not want anyone else to see him like this. It was not like they had not seen his post drunken self, but the less they did, the better.

Ezekiel flipped open his TIN and held it at a cautious distance from his head. For some reason, he felt way worse than usual after his average blackout.

"Zeke! Where are you?" Chester's voice rumbled, low and soothing, though the speaker. The Tardigrade-Ziz pressed the vibration to his forehead, and tried to say something in reply, but words were having definite difficulty coming out. "What? Are you okay?"

"'M by the fountain," Ezekiel finally managed to mumble. He managed to stand, and pain shot down his leg, agony making him swear and fall back to the ground. "I can't walk."

"You don't sound too good," Chester remarked, and Zeke did not hold back the smart remark on his tongue. Chester only clicked his own, unimpressed. Sweat broke out on his shoulders, curling in on himself. He could feel his gray pants were absolutely soaked through, and not just with water, and he flinched his hand away with discomfort. "I'm sending the golf cart with Max and Marlin to-"

"Wait, no-" Zeke inhaled sharply, feeling his face grow heated behind his glass PPE. There was a pointed silence on the other end of the line, hearing clearly that Ezekiel did not want the youngest members to pick him up not for their usual incompetence, but something else. Worry. "Chet, I think- I know - I haven't been- please, just pick me up- and bring a rag so I don't stain the seat."

He hoped Chester would get the point, and from the exasperated sigh he got from him, he did.

"I'll be there in a minute."

"Thank you," Ezekiel groaned. Pangs of pain ran down his stomach and legs. "On second thought, bring some pain killers with you."

"Zee, you can't mess with your meds like that," Chester reprimanded. Ezekiel rolled his eyes, but thankfully could hear the soft rattling of the medicine cabinet. "I'll be over in a minute, again. Try to keep yourself in one place."

"Trust me, I am not going anywhere," he grumbled, hunching over. "Just hurry up if you don't mind, I'm getting a little nervous."

"If you wanted speed, then you should've accepted Max and Marlin," Chester reprimanded, but Ezekiel could see the hover cart heading fairly quickly over to him, rippling waves of wheat and grass. Zeke waved limply at the big white cat man, the D'mas'de appearing quite unimpressed. Chester hopped out of the vehicle and headed over to his boss. "Dang. You don't look so good."

"Wow, I couldn't've known," Ezekiel sarcastically replied, rolling his eyes. Still, as he pulled himself into the hover cart, wrapping the old towel around his waist, he put his hand onto Chester's wrist. "Chet. Thanks. It means a lot to me that you bother to pick up this hungover sop from the fountain he fell in."

"Ay, don't worry about it," the D'mas'de reassured him, though he rolled his eyes a bit. "But you really should try to tone down the sauce."

"I know, I know," the human sighed, sinking into his seat, squirming uncomfortably, and he snapped his fingers as he remembered. "Where's the pain meds?"

"Seat pocket," Chester answered without even looking. "I brought two."

"Thanks, Chet," Ezekiel murmured, and downed them both without water. He made a face and fisted a hand over his stomach. "Maybe I shouldn't've done that without eating."

"Maybe," Chester agreed. "But I forgot, too. It's okay."

"Yeah," Zeke tried to smile, but it came out as a grimace. A harsh bump made his insides, including the tylenol he had just downed, protest with pain. "Ugh. Slower, please."

"You're really not looking so good," Chester remarked with concern. "Maybe you should take the day off."

"No way!" Zeke snapped, then caught himself, rubbing his temples. He continued through grit teeth; "I just need to wait for these pain killers to do their job and kill the pain."

Chester did not say anything, just raised an eyebrow. Ezekiel pulled out one of his stashed clipboards and proceeded to scribble on it, tapping a pen to his cheek every now and then.

"You're looking worse by the minute," Chester commented. Ezekiel glanced at himself in the mirror and grumbled. "Maybe have a nap in your office."

"Maybe," he unconvincingly, slowly, stated. "Do you mind throwing me into the window to my office, anyways?"

"Only if you promise to take a nap," Chester bartered, lean muscle rippling with his grin and the flex of his arm. Zeke groaned, pinched the bridge of his nose, huffed and puffed, threw up his hands, and then; "Fine. Twenty minutes. No more, no less."

"Deal," Chester smiled to himself. Zeke crossed his arms and simmered. Chester maneuvered the hover cart so no one could see them coming, and glanced up at the water sanitation office. "Your window's shut."

"The boys never shut theirs all the way," Zeke pointed out. "Just toss me up there."

155

"Okaaay," Chester replied, though he did not sound extremely enthralled with the idea. Still, he did exactly as asked, and was rather surprised to see Ezekiel making it into the room, allthemore impressed that he managed to keep the towel wrapped around himself. "Nice job, Zee!"

"Keep it down!" he hissed. "Dole out the chores, I'm going to shower, change, eat, and pass out. Try to keep anyone from coming to my office, or better yet, the main building, okay?"

"You got it," Chester shot him a finger gun. "Sleep well!"

Ezekiel only showed him another finger as he shut the window. Chester chuckled, and he sauntered his way over to the other employees waiting on the bench, and surveyed the group. Mary-Anne and Lou were sharing Shells, listening to Lou's newest mix. Andrew, Phillip, and Darnice were listening to Sal gushing over John, who was not present due to an interview with a Ziz. Among the interns, Marlin, Bill, and Max were arguing over some inanity, Theo talking animatedly to Elisa. Ricky was waiting expectantly for Chester, and xe gave him a nod.

"Alright everyone, Zeke, uh, has a migraine," he announced. "He's gonna be in his office resting. Anyway, here are the extraneous duties."

Everyone glanced at each other, thinking migraine to be doublespeak for hangover- and they were not entirely wrong. With only some protesting, everyone accepted their chores and left the house be.

Three hours later Ezekiel woke up, and everyone could hear Chester laughing as the enraged man chased him about, yelling something about twenty minutes.

156

Convergence

2.24.2023

"I've never really been one for religion."

"Really, Becky," Tim chided. The mid-ranking clergyman gave her a smile. "I think you should give Odiology a chance. We're not the kooks that fringe society makes us out to be and not the fanatics the Three would want you to believe we are."

"Even so, we agreed when we started dating that you wouldn't get Evangelical with me," Becky reminded him. Tim paused, realizing that he had in fact been trying to persuade his girlfriend to join his religion, and smiled wryly, apologizing. "It's alright, I know you're enthusiastic about it."

"Of course I am," Tim nodded, his smile growing relaxed once more. "One people, one mind, one purpose - unity. What better message is there to spread? I for one have found meaning and support within the Sanctuary. The other preachers find it odd that my partner doesn't join the services, though of course I respect your decision."

"Well, if I happen to be bored when one of the sermons go on, I guess I could join for a few and watch you at work," Becky shrugged, not quite interested, but willing to humor her partner. "When's your next one going to be?"

"Wednesday night," Tim replied earnestly. "I'm usually scheduled for then."

"And you go on the other nights to listen to the other lecturers?" Becky asked, leaning her chin on her hand. Tim nodded twice. "I guess I can come over on Wednesday."

"Your presence will be highly honored at the Sanctuary," Tim grinned at her broadly, proudly. "I'm sure of it."

"It better be," Becky rolled her eyes, smiling. "After all, you're my boyfriend."

"We don't simply award rank at the Sanctuary," Tim remarked with a half shrug. "But I know I can get you the first few levels, being that you know a little bit from me already. Most of our flock hardly knows a thing about the deeper meaning when they first convert, but they know the truth when they see it."

"Really now," Becky remarked, raising an eyebrow. Something felt amiss, but she hardly could put her finger on what it was. "Well, let's see if I find the truth."

—

Becky listened to Tim's speech with growing bewilderment. It was laced with powerful rhetoric and persuasive insinuations, but on the whole, Becky found herself utterly lost. There was one line, however, that overlaid the whole of the oration.

We are all Void, Tim had intoned. There had been murmurs of agreement wafting through the crowd, nearly everyone nodding along. Becky felt her close cropped hair stand on end at the display of unity for this odd and albeit off putting statement. She shifted uncomfortably as Tim reiterated the point for the umpteenth time in ten minutes. Becky wanted to leave at this point, to explain to Tim later that Odiology really was not for her, but she did not want anyone to see him go. However, that would likely embarrass Tim, and she would have preferred not to shame her boyfriend by making an exit from his speech. So she waited, trying her best to think about other, more pleasant ideas than what Tim was purporting.

"Objectionable, isn't it?"

Becky started at the voice beside her, turning her head to look at the person sharing his table. He was a small Ziz who looked like sleep had been avoiding him as of late, his feathers disarranged and beak unpolished. However, Becky had noted that most of the Odiologists around had poor quality clothes, and it made her ponder Tim's remarks to her at one point that the less fortunate would flock to the religion. Yet something in this Ziz's demeanor made him feel far less impoverished, leaning towards a man fallen from grace.

Becky finally realized that she should reply.

"Well, objectionable is one way to put it," she replied slowly, glancing around to make sure no one else around could hear her words. "I'd put it more along..." a smile crossed her lips, "odious."

"It's like a fragrant flower that the more of it you smell, the more nauseated you become," the other smiled, relief evident in his entire demeanor- his shoulders loosened, his eyes grew less vigilant, and he leaned back somewhat. "If you haven't joined yet, which I assume you haven't, I might suggest to look elsewhere if you seek God. They sure as hell don't come around here."

Becky nearly laughed aloud, snorting into her hand. She found herself warming up to this guy much faster than her usual wariness allowed others to slip through the walls put up around her emotional care and camaraderie.

"Seriously, though," the Ziz shook his head, beak flashing in the dim light. "It's not good here."

Becky and her companion were aware that the others were rising to clap the end of Tim's speech, and Becky was struck with a sudden need to see this person again, out of the confines of the Sanctuary, where he could speak more freely, louder than the whisper they was forced to use during the sermon.

"When can I see you again?" Becky asked him under the din of applause, clapping herself and looking directly at Tim, who seemed to revel like a cat in the praise. "Can you leave to a cafe or something?"

"I…" he hesitated, and Becky was about to retract her words before he nodded. "Yes- I- I can save to go."

Becky did not have time to process the statement before they broke apart. She turned back to the Ziz's retreating back, realizing she had forgotten an important step.

"Wait!" Becky called. Dark eyes met hers. "Your name and CIN."

"Oh," the stranger blinked. "Here's my CIN code."

He brushed his wrist over the back of Becky's hand. She saw the number flash and compartmentalize within her own SIN's system.

"I'll see you later," he said, looking nervously at a person squinting at them. "They're not fans of post sermon conversation in the halls."

"Your name," Becky insisted as the Ziz turned away. He glanced back, and said; "It's T'rill."

—

Becky, after she was able to process the odd parting statements of her newfound friend, frantically texted T'rill that there was no need for him to use any of his money if he were to meet with her, and that Becky would happily supply the credits for the food. Being a foot soldier for the Three had its perks, mainly a good paycheck. T'rill seemed hesitant to accept her offer, but Becky insisted, and T'rill relented.

"I'm going out," she told Tim a few days later. "There's a sermon at the Sanctuary for beginners by a Ms. Patrice. I'm pretty lost in it all right now, so I think it would be a good choice."

"Oh?" Tim perked up, a glint in his eyes. He smirked at her pridefully. "I told you that there's more to it than meets the eye. Have fun, dear."

"I'll try to understand, this time," Becky replied, and made her way to the cafe. She was relieved to see T'rill already waiting there for her- she had worried that he would be a no show, judging by how skittish he was after the sermon. "Hey. Sorry I'm late."

"No worries," T'rill gave a stilted laugh that gave away his many, many worries. "I'm glad to see you."

"I am, too," Becky replied, truthfully. She decided that the best way to go about it was casually, and struck up a conversation about the weather and mining stations as they waited for their drinks.

Eventually he could not wait any longer.

"What's all this about... 'void was the beginning and will be the end'?" Becky asked, leaning back. T'rill winced, gaze breaking away as he shuddered. "I hadn't heard of any of this until those sermons."

"I- I'll get to it," T'rill promised, fidgeting with his feathers. "Let me... go in order."

"Take your time," Becky assured him. Still, her curiosity ate her. She stifled it. "As much as you need."

"They don't tell anyone this, but when you join, they take everything from you," T'rill whispered, glancing around with genuine fear in his eyes. Becky's heart ached for him. "All your money, clothes and belongings- they say they're going to share it with the community, with you, and it's true enough. They say it is to relieve one of their worldly stake, and bring them closer to the Void, to Convergence."

Becky nodded, recognizing the teachings, horrified at the practice. No wonder most Odiologists looked poor and disheveled- they were.

"One finds work in the Sanctuary. Food in the Sanctuary. Clothing in the Sanctuary. Shelter and housing- the Sanctuary. The Sanctuary 'provides' for everyone, all together, all at once, one big family," T'rill went on, his smile warbling and shoulders trembling. "That's how they got me- the family aspect. I loved it, at first. We all were together for one purpose, to be together. United."

T'rill wiped at his eyes with his sleeves. Becky hesitantly reached to take his hands.

"A few months ago there was- there was a Void's Embrace, as they call it," T'rill shivered, eyes growing moist and pained as he curled in on himself. "I didn't know. I didn't know. My friends, my new family- Becky, it was mass suicide. Apparently, there is a huge blotter in the center of the Sanctuary. I'm not supposed to know this – I found out when I was… assigned a new job. They all jumped in."

"What?" Becky breathed, eyes going wide. Her heart rate picked up- she had heard of a sudden spike of disappearances earlier in the year, and there had been rumors that those missing had all been Odiologists, but that had been dismissed as unsupported claims. But here T'rill was nodding, looking more terrified than any other man before her had. "God, I… I am so sorry…."

"I tried to leave, after that," T'rill smiled painfully, sorrowfully and with an immense self pity that Becky did not believe to be misplaced, as she pitied him too. "But how could I? I had nowhere to go, no one to turn to: the Sanctuary made sure of that. I was poor, on the streets, and no one would hire me, obviously. Then… they invited me back. Of course I accepted, I was hungry and afraid. They… they punished me for my insubordination, for my weakness of faith."

"Punished you?" Becky repeated, noticing her hands were shaking as they held onto T'rill's. "Hadn't you been punished enough?"

"I told you they gave me a new role. I was assigned to cleaning duties," T'rill swallowed, blinked, swallowed again. Becky felt terrible for the man. She never knew about any of this. From what she saw from Tim and his friends, Odiology was no worse than any other major group. "I- I need a moment. I might- I might be ill."

Becky pulled a trash can close for the other man, in case he needed it.

He did.

Becky gently nudged forwards a glass of water. T'rill took it gratefully, sipping at it.

"What's cleaning duties?" Becky asked, brow furrowed. "You mentioned that everyone lives in… communal living, so to speak."

She did not need to say the rest; that T'rill's reaction to recalling seemed far too harsh for simple janitorial work, but the man could have been a germaphobe for all she knew. T'rill, however, smiled slightly, sadly, shaking his head.

"You would think so," he quietly murmured. "So did I, I hoped so at least. But no."

He met Becky's eyes, unwavering. There was resignation, pain, horror, and yet strength and desperation in his irises. A pleading instability, a fear and hope of being caught and known.

He took in a shuddering breath before speaking once again.

"I had to clean the corpses that missed the jump and give them to the Blotter."

—

Becky returned home in a stupor. A death cult. A death cult. Her boyfriend was a priest of a death cult. Her boyfriend wanted her to join the death cult, to be a leader of it alongside him. Her boyfriend's ex, trapped in the death cult, had enlightened her to several truths she would have rather left in the dark.

What the hell.

"How did your meet up with the other Newly Converged go?" Becky jumped at Tim's voice, smooth and suave as usual, sneaking up from behind her. "Oh, I didn't mean to startle you."

Part of Becky found herself almost yelling at the man for what he was doing, but the rational part of her knew that if he dared speak a word, T'rill might be hurt further than he already was. She had to tread lightly and not give away her companion's name.

"It's alright," Becky responded, a hand over her chest as she tried to breathe normally. Her gaze flickered behind Tim to see the schedule of Odiology speakers, to see the one she ditched to take T'rill out to the restaurant, as the name had slipped her mind with her intense thought. "Ms. Patrice's teachings were fascinating. Very... enlightening."

"We don't call her the Beacon Deacon for nothing," Tim chuckled, turning away. Becky found herself relaxing, and the thought alone hurt- to be afraid of her boyfriend. "I'll make us some tea. You look a bit strained, Becky. That's alright. The truth is a bit painful, isn't it?"

"You said it," Becky softly agreed, a bitter feeling in her chest. The truth sat within like a heavy, leaden rock that swelled up. Becky faked a yawn, stretching out her shoulders. "I'm pretty tired out from everything today. I might head to bed early."

"What, you don't feel the rush of divine inspiration keeping your lifeblood awake?" Tim teasingly joked, coming over to press a kiss to Becky's temple. Becky forced herself not to flinch away. "Hm. You're cold and clammy. Maybe you're getting a cold. Come on, little sheep, let's get you tucked in to get some rest."

As sleep claimed her, she could not get T'rill's haunted look out of her eyes.

Desperate.

Brash.

Becky knew only one thing in her dreams; she had to rescue him.

—

It took several weeks of lying and sneaking behind Tim's back to help T'rill.

Becky hated what she was doing with every fiber of her being, overhearing conversations that she was not meant to ever know as she sweat in hiding. Plans for Void's Embraces. Convergence pods. Space mausoleums. People erased from public record and knowledge, false death certificates issued to family members who had been ascertained to have no hope of joining the Sanctuary. So much death and misery revolved around this religion that her boyfriend was so staunchly prideful of. Who knew about all these… terrible things.

And let them continue. Furthered them, in fact. Nurtured them into existence. Used his charm and wit and musical abilities to tangle people of all kinds and backgrounds into the Sanctuary's grip.

During one of their long conversations, T'rill had mentioned to her that Tim had once wooed and won him, and then dumped him once he was mired in Odiology.

He realized Becky was dating Tim after he finished speaking, and paled rapidly, apologizing profusely, but Becky waved away his sorries. She was already too weary and wary over her partner, and had no guarantee for how much longer it would last between them. Part of her wanted to fight the notion, that Tim would never do such a thing to her. Yet what differentiated her from T'rill? Who was to say that Tim was not intending the same with her? As she spent more time with the other man, she learned that all T'rill wanted was a family, as he had lightly touched on in their first rendezvous. That stung, doubly so, as Tim had been his partner, and then. Then.

It took hours, days, weeks, months- at times T'rill despaired that he would never be free from the Sanctuary's clutches, but Becky promised him that freedom was right around the

163

corner. That they would reach it, together, and Becky would be there every step of the way.

It was easy to go around Tim's back, and Becky had.

She did everything for T'rill, now.

—

"Are we there yet?" T'rill asked, his hand warm in Becky's own. Becky smiled, giving him a reassuring squeeze as they kept walking. "Where are we going?"

"I'll tell you when we get there," Becky assured him. T'rill sighed and pouted, making Becky's heart feel a bit warmer and happier. Finally. All their work had culminated to this point. Becky led him into the room and carefully stepped behind him to take off the blindfold. "Open your eyes."

T'rill did as Becky bid, and gasped involuntarily as he took in the room.

An apartment, furnished lightly, not a single sign of the Stain or Enigma around. His surroundings blurred, and T'rill furiously scrubbed at his eyes to clear them of their tears. They dripped faster all the same, and he turned on his heel to face Becky.

"It's all yours," Becky gently said, holding out the keys. Instead of taking them, T'rill was suddenly pressed to her chest in a tight hug. Becky froze for but a moment before lowering her arms, her guard, and hugging him back just as firmly. "I have you. It's alright. You did it. You've got a job at the arboretum, your own food, and finally housing, and I'm here for you every step of the way. I'm so proud of you."

"It's thanks to you," T'rill told her through tears. "It really is. I couldn't have done… any of this without your help, Becky. Thank you."

"Trust me," Becky smiled slightly, taking his hands as her own eyes teared. "I know. I'm so thankful that we got you out. And now we can rebuild."

—

Becky's SIN lit up with a message. It was an audio recording sent from T'rill, and she immediately opened it.

"Hey, Becky- I'm trying to remodel, but some things are too heavy for me to move. If you have a minute to stop by and help out, I would appreciate it. Your pal, T'rill."

164

Becky dictated to her SIN to reply that she would be there in the late afternoon. She did not mention that it would be when Tim's night sermon would begin. After all, the best way to keep away from an addiction or craving would be to remove the stimuli or reminders of it. T'rill had mentioned to her that sometimes he missed the Sanctuary, and in response Becky would hold him close and gently assure him that he could press on.

When Tim left their home, Becky waited another fifteen minutes before setting out herself, texting Tim that she was going to help out a friend with moving some furniture. Tim did not reply but acknowledged that the message had been received. At T'rill's doorstep, Tim did send a reply informing Becky that he would not be home that night. Suited Becky well enough; as her boyfriend's presence no longer was the warm and enjoyable one it used to be, now knowing what he represented behind closed doors.

"Hi, Becky," T'rill greeted, smiling at him, feathers ruffled from exertion. Becky looked around the room and nodded with a light smile. "Do you like it so far?"

"I think it looks great," Becky replied honestly. The room, to others, would appear as a wreck, but Becky could see the graceful flow of utility throughout. It was very much like the Ziz beside her. "Now, where's the heavier objects that need moving?"

"My dresser, for one," T'rill breathlessly replied, and Becky reached over to smooth down some of the sticking up feathers. T'rill smiled and ducked his head. "Um. The one in my room."

"Alright," Becky agreed, electing not to bring up what she had done. "Let's go take a look."

"Right behind you," T'rill remarked, and the two set off for T'rill's room. When they got there, Becky paused as she took in the environment, raising an eyebrow as she looked around. T'rill silently closed the door behind themselves. "Is something the matter?"

Becky turned around to face him.

"You don't have a dresser," she pointed out. T'rill looked up at her, and rested his hands on the point where her shoulders met her chest. Becky let him push her down onto the nest, and now she stared up at T'rill, who crawled over her. Her heart beat quick and fast and delighted, sending a pang of guilt down her spine. "Wait, T'rill...."

She bit her lip while the other stopped immediately, coloring sharply. Becky thought long and hard about how to explain this. Yes, Tim was scaring her, and she no longer felt neither safe nor happy around him, but.... Yes, T'rill made her heart sing, was caring and

165

sweet and gentle and she loved him desperately, but- but-

"Let me show you how grateful I am for you," T'rill leaned close to whisper. A shiver ran along Becky's limbs as they warmed with the blood rushing through them. "I'm so grateful for all of your help, and kindness, and protection. Let me show you."

Becky looked at him for a long moment, her heart soothed by his very presence. Her eyes drifted to the door, and then back to T'rill's face. It was startling how eager he was.

Becky nodded.

T'rill flew onto her, wings wrapping over her shoulders and laughing as he pushed her to the soft surface. He held her tightly, under his wings. It was soft and gentle and curious all at once, a sweet desperation soothed by proximity and fulfillment.

Becky noted with fascination that, while she had spent so long protecting T'rill, in this moment, she felt protected by him.

It was... wonderful.

They broke apart after what felt like eternity, only to allow Becky to inform Tim that what they had between each other was over, and she would collect her things that evening. T'rill, at first nervous, was easily assuaged by Becky's triumphant grin, and her arms pulling him back down. This was what unity was meant to be. A convergence of happenstance and circumstance that culminates into something beautiful and wonderful.

Into life.

Prayers Against Temptations

44.2023

1.

Many (it was not that long ago) years prior, Angelo St. Hubert was an arrogant, entitled, and foolish boy.

His arrogance had been terrified out of him, though he had not realized how effectively until he had made his new home far away from his father and his unavoidable roar.

His utter destruction of esteem certainly made some things easier, such as respecting his fellow person, and opening his heart to the compassion that streamed through his veins. Though several humane horrors had led him to this point (starvation, illness, malice) he was grateful that he was no longer blinded by his own splendor. Once a man wakes up in his own vomit from true hunger he can truly understand how meaningless his existence is.

Wickedness ceased to leave him be, however. Angelo found himself glancing over his shoulder constantly in this space that should have been safe, that should have been a fresh start, and now held fresh wounds and invisible knives.

Angelo shuddered as Tracheion's hand slid up to his shoulder, slick with the echos of blood, and he yanked him down harshly.

"Hello, dear," Tracheion greeted in David's tones, making Angelo's stomach turn painfully. "My, I didn't take you for such a schemer. An odd medicine woman here, inquiring after little old me? And sent for by you, no less!"

Angelo did not reply- he did not know what to say, but he glared down at the possessing spirit nonetheless. He choked as Tracheion grabbed his tie, yanking him closer so he could hear him hiss.

"Why was she here," Tracheion demanded, not a question. "How dare you go behind my back and summon one of your companions?"

"She's no companion of mine," Angelo replied, dull and tired. The thought almost made him laugh. "Besides, she would like to meet your acquaintance, if you please, Mr. Tracheion."

"Oh, does she?" Tracheion mused, absentmindedly twirling Angelo's tie round his wrist, watching the other begin to strain for air. Tracheion let go after a sharp yank down. "Well, perhaps I'll take him up on that."

Angelo inhaled deeply, adjusting his collar to loosen the deep green tie. Tracheion patted his cheek, smiling up at him without meaning it. Angelo repressed another shudder.

"There's a good lad," Tracheion remarked, pushing Angelo forward slightly. "Off you go!"

"Yessir," Angelo mumbled, folding his arms with minor defiance. Tracheion rolled his eyes at the display; so lonely that he had to hug himself for comfort. Pitiful. It almost made him smile. Angelo briskly headed off to the art department, head down and eyes on his feet. Oquerys' voice, now so close again, reprimanded him within his own head, and he forced himself straight- and just in time, too, as he bumped into Leo - with his red rimmed eyes and despondent expression. "Oh, hello, Mr. Ember... you seem perturbed today."

"No, I'm alright, don't worry about it," Leo waved him off, smiling tiredly. "Just... a lot has been going on is all. Almost too much to keep track of."

"You look exhausted," Angelo said softly, reaching over to him and straightening his sweater. "Please, would you go home and rest for a bit?"

"Maybe I'll just go home," Leo mumbled, eyes falling away from Angelo's. The younger man's breath hitched and he stiffened, eyes widening. Leo steeled himself and looked back at him, trying to imagine him as David (which was very hard, as the only things that David and Angelo shared visually was their teddy bear dispositions). "For good."

"Mr. Ember, no-!" Angelo shook his head slightly with a mix of worry and fear, dropping down into a kneel to look up at Leo more comfortably. "Please, I know things are rough, but they're going to change for the better soon. I promise. I sincerely do."

"I don't know how much more of this- this two facedness I can take," Leo turned his head away from looking at the other, perhaps out of his own musing or out of the embarrassment inherently attached to the motion. Angelo felt his heart ache and stopper, though he had no idea what to say to him. "It's like David can't tell up from down sometimes."

"Leo- please- please trust me," Angelo implored. "Please. A week. A week and everything will change. I promise."

168

Leo looked at him with tired eyes, but there was the slightest spark of hope in them. The longer he looked at Angelo, the brighter that spark appeared. Yet then his eyes drew away, and it dimmed until it was hardly visible at all.

"Please."

"Fine. Fine." Leo dropped his head into his hands. "I'll trust you. It's like… you're the only person around who's seeing the problems and not getting angry about them. Why, Angelo?"

"Things that would be hard to understand," Angelo said softly. "And not my secret to tell."

"Why are you afraid? You were doing so good until that doctor showed up." Leo asked at last after a long silence between them. Angelo stared at him, and the deep seated fear that he had been struggling to hide for so long rose up to the surface for the shortest instant. "Angelo… you can trust me, right? It's not a one way road."

"I… I've done something that…" Angelo hesitated longer, looking at Leo with a quiet pain. "That will make everything better. But… I don't think it will end well for me, and me alone. And I'm sorry."

"Sorry? Sorry for what?" Leo's brow furrowed, and he examined Angelo's features. "Angelo, what did you do?"

Angelo did not reply, only gave a slight, sad smile before turning away and going down the hall.

"Angelo!" Leo called after him. "Where did you go last night!?"

The tall man stilled and turned to look back at him.

He looked tired.

Exhausted.

Leo let him go the second time, shaken by the absolute enervation written all over the young man's round features.

Haunted and petrified.

2.

David climbed the steps at a snail's pace, hardly able to move his hands along the banister, let alone taking his feet off the ground. His back hurt. His hands hurt. His muscles burned and body ached, used so harshly that even his eyes strained to remain open. Tracheion cared not for how he used his host, as long as he got whatever he pleased done the way he liked. The day was a blank, and David tried not to sob at the loss of time, the fear of what was done in the meantime. There was one thing to be grateful for, however. Tracheion had spent the whole day with Oquerys, discussing the new vessel the doctor would be creating for him. Such a thing meant that David might be freed of this aggressive usage sooner rather than later (a later that may have never come).

There was also the fact that two nights before, Leo had held him once more. His heart felt lighter in the morning, lighter than it had been for a long time, and at least Tracheion let him hold onto that softness until he dropped him back off in his thoroughly bushwhacked body. There was the bliss of sleep waiting for him as well, which could not make up for the lost time, but would assuage the aches and pains that afflicted him. Perhaps Leo would let him into their bed again, and the thought was enough to help him rise up the remaining stairs.

The apartment was quiet when he entered. Which was unsurprising, considering the hour. Still, David gave a sigh of relief, noticing a still warm cup of tea set on the table, a small paper with his name leaning against it. He picked it up and took a long draw, feeling it revitalize his core.

And then he noticed that there were more words on the other side of the paper.

He picked it up and read the note, unsure whether to be relieved or alarmed by the contents. It was from Angelo, that was clear enough, but the terms used were stiff and disquieting.

"Assisting the Doctor. - A St.H"

David stared at the note, feeling nauseated. He wished that the doctor in reference would have been Lawrence, but in that case Angelo would have put the clinician's name. David gripped the cup of tea tighter, wondering about what Angelo could be doing at the moment; especially considering what Tracheion had allowed him to overhear of his and Oquerys' plans. His heart ached for the younger man, as Tracheion reveled in showing Angelo's pained and disturbed expressions to David.

170

Firm arms wrapped around him, a forehead pressing to the side of his neck. David exhaled slowly at the encompassing pressure, leaning against him.

"Are you alright?" Leo asked him, his voice strained and clipped. David's heart ached painfully upon hearing him, almost alien in his tone. David set the tea down and turned around, his hand crumpling the note he held as he wrapped his arms around Leo. Leo's breathing shuddered, and he tightened his hold on David as well, pulling him as close as he could. Everything was far too much. Thinking of the Angelo made his heart cry, and thinking of David made his eyes bleed. Everything was wrong, so wrong, but here and now he could hold David and pretend things were getting better. In this singularity, he could pretend that he believed Angelo's promise, and oh, did that hurt. David murmured against his shoulder; "I could ask you the same thing."

Leo only tightened his arms around him, a quiet gasp escaping David at the squeeze. A hand reached to Leo's face, resting on his cheek as their eyes came to meet.

"You look so tired," David whispered. Leo replied, almost smiling; "I could tell you the same thing."

David's lips twitched into the slightest of smiles, and he leaned up onto his toes. Leo made no motion to move away, in fact, he tilted his head down to meet David. While short and simple, their kiss swelled with emotion, Leo able to feel David's rapid heartbeat slow to a more tranquil, content one. He sighed against the other's lips, pulling him closer. David drew apart after a moment, blinking as he breathed.

"Let's go to sleep," he softly said. Leo nodded, just once, and let himself be guided to their bed. David clamored on first, positioning himself so that he could hold the other. Leo nodded again, seemingly without thinking, and joined him. David's arms adjusted to be more comfortable for the both of them, and Leo felt tears trickling down his face and into his hair. David's heart ached as he silently sobbed in his arms; and he tightened his hold even as they both wept. "Leo... I'm... I'm not going to ask what's wrong- I know, everything's... everything's messed up and it's my fault. I will say that... that I'm sorry. Give me a few more days. A few days and it's all going to change, I'll tell you everything. I promise."

"You and your promises," Leo tried to joke, but it came out tight and wavering. "Such a dreamer."

The term hurt, for once. David tightened his arms around Leo, hiding his face against his shoulder as he too strained not to cry.

"This is a... it's a nightmare," David admitted, eyes shut tight in an attempt to hold back his tears. Yet they made it past the barrier anyway. "It is. I'm so sorry."

Leo turned around, pushing David over as he twisted. The smaller man let himself be caged by Leo's form, looking up at him with a pained reverence. Leo slowly leaned down kissing away the tears, following them to where they slipped behind his ear.

"I want to hate you," he whispered. David's next intake of air shuddered, a moan escaping him. Leo licked his lips, shaking with the effort to speak, hands tightening on David's thin, too thin, wrists. "I want to hate you, so much. All the signs point to you. All the bad ideas, all the painful cataclysmic shifts, they all lead back to you. The only thing I can hate you for is for making me love you."

David turned his head toward Leo's, and Leo could not help but kiss him, slow and loving and painful for, because of, all its love.

3.

David woke up in Leo's arms. His lips hurt, his stomach ached, his wrists pulsed (one had a small bruise from Leo's nail), and his back felt like hell- exhausted from Leo's gentle, loving abuse. He had done nothing but kiss the man, long and slow and rough all the same, sweet and tinged with saltwater. Leo had held his hands away from himself the entire time, even as David begged to touch his face and hold him close, Leo murmuring, 'not now' (though he let him go instantly when David said it hurt, and David fisted his hands into the sheets to keep from touching his love). Leo had pulled David to his chest, holding him off their bed, as he kissed him with more aching emotion than David had ever faced, and it burned like the inferno, agonizing and a quiet sad.

His stomach churned; famished. He had not eaten in... days, perhaps. He did not remember his last meal, and it was more saddening than concerning. He made his way out of bed, already cold without Leo's arms around him. He shivered, rubbing his arms as he pulled a blanket around his shoulders. The soft scent of roses and honey wafted from the fabric, making him tighten it over himself, closing his eyes for but a moment.

David quietly made his way out of the room, getting to the kitchen and finding a tray of lasagna. Mouth already watering, he slipped it inside the oven, waiting for it to reheat. He sat in the dining room, eyes trained on the oven only aways away. His gaze slowly turned the other way, however, into the living room. The door to Angelo's (which was Leo's old) room was open slightly, a bit of greenish light spilling into the dark central space. So he was back, thankfully. David stood, his chair making a quiet noise of protestation. The

172

man slowly made his way over, hand hovering at the door's edge before he simply peered within from the outside, his curiosity eating at his heart.

What he saw within confused him. A soft, light green that hurt to look at too long made his eyes water, illuminating the whole of the room. It was spartan, clean. Everything in its place, nothing sticking out, hardly any belongings visible. The bed pressed to one corner, a neat work table in another, a guitar case carefully next to it. There was practically no other sign that the room was occupied, aside from the man who resided within.

He was not on his bed, instead bowed over it, eyes closed tightly and hands clasped over his chest. David could not quite make out the words he mumbled, and hardly could understand him if he tried.

"— te pido tu ayuda en este día…"

It felt cold in the room, the bowed man shaking, licking his lips and trying to find the words. David took a step forward without realizing, catching more of his fervent words.

"Dame la fuerza y resistencia…" Angelo took in a shaky inhale, curling tighter – a true feat, considering his size. "Resistencia para no ceder a la tentación… por favor."

The silence around was painful. David's ears felt wet, as though they were bleeding, but he reached to touch them and found nothing.

"No me permitas caer en la desgracia," Angelo sobbed without tears, covering his face. "Y en destructora de vidas de aquellos…."

David was not sure if he was breathing or not. Angelo certainly was, but David felt nothing in his lungs, as though he was floating. The ethereal green light of the room seemed to be suffocating him.

"De aquellos que amo," Angelo pleaded quietly, broad palms upward now. "Los amo… protégelos, por favor. Por favor."

David was next to him without even realizing. His heart throbbed painfully, coldness across his entire body. He only understood flecks here and there, yet the strain in Angelo's voice was universal.

"Protégeme del perverso que me controla," Angelo shook as he begged, tears dripping down his hands. It looked toxic in the viridescence, viscous and vivid. "Protégeme. Protégeme. Protégeme de la tentación. Por favor, protegernos."

David did not even realize when his hand reached out and landed on Angelo's shoulder.

The young man flinched and turned around, and the strange green light was gone.

"Mr- Mr. Krammer!" Angelo gasped, his face shrouded in darkness and the window before him illuminated the wisps of his hair. "You- you are awake? It is very l-late."

"I am awake, yes," David replied, skin still prickling from the whole of this event. He tried to smile but nothing on his face changed. "I... are you alright, Angelo?"

"I am." Angelo quietly responded, head lowering and turning aside. He stood up from where he was knelt, and David felt the disconnect wax between them as their differing heights became starkly more apparent. "Why are you not resting?"

"Um..." it took David a moment to remember his own hunger, the situation removing it from his mind for the time being. "I needed to eat. And you probably need to, too. When was the last time you ate anything, Angelo?"

He had meant it lightheartedly, but the young man looked away, curling his shoulders inwards.

"Angelo...? Are you sure you're alright?" David tilted to get a better look at his face. In the pale blue moonlight, Angelo looked like a haunted memory. David carefully reached to touch his arm again. "Angelo?"

"I am certain that I am fine," Angelo replied, monotone and robotic. "I will be going to sleep soon."

"Please, eat with me," David quietly urged. "You're... You're not looking too good, Angelo. Are you ill?"

"I'm fine," Angelo repeated again, brow furrowing and eyes watering. He subtly wiped at them with his sleeve. "Please- please, Mr. Krammer. I can't eat a bite."

"Have a nibble, then," David tried to persuade, taking his hand. It shook terribly in his hold. His heart panged for the younger man. He looked so vulnerable, so easy to break, so delightful to make all his and destroy from the inside- David shook his head to clear it, flushing from the thoughts that had forced their way through his mental barriers. "Please. At least sit with me. The food will be warm soon, Angelo, and the smell can do wonders for appetite."

"I…" Angelo hesitated, his face still tight and worried. David gave his hand a squeeze, looking at him with large and pleading eyes. Angelo finally acquiesced, shoulders dropping slightly, but the slightest smile was on his face. "Fine. Ok."

David smiled and tugged on his hand, leading him out of the room. Angelo was silent, steps firm but light and hardly there, as though he was attempting to lessen his presence. It hurt David's heart, but he was not quite sure why. They followed the scent to the food, and together sat. The timer went off for the oven shortly thereafter, and David swiftly made his way over to shut it off so as to not wake Leo. Plating for two, he brought the dish over before realizing what it was- and instantly feeling his stomach shift.

"Oh- oh, Angelo, I'm so sorry, I didn't realize-" he stammered, setting down the plates. "The tomato. I'll- I'll make you something real quick, okay? I wasn't thinking when I was taking it out."

"It's okay-" Angelo tried to insist. "I told you, I don't need anything-"

"Yes, you do," David rebuffed. Angelo's mouth snapped shut. "I'm going to make you something to eat. Just give me a minute."

"I want the lasagna."

David met Angelo's eyes. He could see the sincerity and resolve in the other's gaze, the actual certainty. He would have asked if he was sure that he wanted a food that would make him feel unwell later, but he could see that Angelo in fact did.

"Okay," he softly replied, pushing over the plate to the younger. He hesitated, but made a quiet blessing and took a bite. David swallowed roughly before following suit. He thought for a moment before broaching further conversation. "I thought… that you didn't believe in any deities?"

"Oh, I believe," Angelo quietly answered between a bite. He seemed dizzy for a moment before proceeding to eat – perhaps realizing how hungry he was. He waved a hand.. "They simply do not love me."

"I see," David, surprised, said. Angelo looked away, embarrassed. "I… thank you for telling me this. Because… because I'm sure they do love you. Because they brought us together, and I could never ask for a more… dedicated and hopeful friend."

David had to swallow down the last word. Angelo looked up at him with sad, tired eyes.

"You easily c-could," he gently countered. He wrapped an arm around his middle, looking dizzy for a moment before continuing to eat. "You c-could have asked for a friend who is less hellbent on his own annihilation. That might have b-been a bit more pleasant than one who seems to be destroying himself at every available turn."

"Angelo," David nearly snapped. "Don't talk about yourself like that."

"It's true, though," Angelo glumly replied, scratching at his elbow. It was a familiar gesture to David. "We both know it is."

"Angelo," David found himself repeating, now with a strain in his voice. He stood, and was now next to the man's side. He was not sure how he had gotten there, nor how his hands ended up on Angelo's shoulders. He did not know what to say, looking into those pretty brown eyes and seeing how sad they were. His hands slipped up (avoiding Angelo's neck, knowing it to be sensitive) to the underside of his jaw. He cupped his cheeks, seeing the younger man's eyes widening. "Angelo."

Two large hands reached around his wrists, pulling his hands away from the other's scruffy face. Angelo looked wary and worried, and his hands were so large around David's wrists... the smaller man repressed a shiver of thrill at the thought of how easily Angelo could crush him, but the spark had not come from that thought- it was from the knowledge that Angelo never would. And, perhaps from the memory of the night, the memory of Leo holding him close and tight as though he would never let him out of his grip, kissing him so hard he was sure that he was still seeing stars.

He wanted the same from, or for, Angelo. He could not tell. He was tired, yes, weak and exhausted, but Angelo would never let him fall.

David, even with his hands held away, tried to lean up to the younger man. Angelo carefully, gently, held him away.

"No," he softly said. David stared at him, trying to process. "You're not thinking, Mr. Krammer. You need sleep and rest."

"That's not what I want," David whispered. He watched the younger man swallow roughly, following the motion with his hungry eyes, searching for a fulfillment of something he did not know how to word. He tried anyway. "I want-"

"No," Angelo repeated, more firmly, trying to hide the worry and fear in his eyes. "No. Please. Please, go rest, you are not thinking."

"Maybe not," David quietly agreed, looking down. His cheeks flushed with shame, regret, worry. "I just want to make you feel better. Because you deserve it. So much. You deserve to be happy, Angelo."

Angelo did not reply, simply holding David's wrists. He stood, careful not to jostle the smaller man, and he pulled him into a long hug. There were more emotions than could have possibly been fit into conversation or words in that hug. Desperation, fear, care, worry, all of it was right there, and it made David choke painfully. His eyes welled, and he wrapped his arms around Angelo in return, finally moving them now that they were free of Angelo's gentle restraint.

David felt floating and drifting, only to realize through his muddled state that he was being carried, so gently and kindly, to his room. He was lain in Leo's arms, slow and steady.

Angelo would never let him fall.

David turned to press his face to Leo's chest, the other holding him instinctively.

Part of him wished that Angelo let him slide.

4.

Angelo barely kept himself from vomiting. His gagging remained trapped in his throat, the hissing stench of flesh so hot it was melting singing his nostrils and stirring at emotions long buried. Regret and pain were the two most obvious of the lot, though some of the others included were mourning and mortification. He tried not to look at the woman working happily before him, nor the other watching silently behind. His hands shook, and he nearly dropped the acid syringe. He had to stop, breathe, and return, using one hand to stabilize the other.

"Don't fuck up, Angelo," Tracheion drawled, smirking. "Never know what Mother would punish you with if you do."

"First of all," Oquerys remarked, turning around with a smile as sharp as a blade and a blade as bloodied as a butcher's knife. "Do not tell my son what not to do in this context. Especially not with such crude language. You may inform him as to what you would prefer, but in my lab, that course of language is unacceptable. Understand?"

"Yes, madam," Tracheion rolled his eyes, smirking sardonically. Angelo felt sick at the expression on David's face, like a man wearing a mask of the cartoonist and making it say and do such awful things. Poor David, puppeted about so easily, tricked by putting his heart in front of his head. Angelo ignored both of them best he could, working quickly and quietly. "Anything else, Doctor?"

"Secondly," Oquerys returned to the Frankensteinesque project on the medical work table. She smiled brightly, humming. "You're very right. The limits to my wrath and course of reprimand can be quite extensive. Wouldn't you say, Angelo?"

"Yes, Mami-"

"What do you call me in the surgery."

Angelo swallowed roughly at the not question.

"Doctor. Yes, Doctor, madam." He softly corrected himself. His hands tremored, trying to work as quickly as he could. "Yes Doctor. I apologize for- for using the wrong term, madam."

"You really have him under your thumb," Tracheion mused, leaning against a wall across them to better watch their work. Oquerys chuckled with amusement, tinged with nerves, and Angelo put another of his emotions into that box locked up deep inside. "Even I struggled to contain him. Right when I thought that I wrangled him into place, he goes behind my back and calls you."

"Oh, he has a tendency to do that," Oquerys remarked softly, sliding a hand over Angelo's wrist, patting it once. There was a kindness in the touch. The fear of losing control – made evident by her next words. "Don't you, you imp."

"Yes, Doctor," Angelo softly replied, blinking rapidly with anger as he tried to continue working. The gloves on his hands were stained black and red. Oquerys questioned him for elucidation. Angelo took in a stuttering breath and continued. "It is a habit."

"What is a habit, Angelo?" Oquerys pressed, smiling. Tracheion watched, fascinated and clearly enjoying the stress being levied onto Angelo's shoulders. "Go on. Explain."

"I'm a backstabbing little shit," Angelo mocked through grit teeth. Tracheion laughed, amused. Angelo's head twitched as Oquerys stared at him, her eyes flashing with fire. It was a mere warning. "I apologize for my language, Doctor... I mean that I am an ungrateful child."

"That's better," Oquerys remarked, returning to her work. Angelo blinked faster, biting his lip harshly, shoulders curling in as though he could disappear into himself – impossible with his size. "Get back to work."

Angelo continued to work in silence, only answering when spoken to. Time was running out. Tracheion gave him two weeks, and he could not bear the thought of failing. He would sell his own soul to save that of Winnowa. Everyone else was recovered, everyone safe, everyone but her. All Angelo knew was that Winnowa was near a window, a cruel joke, but despaired when Tracheion laughed and laughed at him, grinning and telling him he was free to tear down the whole place to look for him- and that she would probably be dead before Angelo could locate him.

That was when Angelo had made the contract.

Damn him, he had to. At the moment, he did not want to think of the details, that human skin parchment signed with his own blood. The way he desperately called a dead woman for help, greeted by a ghost.

The body was nearly complete. Tracheion came over to look, curious, glad to see that it was being created as to his specifications to the letter. He pressed a finger to the top of Angelo's forehead to make him raise his head from his concentration.

"Why the hurry, Angelo?" Tracheion smiled broadly. "It's not like someone's life is on the line."

Angelo did not reply, frozen as he waited for Tracheion to release him so that he might continue working. Rage simmered in his eyes. Tracheion's gaze dropped to the corpses, tilting his head. He smiled again, and Angelo's blood boiled at the thought that he was showing them to poor David.

"Please stop doing that," Angelo quietly said. "Your contract with him is terminated, to be fulfilled by me. Must you push the boundaries of allowance?"

"Of course I do," Tracheion rolled his eyes. "Might as well get every last drop out of ol' Davie boy. Can't say I won't miss the fun."

Angelo did not say anything for a long moment before stepping back and picking up a pristine cloth to run over his face. His eyes landed on the clock, and his stomach panged painfully. Oquerys met his eye behind her thin glasses, and flashed a smile.

"Go prepare a meal, Angelo," she instructed him right as Angelo was about to ask if he could go to cook. Angelo nodded once, though he hesitated. "Yes, Angelo?"

"Will Mr. Tracheion be joining us?" he asked them both, eyes on the floor. Oquerys shrugged as she continued working on the corpses. She replied; "That is up to Mr. Tracheion."

Angelo's eyes met his for just a moment, and Tracheion's smile faded at the lack of contempt in his gaze. While Angelo was always courteous and respectful towards him, in spite of his anger, Tracheion marveled at the moments of kindness offered by him.

He shrugged.

"Sure. I guess."

5.

"Of course," Oquerys remarked, and Angelo shirked away from her, the eye roll audible. "Vegetables. When will you grow up, Angelo?"

Angelo swallowed and did not reply, looking down at his shoes. He was holding another covered tray in his hands and he silently walked to Oquerys' side and set it down before her. He opened it, and the steaming cuts of meat made Tracheion's mouth water. Oquerys raised an eyebrow, looking at her son from the corner of her eye.

"Which?"

"Lamb, madam."

Oquerys waited for Angelo to plate the food, the young man carefully serving her first followed by Tracheion, though he had hesitated, unsure who he would rather offend less. He did not add any greenery to Oquerys' plate, though he did place some beet salad. Angelo carefully set both salads onto Tracheion's plate and moved to his own seat, his dish empty.

"Eat," Oquerys instructed. Angelo looked to the white glass, and murmured a response. Oquerys' smile grew cold. "Excuse me?"

"I- Yes madam," Angelo quietly replied, taking from the vegetation. Oquerys obviously did not fully approve, but let it slide. "I will eat."

"Good," Oquerys nodded, smiling. "Now...." Tracheion found himself pulled into conversation with Oquerys, lightly brushing over their pasts and how they had both left their old lives behind for one on Earth. The more Tracheion spoke to Oquerys, the more amazed he was for a multitude of reasons. He was mildly surprised to know Oquerys' origins were not of Earth at all, though he had known her to be supernatural – he could sense it. They were similar, but different. The small pieces of information they shared were challenges, Tracheion found. Though, there was the additional perplexing nature of-

"Angelo. Where do you think you're going?"

"I had finished eating, madam," the timid young man said, holding his own hands tightly. Tracheion rolled his eyes. "I was going to go clean the kitchen-"

"You have not had anything with enough energy," Oquerys serenely remarked. "Eat some meat."

"No, thank you," Angelo quietly murmured. Oquerys did not respond, and Angelo shifted uncomfortably, trying to leave once more. Oquerys snapped her fingers, making the man stay in place, trembling and looking ill. "Please, madam, I don't want-"

"You need energy, Angelo," Oquerys shook her head, smiling. "Silly boy. You'll collapse once again and you will be angry that you wasted precious time because you refused to refuel your body. Sit. And. Eat. Some. Meat."

"No," Angelo replied, increasingly distressed. "No, I don't want it. I'm nauseated, and it'll make it worse."

"It's not bloody, or tough," Oquerys rebounded, looking at him over her glasses. "Not only that, but you had cooked it yourself, and quite well. You disappoint me. Acting like a child."

"I am not a child," Angelo tried not to snap, hands shaking. "I am an adult, I have been taking care of myself and-"

"Taken in by two men who had pity on you," Oquerys corrected smoothly. There was a latent anger in her eyes. "Additionally, according to my sources, at least one of them has a fancy for you. Who knows how long that had been going on for, hm, Angelo?"

"That's not true," Angelo said quietly, flushing. "It's not true."

"Regardless of truth or not," Oquerys continued, as though the tremors in Angelo's voice were nothing. "It is obviously rather irresponsible and foolish of you, to bed near strangers. To eat and grow comfortable without knowing what hand feeds you."

Angelo looked as though he were about to cry, and Oquerys clearly noticed, laughing to herself.

"You're still a lost, silly little boy," she reminded, moderate of tone and jagged of meaning. Angelo's fight with his furious tears slowly became a battle he was losing. "Wouldn't you say so, Tracheion?"

"Hm? Oh. Yes." Tracheion snapped out of his thoughts, his fascination with this exchange. Oquerys seemed to so easily break Angelo down, expose his most vulnerable sides and tear into them with something akin to delight – or a strange terror. "He always struck me as naive."

"You've mentioned, sir," Angelo quietly replied, voice tight and wavering. "Please, I don't- I don't want to eat meat, must you reprimand me so?"

Oquerys gave a long suffering sigh, which was more than enough to make the young man flinch. Reaching into her medical bag, she drew out two items and set them on the table. Angelo instantly recoiled and staggered back as though Oquerys had drawn out a venomous snake. Tracheion observed the syringe and a crystally white semi liquid in a vial.

"No," Angelo whimpered, shaking where he stood. Tracheion, still bewitched by this odd scene, recalled how much more firmly Angelo had rejected his offer. "Please, no. I'm trying so hard not to, please-"

"You need your energy somehow, Angelo," Oquerys guiled. "If not with flesh, then with chemicals. Make your choice."

"I don't want either," Angelo softly cried out, voice aching with restraint and fear. "Please, no."

"Now."

"No!"

"Angelo."

Oquerys' voice was soft, gentle. Dangerous like the shake of the rattler's tail. Angelo stiffened, tears staining his cheeks.

"I am sorry sir, I'm sorry, I didn't mean to shout-"

Oquerys snapped her fingers, and Tracheion was entranced to see Angelo jerk back into a proper position as though he had been yanked sharply. He was crying unstoppably now, looking at Oquerys with no small measure of fear in his dripping eyes.

"If you so insist on misbehaving," Oquerys stood, putting out her hand. Angelo whimpered, shying away, but Oquerys did not move. Tracheion watched as Angelo placed his wrist in Oquerys' hand, the mother tightening her grip harshly. "I will shackle you to the gurney and you will complete the nervous system by sunrise. Then you will go to work, and return to complete the structure of the muscular system. You will not be permitted to sleep until it is completed. Do you understand?"

"Yes, madam," Angelo sobbed. "I understand. I understand."

"You may eat or inject prior to."

"No, I'll work, please," Angelo begged, and Tracheion could hardly believe his ears. Oquerys had lost to her son in this battle of wills. "Chain me."

Oquerys looked at him dully, and then smiled at Tracheion.

"Excuse us for a moment."

6.

Tracheion woke up with Leo's arm over David's middle. He gingerly removed it, trying not to cringe. Sometimes he wondered if David's continuous relationship with Leo was a minor way to get back at him, but he knew that such a notion was very likely untrue. Well, soon he would not have to deal with the awkward and uncomfortable moments that David and Leo shared, and the notion was more relieving than he expected it to be.

"Where're you goin'?" Leo slurred, eyes blearily squinting. Tracheion patted his arm, replying, "To check on Angelo. You sleep tight."

"Mm." Leo did not speak further, nudged back into sleep by Tracheion's shadowy influence on his brain. The trapped spirit rolled out his shoulders as he stood, tossing on a bit of clothes that he knew David would be mortified with and would probably have to return to the apartment to change. At this point the human should have wisened up by now and left clothing in his office, but sometimes he hardly seemed to realize left from right. Leo mumbled, "tell him I say hi."

"Will do, Leo," Tracheion flashed a smile he could not see. "See you at work."

183

He left the apartment with a saunter, making his way down the stairs and out into the dark streets of the night. A quick hail and taxi ride later, with a generous tip (David would not bristle too long for that one) added, he was outside of the manor Oquerys had gotten built in not time at all. Or maybe she had it repaired. Tracheion wondered for a moment at the woman's seemingly endless funds before deciding it was none of his concern. Applying the code to the door, it opened for him through a means of mechanical engineering that Angelo had installed for him. Angelo had put a similar function at the studio's front door, though more grandiose and whimsical, fitting for a toy company. This door opened as if to a graveyard.

He made his way through the eerily quiet halls, trying to remember exactly which way to turn and go in the maze of an estate. Eventually he did find the surgery, the pale blue light streaming out from beneath the door. He pushed it open and stepped within.

Angelo was shadow shrouded by the light as he worked silently. If Tracheion believed that his hands had been shaking earlier, they were practically vibrating at this point. He silently observed him, looking at the body that would be his with a sense of curiosity and....

"Angelo?"

"Yes sir?" Angelo murmured, not surprised to hear him. "How can I help you?"

"What's your favorite word again?"

"Anticipatory?"

"Yes, that's the one." Tracheion nodded with satisfaction. "Yes, that is the one."

Angelo did not speak further. He moved to the other side of the body, reaching over to another corpse and extracting a material. Tracheion saw the silvery glint of a thin chain keeping Angelo in a radius around the center table.

His gaze eventually landed upon Angelo's face.

He had to blink to recognize him. He looked sick, shaky, sleep starved.

"You can go longer than this," Tracheion scoffed. Angelo looked at him as though he did not understand the words he was saying. "Staying awake, that is."

"Oh," Angelo mumbled. "I've already been awake for... for two days. Or was it three?"

184

Tracheion stared at him, recalling that Angelo had not gone to sleep, for, in fact, three days. A sardonic smile tightened on his face. He did not know what to say to him, and honestly was not sure if he wanted to say a word. Angelo struggled to thread a needle, eventually using another needle to put it into place. Tracheion watched as he proceeded to lower the needle before realizing that he held the unthreaded strand. That was the final straw for the spirit.

He left the room, making his gradual way to the coffee room. He stirred together a drink, marveling at the utility within Oquerys' estate- an entire room dedicated to caffeine. Now that is some substantial societal progress. He did not pay attention as he grabbed another mug and poured some tea within, swirling in some honey. It cooled as he returned to the surgery, leaning against the wall as he watched Angelo work.

The man's motions were jerky and slow all at once, as though encased partially in molasses. It was disturbing to Tracheion, and he whistled to get the young man's attention. There was a definite delay to his reaction, and Tracheion did not like that considering that Angelo was working on *his* future body at the moment.

He shoved the drink into his hands. Angelo nearly spilt it with how his hands tremored.

"Drink that," Tracheion firmly instructed him. Angelo stared at him, then the drink. He looked into it for a long minute before nodding slowly, sipping at the hot liquid. He seemed to have lost any care if the drink was poisoned or not, unsure if he was more likely to pass out from overwork or drop dead on the spot from poison; and he was too tired to decide which he would prefer. Regardless, if he would not finish his work, a fate far worse than death would steal up on him, so getting it done was more than simply imperative. Tracheion, satisfied, nodded in return, unaware of Angelo's rambling sleep deprived thoughts. "I'd rather that you don't screw up when doing my senses. After all, that's the main point of the deal."

"Right, sir," Angelo sighed, rubbing at his eyes and yawning. "Thank… thank you. I'll get back to the… the vessel shortly. I apologize for the delay and slow progress."

"You should take a rest," Tracheion observed with a tilt of his head, folding his arms. Angelo looked at him with obvious fear. "Why the big spooked eyes? Is it because of the Doc? She'd never know if you nap for a couple minutes."

"She'd know," Angelo replied, eyes wide and terrified. A scared smile danced on his lips. "She definitely would know. Anything with the soul, she can read. Please, don't tempt me with the thought of rest. I must do as she says, and she told me not to sleep."

185

"She's really got you scared to hell and back, huh," Tracheion murmured. "Whatever happened to you, kid, that made you run so hard and fast?"

Angelo glanced at the dead bodies in the room, as though wondering if they were there, or if Tracheion could not see them.

"Do you really have to ask?" Angelo quietly questioned, gesturing around the room, brow furrowed and a sick look crossing his face once more. Tracheion briefly wondered if the man was falling ill from his own abuse of his body. The probability of that seemed more than likely. "She is... incomprehensible to me."

Angelo fell silent, brow furrowing and trembling. He rubbed his arms, trying to shake out the feeling of fear and exhaustion battling, knowing that he had to focus.

"Please let me return to my work," Angelo whispered. "Thank you, for the tea. I will complete the vessel soon. On time."

"I'm sure you will," Tracheion rolled his eyes, but he found upon deeper thought that he sincerely meant his words. If there was ever anyone who knew exactly how to traverse a deal with the devil, it would be Angelo- and if there was anyone who could do so running on no sleep for five days, it would also be Angelo. He felt his sarcastic, malicious smile slip off his face. "I mean it. You're really a monster's worst nightmare come true. I'm glad you're not the one I made the deal with."

"I might have done this in the first place if I was," Angelo stated, but without the icy bitterness one would expect from his words. He sounded far sadder, the anger on a back burner. Actually, there was none of the anger that should have been there. It made a chill run down Tracheion's spine, rebounding from David's psychosomatic and unconscious reaction as well. He hummed David (the body's owner, it was not his and this was an uncomfortable, burdening reminder) back to sleep. Angelo returned to working on the vessel - the corpses. So many corpses. There were about six lain on one table, and another one, fresh and stripped of its flesh, on another. "Or at least, something less gory. It would have taken more time, but at least my conscience would have remained untouched. I'm sorry. I'm so sorry. I need to get back to working."

Tracheion bit back the logical response of telling Angelo he need not apologize, instead silently watching him continue to slave away to complete the body, to make it functional and usable. He placed a small wire, coated with some salt based mixture, against an open strand in the vessel, and Tracheion tried not to show his amazement as the fingers in the dead body twitched and flexed.

186

With a few more electrical nodes and probes, it sat upright. It was clearly puppeteered and nothing living, but Tracheion could only imagine what it would be like to breathe air not tinged with blood, to touch and feel with fresh, new hands only his own.

He reached out and touched his own- future- face. It was cold, dead and lifeless, but... only for now. Soon, soon it would be his, with blood and blood running through its veins, his veins.

It was perfect.

"Sir?"

"Yes, Angelo?"

"Are you alright...?"

"Absolutely excellent, that's what I am," Tracheion said with admiration, grinning broadly with David's mouth- it never fit right, too tight, did not get his words across the way he wanted them to sound, always had a distinct soft side to it. Tracheion was not soft, detesting that he had to rely on blood and sinister manipulations to get the respect he deserved. But soon... that would all change. The simple oddness of Angelo's question only struck him after his musings. "Why wouldn't I be?

"You seem... highly affected, sir," Angelo noted. "It is unusual to see you so excited."

"What, am I not a fun guy?" Tracheion asked, wrinkling his nose. Angelo hesitated to answer. Tracheion scowled, figuring the reply. "Nevermind. Can't a man look forward to having a body of his own?"

"Of course you can, right, yes," Angelo hastily placated. "Yes. That's very true. I'm working on it as fast as I can, you know."

"I'm sure you are, Angie," Tracheion murmured, still admiring his soon to be body. "I can't believe it. Not being tied to that awful book anymore. Being able to touch things with my own hands. Looking how I want to look and not pretending that I'm someone else."

"Do you have a name you would want to use, Mr. Tracheion?" Angelo asked, tilting his head as he worked. Tracheion stared at him, mouth falling open. It had been too long.... "We would need one for your documents. We have most of them ready- you're going to be listed as an orphan from Sweden who needed new papers because they got destroyed in a fire. But for that, we still need a first name. Or a last one, though 'Tracheion' is not a common first name- even in Sweden."

"Oh," Tracheion said rather dumbly, struck by the question and its simple logic. He looked at the bodies in the room, at his own- David's- hands. He found himself remembering, murmuring, a simple name that had been settled in his brain for the appeal of anonymity, the way it rolled off his tongue. It had been a name he had nearly forgotten. "Well, my name's Elron."

Angelo looked up from his work, head still at a tilt, though he seemed not to realize.

"What?"

"My name is Elron." It felt strange to acknowledge again.

"It... it's a good name," Angelo remarked, blinking once. He gave a slight smile. "It really suits you."

"You think so?" Tracheion tried not to seem too earnest, going more for a preening lilt. "I always thought it has a great ring to it. Elron Tracheion. Flows right off the tongue; even David's."

"It sounds very nice," Angelo agreed quietly. "Mr. Elron Tracheion."

Tracheion grinned.

7.

David walked into the art department. It was shocking how joyful it was within, how optimistic it had become in such a short time. David did not know how Angelo managed to do it, carefully cultivated trust and regrew bonds. There were some rumors about Angelo using certain, achem, 'charms' on Lynn to keep her in the studio, but David and Lynn were able to dispel that gossip carefully. Certainly, it took time, but little by little Angelo's reputation began to recover. After making his way through the animators, giving encouraging smiles and soft words of gratitude, he came to Leo's desk. Angelo, who was working in the same room, seemed not to notice either of them at all.

"I'm going to drive Angelo to the doctor- Lawrence, that is," David disclosed to Leo in a low murmur, glancing at the younger man. Angelo looked in no way fit to stay at work, but he was diligently drawing and flicking through frames nonetheless. "He requested that I drive him this morning, and to remind him in case he forgets- and it seems like he's forgotten, poor dear's been absent minded lately. I'm going to accompany him where he needs to go, I... I don't like how sick he's looking."

"Yeah," Leo echoed, eyes locked on the youngest animator. It seemed that while things were, so shockingly and sudden as if by magic, improving, Angelo himself was deteriorating just as rapidly. Leo did not want to think about how that was happening, and nor did David. David suspected and feared that Angelo had sold his lifeblood for the company, but Angelo had laughed, nearly hysterically, when David had cautiously brought it up. He very gently told him otherwise, but David was not so certain about that. "Okay. Please take care of him... I'm really worried."

Neither said a word about how this very much was the week they had been dreaming for, praying for, and yet they were not so sure if the price to pay was Angelo himself. Even with Angelo's promise to David that it was not the case, he seemed to be working himself into the dirt regardless. Those around him could only pray that he was not working himself a full six feet. David gave Leo's hand a squeeze and slipped away to the young man, tapping his shoulder and letting him know that it was time to go to his appointment with Lawrence. It seemed to take Angelo a long moment to process the information, and he shakily stood, leaning heavily on his boss as the two of them left the building.

They got in the car quietly, Angelo thanking him once more for the offered ride. He seemed so sad, and David could not understand why, as things were finally getting better. David tried to cheer Angelo up with small talk and easy questions, but the young man seemed so utterly exhausted that he eventually gave up and took his hand instead. Angelo's slender fingers twitched before wrapping around David's, hesitant and uncertain. David held back tightly and achingly.

Angelo nearly fell asleep in the waiting room. David's worry spiked at the way he forced himself to stay awake, shaking his head violently and looking about with wild, terrified eyes, as though he feared someone was watching him. Paranoid. David did not know how to assure him, how to tell him that he was safe; how to tell him he was loved.

Angelo's name was called, and he stood, putting a hand to his forehead to still the motion of the floor.

"Good luck, Angie," David told him softly. "I'll see you soon."

A lazy tendril in the back of his thoughts laughed, the tips of his fingers already no longer retaining the same feeling as if he were alone in his body. He could almost hear

189

Tracheion teasingly ask if he was sure about that, and even though he was not, he wanted Angelo to hear it. He wanted him to feel safe.

His eyes drifted shut and closed him out, sending him drifting among stars as Tracheion settled into his flesh and bone. The spirit picked out a chair and sat, taking a magazine and flicking it open to wait.

In the office, Angelo found it beyond difficult to focus on Lawrence's words. The doctor was clearly growing increasingly concerned for the young man, but he was at a loss as to what to do. He noted severe sleep deprivation, though when he asked about Angelo's sleeping habits, he lied by omission and said that he was very busy. Lawrence could believe that, but if he took it as an excuse was another question.

"How have you been staying awake?" Lawrence asked, not sure if he wanted to hear the answer, especially considering that he knew Angelo's medical (and street medical) history. Angelo hesitated, looking embarrassed. "It's ok if you relapsed. I just need to know."

"I've just… been making myself," Angelo mumbled. "But the Doctor had offered a… a boost."

"She…" Lawrence stared, trying to comprehend. He snapped shut the case file. "She offered you drugs."

"She made me choose between those crystal shards and sleep deprivation," Angelo explained, far too calm for the situation. Lawrence stared at him. "I managed to choose the latter."

"How long have you been awake for?" Lawrence asked with a growing sense of horror. Angelo blinked, slow to process the question. "Please don't tell me it's been more than two days."

"Three or four," Angelo quietly replied. He looked vulnerable, guilty. "Please don't be angry…."

"I'm not angry," Lawrence soothed in a half lie. He was not angry at Angelo- that fucking doctor who had strutted in and started bossing him around as though she had owned the sweethearted artist was pissing him off. "Shit, Angelo… are you… shit, you're not okay."

"Please help me," Angelo did not sob- he was too exhausted and sapped to do so. It frightened the young doctor. "Please, Lawrence. Protect me from temptation."

"That's a tall order," Lawrence weakly replied. He briefly thought back to when Angelo was the most simple of the cases in David's Artimation Studio, where he had an addict patient to some magical blood and another case of possession, to name the smallest details. Angelo looked down at the ground, as if knowing his plea was futile. Leo's heart stung at the sight. "I can't... protect you from most," he slowly said. "But I can help with some. I'm sorry I can't do more."

Angelo slowly looked up at him with a light in his eyes, the faintest flicker of hope. It hurt in Lawrence's soul. He walked over to his medicine cabinet and prescription pad, jotting down a number and drug name and then pulling out a bottle from the shelf. He hesitantly walked back to Angelo, handing him both.

"Take these as needed," Lawrence quietly instructed. "For temptations. Any and all. I know you think you can't sleep until whatever batshit mission you have is laid to rest, but please, for my sake, try to get even a little. Please. For me."

Angelo clutched them both to his chest. His brows were knit and his eyes brimmed with tears that dripped out, unable to stop them in his vulnerable and hardly conscious state. A wave of nausea and guilt wafted over Lawrence once again as he took in his dear friend's appearance.

"Please," he repeated, the word slipping away from him before he could even think. He, however, knew that he meant it, each and every time. "I care about you, Angelo, and I don't want to see you suffer."

"Thank you, doctor," Angelo finally whispered in response to the medications. He hesitated before answering Lawrence's request for him to sleep. "I'll try. I promise."

"You're not looking well, Angelo," Lawrence whispered, haltingly going to place his hands over Angelo's, the one devoid of the prescription and medication. He did not care that it was a breach of conduct, he loved the man sitting across from him, and needed to let him know that. The words slipped away once more, each one intended and true without meaning to or knowing how to say them. "I... I care about you deeply and I don't want to see you hurt. Please take a bit more care of yourself... it's like you've traded in addiction for workaholism. Don't do this to yourself."

"Do what?"

"Work yourself to death," Lawrence replied. He had not meant for it to come out as biting as it had. There was a sudden urge as though Eleanor was reprimanding him for

191

his sharp tongue, ordering him to kiss the hurt away. He did not do so, and instead pulled his hand carefully away from Angelo's. "The doctor's ordering you not to overwork. You can be good for Doc Trace, right?"

It was difficult not to add a teasing purr to his voice, not to slip in a sweet pet name at the end of his words, knowing that those temptations would have been impossible for poor, gentle Angelo to resist. Especially not now, in his weakened physical and emotional state. He had used his guiles against the young man in the past as quite effective psychological tricks, but here and now they would not only be inappropriate but also damaging. Angelo needed, as much as Lawrence hated to admit it, as little intimacy and loving support as possible. For some reason that Lawrence was too hurt to understand, love agonized Angelo at the time. He could see it in his eyes, plain as day, from the way David spoke to him, gentle and ardent, not seeing, or not wanting to see, Angelo's pain. The young man had kept his gaze away as any respectable gentleman might, even if it was screaming against his heart and desires.

Angelo had not answered him, his eyes drifted to the ground and expression a tumultuous storm of emotions too difficult to discern and understand. What appeared to be resentment turned out to be sadness, and anger was pain. It was a complicated web of agonies and miseries, a sullen shine in his eye like that of a man being led in two directions at once.

Lawrence could only pray that Angelo would stay by their path, and that it was the right road to take.

Protect me from temptation.

Very well.

"You had best be on your way to your almighty important task," Lawrence nonchalantly, though not unkindly, reminded him. It took a moment for Angelo to realize that Lawrence was sending him off, just like that. Nodding once, he stood, wobbling a little until Lawrence handed him his nearly forgotten cane. "Good luck, Angelo. Please call me if there's any complications."

"I will, doctor," Angelo quietly replied. His eyes watered as he shook his hand. "Thank you. Thank you."

Lawrence silently watched as Angelo left. David was waiting for him, leaning against the wall and glancing at his watch. A smirk that was decidedly unlike David's spread over his face, and Lawrence repressed the urge to punch that stupid smug shade back into the realm from whence he came.

"All ready to go, Angelo?" Tracheion drawled in a smooth accent that was marred by the formation of David's mouth being unsuitable for the tones. "The doc- not you, Trace- is waiting, you know."

"Right," Angelo whispered, almost sadly. "Yes. I'm ready. Thank you again, Dr. Trace."

"Anytime," Lawrence replied quietly. His eyes met Angelo's. "I'm serious about that. Anytime."

Angelo hesitated, and then nodded. The two of them left together, Tracheion strutting and whistling as he twirled David's keys on David's finger, Angelo's steps tumbling and head down, focused on the ground so as to not fall.

"God protect us all," Lawrence sighed, brow furrowing in pain and eyes shut tight. His shoulders dropped and he rubbed his face, looking to the space where Angelo stood but a few minutes ago. A pain welled up in his chest, tight and aching within his throat. "And save him from himself."

Burnt Offering

Oquerys wanted him. Plain and simple. She wanted him any way she could get him. It was difficult to admit that, it was hard to acknowledge, and it was even more infuriating to live with.

The only person Oquerys had trusted to work on the other spirit's body was Angelo, and only him because she knew with absolute confidence that her son cared for Tracheion in that innocuous way of his, feh. Though quite frankly, saying so (that Angelo was the sole permitted individual) felt in and of itself discomfiting, because it required her to concede that she did not even trust herself around the vessel. Alone, her thoughts plagued her, tempting her to run his ethereal hands along the empty body, shuddering at the very notion that it would be Tracheion's. Oquerys had disliked the demon upon the initial meeting, yet by the second, found himself gradually entranced by him. Currently, she found herself reaching a similar point of enamour and obsession as she had with his Lordship.

Oquerys hungrily looked over the vessel, picturing it animated with Tracheion's behaviors, so hindered by the meat puppet he was currently commandeering. Oh, Oquerys could see past the janky motions and awkward stilted behaviors. She could tell that the man beneath was completely different than Krammer's body allowed.

Oquerys wanted to see him as himself. Wanted to murmur to him, grin at him, see his true responses. She licked her lips, wishing Tracheion's presence in the room- if not in the vessel, then watching through Angelo's eyes. The desire to ravage his body before him, to show how much she wanted him, to look him in the eyes as she used his future form- Oquerys fought another shudder, shaking her head to clear it. Growling, she stepped back. Too long. It had been too long. Doing so would no doubt push the other spirit being away from her, and her desire would go utterly unfulfilled, only spiked with the taste of potential and thus made allthemore bitter.

The body was completed, yes. She could call Tracheion for her fantasy, or she could inform Angelo to call him, and be with her son to fortify his constitution. Allowing herself to falter would so not be a good look. Deeply inhaling, she cleared her throat, and lifted her voice.

"Angelo."

The boy appeared quickly, twenty two seconds and a half, and stood silently after greeting her, awaiting his orders.

"You are aware the vessel is complete."

"Yes, madam."

"Have you informed the consumer?"

"No, madam."

"Why not?"

"I was waiting for your permission, doctor," Angelo replied easily, eyes wide and unassuming. "I had been aware that you were running the final checks."

"Well, everything is in working order," Oquerys gestured over the body. "Call up the contractee, and deliver the good news. I will be in the Red Room if you need me."

Angelo swallowed harshly at the utterance- he would do his damnedest not to need Oquerys, then. Silence reigned in the Orange Operation rotunda, and Angelo tried to shake off the fear from the other Room's mentioning. He swallowed and rubbed his sleep deprived (how long has it been at this point? six days, seven?) eyes, stumbling to the telephone.

David answered the phone. Angelo felt a pang of pain for it.

"Hello, Mr. Krammer."

"Angelo...?"

"The vessel is done. For Mr. Tracheion."

A pause.

Angelo gripped the phone's wire.

David replied, thankfully (or painfully, as Angelo did not want him to see that awful amalgamation of corpses and death), in a murmur.

"We'll be there shortly."

Angelo waited by the front door, foot tapping with anxiety. He could not wait for this to be settled, to get Winnowa's location and rescue her from wherever Tracheion had her shackled. The studio. The company's building was massive, and Tracheion knew it.

195

Taunted him with it. Watched him weep and laughed. Now, now, now the deal was settled. They would both get what they wanted, and they would both be freed from their awful bindings.

David's knock. Angelo opened the door instantly, letting him into the yellow floor. David blinked, never having personally been inside the estate as himself. Angelo put out his hand hesitantly for David to take, and led the man down the hall and around the corner and to the stairs that led to the Operating floor. If David was surprised by the color coordination, he said nothing of it. Angelo reached for the curtain shielding the vessel, hoping David did not smell the stench of death lingering in the room.

David's hand caught his wrist. Angelo froze, turning slowly to face him. The look in David's eye, of worry, care, respect, awe, love- it hurt and frightened him.

"Angelo," David whispered. "I can't thank you enough. For everything you've done. All of this, putting yourself through Hell, worked yourself so hard, did everything you could- all to pay a centuries old family debt that's not yours. I... I'm so grateful, Angelo. And yes, thank you too, for letting me tell him. I'll let you get to your body now. Angelo... how does this work?"

"We need Mr. Tracheion in control," Angelo softly said, trying not to think of David's other words, though they buzzed around his head sweetly like flowers. "It's a conscience transfer. I'll see you soon."

"Okay," David nodded. "Okay. Thank you, again, Angelo. I can't... I can't tell you how much this means."

"You don't have to," Angelo replied. "Rest, at last."

David's eyes watered, and he closed them. When he opened them, they were not his own.

"Alright, Angelo," Tracheion beamed, excitement in every facet of his- David's- face. "Let's get this party started."

"Yes, sir," Angelo nodded. "Right away."

Angelo pulled off the cover on the body. Tracheion marveled at it, eyes trailing along his future form, shuddering with anticipation and delight.

"Sit here, sir," Angelo instructed, gesturing to a chair positioned near the head. "I'll get you all wired up."

196

"Wired?" Tracheion questioned. "Nothing demonic?"

"No, sir, purely technical."

Tracheion nodded once again, sitting where he had been told, leaning his head back and closing his eyes.

It was finally time.

—

Tracheion's senses returned to him gradually, the feel of the cold metal beneath him, the sound of movement, and then, blurrily, the sight of the doctor at work. His eyes fixated upon him.

David was gracelessly swung onto Oquerys' shoulder, the doctor handling him as easily one might with a sack of potatoes. He did not seem to notice Tracheion's return to consciousness, but it was always hard to tell with him what he did and did not see. Tracheion's eyes followed him as he exited the room, and then drifted about. Things looked... differently. More clear- he had a passing thought that David needed to update his prescription- and vaguely different of shade. Angelo was looking at a screen, brow furrowed and glancing at papers to the side. The young man looked shockingly more exhausted than Tracheion had ever witnessed him appear; but maybe it was the fresh eyes.

Smells that David did not notice were stark to him, the scent of cotton hiding death, though smells that David had found were gone, like that of disinfectant and other chemicaline scents, or they did not register in his mind as such- was he- he-

He was finally himself again.

"Mr. Tracheion?" Angelo's soft voice sounded sweeter than ever, despite Tracheion not noting any difference in hearing between himself and David. If anything, Angelo's slight accent only seemed a bit more accentuated, as if unfamiliar to Tracheion. "Are you... there? Did it work?"

"Mmmmm..." He only groaned at first, familiarizing himself with his jaw and its movements. Slowly, he pushed himself forward, appreciating how his muscles flexed and compressed — a good thing that nervous system was not affected by Angelo's sleep deprivation. "I... yes. Yes, I do believe it did...."

Angelo came to his side, eyes wide and hopeful. He carried with him a few papers, fiddling with them. After a moment, he handed them to Tracheion. Tracheion glanced over the first page, a bundle marked with "Tracheion's paperwork". A small smile rested on his face, taking in a deep breath as he thumbed through the papers- the air caught in his throat, his smile freezing and falling. An all-too familiar sensation, seared into his memory, equally burned his skin. He dared not look down, knowing exactly what was forming upon his chest. He curled in despite the agonizing pain with a horrified, fearful, almost inhuman noise.

"No, no, no no no-!" He cried, vision blurred now with immediate tears. Angelo's own cautiously jubilant smile was gone. "It can't-! Not here-!"

"Mr. Tracheion?!" Angelo desperately questioned, dropping whatever else he had been holding and reaching for him. "What's w-wrong, I- I don't know- I- please, breathe-"

Tracheion whipped back from his touch, panicked and clutching at the smoldering mark emblazoned across his chest. "It's supposed to be done! We're done, that damn curse, I thought-!"

Angelo's arms shot around him, partially to keep his hands away from the mark, mostly in the embrace he pulled him into. Angelo's tired tears dripped onto his shoulder.

"Please," he whispered. "I'm here, I'm sorry, I never- I never would force you to do anything, it's not my doing, I promise. You're free, I promise, I promise I utilized the book so as to assure your freedom, I- I did not mess up, I swear. You are free. You are free. I didn't know this would happen, I would have given you painkillers before, I- I am so sorry- I'm sorry. Please breathe... it'll be okay. You're free."

For a moment, one long, long moment, Tracheion accepted the embrace, trying to still his racing heart and panicked thoughts. When he returned to himself enough to realize what he was doing and with who, he pushed him away. "She's... halfway between the toy man's bench and the stairs. Five boards from the support beam on the left side. By the window. There's a very small carved 'X'. That's the one," he stammered out, pulling entirely back. "My end of the deal is done."

"W-what- oh-" recognition clicked in Angelo's eyes and he quickly wrote the instructions on the palm of his hand with a surgical marker. "Thank you. Thank you- can- can I get you anything before I go?"

"No," he firmly replied, curling in on himself once more.

"Are you sure you d-don't need anything...?" Angelo hesitated, hovering in the doorway. Painridden, Tracheion waved his hand forcefully. "Sir-"

"Get out before I change my mind," Tracheion snapped. Angelo swallowed harshly, shirking away from the door and blinking rapidly. "Now! I told you where she is. Go and get her before she kicks it."

Angelo backed away and then turned, running. His footfalls were fast, yet stumbling, tripping over himself in his dash to the studio. He heard the rumble of Angelo's motorbike from the vine covered window, speeding off. The mark on his chest burned as though it had just been set alight that first time, cherry red and making the ghostly scent of burning flesh fill his nostrils.

Tracheion curled tighter in on himself, tears slowly tracking down his face and falling onto the white cloth covering his lap. The indignity of only wearing a sheet felt like nothing in comparison to the singing embarrassment from the mark on his chest. He tried to breathe as Angelo told him to, but his breaths came shuddering and choppy, still much calmer than initially.

He took in another breath of air, and the burning grew intense once more. He grit his teeth and shut his eyes tighter, willing the mark away. It was supposed to be a fresh start. It was supposed to be a body all his own. It was supposed to be new, clean...

It burned, oh, how it burned.

It was not fair. It really was not fair.

But if there was one thing that Tracheion learned about life so far, it was this:

Life wasn't fair. He had better get used to it already, because wishing it was different only made it hurt more getting bit again.

—

Tracheion was not sure how long he had stayed like that, silently crying and staring forwards. His chest ached terribly. Even simple breathing hurt, making the mark stretch across his fresh, raw skin.

The doctor's tread made itself known to Tracheion's ears, and there actually was a slight difference between his own and David's hearing- he could hear the stride of the predator in her steps. The door swung open, and Oquerys stood still, looking over her patient.

199

Then she approached him, coming to stand by his side, lifting his face with two fingers under his chin.

"You look gorgeous, my dear," Oquerys remarked, smiling as she usually did. Tracheion was able to perceive the slight tilt in her lip towards concern. "Why the tears along your pretty face?"

Tracheion sucked in a shaky breath. "I... I thought I would finally be free of this mark," he admitted softly, gesturing towards his chest. Oquerys pulled back just enough to examine it, letting his fingers drift down to the burn. It was less searing red than it had been initially, looking as though it were a few days old. Oquerys hummed, examining it. He snapped on a pair of gloves, gently prodding at it. Tracheion winced. "Ah- ah."

"Does it hurt?" Oquerys asked calmly. Tracheion curled tighter, pulling the blanket back up. "It does not appear to be as fresh as it should, considering you have just now occupied your new body. Also, considering that it appeared without prompting, I doubt removal is possible, seeing as this transcended your forms."

A gap grew between them with his words, Tracheion's eyes watering allthemore once again. In the silence, the starting of David's car was extremely clear, and the knowledge that they were separate beings at last grappled with his thoughts. It seemed so... impossible. Yet here he was, breathing and feeling on his own, no longer shackled to any other.

"It doesn't hurt as bad," Tracheion whispered. He sucked in a deep breath, expecting the pain to grow sharp and stark once more, but it remained dull and ebbing. "Not as bad as I was thinking it would, not as much as it used to... it used to burn. Searing, no matter how long it was there, how much time had passed. This... it's not like that. It's... quiet."

"Quiet?"

"Inactive," Tracheion clarified in a mumble. "Dull. Just...."

He fell silent, trying to figure out how to word his thoughts and emotions. His emotions were so clear and stark now, so obviously his own- and thus so much harder to name. Oquerys sat beside him, opening her arms for Tracheion to settle within her embrace. Tracheion leaned into the touch without meaning to, but once he was within the doctor's grasp, he found it impossible to get out. Oquerys' arms were warm around him, secure and comforting. Tracheion felt himself shudder and sob, clinging to her as he mourned his skin and freedom. And yet, and yet, in Oquerys' arms... it did not hurt as bad. He was not nearly as embarrassed as he thought he would be.

"So, Elron- that is your name, right?"

Tracheion lifted his head, and nodded, eyes wet and blinking slowly. Oquerys' gaze was shockingly gentle to him, open and understanding. Tracheion wanted to lean up against him, though merely returned to her embrace that he had inched out of to look at her.

"Good. Good name. Anyways, Elron-," Oquerys' arm was gentle around his back, her hand rested on the other's leg in reassurance. "You're not going to let this old scar define you, will you? Insofar as I can tell, it does not appear to have any strong hold over you, besides emotionally."

Tracheion felt his jaw clench, preventing him from answering in a positive manner. The centuries of burning servitude spoke otherwise, that it would only be a matter of time before he was forced to serve again. Oquerys tilted his head, still smiling, and moved his hand under Tracheion's jaw again. He did not move his head, though, allowing him to choose if he wanted to move it himself to meet his gaze once more. Tracheion slowly moved for their eyes to meet, and Oquerys' hand followed the motion.

"You are no longer shackled to your past, Tracheion," Oquerys told him. They stared at one another for a long moment, neither saying a word. Oquerys patted Tracheion's back, and a thrill went out from his touch, quiet and his own. It was his feeling. It was his own body once more. It felt wonderful, even with the dull ache ebbing away on his chest. Tears pricked his eyes once again, but these were not unhappy. Oquerys stood, rolling out his shoulders as he did so. "There are fitted clothes arranged for you right here. Hopefully they are to your liking."

Tracheion caught him by the hand as he was leaving the room.

"Doctor," he breathlessly remarked. "Thank you. For... for coming and making my body. And for being here for me now. I only wish I didn't make a fool of myself."

"Nonsense, dear," Oquerys shook her head with a smile. "Your reaction was completely natural and understandable. I will be in the reading room when you are ready."

"Got it," Tracheion nodded. Once the doctor was out of the room, he made his way to the clothing, but not before admiring himself in the full length mirror Angelo had brought in. He was undeniably handsome, and it surely assisted in making him feel a little better. He put on the clothing, carefully buttoning the shirt- but upon reaching the scar, he paused.

He had covered it since- since then. But it was his mark, was it not?

Tracheion left the shirt where it was, slipping the vest on and finding the way the clothing framed the mark rather dashing. It was all very well suited, and he came to the reading room.

Oquerys stood to greet him.

"You look fantastic, dear," she remarked, looking him up and down. Tracheion replied, "You made me look this good."

Oquerys grinned.

The Three B's

"Do you want to go home to your family in a body bag?!"

Winston could clearly hear his father's words echoing around his head, ringing in his ears.

"Or would you rather be beaten, bruised, and bloody?"

His hand left a mark where he had pushed off from the shale beneath him. He stared at the flickering, aushi maroon, watching with fascination as it pulsed.

He would take the triple B's over the black double B any day.

Beaten meant your lungs were still drawing air.

Bruised meant your muscles were still functioning.

Bloody meant your heart was beating.

Body bag is dead.

—

Winston staggered forward, as if to prove that he was not a corpse risen from the gloam. His arm instinctively moved to his middle, feeling where a jagged piece of the shale punctured him like a balloon, and like a balloon, in order to not lose his lifeblood, he would have to keep it within himself like a fancy bit of opal he jammed in himself for decoration.

His lips twitched into a facsimile of a smile, tasting iron and smoke. The smoke meant that he had sustained a Soul injury- probably his concussion. Drunk on the blood loss and pain, he stumbled forward, relying on his muscle memory to take him somewhere safe. A place where gentle hands would ease that pain on his mind, rending him into two awkward, uneven halves.

Winston latched his mind on that slight tug towards those hands. Those sweet hands, those loving hands, those gentle hands; beckoning him back. His own hand left a blotchy mark on the door's handle, and he let himself into the house after remembering that he had to unlock the door.

"Win? Winston, is that you?" Sweet voice, loving voice, gentle voice, it called to him with concern. He mumbled some response, some affirmation, that it was now him, now whole, her very voice alone a soothing presence. Soft footfalls approached, stopping suddenly with a strangled gasp and a sharp pang of pain that made him cry out in sympathetic agony. Sweet hands, loving hands, gentle hands, they caught him as he stumbled forward to comfort her. "Winston, what- what happened?"

"Better three B's than two," he said, rather inanely. "Soph. Sophie. I love you. Sophia."

"Winston, breathe with me," she commanded, and he let her take over his parasympathetic system. "There, that's good, there... no, no Whit, stay upstairs. Your father had an accident. Stay upstairs."

Winston had said those last two words along with his wife, lips moving from their intense connection. She hissed in pain as she assisted him to the couch, kissing his forehead- Winston could taste the smoke through their bond.

"I'm calling your father's doctor-"

"He's dead."

"He's- well, damn." Sophia stared at him. Winston could sense her vision of him- beaten, bruised, bloody. But not in a body bag. She took in a breath, and Winston's body breathed along with her, deep and slow and calming. She was so calming. Sweet, loving, gentle. "Okay. Okay. I'm calling my doctor then."

"He won't know what to do," Winston grumbled, not meaning to damper her soul, but speaking the truth. "I need someone who specializes with... Auræic injuries... I've got a split, I think."

"That would take three days!" Sophia protested, giving his hand a firm squeeze, but sweet, loving, gentle. "I am calling my doctor, now, and then we can get a specialist from there."

"Mm." Winston could not argue with her logic. He listened to her speaking frantically with the operator, and then a knock on the door. She glanced in its direction, ignoring it to get through the phone. Knocking again, more insistent. It was not a... human knock. It was distinctly feathered. The woman lowered the phone, staring at that entryway. Winston pushed himself up, eyeing the couch beneath him with mild disgust at the maroon coating it around him. "Sophia... get the door. Please."

She hesitated, but set down the phone, and opened the door.

A long beak, dark eyes. A medical bag in hand.

"Mrs. Farres? I received a call," the plague doctor said. "How badly injured is he?"

"Who- *what* are you?" Sophia asked, aghast and mystified. How could a doctor have shown up so quickly? Winston nudged her mind, urging her to let the other man inside, though he himself was uncertain as to why or how he had appeared. "Winston, are you sure that it's alright?"

"Yes," he mumbled. She stepped aside and Siwwil bowed low in greeting, kissing the back of her hand. "Grateful to meet you, Madam. Your mate rendered me an invaluable service. Allow me to perform one for you. I am Doctor Siwwil."

"You know what? Sure, yes, please, actually," Sophia ran a hand through her hair. "I don't- I don't know what happened to him, he just got home- how did you know?"

"I have my ways, thanks to a friend," Siwwil shrugged, entering the living room and setting down his bag. "Anyways, this will likely be unpleasant for you to stay around- and your husband's rampant inability to control his bonds would make that much, much worse."

"Right," Sophia faintly replied. "I'll go- I'll go check on Whit, then. Please let me know when... when you're done."

"You'll know, Mrs. Farres," Siwwil remarked blandly, still smiling as he withdrew a few tools neither Winston nor Sophia recognized. He turned his head toward her as he tapped a syringe to make sure no air was within it. "Carry on, now. I won't be long. There is no healer better for your husband than I."

She stayed for one more moment before turning around and fleeing up the stairs to their son. It was more to assure herself more than him, but then again, both would be accomplished in one swoop. Siwwil administered the shot in the meantime, Winston hardly noticing it coming and going.

"What was that for?"

"Your dissonance. It's a soul binder. It won't make your concussion go away, but you'll certainly feel more yourself. And feel more in general."

"What do you mean by that?"

"Increased sensitivity."

"Ah."

Winston watched with fascination as Siwwil quickly set to healing him, and he had to admit; the doctor certainly knew what he was doing. And like a dentist, he seemed to think small talk was the perfect thing to do while his hands were inside of Winston.

"So, a child?"

"Hm? Oh, yes," Winston remarked, then let out a hiss. "Yes. A boy. Whit."

"Cold shell," Siwwil replied, and Winston vaguely recognized it as a Ziz blessing. "How old?"

"Just turned six," Winston said, breathing slowly and letting the doctor's skillful hands stitch him up with well practiced, efficient ease. Curiosity gripped him while he stared at the doctor. "And you...?"

"We're expecting," Siwwil answered, matter of factly. Winston took in the information, both surprised by it and not. Without thinking, he questioned, "When?"

"Within the next few months," Siwwil hummed, finishing up a wound. He turned Winston to his side to focus on his back. "My, what did you do? Jumped off a cliff?"

"Exactly, actually," Winston grimaced. Whatever the doctor had given him was doing wonders for his conscious thought and controlling his body, but damn if it did not make those aches and pains all the more stark. Increased sensitivity, he said. Siwwil chuckled as he got to work on his back. Winston spotted the shale pieces set on the table, somehow already cleaned of gore and grime. They were almost shining. "Chasing a bounty. They jumped across the gap."

"And you thought you could make it yourself," Siwwil finished the story. "Well, all I can say is you pissed off one angry cat. Arm out, please."

Winston practically screeched as Siwwil swabbed the scratches with the most painful solution that ever touched his flesh. The medic jabbed down with his beak to keep Winston from jolting away, applying a strangely warm cloth and binding it down with bandages.

"That stung like a thorn coated in poison!" Winston grit, pulling his now bandaged arm to his stomach. "Goddamn, doc!"

"You're welcome," Siwwil replied, dipping his hands into a strange clear liquid that turned dark purple as soon as his hands entered it. The soft smell of smoke filled Winston's lungs for a moment, and then dissipated. Winston only then realized that he felt like the man he was before his fall, leaving him in a shocked stupor. "How are you feeling, Winston?"

"I-" he blinked, startled with how little pain he was in. "Shockingly good, for a man who just fell fifty feet into stone. You... certainly are skilled."

"Mm, yes," Siwwil smiled, then stood in front of and called up the stairs. "Your husband is soothed, Mrs. Farres. You may come down, and you might want to bring a towel you don't mind disposing of afterwards. Ah, there you are."

Winston took in his wife as she rushed into the room, hesitating to jump upon him, but pulled herself close regardless, cupping his face and kissing him sweetly, lovingly, gently. He reached his uninjured arm around her, sighing with relief as their souls brushed together once more, hers relaxing as it became clear that his pain was little to none.

"Doctor," Sophia turned to face Siwwil, sitting beside Winston and holding his hand tightly. "Thank you…. I'm sorry, though, I feel as though I recognize you. What was your name, again?"

"Siwwil Orionvi," he promptly answered. Sophia's brows furrowed for one moment, and then her eyes widened with shock. She sat straight up, and exclaimed; "You're the doctor that married The Orionvi! Oh, my god!"

"You married who!?" Winston sputtered, becoming a carbon copy of his wife, sitting straight up with wide eyes. Siwwil looked quietly prideful, but- that Auræic, the one Siwwil risked everything for- "What about Adam?"

"Addie loves me," Siwwil replied sincerely, "Orionvi and I benefit each other. Our relationship is rather a formality. My love for Adam is not diminished by my admiration of The Orionvi."

"I see," Winston replied, still mystified. Siwwil, Adam, and The Orionvi… what a powerful union, even if one party was not quite involved in their romance. And one of them was expecting…. Winston glanced at his wife, the doctor, and then the stairs. Dark blue eyes just like his stared back at him from the top. He gave a tired smile, standing up. "Excuse me, Doctor. If I may pay you for your service, I have my own duties to attend to."

"No payment."

"What?"

"No payment," Siwwil repeated. "You rendered me an invaluable service. I am forever indebted to you for your actions. If you ever need a healer, do not hesitate to call upon me. Now, if you excuse me, I must return to my family. Au revoir, Mr. Winston, Mrs. Farres."

They watched, astounded, as he picked up his bag and walked out the door. Their gazes were drawn to the table, where the polished shale pieces were. A small bottle of liquid medication was on the table with instructions to drink a tablespoon with every meal until the bottle was finished.

Whit ran into the room, skidding to a stop before he could crash into Winston, but quickly wrapped his arms carefully around him. Sophia had luckily covered the bloodied couch with the towel already, and was making arrangements in her head to have it properly cleaned, if not replaced entirely. Winston knelt to his son and put his hands on his shoulders, inspecting him. Soft, yes, a bit naive, but he could learn for certain. He gave him a nod, and patted his shoulder just once, standing up once more.

"I am ready to go to sleep now," Winston remarked, and Sophia quickly came to his side. The three of them went up the stairs, Whit hugging his parents goodnight before being sent off to his room. Winston kissed Sophia as he laid down, pulling her close. "How bad are my bruises?"

"Quite bad, if I'm honest."

"Good," Winston murmured, holding her tight.

—

Whit snapped back like a rubber band, crying out as his arm shifted painfully. Winston's grip on him did not let up even as he stumbled back, staring at his father. Winston clucked and shook his head, whistling for the dog they were practicing with to jump back.

"I could have made that jump!" Whit defended himself, eyeing the gap. Winston cocked an eyebrow, and asked; "Could you?"

"I mean- sure I could," Whit replied, but now seemed a little less sure of himself. "Probably... I think I could make it."

"What is the first rule of bounty hunting?" Winston asked sternly. Whit sighed, looking at the ground. "Never, ever-"

"Take unnecessary risks," Whit mumbled, shoulders slumping. "I know."

"Sure, you *could* have made that gap," Winston went on. "But *would* you have? Can you say without a shadow of a doubt that you would have made it safely, and without any stumbling that would leave you vulnerable?"

"No," Whit admitted, face heating up with embarrassment. Winston let go of his arm at last. "I don't think that would've… happened. Getting across without stumbling, that is."

"Right," Winston agreed. Whit was, at times, just as stubborn as he, and sometimes it felt like talking to a younger version of himself. What had changed for him, why did he stop taking so many risks… Sophia. Yes, she was why he grew more sensible in his actions. It was not only about him after she had come into his life like a paper crane, settling in his grasp and bringing him luck and love. Then his son, too, became cause for sensibility. Carefully, he reminded; "Don't forget that you're betrothed, Whit. What's worse than the triple B's?"

"The double B's," Whit grumpily replied, looking none too happy about the reminder that he was scheduled to be married to someone before he could even understand what marriage was. "I don't see what me being betrothed has anything to do with-"

"If you're killed, you will make someone incredibly sad," Winston remarked. Whit swallowed a lump in his throat, biting his lip to keep from talking back. "Not to mention it would devastate your mother and I, but how would you feel if you learned your future spouse perished in a completely avoidable and stupid manner?"

Whit would have liked to say: 'Well, I don't know them, so I wouldn't really care'; but he felt his stomach turn violently at the very thought alone. Winston, seeming to read so in his eyes, gave a nod.

"Whether you like it or not, you have someone else to think about," Winston said to him, more soft than he usually spoke to his son. "So keep them in mind when you're beaten, bruised and bloody."

"How can I keep someone in mind when I've never met them?" Whit protested unhappily. "I might not even like them!"

"But you may love them," Winston countered easily. "With that heart of yours, it would be shocking if you didn't."

They both fell silent for a long moment, staring down at the river below.

"So," Winston stirred, "don't break your betrothal from a body bag."

Helpless – Human

2.2.2024

To scream for help is one of the final defenses of a human.

Do you doubt me?

Go on, give it a try. Think of something you have been struggling to accomplish, struggling to confront, struggling to deal with, struggling to run from- and ask for help.

Trust me, if you are reading this story, you are most likely not in any mortal danger, unless you like to live life on the edge. You might want to spend your final moments doing something else, but if this is how you would like to spend your time, I am more than honored.

Regardless, my friend, have you asked? Have you sought the advice of an expert, a friend, a parent or parental figure? No? Why?

Are you afraid?
Are you afraid?
Are you afraid?

You should be.
To ask for help, is the final defense of a human.

You display your vulnerabilities, your insecurities, you place them on your sleeves, and you open your soft, flesh and blood mouth and utilize the miraculous mechanism of your body or hands to request that you be shielded from your own incompetence.

Are you helpless?
Do you think you do not deserve help, understanding?
Please, take my hand. Lean on my shoulder. Bring me comfort, ask for help.
If you ask for help, I will too.
Maybe.
I like to help.
I do not need help.

I am fine.

Self Confinement

4.4.2024

Yaakov needed his privacy. Really.

Like, really needed his privacy.

If he did not have it, the creative wells in his mind dried up, became stagnant and sludgelike. Truthfully, Shmuel's presence was one of the few that he could tolerate- if not the only one he could accept at all. Now, don't get him wrong, he enjoyed company well and good enough! He loved spending time with Chaim and Natanel but-! Being around them made him forget his camera, what with the calmness they exuded and how far removed they were from the street shots and pictures Yaakov worked to obtain. With some help from Rose Robotics, he had developed a process that printed their pictures *in color*, and that alone knocked the competition out of the park, made them green with envy.

Unfortunately, the only way Yaakov could make pictures like that was if he was alone in his darkroom.

So he was hidden away in that chemical laden room, where no one bothered him, and where he retreated hard enough into his head so as to comprise excellent, vivid lights that beat out the stench of his environment.

It worked like a charm! Really! There were no problems at all with this system, ever.

For years, Yaakov was more than content to work away in the chemical room, coming out and showering in the theater next door. Then changing into clothes that did not bear the smell of his labor, and going out to meet everyone else. Yaakov's hours, in order to conform with everyone else's without having to change more than twice, meant that he came in early and left early. Not a big problem for him either! Gave him his afternoons. That was good enough for him. Nice time to spend in central park and feed the pigeons. That was a good day in his eyes, when he powered through a couple of sheets and then a few slices.

It was a good domain for him.

So when Iyov showed up, with a safety inspector in tow, he was none too happy with the proceedings. Iyov tried his best to placate him, told him he would receive a bonus and an extension on his deadlines, but...

"Two weeks!?" Yaakov stood so sharply that his chair tumbled back and landed with a splash, having knocked over a chemical basin. "What do you mean, two weeks, minimum?"

"Yaakov, Kobie, it's not safe in here, really," Iyov attempted to reason with him, but to no end. "As the inspector noted, there's a serious safety issue with the studs, they're rotted. That needs to be fixed before I can feel comfortable allowing you back."

"But Iyov!" Yaakov protested, "You can't! You can't do this to me! I can't work anywhere but here! What am I supposed to do for two weeks, your extension isn't enough time for me!"

"It will have to do," Iyov said as calmly as he could. His grey eyes were solemn, for once. "Please, Reb Fabian. Be reasonable. Might I arrange for you a temporary private office?"

"Where?" Yaakov questioned, almost sneeringly. He gestured outwards with his hands, at the whole of the space, towards the murmuring of voices outside the gratings. "Where in this studio are you going to find a 'private office' that's actually private, where I can get work done–"

"Devorah's spare development room," Iyov replied easily. "It's not in use. Very dark and quiet."

Yaakov stopped mid rant, gaping at Iyov, blinking twice. His mouth snapped shut, he blinked again, nodded without realizing, nodded with being aware of it, and cleared his throat with some embarrassment.

"Uh. Yeah. Um…" he smiled sheepishly, apologetically. "That can work."

Yaakov was settled in the dark print room, and he had to admit, it was almost perfect. If only he could listen in to the numerous conversations that flitted about the press, then it would be right near that level. As it stood, on such short notice, it was just fine.

Quiet.

Peaceful.

Just that touch of an off scent that made his mind turn a little faster to distract himself.

It was hard to tell what time it was, on that dark floor, but there would be flickers of light coming from that room down the hall every now and then, and while it bothered Yaakov at first, it blended into the monotony and silence.

"Hello, Fabian."

Yaakov jumped out of his seat, clapping a hand to his head to clamp his hat down. He spun around to see Devorah illuminated in the doorway, and mustered a small smile.

"Ms. Wasser," Yaakov managed to gasp out, trying to quell his racing heart. "Apologies, I'm not used to being interrupted, not where I usually work. Iyov let you know I'd be here, right?"

"Yes. Who do you think set up that little office space for you, with all your magical chemicals?" Devorah replied, cocking an eyebrow. Her eyes flashed mischievously, but not without softness. "I take it that you're not very happy about the shift BenAcher did to you."

"No, but…" Yaakov shrugged. "He's the boss. Have to do what he says."

"I see," Devorah nodded. She leaned against the doorway, looking at her nails for a moment. She gave a sigh and another nod. "Well, if you need anything, let me know. I'm down the hall, in that room with the flashing lights of the printer."

"I thought so," Yaakov replied, but he did not really know why he said it. He cleared his throat, slightly embarrassed by his words, and gestured to his work. "Well, I gotta get back to it…."

"Right," Devorah said, though she seemed oddly disappointed. "See you."

Yaakov could not help but feel like he was missing something important as Devorah turned away. He had half a mind to call her back, but then his watch beeped, and he mindlessly returned to work.

Yaakov was going to lose his mind. He was stuck on one line, one silly little line, but it was the final line of the photograph which meant that it had to be perfect.

For some reason, it was nearly impossible for him to think it up. It was already the second day that he was working on it, and had already finished a different picture, hoping that he would have gotten the inspiration while completing the other one.

Nope, he was still missing the final line.

Frustrated, he shoved aside the work, ready to tromp up the stairs and escape the void of his mind, to leave the abyss of floor K, his path illuminated by the flickering lights down the hall.

He stopped short of the stairs, staring down the hallway and to that room with the flashes of brilliance emitting like sparking stars.

Yaakov knocked on the panel beside the door, unsure when he had made it to its open maw, and Devorah tilted her head to view him from the corner of her eye, shrouded in shadow. She smiled, and her teeth glinted pure white in the light. It hurt Yaakov's eyes, making him squint.

"Come right on in, Fabian."

"Er, hi there, Ms. Wasser," Yaakov waved a round hand, then realized he had been requested into the room, and awkwardly shuffled in. He had to lift a hand to be able to see in the blinding flashes of light. "May I ask why you generally leave the door open...?"

"It's the way folks see if they happen to come down here," Devorah shook her head, and pointed to a comfortable looking chair near her desk, an armchair with shoulder wings. "That should help keep the flickering from bothering you."

"I see," Yaakov mumbled, though he did not at the moment. When he sat down, however, he realized that the winglets were perfectly angled so as to cast his eyes in shadow. "Neat. Thanks."

"Course," Devorah replied simply. She carefully reinserted a spool of microfilm, and flicked through the massively projected pages displayed on a white sheet. She nodded with satisfaction. "These things can be mighty fickle. Iyov has me make at least four of the same page. If you ask me, we should just get them copied out, but he's right that it loses some quality if you do it that way, and we don't know which version is best."

"Interesting," Yaakov said, though he had no idea what Devorah was talking about at all. He mused on it for a moment, and then decided that it was genuinely interesting, but he did not know enough to question anything about it. He rolled a few ideas for conversation starters in his head, and then gave up with anything particular. "How's your day been treating you, Ms. Wasser?"

"Just fine," Devorah smiled again, her smile like the sun for a moment. "And yours?"

215

"A bit good, a bit frustrating," Yaakov admitted. "Adding tint and color and boldness but can't get the final line solid. Finished a different picture in the meantime."

"Damn," Devorah laughed quietly, shaking her head. "And people call BenAcher the workaholic. I take it that it didn't work out so well for you, huh?"

"No, not really," Yaakov smiled sheepishly, flushing at the comparison to their boss. "I'm not that bad, either. I take breaks! A lot of them. I was just on the clock, so I'd feel weird not working. Or at least trying to work."

"Understandable," Devorah nodded. "Well, what're the pictures?"

"The first is of the hermit's home. Lonesome place," Yaakov shrugged a shoulder, accidentally getting a faceful of light with the motion. He blinked, purple and green stained on his retina and providing sunspecks along Devorah's tall frame, discoloring the dust motes in the air. "Huh."

"Hm?" Devorah questioned his blank statement, and Yaakov's dying blush resurged. "What are you wondering about, Fabian?"

"Oh, nothing, I'm not sure," Yaakov assured her, rubbing the back of his neck, once again blinding himself with that not quite white light. New colors dotting over Devorah, deep pink and gold tinged yellow joining the fading green and purple. "Something about the way light works, I think."

"Mhm." Devorah hummed, then returned to working. Yaakov watched in silence, relaxing to the quiet clicks of her kerning and setting. It was almost musical, exceedingly rhythmic, and before Yaakov knew it, he was dozing off to it. "Comfortable there?"

"Mm. Yeah," Yaakov mumbled, eyes half closed, light dancing on his lashes and streaking sparks in his limited vision. "Very. Thanks. Good chair."

Yaakov heard Devorah laugh quietly again. Once more, her teeth flickered, fascinatingly.

And then it all went dark.

Yaakov woke up with his throat and nose feeling a bit stuffy, and he was cognizant of the fact that it was from the dank environment the printer and picture development fluid before he realized he was there at all, and faced some minor disorientation by shifting light, staring at the old articles and blurbs playing in front of him in the empty room. One had a section marked 'placeholder', and he understood that was where his photo would be set. After reading through the pages in the near silence obscured by the hum of

216

the projector, he got up, stretching out his arms to the sides, and heard the schlump of a fabric sliding on another material and falling to the floor. He looked down to see Devorah's long trench coat a pile on the floor, having been resting on him as a makeshift blanket. Yaakov observed that a note had been pinned to it with a small clip of metal.

Leave the coat on the chair, take the flashlight next to the projector, unplug the projector. Thanks - Devorah.

For some odd reason, Yaakov felt incredibly sad as he followed the instructions.

He failed to shake it off on his walk home, strangely alone.

"Good afternoon, Fabian," Devorah remarked as Yaakov sat down in the armchair with his lunch. "Any luck on the missing line?"

"No, unfortunately." Yaakov replied with a groan. Devorah gave a hum, opening the door for Yaakov to voice his vexation. "Still stuck on it. It's been three days, you'd think that I'd have a better grasp on what to put for it by now. It's just a splash of color!"

"Inspiration comes and goes, but the impact will always leave you reeling," Devorah commented, making Yaakov startle and stare at her, tilting his head. It made Devorah laugh again, that self same low chuckle that Yaakov was starting to become familiar with. "What, don't think I'm a creative sort? All ridges and straight lines?"

"No, no, I wasn't startled like that at all," Yaakov shook his head hastily. "It was just… a very good statement that I needed to hear. So… thank you. I guess I've been beating my head against the wall and expecting it to come easy."

"We all sometimes need some sense smacked into us," Devorah joked. Yaakov silently agreed. "Here, though. This reel's got music- it's one of Carl's shows all finished up. We got it recorded today. Want to watch it?"

"Sure," Yaakov replied, curious to see it. He smiled at Devorah as the woman set up the film, and moved in the chair so as to give Devorah some space. Devorah raised an eyebrow, and Yaakov smiled sheepishly. "There should be enough room here for the both of us. It's almost a couch."

Devorah observed him, then shrugged.

"Okay."

Yaakov was startled a second time by how warm Devorah was, warm enough to feel her presence outlined through his relatively thick woolen clothing and the space between them. He glanced at her, only able to see her profile with how the light struck her.

Yaakov refocused on the musical.

Really, he had to hand it to Meir, the music was absolutely lovely, and complemented Susanna's compositions perfectly. The dances and concept all melded together in a fantastic wave of sounds, colors, and lights. The reprieves were touching, and the humor was excellently timed. Everything was perfect.

He smiled and hummed along, curling up as he watched the film go by. Kudos to Andres and Tiffany, too, it truly came to life on the screen. Well. The sheet. Regardless, it was an adorable musical and Yaakov was thrilled to be able to watch it first.

"That was really good," Yaakov praised when it ended. Devorah hummed in agreement, and for the third time that day, Yaakov was startled by the tall woman, jolting off the chair and landing flat on the floor. Devorah had stood up quickly to help him up with her umbrella, to ask if he was alright, and Yaakov let her do so, but was flushed with absolute embarrassment - he had been cuddled up to the lady, her hum still reverberating in his chest from their closeness. His face was dark red, and he stammered, trying to sort out his words. "I'm- I'm so sorry, I didn't realize I had- oh, gosh, I'm not really much of a, um, cuddler, I didn't realize- I'm so sorry-"

"Yaakov." Devorah's voice was smooth like cold milk on a hot pepper; soothing, relieving, almost jarring but in a good way. Yaakov shut up immediately. "It's okay."

"Oh," Yaakov exhaled, long and hard, unable to stop blushing and trembling. "Okay. I…"

"Really. It's okay," Devorah gave him a smile. "If it was a problem, I would have told you."

"Right," Yaakov swallowed hard. "Thank you for showing it to me, Ms. Wasser," Yaakov murmured, looking to the floor. He wanted the earth to swallow him up, wishing that the wood would jut up from the ground and consume him like thousands of tiny teeth. "I appreciate it-"

"Devorah."

Yaakov looked up, the mortification slipping away at last.

"What?"

"Call me Devorah," Devorah repeated, smiling at him. That bright, brilliant smile. Yaakov managed to smile back, or rather could not help but smile back, eyes crinkling and covering Devorah with glimmers of stars. He took off his cap with a little bow, replying: "Yaakov."

"Alright, Kobie. Yaakov it is."

Yaakov felt a warm wave crash over him.

It left him cold when he walked out of the room.

"Good morning, Yaakov," Devorah greeted with a smile. Yaakov came in and stood behind her, waiting patiently for her to turn around. They had been 'floormates' for nearly the full two weeks, and for the last three days, Yaakov had been nearly avoiding Devorah - not that either of them would admit that. "How are you? Haven't seen you around much."

"Fine."

"You don't sound fi-" Devorah chuckled as she turned around, immediately struck dumb by Yaakov's presence for no apparent reason. Her mouth remained slightly open, smiling just a touch, though it froze on her face. "Yaakov?"

"Hello, Devorah." the picture man replied, calm yet with some energy burning within him. He was holding a small stack of papers tightly between his fingers. "I wanted to talk to you."

"Oh- oh?" Devorah cleared her throat, glancing away. A nervousness was building in her chest, and she tried to shove it away. "About what?"

"I have a question for you," Yaakov said, glancing at the papers. "It's because of the picture."

"Did you manage to think of your line of color at long last, Yaakov?" Devorah asked him, a bit off put by the way Yaakov was looking at her, bright eyed yet rather silent. Yaakov nodded. "Are you going to share it then, or just keep it to yourself?"

"Have you ever been alone in a crowd, and crowded alone?" Yaakov asked softly at the same time he answered Devorah's request, passing her the picture. A shiver ran through Devorah as she stared at him, gripping the picture of that sole lonely house, hesitant to reply in return. Yaakov decided that he would answer his own question first. "I have... I feel that way a lot."

"I see," Devorah replied, then swallowed harshly, looking away, into the light of the projector. She could sense Yaakov stepping towards her, standing next to her. "Maybe... I feel that way sometimes, too."

Yaakov carefully put the pages aside, next to the press. His hand came to pinch the corner of Devorah's sleeve to regain her attention. Devorah's gaze snapped over to his.

"Do you feel like that alone with me?" Yaakov questioned quietly. Devorah found herself unable to answer him this time either. Yaakov, again, spoke first. "Because I don't feel like that with you."

"I don't... feel alone with you," Devorah agreed after a long moment. Yaakov's hand tightened on the fabric, making her swallow roughly. "Yaakov?"

"I really have been enjoying your company," Yaakov stated, stepping back to gesture around the room. There had been a startling transformation within the last week, a desk added with a safelight, more development chemicals and basins, a wire for pictures strung up where Devorah's head would not get caught, an extra chair added next to the armchair, also at the perfect angle to shield eyes. "The way you've let me into your space makes me feel... welcome. I feel like I can talk to you forever, sit with you forever. I'm sorry I've been avoiding you. After you invited me to dinner, after we've been having lunch together for nearly every day, I suppose I got a bit spooked. Then the dinner was great. I loved it. I loved spending time with you, Devorah, and I just... I just wanted to do it again."

Devorah gaped at the photographer, who finally had found his tongue around her.

"I don't really care what we call this," Yaakov went on, eyes bright. "You light up the room. You're amazing and relaxed and generally so nice to be around. I want to get to know you."

"I... wouldn't mind that," Devorah quietly replied, mustering a smile. Yaakov returned one in response, finally letting go of her sleeve. "What do you suggest?"

"I've got a reservation at a Lithuanian rooftop restaurant if you'd be willing to join me for dinner," Yaakov grinned at her, unable to keep from doing so. "Chaim found it. What do you say?"

"I'd be happy to give it a shot," Devorah smiled genuinely and nodded. Yaakov's smile was completely uncontainable, making Devorah laugh softly, warming Yaakov's heart even more. Devorah nudged him, pushing his pictures towards him. "But isn't someone on the clock? Shame on you, Yaakov! Alas, behold how the mighty have fallen."

"Oh, you hush," Yaakov scoffed, smiling and slightly blushing. "You're right though. I'll be right back!"

He bound up the stairs, feeling warm and with a tranquil excitement bubbling beneath his skin.

It was a wonderful sensation, one he hoped to have again and again.

Iyov raised an eyebrow. Yaakov searched his face, trying to understand the emotion that was on it, yet it was such a playful look that he gave up after a moment.

"So," Iyov broached at last. "You want to stay over by Devo?"

"Yes," Yaakov replied with a nod. "I hope it's not a problem…?"

"No, not at all," Iyov shrugged, eyes flashing. "Glad to see that you like it there. Ironically, it turns out that there's no stud issue."

"Oh, that's funny," Yaakov blushed, nodding. "But I really am happy there."

Iyov studied his face for a moment longer before smiling warmly.

"What changed your mind?"

Yaakov hesitated, then said;

"I like being alone less than I thought."

"Amazing. When's the chupa?"

Today

5.16.2024

Today is the day you are going to make a game. Isn't that exciting? You've wanted to make a game for a long time.

It's always been so cool seeing developers create amazing things, and a lot of your friends have experience with coding and development. You've got a whole thing set up and you've got a couple games planned.

It's hard sometimes, because your friends all have experience that you don't, or maybe it's just easier for them to grasp the information. But you're determined to be a valuable part of the team.

So you get up, and tell yourself that today is the day you're going to make that game.

It's funny, almost, because that's what you said yesterday. And the day before that. And the day before that. And so on so forth.

Just like that book you promised to publish, two, three years ago?

Today's the day you're going to make a game, you said yesterday. A week ago. A month ago. A year ago. Today.

Today's the day you are going to make a game. Today is the day you are going to write that book. Today is the day you are going to make something, *anything.*

Today is the day that you are finally going to do it.

Except you're tired. Your eyes hurt to stay open, teeth ache in your gums, shoulders spasm, legs twitch, knees pop and twist.

It's sad.

Today *was* going to be the day you would make a game.

Projection

8.13.2024

Everyone had a crush on the projectionist.

He fit everyone's type- he was tall, dark, and handsome. Of course anyone would find themselves eyeing the man whenever he was around. Following his gait, and appreciating the cloudy gaze of his eye when he would turn it towards a person. It was a look that exuded confidence and a tranquil, relaxed perception. A look that made someone's skin go hot and cold.

Everything about him was extremely pleasant to look at, to observe, to internalize and mechanize.

That, at least, was what Tiffany told herself, when she found herself staring at the light tech for a moment too long. It was totally fine and normal to be attracted to Andres. There was nothing weird about it. Or uncomfortable. Because everyone liked Andres.

Probably.

The way that Susanna looked at Tiffany when she confronted her on the way she would look at the spotlight man said otherwise. Maybe it was because she lied and said that she was not staring at Andres, how dare she accuse her of such things. They simply worked in the same booth for hours at a time without saying a word. Et cetera.

Perhaps she had a problem. But if she had a problem, that meant that everyone else had a problem as well, because obviously everyone had a smidgen of a crush on Andres. Most likely. As far as Tiffany was aware (which meant, asking no one and trying not to think of anyone else) everyone did. It was. Perfectly fine. To like a man. That no one knew the remotest, slightest thing about. Aside from his name and job.

The mystery of the man was a bit maddening- Tiffany would be the first to admit that. Though! Though- Tiffany's excuse for this slice of insanity was the fact that she was an engineer, an architect of sound- it was in her very nature to determine the roots and structures of a substance, be it a person or audio effect. So, of course Tiffany would find herself fascinated with the dark man- unknown, silent, but so very aware of the gestalt of the studio and its inner workings. Tiffany wanted to understand him, wanted to comprehend why Andres was so quiet and observant. There had to be a source, a reason, or at least a psyche behind that stoic façade. Unless the man was a blank slate, and simply took in information for no reason; robotic and route. Even so, that too entranced Tiffany, her adoration of the mechanics of entertainment engineering, something she keenly shared with Devorah from the paper next door. And, apparently, Andres.

Tiffany had to learn more about him. She had to. It was becoming an obsession – and any obsession around Andres was a problem, the damn ghost. One could only imagine how much worse an obsession about Andres would be. Tiffany constantly had the passing thought that Andres was well aware of the sound technician's crush, but she dismissed it with the knowledge that everyone had an attraction to the secretive projectionist. Therefore it was totally fine if she had one, too, and Andres hardly was aware of Tiffany's little crush specifically.

Maybe.

Or maybe Tiffany was projecting, really, really hard. But that would be ridiculous to assume that. After all, Tiffany was a rational minded, level headed Brit. Therefore, projecting her emotions onto other people was a stupid, nonsensical notion.

Susanna was getting sick of Tiffany's excuses and stammered brush offs. Eventually, she whipped around to face her (while she was rambling about these exact things, to be precise) and pointed a pencil in her face.

"You really need to stop ignoring the fact that you got it down bad," she remarked, in a vaguely threatening manner, haphazardly waving the writing utensil around. Tiffany gawked, and she went on, apparently quite annoyed at the woman's skirting around the issue. "It's been over a year of this silly crush, Tiff. Just fortify and talk to the guy, damn it."

After a long moment of silence, Tiffany managed to squeak; "But what on Earth am I going to talk to him about? He hardly talks to anyone! And, I do not have a- a crush! That's utterly preposterous to even suggest that I have one! I'm not some, some teenager, I'm one of the world's first female sound engineers! I am the great Tiffany Smith! I'm not scared of a projectionist! Even one as mysterious, and handsome, and fetching as Soledad. Even if it is Andres."

Susanna's half lidded gaze was entirely unamused.

"You're doing it again."

"Doing what?" Tiffany scoffed. "I'm doing nothing!"

"You're doing that 'puff up' thing," Susanna replied, making air quotes with her fingers. "The one that you use when you try to pitch to people who don't know better. I'm not one of those people. I'm your friend. Your best friend, in fact. Is that too childish for you, too?"

Tiffany, her mouth in a straight line, shook her head.

"Good." Susanna gave a slight smile, almost a smirk. "And, you should know, that as your friend, you're not fooling me. Go talk to him. Ask him about his work, what he does. You know that's the best way to start."

"You're right," Tiffany sighed, shoulders dropping slightly. "Yes, you're right."

"When have I ever been wrong?" Susanna did smirk then. Tiffany rolled her eyes. "Of course I'm right. Now shoo. Get out of my soundroom before I turn *you* into a projector."

"Okay, alright, I'm leaving," Tiffany brushed off her blouse as she stood. "What do you think, though? You hear everything that goes on in the studio. Has he mentioned anything?"

"No," Susanna shrugged, already back to tinkering away. "He can be pretty dense when it comes to observing people who are observing him. I think that this will come out of left field for him."

Tiffany hesitated, but nodded.

"Alright," he resigned herself to her fate. "I'll talk to him."

Well, there was a slight caveat to that. Tiffany never said when she would talk to Andres.

So she was off the hook.

That was, at least, what she was telling himself. She was, once again, attempting to persuade herself that it was not a big deal, that everyone had feelings now and then for the tall, relaxed man. That it really was not just a Tiffany thing.

But it was getting... almost painful.

Dancing on eggshells whenever she was around Andres. It was painfully frequent, as they worked in the same engineering booth. The studio was doing rather well, that was a fact, which meant that they were constantly working together through the shows of the season. Additionally, they helped their boss with advertising and promotions, constantly out with

225

him. There would be Andres, showing new clips of the plays, shows, and musicals that Carl Goodly's theater was showing, and Tiffany would be there to add the magic of music. Working side by side for years with nary a sentence between them.

Tiffany was determined to bypass that issue, though.

Or maybe she was not, and was actually more than content continuing to pretend that having a crush on Andres was standard procedure.

Though since Susanna essentially banned her from conversing about it with her, she was out of options for talking about the matter, unless she wanted to talk to a microphone or the wall or BenAcher's strange dream catcher.

That left bringing it up to Andres.

Tiffany held in a sigh as she looked over the newest edition to the theater's 'hip mobile', a little metal device that showed off various clips all at once. She had an assistant take over the presentation once she finished her chatter about the updated audio machinery, and made her way over to the darkened room where Andres did the showings for the extended clips.

The bright light of the projector stunned her for a moment as she entered the miniature practice theater. It was impossible to tell if Andres was in his booth or not, enshrouded by darkness. She could tell, though. Tiffany quietly took in a breath and made her way up the stairs, slipping past murmuring potential donors and giggling kids who were eager to get an extra peek at the shows to come. She knocked quietly on the projection booth door, knowing that Andres' keen hearing would catch the soft gesture.

There was the quietest sound of sanded, clean wood on smooth, polished wood, and Tiffany saw Andres' outline, an abyss in front of the yellowish glow of the projector's light.

"Evening, Tiff," Andres' low, graveled tones greeted her. The slight southern drawl that Tiffany found herself so enchanted by was a gentle tinge in his generally light words. "Here to watch some ballet?"

"No," Tiffany replied honestly. It earned a snicker from the man, who Tiffany could now see now that he was past the blazing bulb of the projector. "I wanted to talk to you."

"Oh?" Andres raised an eyebrow. "Well, have a seat. I'll be with you when I change out these reels."

Tiffany nodded, sitting in the seat that Andres indicated. She watched quietly as the cloudy-eyed man carefully switched out the reels, putting in a new set of the trailers and playable teasers. That was something Carl was working on – interactivity. It boggled Tiffany's mind, to say the least, and so, she tried not to think about it too hard. Chaim had spent far too long attempting to explain the vocal tech to the sound engineer- though she was slowly figuring it out. It truly was cutting edge technology, courtesy of Rose Robotics down south.

Andres heavily sat beside her. Tiffany felt a drink pressed into her hands, though she hesitated to drink it, unsure what it was. Everything about Andres was a mystery - even whatever the cup in her hands contained.

"It's champagne," Andres snorted, able to see in the dark much better than Tiffany, having spent several thousands of hours working in the confines of mines prior to his lighting work. Tiffany nodded a bit hastily, trying to cover up her minor embarrassment at not realizing what the simple drink was. Andres gently tipped a glass of his own against Tiffany's. "Successful night, from what I've overheard."

"Yes, it's gone rather well," Tiffany replied, attempting miserably to figure out how to… talk to Andres. "I take it that the crowd has been perceptive to the new technology that our mysterious southern friend is working on?"

"Yeah," Andres confirmed, smiling down at the crowd. He had moved to lean over the lip of the window, his eyes reflecting the clips in front of them. His gaze, though, was drawn to the people. "Sure is nice to see folks appreciating art."

"It is," Tiffany murmured, looking down at her glass. The bubbles in the drink were like spheres of gold, gentle and brilliant. Her chest felt a little tight, and she resisted the urge to rub at it. Then, once again, Andres sat beside her. The projectionist drained his glass with a slow tilt of his head, exhaling softly as he relaxed in the seat. He nudged Tiffany, prompting her to speak. "Ah, mm." Her mind went blank. "I… well, I suppose I wanted to talk to you. We've worked together for… a long time, now, and we've hardly exchanged words."

"That's… true," Andres slowly responded. Tiffany took a sip of her champagne to avoid having to continue speaking. She was glad for the dark; it hid her nervous tremoring, and the slight flush that was sure to be on her face. If it was not a more intense one. "Truth be told, Tiff, I had gotten the impression that you weren't the biggest fan of me."

Tiffany choked on her drink. Of all things, that was the last thing she expected to hear. Flabbergasted, she stared at Andres for a good long moment.

"I'm the biggest fan of you, damnit," Tiffany sputtered. "What in Heaven's name gave you the notion that I didn't like you?"

"Well, the way that you'd watch me," Andres replied, surprised. "Pretty intense."

Tiffany stared.

Then started laughing, desperately trying to keep from guffawing.

"Andres."

"Yeah? What's so funny?"

"I like you," Tiffany said, grinning. "What're your dinner plans after this?"

It was Andres' turn to laugh.

Fluid Lines

8.15.2024

Equations were only a multitude of lines.

Numbers – easily shown in the form of tallies, in firm, sharp lines. It was the easiest form of speaking, a simple streak, straight and swift. Numbers were lines. Art was lines; be it written or drawn. It was all the same, you see, numbers and words and pictures, all lines in different forms.

Supposedly, according to the two comic artists who were ganging up against him, that was why he had to sign off on them getting more funding for the next 'big project'.

Natanel stared at them through his hexagonal glasses, though he knew they could not see his eyes with the slight silvery tint. Chaim was inching towards Iyov, trying to discreetly step on his partner's foot so he could stop shoving it in his mouth, cluing in on the fact that Natanel was entirely unimpressed far sooner than his motormouth companion.

Eventually, though, Natanel decided that he had enough of them wasting his valuable time.

"BenAcher. Levy," he rumbled. Chaim went pink and Iyov's mouth snapped shut. "You two fools have no clue how business works, not a single one. See here," he wheeled himself over to the revenue chart, his office chair smoothly gliding on the white oak flooring. "You make money, you can get funding. You lose money, you don't have funding. Khap?"

The looks of dismay on the two men's faces were enough of an explanation that they very much did understand, but Natanel did not like the look on Iyov's face- a cheeky one, hesitant but determined. Natanel held his breath as he waited for his boss' next words, almost certain that they would be nothing good to hear.

"Well, can't you just... pull it? From somewhere?" Iyov asked, raising an eyebrow and giving a lopsided smile. Natanel's expression darkened, eyes narrowing and lips twitching downwards into a frown. Chaim, the quicker of the two, grabbed Iyov's arm and began pulling him towards the door. Iyov, finally getting the picture, paled slightly as he backed out with his business partner. "Actually, on second thought, can we scrape together abisl of cash? For a fundraising event?"

"Maybe make like Levy," Natanel growled, standing up, and started stalking towards them. "Shut your pisk, and get out of my damn office before you find yourself in deeper drek!"

Chaim quickly closed the door behind them.

Iyov's face was pink with the embarrassment, dark brown eyes with little remorse but plenty of regret. Chaim shook his head as Iyov reached towards the door handle again, and the other man's hand fell to his side. He gave a sigh, shoving his hands into his pockets and heading away towards the studio's rotunda library. Chaim followed after him, a mite dejected himself.

Iyov sat down with a long groan, rubbing his face, adjusting his kippah. Chaim seated himself across from his khevruse, silent and lost in thought.

"What are we going to do, Chaim?" Iyov asked, looking at him like a bit of a lost puppy, eyes big and mouth slightly downturned. "We need the money for funding our projects, yes, but we also need the money to keep this place afloat."

"Look, I don't know what to tell you," Chaim crossly replied, folding his arms over his chest. "Natanel already gave it to us straight. We don't have the money for this right now. We really should... should work on getting another strip out, and maybe we can work on a cartoon for the theaters."

"We have one ready!" Iyov splayed out his hands, and his arms. Chaim blinked, surprised. "You know, the three that we have in backup!"

"Oh, right," Chaim murmured. He pinched the bridge of his nose. "Right. But Iyov, we shouldn't use the backups all willy nilly like this. It comes across as... a rush? I don't know. It's just... not a good idea."

"Well, I..." Iyov tapered off. Then, he rebounded with a smile as big as a rainbow, making Chaim tense up with what was sure to be a bad idea incoming. "I was thinking that we could make a bigger cartoon. For fundraising. Something... feature length, maybe."

"Iyov, that's a terrib-" Chaim caught himself, blinking twice. "Did you just say to make a longer cartoon? That's it? A movie?"

"Yes, that's 'it'," Iyov replied, irked and mildly offended by Chaim's surprise. "What did you think I was going to suggest? A strip show instead of a comic strip? Khas v'shalom?"

"You would enjoy that, you farze'enish," Chaim grumbled, though with a light in his eye. Iyov glared at him with mock offense, calming down from the genuine upset of a moment prior. "Either way... it's something that could work. The only problem is...."

"Reb Shechter," Iyov glumly finished, nodding his head towards the bookkeeper's office. "He's never going to okay this, not with an episode half finished."

"So let's finish this line, and then we can pitch our idea to the almighty check signer," Chaim said with a smile, encouraging him. Iyov gave a small smile in return, nodding. "And I'm guessing you want to make it a musical, right?"

"How do you know me so well?" Iyov asked, eye twinkling as he winked. Chaim laughed a bit and clapped him on the shoulder as he stood up. Iyov kissed his own fingers and pressed them briefly to Chaim's hand, standing up himself. "Ach, Chaim sheli. Let's get to work."

The pair of them quickly made their way up the stairs, in a comfortable silence as they entered the art department and slipped into seats- Chaim into his usual one, and Iyov into whichever he pleased – which meant the seat across from Chaim, as it was one of three available. Within a few moments, the soft scritching noise of sketching filled the room, conversation passing between them every now and then. Chaim eventually stood up, stretching out his back.

"It's time for mincha," he informed Iyov, pulling him out of his focus on the work. The other man glanced at the clock with surprise, then nodded, and stood as well. He gathered up their papers, dropping them off in Stanley's box for the developer to synthesize and set up for the film reels. "Be right back. Getting the Broadway trope and the inkers."

Iyov nodded in acknowledgment as Chaim slipped out the door to get the remaining members of their minyan from the theater next door, and the printing press across the street. When he returned with the group, he was glad to see the studio was already gathered and waiting for them. Meir, as their khazn, nodded in greeting. They began shortly after confirming everyone was present, the services adding in aravit. Soon, Iyov was thanking everyone for coming, and adding in a small Torah remark- one that made everyone groan, though appreciatively (this one was about how since the Torah was not

231

in heaven, God judges for the actions done – not the thoughts one may have). Then once everyone had filed out, Frank the janitor came in with a smile, Iyov thanking him personally (as he did every day) for his hard work. Chaim wrapped a hand around Iyov's wrist, tugging him back to the art room. After chugging an entire pot of coffee between the two of them, they sat down and got to work. The pair worked until tikkun chatzot, and after that post-midnight prayer, both of them stumbled over to the break room and passed out- Chaim not even making it to his usual spot on the couch and falling asleep next to Iyov's cot as they chatted quietly.

The sun beaming across his face woke him. Iyov was already awake, washing negel vaser in the connected bathroom. He waved at Chaim, murmuring the morning prayers after he stepped out, gazing out the window to the sunrise.

"I'll see you downstairs," he said in way of good morning. "I'll see if Susanna brought for us some coffee and bagels."

"Two bagels," Chaim murmured, pulling Iyov's blanket over his head- as, once again, he could not find his kippah. After reciting the brief gratitude of the return of the soul, he got up. Stretching out, he too made his way to the bathroom, noting that Iyov had refilled the double handled cup already for him. Soon, he too was back in the main room, finding Iyov was in fact munching on a bagel. The man pointed at a plate with another two bagels on it, making Chaim smile.

There was a third, extra bagel, though.

"Who's that for?" Chaim asked, nudging a hand towards the plate. Iyov glanced at him, and then upwards with his eyes closing slightly. Chaim fought a snicker. "Natanel's office is down the stairs, Iyov."

"Aye, yes," Iyov nodded 'sagely', pinching a few fingers and emphasizing his words with the gesture. "But we must beg haKadosh barukh Hu for the man to sway. For only They know what lies in the mind of a person. And maybe, just maybe, They might give him a nudge. Who knows? Maybe I will put Their name twice in the credits."

"Are you trying to bribe God, Iyov?" Chaim questioned teasingly. Iyov only smiled. "I don't think He really goes for stuff like that."

"Damnit," Iyov sighed in mock defeat. "Maybe She'll take a cut of the revenue? Our biggest and best investor and fan."

"We'll see about that," Chaim smiled, patting Iyov's shoulder. "Let's finish up this episode, at least."

Iyov, reinvigorated, nodded. First, they went back to the in-studio synagogue. Once shacharit was done, though, Iyov beelined to the art department once again, savaged another mug of coffee, and dove back into trying to finish up the entire paper – including the English side, which he usually left for their Goyische workers, but they were out for the holidays. Chaim joined him soon after, as did Benyamin (their 'intern' [Chaim was sure that Iyov simply liked the kid being around, and was glad to be able to support him]), once he finished up at school. Chiam's head shot up, however, when what that truly meant clicked in his brain. If Benyamin was there, it meant that it was late in the afternoon.

"Iyov."

The head of the studio hummed in response.

"We didn't eat lunch."

The other man raised his head, blinking with surprise as he recalled that Chaim was in fact correct.

"Ah. Oops." he stood up, smiling apologetically at Benyamin. "Well, Benny, Chaim and I will be right back after we devour some potatoes. Or something. You can keep working on those midframes– you're doing absolutely fantastic."

They left the teen glowing with the praise. Iyov whistled as they walked to the lunch room, Chaim shaking his head at him.

"You like walking on a thin line, on the breg," Chaim nudged Iyov, "Stop that whistling."

"It's not Wednesday," Iyov replied with a cheeky smile, and promptly resumed the high pitched titter. Chaim rolled his eyes, but let the matter drop. The duo scarfed down a soup that Iyov had put in the freezer a week ago, discussed the upcoming parsha in brief, and then returned to work. Iyov glanced over Benyamin's work, smiling brightly. "Looking good! We'll be done with this episode in no time!"

Chaim rolled his eyes once again at Iyov's entirely unserious demeanor. Though, it turned out that the dark haired man was absolutely correct when it came to speed. The three of them managed to crank out the remaining panels before the end of the week, beating out the deadline by nearly two weeks.

Tired but exhilarated, Iyov gave Benyamin a bonus from his own funds, the student practically skipping with joy out of the studio at the end of the day they finished. He was also extremely pleased with the long weekend he had earned for himself.

Deadline- beaten. They now had an episode to air, a completed comic strip *and* entire newspaper, as well as the three comics in the archives for backup. There was no way that Natanel would reject the feature length idea now, considering how prepared they were for the workload. And, their non-Jewish employees would be available again after their holidays were concluded. Which would mean that the eight empty seats in the newspaper's halls would be filled up once more, and developing the flashes from around the world would be a breeze.

Chaim drove Iyov to their apartment, both of them talking excitedly once more along the way. After a brisk dinner, Chaim was on Iyov's lower bunk beside him as their animated conversation flowed back and forth between them. There was a paper pinned to the bed above them, Iyov sketching ideas upon it as they talked. Chaim found himself growing drowsier, slowly tapering off into silence, dozing off. Iyov happily curled next to him, doodling until he too felt sleep tugging on his ankles.

He quietly recited shma, keeping Chaim in mind, and went to sleep feeling extremely hopeful for the next day.

"No."

Chaim's eyes widened at the same time Iyov's rapidly moving mouth snapped shut.

Weakly, Iyov asked; "Can you repeat that?"

"I said, 'no'. Beshum oyfn nisht." Natanel repeated, narrowing his eyes. He leaned back in his office chair, steepling his fingers into a small pyramid shape. "Loy v'loy, if you need it in straight Hebrew. No, in plain English."

"But- why not?" Iyov struggled to keep himself from whining, forcing his mouth into a smile. Surely Natanel was mistaken. "The studio is completely ready for a big project- and we finished the current one way ahead of schedule-!"

"What Iyov means to say," Chaim cut him off, trying to salvage the situation as well, and was well aware that he was more equipped to do so than the chatterbox. "Is that we're confident in our ability to pull this off. And there have been funds coming in. And there will be more funds coming in as well. So-"

"Not in a thousand years," Natanel denied, stamping the request for funding with his red rejection. "Tsvey mol di tsores when you're together! No means no! Maybe after you have ten episodes in the vault, then we can talk!"

"I'm not nearly as bad as he is!" Chaim protested. Iyov looked at him sharply, wounded by the other artist's attempt to distance himself. Natanel rolled his eyes, and replied; "You're seventy, and he's one hundred and thirty. That makes two hundred percent!"

Thoroughly chastised, Chaim's mouth turned into a thin line. His ears even turned slightly pink. Iyov did not say anything in spite of the thick words on his tongue, shoulders raising slightly as he tried not to dwell on the unfairness. Chaim noticed that he was biting the inside of his lip, a nervous tick of his when he was attempting not to say anything negative or upset. Chaim felt bad for a brief moment, but then he snapped to attention when Natanel knocked his nail on the desk twice.

"Times ticking, nu?" he waved them out of his office again, shaking his head. "Shoyn!"

Iyov's face burned with an indignant shame as he, this time, pulled Chaim from the office. What really was getting under his clearly polished nails, though, was the slight gaze of satisfaction he caught on Natanel's face. The jerk! Chaim, still dismayed, was yet to see the look on Iyov's own visage, but when he did, his down put expression faded somewhat as he tried to cheer up his friend.

"Well, let's get to pouring more of our hearts and souls into making those moving pictures, and maybe we can spread more awareness of our brothers' plight," he told Iyov, but Iyov's scowl only deepened at the suggestion. "Iyov? Is something... wrong?"

"Of course something is wrong!" Iyov snapped, though he tried to keep his voice low. "That farssiener! I'll wipe that look off his face!"

Iyov whipped out his turquoise eye liner, marching over to the bathroom to apply it. Immediately comprehending what his friend intended to do, Chaim reached desperately to stop him, but missed the man's waistcoat by a fraction of an inch. Still, he caught the dark haired man on his way out of the restroom, slinging his arm around his waist and pulling him swiftly into the small closet right before Natanel's office, a small, tight smile on his face for anyone who saw him drag Iyov off. To Iyov's credit, he did not make a word nor sound of protestation, letting the other twirl him away.

"Iyov. Yoyo. My friend, balibter, do not do this," Chaim pleaded with him. "Natanel will not take well to it. He will not. Being... quirky will not go over well. Please."

"It's not a big deal. I'm his boss. He should listen the first time," Iyov, still upset, replied. Chaim pursed his lips as he looked into his eyes- the blue-green makeup brought out the brighter colors in Iyov's typically dark eyes, like an aurora borealis with exposure. "I'll break his brain a little. Then we'll get the checked line."

Chaim pursed his lips, brow furrowing.

"Fine," he sighed. Iyov's unhappy little scowl turned into a hopeful half smile. Chaim pointed a finger in his face. "But, I'm coming with you – no funny business beyond a crack, khap?"

"Works with me," Iyov beamed brightly, leaning over and pecking Chaim's cheek, making the other turn a remarkable shade of scarlet. Iyov slipped out of the door, Chaim following his swagger infused gait. The two of them silently approached Natanel's office, Iyov turning his head towards Chaim - checking to see the reaction of the other man. A slight, half lidded smile met his gaze, assuring him that he looked enticing and alluring- as much as he could, being so goofy as he was. That probably was part of the charm. He knocked on Natanel's office door, and without waiting for a yes or no, entered the room. He was, after all, the boss. "Shechter... maybe I could... convince you that we deserve the funds."

Natanel had not moved from furiously scribbling on papers, and sharply shook his head.

"No." he snapped, not looking up. "You might own this company, but you hired me to keep it on track. So get it into your head, tumpik. You're not getting it."

"Reb Shechter," Iyov said, his voice low and chiding, almost amused. He carefully moved to lean against Natanel's desk, striking a flirtatious pose. "Look at me."

Natanel, about to tell Iyov off, only stared as his gaze landed on the other man.

Chaim could feel the tensity growing, thick and slow.

Iyov's fingers slid under Natanel's jaw, making their gazes align.

"I can guarantee," Iyov murmured, "That we will be successful. Emet."

"'Truth', you say, you promise," Natanel was slow and uncertain in responding. "But we all know you to be a big promiser, Iyov."

"Tsuzogn aun lib hobn kost gornisht," Iyov replied, the silver tongued bastard. There was that slight smile on his face again, eyes twinkling beneath the blued eyeliner. The

236

expression was a cross between desperate and determined, and Chaim sympathized with the mixed feelings in poor Natanel. He had gotten that look frequently. Iyov's fingers found Natanel's hand, giving a light squeeze, still looking in his eyes. "Zay azoy gut."

"Fine. Fine, you glatiker," Natanel gave up, tearing his gaze away. His eyes landed briefly on Chaim, shaking his head with exasperation. "Take it and go."

Iyov triumphantly presented Chaim with the blank check.

Секрет

8.16.2024

Есть что-то очень страшное в этом месте. Если кто-то умирает, никто не знает, куда труп уходит.

Есть шёпот в темноте, в темноте густой, как старые черные чернила, что трупы растворяются.

Но это не работает, учитывая закон о сохранении массы- у тела имеет кости и органы, не может такого быть.

В этом месте сильный мор для мозга и для души, эта болезнь течёт через глаза и уши, и все поедает.

Этот секрет один из многих, многих секретов в этих деревянных стенах-

но если человек спросит:

«что они делают с трупами?»

ответа не будет- ничего нет, ни человека, ни тела- все умерли.

Transformation

8.27.2024

To be transformed is, generally, a mixed bag. Some individuals yearn for change, for shifting into something new, to match who they are within their soul. Others fear such a shift, a holistic destroying of what was before, never to rise again. And then, there are those who seek to enhance others, to cause that anatomical rebirth, forging something anew from the old.

There is an innate bond between the creator and the creation.

A vulnerability, the whispering knowledge that there is one that will forever know you better than yourself. The doctor knew that well, the discomfort of his craft assuaged by the fact, or what should have been the fact, that their creation would never live in a way to be aware of its minuscule place in the world; of its sheer pointlessness – a tool, one that will be outshone by a later prototype.

No, it would never be aware, sentient of the futility to carve out for itself a new meaning.

That was how it was supposed to be, at least.

However, regardless if the beast was machinery come to life, there were... other people irreversibly changed in this gaping abyss, fundamentally altered by the toxic waves from the EMP. The obsession with change and perfection made Raymond uncomfortable, certainly, though as long as he was left alone, he was content. As content as a man in a personal Hell could be.

The Soothsayer – attempting to become a true messenger of God, without knowing Their Nature, and hoping that with enough internal change, he would never have to learn. The knowledge only tore him asunder when he accomplished his goal.

The Designer seeking to change herself for herself, to become Perfection and thus destroy everything. Already thrice dead from her relentless pursuit of her own reincarnation, she continued with tools of iron and the burning lasers.

And the Constructor....

There was an unnerving, disquieting aspect to that creaking, metal behemoth as Raymond entered the room.

Silent and overbearing.

The obvious trap was almost humorous what with how transparent it was, like a thin sheet of paper illuminated by a light table. Yet there was no way but forward, onward into oblivion. With a soft breath, a whispering wind in and out of an empty vessel, Raymond approached the slumbering giant. His hand reached for its Core, pulsing and oozing.

No, he felt no serious desire to actually touch it. On second thought, why bother? There was no need – he had his medical bag, the bone saw sharpened to cut through metal. With ease, he could simply break through the door sealing him in this tomb. Although vaguely aware he required that Core, he would have preferred not to deal with it. Resolved, Raymond turned his back to the still sleeping hulk of metal and made his way towards the exit.

A nigh silent creak behind him had Raymond gradually turn back toward the spindling wire and metal. There was not a single sign of any motion, however, not even a puff of dust. Apprehensive, Raymond continued to edge his way to the door.

Faster than a viper, a leg of the mechanism shot forwards, whipping Raymond in the back. It was sheer luck alone which kept him from slicing off his own hand. Breathless, and knocked to the floor, the old man was incapacitated swiftly, bone saw flung out of his grip. It embedded itself in the wall across the room, and Raymond grimaced as he prepared to retrieve it. Now that a struggle was inevitable, he had to defend himself or die.

Ended up being a pipe dream- or even, a dream for a pipe with which to fend off the arms that assailed him. Instantaneously, he was swarmed, an uncomfortable grip that lifted him clear off the ground. Eventually, he found himself tumbling into a cage of shifting and slinking metallic bits and pieces, nauseated and off kilter. The brass bars kept him in place as he was dizzyingly pitched forward to face the Core once more.

Haydan, the Constructor, reduced to only his skull and the two gloves of what were once hands, suspended in wiring within an Iron Maiden of his own making, swung forward to greet him, Raymond lurching back as it felt as though he was eager to crack open his skull.

Knowing Haydan, it was entirely possible.

"If it isn't Raymond!" the hulking mass cried, the bloated, overcharged head staring at him unblinkingly. Foul green light poured from his mouth and eyes as he spoke. "I'm so very glad to see you, old friend. Dear me, you look worse for wear!"

Raymond did not reply, only stared silently back at the Constructor. The bodiless man's smile, that of an electrocuted man, did not fade.

"It's been some time since I've worked on an upgrade for dear Jo," the builder mused, bringing Raymond closer for inspection. He gesticulated wildly, constantly, as if his hands were merely pre-programmed devices. "I doubt that I've gotten rusty, though. Let's give it a shot, eh?"

The arm holding Raymond spun around rapidly, then twisted to the side- all the way upside down. It deposited him atop Haydan's old workstation as he tumbled out of that shifting cage, the small man immediately attempting to scramble away and escape. To prevent that, two metal arms cinched tight over his wrists, nearly cutting off the circulation. A quiet grunt of pain escaped him, converted into a huff of air as he was slammed back onto the table. A screeching, creaking groan followed the table being dragged across the room towards the Constructor. The head smiled down at him, with that empty, blown-eyed gaze.

"My, I was mistaken. Time *has* been kind to you, hasn't it?" Haydan murmured, a sort of delighted lilt to his tone. Raymond kicked and tried to use his legs as leverage to escape, but the metal tightened, pain lancing up the center of his wrists, skyrocketing up his arms to the nerves in his elbows. A half-choked whimper of pain, and he went limp (yet uncomfortable) in the pinching grip. "Your muscle structure appears to be in remarkable shape, and your stamina is rather unyielding from what I've seen. Yes, you would make a fine basis for a robotized specimen."

Raymond decided that he very much did not like what Haydan was suggesting.

With a renewed effort, he attempted to break free vigorously, only to gasp with the sharp pain of one of his wrists fracturing under the pressure of metal winches. Horrified, his head swiveled to face the limb, seeing red oozing into his flesh- the burst vein seeping through his body. The nausea from before resurfaced violently, swallowing down the need to retch.

"It's been quite some time since I've done this," Haydan hummed, raising another many jointed limb, his hands still flailing in their repetitive pattern- and to Raymond's rapidly increasing horror, he saw his bone saw in its unstable grip. Without thinking, Raymond desperately tried to escape once more. A broad round pressed on his chest, pushing him back down, gradually winding him as it crushed his lungs. He gasped, feeling his ribs creaking under the force of pressure. "If you would stop squirming, Ray, it would be much easier for the both of us, you know."

He tried to reply, but the circular press moved down once more and winded him entirely. Then, he held his breath unwittingly as the saw pressed to his sternum, directly above his solar plexus. Oh, hell no. If there was one thing worse than a non consensual surgery without anesthetics, it was non consensual surgery without anesthetics by a man who was now merely a head rigged to power a giant confusing mess of wires and metal with an extremely limited range of motion and practically no precision at all.

The saw cut surprisingly straight for those facts, tearing through fabric, skin, bone, and flesh with ease- just as Raymond knew it could. A substance like blood welled up in the cavity, spilling out over his side.

It was both hot and cold at the same instant, the chills of loss shock hitting him- especially with his broken hand; and the lava-like warmth of his ichor. Raymond ceased any and all attempts at escaping, understanding now that it was futile.

Haydan used a random pincer to spread open the wound, the bulky mass pressing now directly on Raymond's lung. It was electrified ice along his exposed veins.

A giant hydraulic made itself visible, gripped to the point of cracking between another pair of I-beams. Raymond stared at it, unable to even muster any horror as the cloudy shock took over.

The hydraulic was carefully placed at the space made in Raymond's chest, not quite a cavity- yet. The pressure of the metal entering his body was unbearable, forcing a space for a huge, heavy cylinder that did not belong in his corpus.

Haydan, losing patience, slammed several arms onto the hydraulic. Raymond's vision went black as it jammed fully within his corpus. The ringing in his ears only slightly faded as the saw pressed against his arm.

Raymond was far too delirious in pain to fight as Haydan slowly tore into each of his limbs, replacing the bones with those massive hydraulics. Blood splattered along the ground, pooling around the table. Raymond could only hear the crack of his bones, the dripping of blood, his own heartbeat in his ears, his groans of pain, and Haydan's familiar quiet humming.

Cut, open, hydraulic. Cut, open, hydraulic.

Eventually, each and every bone in Raymond's body was replaced. Against his will, he stood.

"Behold!" Haydan announced to the Void. His hands continued their motions. "The designing doctor!"

The husk of Raymond stood, without drive or purpose, a silent and unmoving exhibit forevermore.

Trace Patterns

10.6.2024

There is something humanizing about fingerprints. They are all different, unique, even those of identical twins are not perfectly alike. Yet every person has them; swirls and ridges that hint at one's life, DNA or past. They cannot be burned away with acid, nor erased with chemicals. Fingerprints can be partial or whole; and they are seen on the smallest, newest human to the oldest, most frail.

Holding his wife's hand, palm up in his own, he traced the lines in her skin, fingers on the center of her hand while his eyes were on the tips of hers, he mused.

She disclosed to him that in a past life, she had read people's fingerprints for a large fee, waxing to them poetic about their follies and warning them of dangers to come. Never would she give them a positive response, only cold, realistic ones. Therefore, they were more likely to come true, and her desperate clients would appeal to her for salvation.

Atabulus studied her fingertips as she read a book, pointedly ignoring her husband's presence; although it was she who had requested that he caress her hand. Perhaps she wanted the sensation, reminding her of a devoted spouse even as she would turn her gaze away. A small pang of pain nestled somewhere in Atabulus' ribs, like a dagger slipped between his opalescent skin. He knelt further, touching the tips of her fingers to his lips, feeling the slight, minute ridges where the prints were, imagining in his mind's eye the way they imprinted on his face, savoring a world which they would never leave.

Yet they drew away, moving to turn the page. Then the hand returned, palm up once more, and he silently accepted her empty offering. He carefully pressed kisses to her wrist, around her palm, and down her fingers.

He wondered if she felt his inhumanity in his touch alone. Was there something that made his touch different, aside from the lack of fingerprints? For indeed, his skin bore no lines- it was smooth, unnaturally (to humans) so. Did she feel it? Did she suppress a shudder each time his hand drew across of hers?

"Atabulus," her voice murmured, commanding and beautiful. His head lifted to meet her steely gaze, unpigmented eyes boring into his soul with ease. He replied, "¿Sí, mi amor?"

"Venga a mi regazo," Alessandra instructed, and he quickly stood, looking at her with wide eyes, searching her face for a lie. She rolled her own, impatient. "Apúrese. Tengo frío."

"Sí, mi señora," Atabulus complied, slowly bringing himself to rest on her legs. One arm wrapped around him possessively, and he suppressed a shudder. She laughed softly, kissing at his neck- making him melt against her chest, face flushed. "Te amo...."

"Me preocupo por ti también," she quietly said in response. Atabulus felt that uncomfortable shift in his chest once again, looking up at his wife. She gave a thin smile, kissing him. "Te quiero."

Her shiver did not go unnoticed.

Thermal Fracture

10.24.2024

There was a draught coming in through the crack. Marina tightened her cloak around herself, staring at the bit of glass as though it could vanish into the night as dusk turned to twilight. As though the moon's healing rays would mend it.

She shivered. The cold was seeping gradually into her bones, yet she was out of firewood, with only a few matches left in the box. Her lacking these items threatened to overwhelm her as she stared out into the darkness. Marina placed her hand onto the crack, feeling the cold air slip between her fingers.

Marina fought a shudder. She rubbed her arms, scarred hands smoothly gliding across her motley skin, flattened by the chill. Despair trickled into her veins just as the frost slowly crested over the cracked window. Glass was just superheated sand, though. Melted. Perhaps she could rescue the situation.

Tightening her cloak around herself, Marina crept out into the freezing dark wood. Branches would do fine- she would be able to take off her bandages, soaked in oil, and utilize them as a makeshift torch. It hurt her hands to attempt tearing them off trees, so she resorted to scavenging along the ground, hoping that she could find enough dry twigs and sticks for kindling. Through sheer perseverance, she collected enough for a concentrated fire.

Marina slipped back inside the shack. Starting the blaze took a few infuriating tries, though she eventually managed to get the flame to catch on the bandages. With satisfaction, she looked at the dancing fire, relaxing as she observed it. Finally. Warmth. She closed her eyes, the flame edging and flickering towards her face from the draught in the window. Marina let it heat her for another moment before exhaling her stress, smiling slightly. She would be able to seal out the cold at last. That alone provided a strong basis of comfort, igniting her hope.

Humming quietly to herself, she placed the flame beside the crack. There were soft noises- not exactly those of melting, but she was encouraged by them. She felt a smile spread on her face as she traced the fracture with the fire. Curiously, she noticed that, like her smile, the crack seemed to be growing. Slowly, the grin on her face faded, slowly pulling away the flame. The crackling noise now was a siren of alarm, louder now, almost angry.

Marina barely managed to throw her hands up over her face to shield herself from the glass shattering. Shocked, she did not even have a moment to shout, startled like a young child who had fallen roughly. Eventually, she lowered her arms from her face, gooseflesh all along her skin.

Marina stared with horror out of the broken window, the howling wind outside buffeting her face and tousling her hair. The small fire at the end of her makeshift torch sputtered violently, in death throes.

Quickly, she dropped to her knees, curling around it.

Praying that they would keep each other alive.

Sound Waves

The sun was pleasant on her face – eyes closed, ukulele in hand, a nice breeze rustling through the tall grass: all of it added up to a calm, tranquil afternoon. It would have been extremely nice... if she was not so worked up over small things. Although she was trying her best to keep her face completely neutral and calm, Magnolia was well aware that a grimace was crossing her expression, souring it. The nice weather and sunshine only went so far in making her feel any better in the moment, struggling to draw inspiration from the surrounding nature.

The song that she was attempting to write was not going well at all. The beauty of Earth and the simplicity of mortality was not appealing to her in the way that it normally did. Nor was her love of knives tapping into the wells of inspiration. Nothing seemed to be clicking today, and it was grating on her thin nerves. Magnolia would admit that she did not have a lot of patience- especially not for an archivist, but she had given this attempt a good try. A long sigh escaped her, eyes finally opening as her meditative state was broken by her overcrowding thoughts.

Six hours of sitting in the crow nest that she and Caroline added to the cottage, hovering above nature, and absorbing all of the little details she could hear, and not a melody to come to mind. It was supremely frustrating, and she finally took to her last resort with pursed lips.

Peter was quick to answer his phone – unlike her, the tech aficionado kept his phone on hand.

"Mag!" his joyful voice came through her receiver. She held the phone at arm's length from her ringing ears- having forgotten that she had turned on the speaker function. "How are you doing?"

"I am not doing, thanks for asking," she replied in a grumble, shifting in her seat, watching a bird fly by. "I'm trying to write a song, and, well, it's just not going so well. I feel like a moth."

"You're not a moth, Magnolia. You're Magnolia," Peter assured her. "Hey, how about I stop by for a bit and see if I can help you out? I'm just going with Rita to get some ice cream donuts later, but that's not for a while."

"That may be acceptable," Magnolia tentatively agreed. "I will be waiting by the stop to greet you. Do you want lemonade? Caroline made it."

"I'll... I'll pass," Peter hesitantly replied, trying to wipe the taste of Caroline's previous, poisonous concoctions from his memory. "But I will be there in a jiffy!"

—

As she said, Magnolia was waiting by the bus stop for Peter. The older gentleman had brought his own banjo to help her out. Peter, respecting Magnolia's space (especially knowing that she could get sensitive when she was frustrated), gave a wave instead of a hug.

"So, miss, what seems to be the problem?" Peter asked, giving a goofy grin, lowering the heart shaped sunglasses that he borrowed from his girlfriend to be 'suave'. Magnolia, focused on her issue and not understanding that he was joking, immediately launched into an explanation of her problem; "Well, I've been trying to make a song and it's not going well at all. I think I already told you that."

"Yeah, uh, you mentioned it," Peter responded, rubbing the back of his neck. "Let's see what we can do, then! I'm sure that together, we'll be able to come up with something!"

Two hours later, Peter was starting to feel a bit frustrated himself. Almost every prompt or bit of insight that he could offer, Magnolia turned it down. Not because any of his ideas were bad, rather that none of them were hitting on what Magnolia was aiming for. It slowly dawned on Peter that he had no idea what Magnolia wanted to make a song on to begin with. After a few more suggestions that went nowhere and failed to milk it out of her, Peter decided to be direct about it.

"Magnolia, since we're going in circles," he opened, tilting his head, a small smile growing on his tired out face. "What exactly *are* you trying to write the song about?"

"It's not a 'what'," Magnolia managed to reply after a minute. "It's a 'who'.... Well, um, *for* a 'who'. I'm trying to write something for Caroline. I really appreciate her, and I want to make her something really special to show it."

"Aw, that's so cute!" Peter's hands came to his cheeks, beaming at her. "No wonder we're going nowhere with it- we're in the wrong place! Come on!"

A quick bus ride later, they were at the pond. Magnolia was frowning slightly, but she followed Peter down to the edge of the water. He sat down, patting the grass beside himself. She turned in a circle before sitting. Then she flopped back, staring up at the shades of sunset.

The sound of water splashing lulled her eyes shut. A comfortable feeling, a familiar feeling. It reminded her of the white noise that Caroline would set up to help Magnolia fall asleep. A slight smile began to grow on her face. She sat up before sleep would claim her then and there at the pond, contemplatively looking out towards the water. Soon, she gave Peter a tap on the shoulder.

"I think I got an idea," she told him, standing up and offering a hand to help him get up as well. "Thanks for this. I needed the break from the countryside."

"No problem!" Peter brightly replied, pretending that he was not tired out himself as he fought a yawn. He stretched as he got up, smiling at the sunset. "Glad I can help."

The next time Peter came over, he heard Caroline humming an unfamiliar song as she tended to the cottage garden, but it reminded him of the ocean. He smiled- it seemed like Magnolia had been successful in making her song.

He came up to her, offering a smile.

"So? How'd the song making go?" he asked, unnecessarily. Magnolia smiled back, and answered, "Pretty good, I think."

Peter laughed.

Elevation

1.7.2025

1.

A cup of tea steamed on his lab counter, the warm dry air of fall drifting through the window. It had been one year of maintaining his practice - the 'test' year that concluded his studies and would award him with his doctoral degree. At first, he had been concerned that due to his infamy, he would struggle with getting enough patients to account for the conferral, but he need not have worried. Desperate, destitute, and desolate individuals flocked to his door – Auræics that were too damaged to be treated by their own, poor D'mas'de, curious and needy people from all species. Perhaps his infamy even gave him a significant boost when it came to his popularity.

Morbid curiosity indeed.

At the moment, he had no patients, allowing him to focus on his studies and experiments instead of the moans and weak cries of the suffering and dying. It was, admittedly, an enjoyable break from the violence that often wreaked through communities during the fall months. The almost-doctor was bent over a microscope, carefully pulling the veins from a ruddy leaf. He reconnected them to a small device and waited for the minute liquid to drip feed into the micro metal frame, and turned it on.

He watched as leaf and metal disappeared into thin air. Satisfied, he leaned back. If his calculations were correct, he would see it again in five days, five meters to the right. He stalked over to his drink, smilingly nursing it as he looked around the rather barebones medical facility. After the fire, it took time to rebuild, but he ensured to utilize fireproof materials when fixing it up.

A sudden knock on his door made him nearly drop his tea, but he quickly collected himself- not without heavy internal rebuke. Atabulus swiftly moved to the door, glancing outside the eyehole before opening it with no small measure of confusion.

"Atabulus, general medical de-facto," he announced himself as he opened the door to the Royal Guard officers with a bow- careful not to allow his neck to be in range. He felt a twinge of impatience for the ability to finally stop using the term for his incomplete studies. Soon. Five days. Five days, and so many things would change. He would officially become a doctor. He would be finished paying for the clinic. His experiment would be successful, he was certain. Still, he had this Royal brigade (it was only four

251

representative guardians, but he was still bitter at his lull interrupted) to deal with. "How may I assist you on this fine day? None of you look particularly injured."

"None of us are," a Dagon spoke, their scales shimmering with pride, and a slight disgust or discomfort - perhaps towards Atabulus, though potentially towards the dry heat as well. "We are here for a brief interview. That you may potentially shed some light upon. Potentially."

Atabulus bowed once more, allowing the troop into his foyer. It was clear that they were officially of the true guard, as no Auræic, D'mas'de, Dagon, and Ziz would willingly work together otherwise. The D'mas'de looked around as she sat heavily in a chair, clearly unimpressed and bored. The Ziz shifted, watching and following after the D'mas'de's lead. The Auræic hovered about, inspecting various tinctures and remedies that were kept in the public eye. And the Dagon, clearly in charge of this entire operation, whatever it was, faced Atabulus. The doctor was getting for them a glass of salted water- and was interrupted by the stoney faced guard leader.

"When are you graduating, tardigrade?" they said, speaking down to him in more ways than two. Atabulus refrained from bristling as he presented the refresher, and replied respectfully, "I will be approved in five days, Commander."

"We heard that you treat all species," the bored D'mas'de rolled her eyes as she spoke. Atabulus attended to her needs as well, providing a hand fan. She accepted it without thanks. Ignoring the rudeness, Atabulus answered, "You have heard correctly. My studies were involved with as many species as I could gain insight from."

"And you make medicines," the Auræic commented, holding one of the fragile bottles. Atabulus said nothing as he tossed it into the air and caught it repeatedly with his shifting body. "Some new, and not always regulated because of that."

"I would not administer a dangerous drug to a patient," Atabulus responded, feeling the latent anger spiking slowly. He tamped it down, and smiled. "The one you are holding is currently undergoing the review process, though testing has been going well thus far. Most of those in the clinical trial have reported a stronger connection to, well, their partners- it's a temporary soul amplifier for non-Auræic individuals, and an inhibitor for Auræics."

"These patients that agree to your clinical tests – are they not forced?" the Dagon interrogated, refreshed after splashing the salted mineral water over their head. "We are

252

aware that those who come to your door are not always the most well off- and thus, as you yourself might have gathered and have been exploiting, may be extorted."

"If I may be bold, your honorables," Atabulus calmly responded, in spite of the righteous rage flaring up in his heart. "I would like to refute any accusations of illegal medical procedures or activity. All of my work is heavily documented, and there are several, untamperable spirit cameras in this lab as required by the medical board. If this information is required, I can provide it immediately."

"Shut it," the Ziz snapped, standing sharply. Atabulus immediately turned all of his hands palm out in a placating gesture. "We're not here for that. We got what we came for."

Atabulus was stunned into silence as the group all moved to the exit. He bowed once more as he followed them out, and was wise enough not to ask any questions. Even so he felt a vague unease about the odd visitation.

He made sure to lock his windows for the night.

2.

Four days later, Atabulus waited impatiently at his terminal, pacing the room and constantly glancing at the device. His night time concoction had been consumed, though it hardly helped the strain in his nerves. Weary from the long day of treating and caring for patients, yet invigorated by anticipation, he waited for the ping that would commence his career – a doctor at last. Perhaps he was being driven by young stupidity, fully aware that sleeping to be energized for the next day would be more wise than waiting until midnight to receive confirmation for what he was certain was coming.

The ping alerted him, head swiveling from the ticking phaser to the terminal. He quickly made his way to it, opening the letter that would begin the turnaround of his life.

He read through it quickly, pride morphing into confusion, and a slight worry. There was an assurance of his graduation, and a stamped certificate to verify, yet the actual diploma was currently on hold due to some bureaucratic nonsense. While holoprinting the placating paper, he read through the letter once more. Atabulus found a touch of peace in the assurance that he would definitely be receiving his diploma that day, but was still vexed by the fact that he would have to wait.

An odd mix of frustrated and elated, Atabulus put up the certificate above the terminal, smiling at it for a moment, and retreated to bed. By evening, he would officially be a graduate – and now, he could rest with the knowledge that he was an approved doctor.

Suddenly more exhausted than he had been twenty minutes prior, Atabulus fell into his bed and dreamed of cascading stars.

Emergencies woke Atabulus frequently- a night worker injured; an abused individual seeking private help; tardigrades furtively approaching for his expertise- and this night was no different. No later than two hours after he had drifted among the cosmos, the buzz informing him that someone was on the property came to his ear, rousing him. Feeling rather heavy, Atabulus pulled himself up to get to the door.

A pregnant D'mas'de hobbled inside, grateful for him being at the ready. Her partner, presumably, a Ziz, stared at Atabulus with suspicious wariness. He quickly discerned that, from the way she was walking, the baby was pressing on the nerve of her spine.

Atabulus quickly provided a light-chair, bringing her to a private room further into the practice, outside of the main rotunda in the foyer. He stood outside the door and waited for the Ziz to join them. He asked her what the matter was, and she confirmed his suspicions in other words. Still, he performed two tests along with an x-ray to be certain, and verified his diagnosis.

Atabulus explained to the couple that due to the Ziz's nature, she was suffering from a calcification within her womb – nothing serious, but certainly painful. She seemed to relax at the clarification, and her partner asked what could be done. Atabulus admitted that, conventionally, there was no specific methodology to healing the issue aside from waiting for the baby to be born, and using copious pain killers in the meantime. However, he added at their unhappy faces, he was currently under review for a medication of his own creation that would promote the metabolization of the calcium into the mother: giving her stronger bones and teeth, as well as protecting her from any calcium cannibalization from the child. The pair seemed intrigued – a good sign, from Atabulus' experience – and he provided the documentation on the clinical trials as well as the approval for testing. The D'mas'de and Ziz discussed for a long moment, Atabulus giving them the needed privacy to do so.

The moment he stepped out of the room, he saw another patient approaching, and he came to the Dagon's side. The cruel heat of the fall had caused his scales to grow sharp and painful. Atabulus hardly had to leave the rotunda, simply prescribing a moisturizing cream along with providing instructions for use. He told Atabulus that he would be sending others suffering from the same issue his way, as the Auræic doctor that they often went to had raised his prices and had turned rather dismissive of their needs, shifting towards a Auræic only practice. Atabulus expressed sympathy and thanks, assuring the

254

Dagon that he would not fall into the same pattern. Silently, he acknowledged that if he would, he would quickly be run out of income.

After getting another patient settled, Atabulus returned to the couple, who told him that they were opting for the experimental treatment. Atabulus could hardly hold back a smile at the response, and bowed his appreciation. He provided for her the first dosage, explained how she should take the medication, and let them know that if they ever needed any more assistance, he was always available.

Then, he returned to the new patient- cloaked, so as to avoid their identity from being discovered. Atabulus let them speak, silently taking in their terrible tale. He asked, when they were finished, if he could see their arm, and carefully splinted the damaged bone. Atabulus knew better than to question if the stranger would be safe beyond his walls, and let them leave, providing them with food and medicine.

The next several hours were spent healing, flitting about from patient to patient, pulling curtains to perform emergency surgeries and strutures, snapping quick bites of food between each beck and call, listening to and talking to and treating everyone who came through his doors. Some repeat patients noted the new paper on the wall, making him flush with pride as they congratulated him.

At the end of the day, when all patients were taken care of and accounted for, all the documentation made, Atabulus settled in his seat in front of the terminal. He frowned – no new messages.

A knock on his door – lost in thought, he did not think to look out the glass before opening it.

3.

Atabulus looked up, and immediately felt panic flood his system. The (now official) doctor dropped to the floor in a deep bow, kneeling before the six royals at his door.

"Your- Your Majesties!" he gasped, hardly daring to raise himself from the floor. "What- how- I- I am at your service. Please, may I inquire as to the reason for your presence?"

The royal entourage gestured towards him to cease his honorifics, and he stood ramrod straight.

The Ziz queen spoke first, her soft, trilling voice extraordinarily pleasant to the ear. He nearly relaxed, but kept his respectful manner. It was the first time he heard her speak in person, stunned by the sheer beauty of her tone.

"Good evening, Doctor Atabulus," Veneras spoke. It was music to his ears for more reasons than one. "You seem to have a very busy practice, do you not?"

"Yes, I do," he replied, feeling extremely light headed. "Though it hardly interferes with my research, your majesty. I enjoy the pacing."

"You graduated today, right?" the Auræic leader, Y'fna, commented, looking around with the species' characteristic tranquility. "Congratulations."

"Thank you, your effervescence," Atabulus felt his throat tighten, and he bowed deeply. He still was in a state of shock from the sudden visit. He felt a surge of self consciousness about his skeleton of an establishment. "Though, I have yet to receive my diploma. I was informed that it was delayed."

"We're aware," said Philipe, king of the Dagon. His consort, Sebastian, smiled with gleaming sharp teeth, adding; "We input the request to hold the document and have it rerouted."

Atabulus was unsure how to react, but surprise overrode any other emotions. Further confounding his emotions and perplexing him, the royals all smiled at him with amusement.

"We wanted to present it to you ourselves," the D'mas'de queen, Elaine, said softly. Atabulus stared as her husband, Benedict, pulled out the document- and another, congratulatory note signed by each dignitary. Atabulus felt the lightheadedness return, and Elaine remarked, "Seems as though you need one of your own tinctures, Doctor. Congratulations."

It took the absolutely stunned tardigrade a long moment to respond, and it took him what felt like thirty minutes to realize that she had teased him. A green flush rose in his face, baffled and honored and touched and nervous.

"I-" he inhaled sharply, bowing again. "I am unsure why I am so deserving of this great honor, to have all of you before me, on one of the most important days of my life. It truly... truly is a privilege."

"You are the youngest graduate from the Union Medical Program," Sebastian eagerly answered. "Furthermore, the first Tardigrade to join the school at all."

"We agreed that your bravery had to be acknowledged," Benedict remarked. "And additionally, we found you highly worthy. Perhaps today will be even more important to you than you had previously anticipated it to be, Doctor Atabulus."

"How.... Your sagaciousness, I cannot even fathom, how so?" the youngest doctor asked in a daze, feeling quite faint. "I already have been graced with your grand appearance. I cannot imagine anything more striking than this."

"We potentially have a proposition to you," Y'fna said. That faint feeling intensified, stars dancing over his vision. Along with a slight fear that built up in his chest. What if they knew about the shadows? What if they were seeking him out to testify to it...? Perhaps if he would not, they would withhold his diploma from him. Already he could see his dreams going up in smoke. "If you are willing to hear us on it."

"Of course, your effervescence," Atabulus bowed again, struggling not to fall. "I am at your service."

"We shall see about that," Philipe said coolly, glancing at his wrist, where an ornate watch rested. Atabulus felt that sinking feeling grow, spreading around his feet and welling upwards. "Now, then... who has the proposal?"

While the royals checked themselves for a document that was sure to seal Atabulus' fate, a ruddy glimmer caught the doctor's eye, and that faintness grew allthemore. For, five meters from where he sent it, the leaf was slowly drifting down to land on Queen Elaine's head.

When it did, she plucked it off her head and examined it deeply, an odd emotion on her face, eyes blowing wide as she inspected it with every muscle of her eyes.

"That's, um, that's mine, your sagaciousness," Atabulus managed to bring himself to say. "It is, ah, an... an experiment."

"I know it is," Elaine triumphantly replied, and gave a delighted laugh. She waved the leaf in Benedict's face and beamed, "I told you! I told you it would be him!"

"I believed you, my dear friend Elaine!" Sebastian grinned widely, reaching over and shaking the absolutely bamboozled Atabulus' hand. "Congratulations, congratulations! Philly, darling, get the contract out!"

"I… am not following, your illustriousness," the dazed tardigrade said, feeling very far away. "Contract? Congratulations…?"

"Come, Doctor," Y'fna commanded, and Atabulus followed him to his workstation. "Bring your time-travelling leaf. Queen Elaine, write the inscription that is on your own."

"Her own?" Atabulus echoed, confused even more, but he obeyed the Auræic leader. The D'mas'de queen brushed by him, and smiled. He bowed again, "Your sagaciousness."

The Queen pulled out a small parcel, and opened it. Within, there was the same leaf-worn down with time. Upon it, Atabulus read, 'You will see this leaf once again in precisely one year from now at the office of the Royal Doctor.'

Atabulus stared.

The next thing he knew, he was seated on his own operating table, several eyes upon him, some bemused, some worried, all trusting.

"Do you not have a doctor?" he asked. They collectively shook their heads, and Veneras took over. "Each of us from our own species. We would like one, to at least unify us in health. You will be our collective doctor, our confidante, shared between us. Do you understand?"

"I do, your tempestuousness," Atabulus murmured, quickly getting up as he realized he was still on the seat. "I understand. Your majesties, I am sure you understand that you take a risk, as I am subject to emotion as any other individual is…."

"We certainly hope you are," Veneras remarked, and the other royals laughed. Atabulus felt his face flush once more. "We'd hate to share an automaton."

Queen Elaine finished writing her note, and then handed the leaf to Atabulus.

"Send it to my bedroom vanity," she instructed. "One year ago."

Atabulus deigned it fit to avoid remarking upon the fact that he did not know how to send an object back in time. Clearly he was able to, as Elaine had the leaf. Feeling extraordinarily nervous, he rigged the device once again, and checked his calculations, desperately trying to figure this out on the fly. Calculations flooded his mind as he carefully reset and refueled the leaf.

Atabulus held his breath, and sent the leaf back. They all watched as it rose into the air, turned green, and blinked out of existence, into the past.

Two documents were then presented to him – one, his new diploma, and two, a contract for the position of Universal Royal Doctor. Each of the dignitaries had already signed it at the bottom.

With shockingly steady hands, Atabulus signed his name, pausing.

Doctor. He was a doctor.

Not only that, but he was now the Royal Doctor.

With anticipation, he signed it.

Details could be worked out later.

Steaming Cold Shower

1.14.2025

it's a special kind of hell to shower
and be cold
yet you can see the steam billow
it reminds me
of that silly little thing, a fear of missing out
but it's not quite that
it's the feeling
of looking out the window
when you're sick
on a summer day
and all your friends are outside
having a good time
it makes you happy
since you dearly love your friends
though with time
the happiness wanes
as not one of them waves to you
you're left cold
it's a special hell to be alone
like a steaming cold shower

Reason

4.19.2025

1.

He was supposed to be his.

Andrew was supposed to be his.

Not that horrid Lou's.

Phillip stared at the other technician's back, that smug asshole who came in with the groundskeeper today- an arm around his waist and with love bites pocked on his pale skin.

Damn that. Damn it to hell. Damn him to hell. Andy was his, not Lou's. Stupid Lou, who sang all day while he worked. While everyone else agreed that Lou had a pleasant voice, Phillip would prefer Lou to eat a brick and choke on it. That would be a much better use of his mouth.

Maybe that idea sounded better than it should. Much, much better than it should have sounded. As it was, the thought of the acidity expert's face going red as he struggled to breathe through fragments of hardened clay gave Phillip an undue amount of joy. His hands itched to feel the lumps of stone in the alchemist's throat, and he tried to put the fantasy out of his mind.

Well, he knew that if anything were to happen to Lou, there would be a back up plan for the water purification plant, and thus how bad would the guilt be?

It would hardly be there. He could envision his hand closing on his neck and crushing it as easily as sealing a pipe.

Phillip shook his head to clear it. Still, that fantasy replayed in his mind's eye, over and over. Lou gone, Andrew crumpling against him in the shock, leaning on him and then becoming his. That would be absolutely perfect. Really, he had no qualms with the other tech, aside from... Andrew. The only reason was Andy.

And he was reason enough.

Phillip was not sure how he ended up outside, wishing he could smoke, but not willing to give himself away with the strong scent of his vaporizer. The cold brick in his hand was grounding, reassuring, and thrilling. He was in the opposite direction from home, waiting in an alley towards Lou's apartment.

Hey. Do not judge him. It was for merry, sweet Andy.

Soon, the steady beat of his target's footsteps came into his hearing, which may have been weaker than Lou's- shit. Phillip froze. Forget smell, what if Lou's acute hearing heard him coming? Shit, shit, that would-

He waited without breathing as the red coated PH detector walked right past him.

Phillip stayed frozen in the alley, watching the other glide by silently
he was getting away.

He was getting away, and he would take Andy with him.

Phillip acted without thinking. The brick collided with the base of Lou's neck, a bit lower than where Phillip was subconsciously aiming, and he crumpled to the pavement.

Phillip stared for a long moment, breathing hard now. He quickly rushed over, grabbing the brick and kicking the knocked out water inspector over. Hefting the brick in the air, he slammed it down on the man's face. The crunch of his teeth breaking was a heavenly chorus to the mechanic. The brick, however, did not crumble, but that was just fine to Phillip. He jammed it down his mouth as much as he could, pressing his knee onto his chest- hard.

Something broke.

He was not sure what, but something broke, and a gurgle managed to slip past Lou's lips- no more sweet silver tongue that sang without reprieve at work- and then he grew completely and utterly still, no longer breathing.

Silent at last.

Phillip slowly pushed himself away from the corpse. He pulled off the clothes he had stolen from a laundromat, his own underneath the vestments. He wiped himself clean of any blood that could have been on him, glad that none of it had ended up on his clothes or face. Throwing the garments away in the garbage in the back of the alley, he broke into a run, hard and fast. Before he knew it, he was in his apartment, and was sipping at a cup of cool water. Honestly, that was much better done than he could have dreamed. It felt so good, and he felt calm and tranquil at last. Phillip gave a contented sigh, and went to bed.

His ringing TIN woke him up.

"This is Phillip Putnam speaking," he mumbled into it, not awake at all yet due to the lack of coffee in his system. "How can I help you-"

"Work's canceled," Ezekiel – the manager of the treatment plant – cut him off abruptly. The man sounded... awful, his normally dry but kindly voice rough and abrasive, a sponge turned to a steel wool. There was a pause, and then a grumble, a swear, and a sigh. "Lou... Lou's been murdered."

"Oh," Phillip replied, feeling wide awake. He struggled to not smile. "That's... terrible. What happened to him?"

"The junks say it was a crime of passion," Ezekiel sighed – clearly lacking faith in the investigators. Phillip swallowed roughly, feeling a rush of cold flooding him, along with snug satisfaction. Another heavy pause. "Andrew... Andrew found him."

Phillip said nothing.

It was all for him.

2.

Ever since Lou had 'died', there was a sort of muted quality overlaying the entire treatment plant – hard to truly describe, intangible yet heavy and pervasive. The workers had banded together in the way that only a death can knit people, a silent nudge into one another's orbit often defined by the lack of words, driven to seek comfort in quiet connection. With violent, sudden deaths, it either tends to be a shattering experience that drives loved ones apart, or draws them together, and Ezekiel did his utmost to keep everyone close, providing support where he could to all, encouraging everyone to speak their emotions and minds. It surely helped.

Yet, of all the people to be affected, Andrew seemed to be the most heavily struck, shambling around at times as though lost in the treatment plant's labyrinthine grounds. Often in the wake of Lou's murder, one could hear him gasping as though he were drowning, stuffing himself in a secluded tower or corner where hopefully no one would stumble across him. There were times, infrequent, that Phillip would feel a twinge of empathy for the groundskeeper, and then he would recall that Andrew was the reason why Lou was dead. Andrew was why Phillip had to get rid of their co-worker.

It worked, as far as Phillip could tell. Andrew did in fact collapse sobbing in Phillip's arms a few times, thanking him for being such a good friend. Friend. At least it was progress. Andy just needed a little bit of time to acclimate, now. Phillip was there for him. Phillip would always be there for him. Andrew was his – it would only be right for Phillip to take care of him. Yes, others also comforted him, but as long as Phillip was at the forefront, he was content.

Mary-Anne, one of the longest standing technicians and Lou's best friend, had been promoted to plant director, though she had been given a few days off to mourn the loss of her closest and oldest friend. Those who checked on the shocked, gutted chemist were treated to tales of two scientists waxing poetic about the music of moisture molecules. When she did return to work, however, Mary-Anne was unsure which of the technicians should take Lou's place as head analyst, hardly able to look through the names. Zeke suggested Marlin, their level headed and skilled quality specialist, mainly working on underwater welding repairs – and Mary-Anne agreed. It was difficult for Mary-Anne to comprehend why he did not come to her mind immediately. Phillip thought that it was because Mary-Anne was too sentimentally attached to Lou. He smiled to himself, noting it as another good to come of his elimination.

Andrew may have been the reason, but there was plenty good to come of it. A big facility shakeup had been coming for a long time, and Phillip was privately proud to be the one to bring it about. Andrew may have been the reason, but Phillip was the catalyst. Perhaps there was more shifts that he could instigate for Andy. He had to keep an eye on him.

During his observations, Phillip noted an interesting shift. While in the past, Mary-Anne and Andrew rarely had much to do with one another, as their departments were rather far apart and their needs rarely overlapped, the pair seemed drawn to one another after Lou's death. It occurred to Phillip that both the chemist and the groundskeeper had been close to Lou, and apparently, with his death, they edged closer to one another for comfort. At first, Phillip considered this to be another glowing success sprouted from Lou's elimination; but as he saw Mary-Anne and Andy spend an increasing amount of time together, he was dismayed to learn that Andy was beginning to lean on her instead of him.

That was unacceptable.

Andrew was supposed to be his.

His, not hers.

Anger welled within him, but he chilled it with the memories of Lou's ribs cracking beneath his knee; the soothing gurgle of his last breaths. A deep inhale, and Phillip was calm and collected once more. Another plan was in order. Another stroke of genius had to cross his mind before he would pursue his goal.

It was for Andy, you see.

She was just not right for him, obviously.

Phillip lurked around the studio, pacing and pretending to be eyeing the pipes to ensure that they were all working correctly. Honestly, though, he was wandering about to catch wind of information that could benefit Andrew. It came from an unlikely source – their 'new' analyst, Olivia. She had been previously assigned to the arboretum, but now with a head missing, she was now working for both.

You see, Phillip was in a sort of meditative state, contemplating Lou's death and what to do about the Mary-Anne issue while 'working' on a pipe in the corner of the plant, when he heard words whispering along the water. It clicked with him that he was catching a conversation taking place in the sewers below him, the pipes liquid flow assisting with carrying the sounds towards him. Phillip did not hesitate to lean his head into the tube to hear them with a bit more clarity.

"I don't know about it, Oli, it feels a little, mm, wrong?" Chester was saying apologetically to his new analyst. "While I understand where you're coming from, we also have to be careful with another switch. While I understand that Mary-Anne liked her previous role more, and you definitely have the skills for her assignment, we can't spread you too thin."

"I see," Olivia replied, sounding extremely disappointed. Phillip latched onto it, straining to hear. "I wish it wasn't all so complicated to get done. I'm much better at the analyses for the chemicals, and Mary-Anne misses her compositions. It just makes sense to switch us."

"It does," Chet agreed. "But don't forget that Mary-Anne was next in line for the position. But I will take your considerations to Ezekiel. He's always receptive to discussion."

At that point, Phillip had stopped listening. He carefully pulled his head from his private little listening post. A peaceful smile crossed his face as he continued working, fantasizing about drowning Mary-Anne in the very pipe he was repairing.

Once his work was complete, Phillip made his way towards the laboratories where Mary-Anne and Olivia were sure to be, analyzing the million cubic meters of water coming in and out of the facility. Mary-Anne and Olivia were in rapidfire discussion, Olivia's more bubbly tones replied to with the other's quicker and more esoteric windlike notes. As Phillip approached, Mary-Anne finished speaking, quieting. It would be nice for her to be silent forever, Phillip thought to himself, so she would leave Andrew alone. Speaking of Andy, he heard the groundskeep's voice from within the room with the angels, followed by a laugh from Mary-Anne. Phillip' blood boiled, and he cooled it as he knocked on the door. Mary-Anne opened it, her cloud eyes soothing his rage. Soon they would be dissipated, and the thought brought him immense peace.

It would be for Andrew. Phillip greeted Mary-Anne calmly, eyes drifting to the man that he would ensure was his. He extended a hello to Olivia as well before entering the room. As he looked around, it was obvious that what Olivia had told Chester in private had been true. It was clear from Mary-Anne's longing gaze towards Olivia's work that their roles were backwards and belonged to each other – just like Andrew belonged to Phillip.

"Hello, all."

"Hi Phil,""Olivia responded with a sweet, innocuous smile. Part of Phillip thought she was naive, but decided that it was not a severe issue. Perhaps it would benefit him. He smiled back at the thought. "What brings you to our humble little lab?"

"Not much," Phillip lied. "Just came to check on a few things. Make sure there's no leaks or rattles. The usual."

"Have at it," Mary-Anne said, and her voice sounded almost mocking in its lilting rhythm. It reminded him too much of Lou. It was the voice of a problem. "I haven't heard anything around here, and my hearing is pretty keen. Oli, darling, have you caught wind of any of that?"

"No, it's all been quiet," Olivia replied with a slight shake of her head, sleek dark hair billowing like a curtain in nightly gales, her plumes shining. Brushing back a few strands that came to her eyes, she glanced at the groundskeeper. "Andrew, you'd probably know better than us, though. Since you have the technical know-how and get around the more."

"I haven't seen anything," Andrew mumbled after a moment of thought, face darkening slightly. He probably had not been paying attention to the pipes while working, simply trying to get through the day. However, his face lifted, and his eyes passed Phillip,

266

landing on Mary-Anne. Phillip saw red, but let himself look at Mary-Anne as well, and felt a touch more tranquil. "Wait, there was that one pipe near the greenhouse that was acting funny, right Mary-Anne? We passed it together this morning."

"Oh, that's right," a light came into the eye as she recalled. Through his simmering thoughts, Phillip watched her finger and thumb stroke down her moon-pearl necklace as she recalled the moment. Phillip imagined her own hand twisting it tighter and tighter until she turned blue. He thought back to times when she would get frustrated, ending up turning a curious shade of mauve. "I forgot all about that. I can show you where it is, Phillip."

"No need," Phillip answered, gauging his words. His mind turned, water in a wheel. "I'm sure I can find it myself. Do any of you need anything?"

"No," Olivia said, and Mary-Anne shook her head. Andy answered, "I'm good."

Phillip nodded, and left the room. He felt vindicated. He had received proof that Mary-Anne was a bad influence on Andrew - she was distracting him from his work. She was going to be replaced by Olivia for the directorial role. Surely there would be another nice wave of good changes with her eliminated from the facility. Andrew was the reason, and Phillip would be the catalyst.

Phillip decided to wait for the opportune moment, going over to the daily schedule to determine when would be the ideal time. Ensuring that there was the correct combination of people in the studio at the same time was vital. Since Lou was gone, a sort of buddy system had been silently implemented throughout the companies by Zeke and John. Phillip and Chester were assigned to one another, due to living near each other, and Phillip could not rightly excuse himself to switch with Olivia to travel with Mary-Anne - not only was it inconvenient, it would also be extremely suspicious. So he had to come up with a better option at getting her alone.

Phillip wrote down each of the names and then made his way to the elevator to leave for the day. Chester was already waiting for him at the door, hanging up his toolbelt. While the other was not looking, Phillip swiped it and shoved it in his toolkit. Time was ticking, but not urgently. In fact, Phillip had nearly all the information he needed for his plan to commence, but he actually needed time to pass enough for conversations to slip from minds and enough coincidence to be able to be established. Phillip pondered the list of employees and scheduling while he ate his supper, and eventually decided on a day. It was soon, but his hands itched for the touch of Mary-Anne's pearls twixt his fingers, tightening evermore - feeling like it was not soon enough.

A few days later, Phillip approached Mary-Anne as she left a meeting with Yunus, giving her an apologetic smile. She smiled back, tilting her head in question at him seeking her out. They were in the lower space of the treatment facility, where the 'magic' happened, as Ezekiel put it.

"I think I overestimated myself," Phillip prognosted lamentably. "I can't find the pipe you were talking about with Andrew. He's busy right now, so maybe you can show me where it is?"

"Oh!" Mary-Anne smiled broadly as she registered what the mechanic was talking about. "Of course I can show you where it is. It's right upstairs."

"I'll follow your lead," Phillip replied, returning the smile. It dropped from his face as soon as she turned around. He had to focus; not allow himself to slip up at all. He had one chance. Phillip put his plan into action: he pretended to trip on his own feet, catching himself on Mary-Anne's shoulder. As he pushed himself away, apologizing profusely, he slipped an extra strength nylon string he picked out from from Chester's toolbelt around the woman's necklace. "So sorry! I wasn't watching where I was going."

"It's ok!" Mary-Anne was quick to reassure him. Perfect - not an ounce of suspicion in her mind. "Are you alright, Phillip?"

"Yeah, like I said, just tripped," he affirmed. "I think I'll take the stairs to get my feet working again. Guess I'll see you there."

"Okay, no worries," Mary-Anne nodded. Phillip felt the string in his hand shift ever so slightly. She still did not notice it. "Take it easy."

Phillip nodded, and ensured there was enough of a strand that she would not feel the carcanet of pearls shifting. He went around the corner and waited to hear the quiet click that indicated the woman pressing the call button. Then, he pulled on the string. He heard a cut off shriek, a thud, and he pulled it tighter. A gargled cry, drowned out by the hum of the elevator chords. He tied the string to the banister as tight as he could.

Phillip smiled, though it quickly was erased by a punch to the back of his head. He whipped around, seeing Yunus staring at him - the underground expert beelining to the wire. Phillip lunged at it, slamming the Auræic against the wall, then threw it to the floor, where he immediately pinned it down, struggling with his confines. A string of curses

268

crossed his mind, blocked out by his furious struggle. Stupid Yunus - it was screwing everything up. Phillip realized that he would have to get rid of Yunus to cover this up now, and another surge of anger cut through his chest. Phillip needed to think of a plausible way to do so, and fast. How did one kill a Auræic, again?

Phillip grabbed the flashlight from his stolen toolbelt, jamming the device into the center of Yunus' manifestation, and turned it on.

Yunus, form shuddering, elbowed him in the throat, and Phillip kneed him in the back, then slammed the flashlight down once more, holding it there. The Auræic's shadowy figure collapsed, pulled into the device. Phillip shoved it into a powercell, hoping to overload it. Yunus struggled valiantly to escape, but Phillip held it in place. He could feel the flashlight heating quickly, Yunus yelling out from the singe. It would not be long now. There was a hissing, crackling noise.

"Phillip!" Yunus roared. "You'll rot in hell for what you did to L-"

Phillip threw himself to the floor right as the bulb exploded, engulfing the room in a ball of flame. He could feel hot sludge splatter across him - less of an issue than Lou's was, in this case. Yunus was silent, its body splatting against the walls, ash drifting to the floor. It smelled like burning rubber, making Phillip gag. Nevertheless, he had very little time to act, now that the sudden issue that had been Yunus was taken care of. He ran from the room, grabbing a fire extinguisher from the hallway, and sprayed the entire place. It helped cover his tracks, too. Then, knowing that it had been over five minutes (long enough for Mary-Anne to asphyxiate), he dashed to the nylon string and cut it, raveling it back as much as he could, and dropped it down the worklift shaft.

He ran up the stairs, hollering for help, but as he came up, there was more yelling. Phillip slowed down as he came upon a gaggle of people crowded around the elevator shaft. It confused him why there was so much yelling going on - she was supposed to be dead.

"Phillip- what happened to you?!" Chester grabbed his arm, staring at him with wide eyes. "Why do you smell like you've been by a barbecue? Is that aushi? Is Yunus okay?"

"Yunus- Yunus passed out working or something, there was an explosion," Phillip explained to the D'mas'de as quickly as he could. The other's face turned from concern to a horrified grimace, brows furrowing as he shook his head. "I... I think its dead. There was only ash- aushi."

"Shit," Chester hissed. He turned around to face the elevator, and began shoving his way past people to get through the crowd. "Ayo! This is an emergency, comin' through, I gotta talk with the big Zee!"

"What- what's going on here?"

"A string from Mary-Anne's dress caught around her necklace and got stuck in the grate below," Chester told him quickly. "There's more aushi. Look away if you're squeamish. Guess the star readers were right; today *is* a bad day for Auræics."

"I've seen it before, I'll be alright-" Phillip started, then found himself cut off as his stomach turned violently at the sight. Mary-Anne's mouth was open to an unnatural, her cloud eyes staring upwards. Her moon-pearls were scattered all around her, but there was a severe indentation on her manifested throat. Inside her throat was a pen. "What the-"

"Elisa did an emergency tracheotomy," Chester cut him off. "She found her with her throat being crushed by her necklace. Tore it off, she did, but that doesn't help when the throat isn't working."

"I- I see," Phillip breathed.

Chester, ignoring him, told Ezekiel and Elisa (who was monitoring Mary-Anne) what happened to Yunus. The facility head's eyes widened, and he got up silently, practically walking over the crowd with Chester to go down and see for himself.

Phillip saw Mary-Anne's fingers twitch.

He felt another surge of anger.

Andrew was his.

It was Andrew's fault.

3.

Mary-Anne's surgery to unblock her throat had gone well. The medbay had assured her several times that the way the necklace had garroted her throat missed her vocal chords, and she would be able to speak again after she would heal. It was a relief for the entire studio, especially Zeke - who had been two seconds from a meltdown ever since Lou's unexpected murder. The studio head went to visit her in the hospital every day, usually going with a small group of other employees (with always at least one other person accompanying him) to see the chemist.

Phillip, his head spinning and hands covered with ash he could not wash off, sometimes elected to go with Zeke. Mary-Anne had smiled at him weakly, and wrote (as she could not talk) that she was grateful that Phillip had tried to save Yunus. Phillip nodded at her gratitude solemnly, undeserved and making a severe chill spread through his core. He attempted to warm himself by summoning up an image of Mary-Anne with her throat entirely torn out; yet it only made him colder, the image of Mary-Anne lying unconscious on the floor of the elevator, pen in her neck completely freezing him. It seemed like the last time he had been warm was the blazing inferno in Yunus's workspace.

It was all Andrew's fault.

Thinking of the janitor used to calm Phillip; his smile and charm and sarcasm - it all had been gentle and sweet on his riotous, tempestuous spirit. However, it had been a long time since Phillip had seen Andrew smile, or heard him joke at all. The bubbly attitude that Phillip had enjoyed was popped, deflated. Since Lou's death, Andrew seemed to be a hollow husk of his former self. Phillip could not understand why. Everything was supposed to be good; better, now that the blockade was out of the way of their destined happiness.

It was Andrew's fault that Phillip had become a murderer. Not that he regretted his actions, but the fact that they had yet to bear the fruit of his labor. Olivia got the role she wanted, and Mary-Anne, once she would return, would regain her original position. There were new fire sprinklers throughout the building and other safety measures. Rumor had it that Ezekiel had paid a fortune for its installation, and Phillip, as the installer, knew it to be true. The facility had gotten upgrades, and Maxwell had gotten promoted from intern to full time. Phillip had done a good thing. Why was Andrew so stuck on that damn alchemist? Why could he not simply move on, and come to Phillip's arms. It would be perfect. Everything would slot into place.

Now, Phillip was sitting and watching Ezekiel talk quietly with Mary-Anne. Andrew sat beside him, but his eyes were on the singer, infrequently adding a bit to the conversation. It was obvious that he was trying to make quips and witticisms, but was doing poorly in that regard. He clearly was too shaken by Lou and Yunus' deaths. It made anger spark in Phillip - why could he not see that it was for the best?

Phillip could not figure out a way to calm himself down. When Andrew used to be the reason for his tranquility, he could always reminisce on the janitor and be relieved of his rage. What was he to do when it was Andrew's fault?

Maybe he could tell Andrew everything. Maybe that would fix it all. Andrew would not be able to refuse him if he told him.

Phillip shook his head suddenly, pulling his mind out of that idiotic pathway. If he told Andrew, then Andrew would immediately tell someone else - he was a chatterbox. Or at least used to be one. Still, there was too big of a risk of someone else finding out from the kindhearted worker. Ricky, Chester, Mary-Anne - if any of them caught wind, Zeke would be quick to learn as well.

Andrew, Andrew, Andrew, always making everything so complicated.

Said man was about to ask Phillip what was wrong, as the mechanic appeared to be rather perturbed - though Andrew was interrupted by the door flinging open. Olivia, accompanied by Ricky, rushed into the room. Mary-Anne's face brightened, opening her arms - the other woman jumping onto the bed and wrapping her into a hug. Mary-Anne pressed a kiss to her cheek. Phillip felt another surge of strange emotion; a mix of rage and something else that made his chest tighten uncomfortably. Ricky casually greeted the group, flopping down to sit beside Zeke.

"How ya doin', Zee?" she asked the lanky studio head, who shifted in his seat with a so-so gesture. She nodded sagely, pulling out a cigar. Or. Maybe it was not exactly a cigar. She lit up, taking in a long drag as silence reigned. Then she exhaled with a chuckle. "Damn. All of ya guys seem to really be stuck inside your own heads." She waved around the roll. "Anyone want a hit?"

"No thank you," Zeke was quick to decline, dipping his head. "I'm good."

"My throat still needs to recover," Mary-Anne rasped, smiling slightly. "But I might take you up on it when I'm out of the hospital."

"I can't either, right now," Olivia apologetically turned hir down. "Not when I'm covering for darling Mary-Anne."

"You're a cutie," Mary-Anne smiled, shaking her head. An itch forced her to cough, Ezekiel immediately standing to give her a kerchief. Olivia watched with trepidation, biting the inside of her lip - worry evident in her eyes. Mary-Anne's entire body wracked with the unpleasant sensation burning in her throat, and when the scratching within her jugular subsided, her eyes blazed with fiery tears. Olivia hesitantly moved to hug her, curling over the blond's shoulder. Mary-Anne pulled away the soiled kerchief with disgust and a hint of fear, but relaxed as she saw no aushi staining the spring green fabric. She looked up at Ezekiel, smiling wryly. "I don't suppose you want this back."

"No," Zeke replied with a slight shake of his head, a genteel smile gracing his angular features, softening the sharp edges. "Thank you for asking, angel. Do you need me to request a nurse?"

"I don't think I need one, right now," the Auræic responded after a moment. "Appreciate it, Zee."

Ezekiel blushed, sitting back down.

Phillip had watched the entire exchange with anger and curiosity blending together in an uncomfortable mix. Were Mary-Anne and Zeke interested in one another? Had Mary-Anne and Andrew ever entertained thoughts of more than friendship? Why had Phillip not noticed that Olivia and Mary-Anne were close in more ways than two?

His gaze drifted over to his lovely Andy, who seemed to be finally dozing off - it had been a long day, a long week, a long month for the sanitation expert.

No, it was not his fault that Phillip killed Lou or Yunus. Yes, he had been the reason, so in a way it very much had been Andrew's fault, but Phillip found himself slowly becoming enlightened as to the true source of all his problems. It was Andrew's fault - but not because he wanted it to be. Phillip felt his brain growing heavy with the conflicting logic. Was it Andrew's fault? Or was it not? It had to be; but it could not be.

Phillip gave a quiet growl in the back of his throat, masking it by standing and stretching.

"I'll be heading out, now," he stated, glancing around the room. Mary-Anne nodded, and Olivia smiled sadly with a wave. He leaned over and tapped Andrew's shoulder to wake him. "C'mon, sleepyhead. Let's get you to bed."

"I'll accompany you two," Zeke commented, standing. Phillip looked up at him with unimpressed uncertainty, Zeke flashing a queasy smile. "The twins are picking up Olivia and Ricky by airide later, so they're both covered. I'd rather you not walk home alone."

"Don't you think you're a little... paranoid, Zeke?" Phillip asked, raising an eyebrow and folding his arms. The smile on the thin man's face flickered before resurging, more nervous, less genuine. Phillip' warm eyes narrowed as he studied his contractee's beguiling expression. "Well, don't let me stop you."

Another positive indication to his new theory.

4.

The walk was relatively silent, Phillip supporting the sleepy Andrew as they made their way towards the janitor's unit. Thankfully, Ezekiel kept a healthy distance, temporarily satisfying Phillip. They got some waves and smiles (many of them tinged with fazed sympathy) as they walked through the compound. Eventually, they came up to Andrew's place, and he suddenly snapped to attention.

"We're here?"

"Yes, sleepyhead," Phillip teased. "Carried you all the way. Anytime."

"Oh, thank you Phil," Andrew sincerely smiled, eyes crinkling. Phillip wanted to give him a hug - then let them into Andrew's apartment, tug him to the couch to hold, soothe, and promise he would always be at his side; if Andrew would promise the same. But Ezekiel was right there, and he would certainly throw a wrench into that plan. Before the doorway, Andrew paused, smile turning a touch skittish as he glanced at the men still beside him as he unlocked the door to his unit. "Um, you guys can get out of here now. I'm home safe, see?"

"It's not a big deal, Andy," Phillip snorted, pushing open the door despite Andrew's delayed, feeble protest. His smile froze on his face and Zeke stiffened, eyes going wide as they took in the space. "Oh- wow. You really weren't expecting anyone, were you?"

"A cleaner off duty, am I right?" Andrew tried (and failed) to wisecrack, face dark with mortification. "Look, it's alright... just haven't had enough energy to take care of it...."

"Don't worry about it, Andrew," Zeke assured, carefully stepping inside. Phillip burned as he watched the lanky plant-bird extend a hand for Andrew to take - which he hesitantly did. Zeke cautiously led Andrew through the wreck, glancing about and identifying where the bedroom was. "You go rest. I'll take care of it."

"But it's my mess," Andrew attempted to deny, sad but not upset. "You don't need to deal with it... it's fine."

"It's not fine," Zeke corrected, shaking his head. "And beside, you helped me when I... was in a similar spot. It's quite honestly the least I could do."

Andrew's gaze had fixated to the pile of dirty dishes in the sink - the uncooked food on the counter, the untouched trash bins. Eventually his eyes wandered to a small portrait on the bookshelf, Lou smiling at him from the wood. After a long moment of internal

274

deliberation, he reached out and hugged Zeke. Phillip stared as Zeke hugged him back, hands clenching and unclenching. Then, Andrew drew away, and Ezekiel pat his shoulder with the slightest smile.

"Go rest, Andrew," he urged once more. "I can handle this."

"I'll help," Phillip found himself saying, in spite of the fact that he certainly did not desire to assist at all. However, he would shove aside his emotions and do it for Andrew - and making sure his Andrew was not alone with that tall bastard was another compelling motivation. "Zeke, you go to the kitchen, I'll take the living room."

"Works with me," Zeke smiled, but Phillip felt it did not reach his eyes. Or if it did, he was a damn good faker. "Meet in the middle in the dining space, then."

"Fine," Phillip barely kept his voice even. It was a damn good thing Zeke would be working in the kitchen, otherwise the temptation to grab a knife and eliminate him then and there could have been overwhelming. The more he observed Ezekiel and Andrew interact the more his suspicions seemed confirmed, but he had to wait. He could not afford another error of judgment (he had been right, it would have only been a matter of time, he just was a little early) such as with Mary-Anne. He found himself constantly staring at Zeke as he cleaned, the alien seemingly oblivious to Phillip' scrutiny. They worked speedily; Zeke focused on the work, Phillip because he wanted to keep an eye on Zeke. The kitchen gleamed after several hours of hard labor, Ezekiel's fibrous feathers snapped back in a loose ribbon and dress shirt rolled up to his elbows. His jacket had been slung over a dining chair, and he whistled as he put away the cleaning supplies. Phillip watched him intently, folding a towel and fantasizing that it was Zeke's spine. All that remained was a small basket of laundry and the bags of trash sitting by the door in wait. Phillip pointed at them, slitted eyes locked on Zeke. The slender man's sickly smile faltered. "Take them out."

"All of them?" Zeke said with surprise, startled and a little dismayed. He surveyed it a moment longer, looking up at Phillip with a nervous glint in his eye. Or was it scheming? Was it fear? "I'd rather get a little help...."

Phillip came closer to Ezekiel, tilting his head. He watched the man take a step back. He smiled wider - unsure of when he started smiling to begin with.

"I'll help then," he soothed. Zeke relaxed just a touch, making his way towards the trash, picking up a few bags in his large hands. Phillip went on, "It's okay to be scared, Ezekiel."

Ezekiel froze, snapping to stare at Phillip, who shrugged.

"I mean, it's pretty obvious that you're scared," he said, going over to grab the last trash bag and the laundry basket. Zeke watched him with a trepidation that Phillip was pleased to see in his eyes. "Everyone knows it, Zee. You're worried about us. First Lou's murder, then Mary-Anne's suffocation, and the explosion in the basement? That's a lot to take in at once. Especially when you're responsible."

"I…" Zeke trailed off as Phillip opened the door and walked out. He hurried to catch up, carefully closing and locking the door behind himself. Andrew would let them in if he had to. Preferably he and Phillip would leave the poor man alone. He did not want to answer Phillip, but the mechanic went on as they stopped by the trash receptacle, saying; "You've always been pretty paranoid and anxious, and I'm sure none of those factors helped."

"I don't think it need be remarked upon," Ezekiel quietly said, hoping to end the conversation there. Phillip shrugged, dismissing his discontent, and replied, "It's all true, though."

Ezekiel, frustrated, returned to silence. They went to the laundry building and loaded in Andrew's stuff, Phillip tempted to shove Zeke headfirst into the machine and slam the lid down until his spine would snap. Clearly, clearly, he was trying to avoid owning up to his responsibility. It was his fault that Phillip had to kill Lou and Yunus, why he almost got rid of Mary-Anne too quick. After all, Ezekiel was in charge of the whole facility. He was the reason why Andrew had met any of them at all. That was why he was avoiding the conversation. As Phillip sprinkled in the detergent, he felt the soot that stained his hands flake off and fall in as well, confirming to him that he was on the right path at last. Unfortunate that it had taken so very long, but at least now he was assured. Phillip gave a sigh, relaxing. He and Zeke left back towards Andrew's apartment, and Zeke finally spoke.

"I was hoping that we could leave Andrew alone, now," he said, voice wavering. Phillip gave him a disapproving deadpan look, making him shirk back. "Really, the man's been through enough… can I just walk you home?"

"Who'd watch your back, then?" Phillip asked lowly, shaking his head. "It's best if you and I go in and get a ride. Maybe the twins just picked up the girls from the hospital."

"I don't think-"

Phillip overrode Zeke by knocking on Andrew's door. The tall man's beak clicked shut, hiding his rapidly growing displeasure for the sake of the man on the other side of the door. Andrew let them in with a smile and tears in his eyes.

"I guess my place is good enough for guests now," he told them, and then reached to hug them both. "Thank you guys, so much. It means a lot to me...."

In the embrace, Phillip felt a little bit of the rage quash down, seeping into a simmer. Yet the fact that Ezekiel was right beside him snapped back at the temptation to take in Andrew, holding Phillip up against an uncomfortable wall. He tried to focus on Andrew's soothing scent, but Zeke's cherry-like scent kept interfering with that. Therefore, Phillip was happy that the hug was brief.

Once inside, Phillip called Mary-Anne's TIN - confirming that the twins were in fact there. Satisfied, he requested that they pick them up later as well. Zeke had excused himself back to the kitchen to cook. Phillip enjoyed his time alone with Andrew. Even if Zeke was right there.

They ate together, and eventually Maxwell's airide revved outside. Phillip rose to leave, dismayed when Zeke made no move to go.

"I'm going to stay and talk with Andrew," he remarked, avoiding meeting Phillip's eye. The mechanic felt cold rage trickle into his heart drowning out any positive emotion that could have come from their meal. Zeke was ruining everything. "I've been meaning to for a while now. So, please, excuse us."

Phillip flashed a smile, each tooth coated in malice and venom.

"Oh, I understand," he cheerfully stated, though his entire body felt cold. "But I thought you said earlier that you wanted to leave Andrew alone."

"No, Phillip, it's fine," Andrew attempted to placate him. He put a hand on his arm, almost startled by the tension he felt in the man's flesh. "Really, Phillip. I wanted to talk to Zeke, too."

"And why can't it wait for tomorrow, at work?" Phillip pressured - quite certain that his suspicion was becoming evident, but he truly did not want Zeke alone with Andrew. He did not trust him - after all, it was his fault. He orchestrated the whole thing, poisoned Phillip against Lou, and had Mary-Anne working with Yunus when he had to get rid of his witnessing. Yes, Zeke must have known about Phillip's unconditional love for Andrew, and instigated him to do everything Phillip was forced to do. Andrew and Ezekiel exchanged a glance, another beep from the waiting hovercraft outside bringing them back to the present. Phillip did not like the look they shared. It was too… intimate. He tapped his foot. "Well?"

"It's private," Andrew softly said. Ezekiel gave a slight, almost imperceptible nod of agreement.

"I understand," Phillip happily stated, because, at last, he did comprehend. His mind ticked away with his plan, suspicions confirmed. "See you tomorrow."

It was all their fault.

Together.

5.

This phase of Phillip's work would be far more extensive. Planning and mindfulness was the most important key to his success. Aware at last of the conspiracy against him, Phillip now was not only strategizing his best course of action, but also his revenge.

Andrew had been the reason, and Ezekiel was fully aware of that the entire time.

Therefore, they would recompense Phillip ounce for ounce. He would ensure it.

Phillip recognized that, unfortunately, suspicion against him was at a record high. The chariness with which Ezekiel had watched him all but confirmed it - suspecting that Phillip had finally caught on to the conjurer's scheming, which he had. Phillip had to admit, the man had played a good game, but the jig was up. Zeke would be unable to avoid the consequences of his actions any longer. Andy would pay for leading Phillip on, for being the delicious bait.

The coming weeks had seen a drastic change in the mechanic's behaviors. He was happier, now that he had been enlightened, and assured of his new path to obtaining his needs. Nothing would get in his way. Phillip was certain of it, and that confidence bled into the various aspects of his daily work and activities. His upped morale spread to other workers (namely other technicians, as they were most frequently in contact with the mechanic; but that too transferred to the arboretum in a ripple effect) and the grim atmosphere gradually eased and lightened. Mary-Anne's return aided with that, as well, and Phillip made sure to observe her carefully to satisfy himself as to the fact that he did not need to finish his earlier job. As of yet, she had given him no reason to consider it, so Phillip was content with allowing her to go about unhindered for the time being. After all, his watch was currently fixated onto Andrew (as usual) and Zeke (newly).

Admiring the man's cunning did not prevent Phillip from fantasizing about getting rid of him. Unlike his previous plans, however, he debated across many more projects and pathways that would result in his goal. He thought about collapsing the ceiling of Ezekiel's office, of breaking the man's car and rigging it to explode, about locking him in one of the maintenance shafts or even his own on-site home and filling it with fumes - the routes and possibilities were endless in his mind. Hit him with a toolbox. Shove him from a water tower. Et cetera.

However, in spite of the quick and sweet deaths that crossed his mind, Phillip knew that he had to ensure that this final motion would be the absolute last, and thus, he wanted to savor it, wanted to ensure that the grand finale had the proper... what term would Lou have used?

Cadence.

Yes. Cadence. The resolution of a glorious piece. That was the perfect word.

Phillip hummed as his mind wandered down the potential pathways. Phillip had to think of something suitable for both Ezekiel and Andrew, which was an interesting little twist to his usual plans. Thanks to Yunus' interference, Phillip learned to ensure that there was no one around at all before commencing his labor. Luckily, he had far more of an excuse to get Andrew and Zeke alone than Mary-Anne, Lou, or anyone else. He hardly even needed to plan that part - all he had to do was request their assistance for labor, which had been a common occurrence in the past. Claiming that he had been working on updating the systems was a perfect reason to get their attention. Even with Ezekiel's suspecting scrutiny, with the right forged paperwork he would be none the wiser. And Andrew, as the reason, surely would play along.

It would be perfect. Phillip would finally be free of Zeke's secret game; and Andrew would be his. Eternally. No longer would Zeke's interference stop them from having their sweet nook carved out. And if Andrew, as Phillip' dismayed, delayed realization hinted, covertly had been cognizant of the clandestine operation, then he would be rid of his subversive hooks that had been lodged into Phillip' flesh.

It was a bittersweet notion. On the one hand, he would miss Andrew - but on the other, Andrew had not been the Andy he liked for a long time. It was all Ezekiel's fault. Lou and Andrew had no business being so close to one another. That had been Zeke's first mistake. His second was underestimating Phillip, assuming that the man would agree to allow himself to be led along like a worm on a string, powerless to the whims of that thin haunter. Phillip certainly proved him wrong, had he not? Eliminated the initial snake with ease, then destroyed one of his lackeys with nary a care and brutal efficiency. Sure, Phillip had failed to quash the siren, but her song was disrupted. It was a shame, a pity, really. Phillip had put in so much thought and effort, too much for it to all go to waste. Andrew was supposed to be his, anyone could see that, and Zeke had purposefully slid Lou forward to test him. Phillip had succeeded, and it was of course to Zeke's dismay. Clearly he wanted the mechanic to fail; hence why he put the janitor's closet beside the musician's office. It made perfect sense.

If Ezekiel could not see Phillip' actions as positive, it was his loss. If Andrew chose to blind himself as to the great goods Phillip had accomplished, then he would no longer see at all. It was all in all a very simple solution.

The only issue was its execution.

It had to be bold, precise, and admirable. It had to test Phillip, Andrew, and Zeke all at once. Phillip was certain that he could manage such a feat, but the only question was how Phillip wanted to do it. What would truly make his mark, emblazon it into the stratosphere for all to understand that he vanquished the vile spellcaster? How could he accurately define his findings and make everyone understand that his actions, as dismal and horrific as they may appear, were justified and necessary?

Phillip thought about it for weeks, his head swirling with images of the maliciousness hidden in Zeke's eye and the sweet temptation of Andrew. The more Phillip watched the pair, the more he recognized their conniving, their scheming. It broke his heart, it really did, especially because he did adore Andrew still. Even if he was a shadow of the man he used to be.

But there's the catch. The filthy, stinking little catch.

Ever since Ezekiel and Andrew had their little tête-à-tête, Andrew had slowly been returning to himself. Smiling more often, landing his jokes, color returning to his aura. Whatever he and Zeke had discussed made him brighter again.

It infuriated Phillip, fire of rage sparking in his heart and burning all the positive emotions to ash.

Andrew had to have been in on it, the whole damn time.

Zeke must have told him that the game was up.

They absolutely were conspiring against Phillip even as they smiled at him.

He smiled back with sharp jowls, eagerly ready to gnash his teeth through their duplicitous throats.

Another change was that Andrew had begun interacting with him more, again, which made Phillip feel conflicted for a number of reasons. For one, it felt cruel, to taunt and tease and entangle Phillip in less than savory actions, and then come by and ask how he was doing. On the other hand, Phillip could almost feel his mouth water with the umami idea that Andrew was coming around to see reason. That surely was tempting, but Phillip had to keep his head on straight, even if Andrew's smile made him want to fight a thousand demons to keep it on his face. Though, there was the fact that with the correctly chosen method, Phillip would be able to keep that smile forever. And what a pleasant idea that was.

Phillip knew he had to figure out a way to attain all his goals at once.

While repairing a pipe with no small measure of frustration, the perfect plan had come to him - at least the flash of an image before his hands, a thrashing Zeke weighted down beneath all the water in the treatment plant. Phillip slowed his work as the mental image faded, quite aware that he had suddenly been struck with divine inspiration, as Lou would have posed it. Perhaps he should have spent a touch more time with the chemist before eliminating the problem, as he did have some rather quaint terms that Phillip was starting to enjoy. Or maybe they had been Phillip's terms that the chemical analyzing thief had stolen. Not that such a difference particularly mattered in this situation, not at all anymore.

No, it did not matter. He raised a cup to the dead man regardless, as he had started him onto the path to fulfill his dreams.

Just one more step.

The pipe that Mary-Anne and Andrew had discussed did in fact exist, and Phillip knew precisely where it was. He also knew that while he could handle it by himself, he had every right to request the groundskeep's assistance in taking care of the problem. All he had to do was ensure that Zeke was the one to sign off on it, as otherwise Andrew was liable to push off the job. That aspect, however, only would lend to Phillip having an

281

easier time with his plan's execution. All he had to do was get Ezekiel to look at the problematic pipe with him, and then request Andrew's attendance.

This time, though, Phillip knew that he had to ensure that there would be no one around to ruin his orchestration. His skin still flashed cold at remembering Mary-Anne's fingers twitching, the nervous idea that perhaps she suspected his involvement in her near death experience – but thus far, there had been no accusations leveled in Phillip's direction. That certainly eased the flaring nerves. In spite of that, Zeke did regard Phillip with trepidation, which could frustrate his goals. Therefore, he had to pick the time, day, and urgency with absolute precision.

He knew that Zeke was always on site; the law of The Three required him to be. Andrew would be available on call, and oftentimes worked Saturdays instead of Monday, taking advantage of the empty facility to clean in peace. Therefore, Saturday would be a perfect day to enact his plan. He quickly began preparing the rest of it, leaving useful items where they belonged – ordering a replacement pipe with Mary-Anne, faking repairs to the damaged one, a rope in his trunk, and a wire in the main chemical treatment room. Within a week, everything was in place and ready to mobilize at Phillip's whim. All he had to do was wait.

On his latest trip to the depot, he had sent a notice to himself with the company's official letterhead. It remarked that one of the pipes recently sent to the facility – the one that Phillip used to fake the repair – was found to be defective and needed to be replaced immediately. Of course, he never actually installed that pipe. It was sitting in the trunk of his car, waiting for when the moment was right.

He waited until Saturday to report it.

Phillip's arm seemed like it was burning under his TIN as he waited for Zeke to answer. Knowing the lanky bastard, he was definitely up and scurrying about the water plant, getting random work done in the downtime. Did he ever take a break? It only lent to Phillip' hunch of his fiddling with magicks. Who else would have so much energy? Maybe he was sucking it out of the souls of the facility's workers.

The call was answered.

"Phil, nice to hear from you," was the cautiously cheerful response, melodic and yet nervous. "How can I help you?"

"Hi, Zee. You won't be feeling that in a second," the mechanic cut to the chase. "I just got a bad warning issue from our plumbing supplier. It's urgent."

"Oh…?" Zeke sounded taken aback, wary. "What kind of bad news?"

"One of the pipes, the one I just installed?" Phillip prefaced. Zeke gave a hum acknowledging he knew which Phillip was referring to. "Yeah, it's got a recall on it. There's osmium impurities."

Ezekiel groaned. Phillip could just picture him rubbing his forehead; or attempting to while trying to wake from a hard blow. Soon, soon. He would get everything he wanted soon. He would be free from Ezekiel and Andrew's evil influence, and they would be extracted from this world. Such a shame, at least for Andrew. Such a pretty face with such a dark heart. He shook his head, focusing on the task at hand.

"Don't worry, though," Phillip smoothly reassured his boss. "I'll be coming in today to take care of it. I have a spare pipe on hand."

"That… that would be great, Phillip," Zeke said with some marked relief. "But, uh, are you sure you want to do this on your day off?"

"Yes, it's important enough to knock it off as soon as possible," Phillip asserted. "Just one thing, though."

"Yes…?" Zeke asked, slow and clearly uncertain of Phillip's goals. Good thing he had prepared this so far in advance. There would be ample proof of everything he was attempting to achieve. "What do you need?"

"Probably some extra hands. I know you've got six, but it's a big section. Is Andrew in?" Phillip asked. Zeke hesitated, and then Phillip pressured. "We could really use his help here. It's one of the arterial pipes."

"I'm not sure," Zeke quietly replied, sounding a touch distant. "He might be."

"Well, see if he can come in," Phillip casually said, but he felt the urge to throttle Zeke spike up. "It can be tricky, you know."

"Right," Ezekiel murmured. "I suppose I'll see you shortly?"

"Yep," Phillip nodded, even though Zeke could not see him. "It's the pipe in the closet nearest the core cleaner."

"Got it," Zeke acknowledged. "Okay. I'll be here."

"Adios," Phillip hung up with a smile, exhaling. Well, that was easier than he expected it to be. Zeke hardly put up a fight. He clipped on the tool belt he swiped from Chester, and nearly skipped out of the house with brimming excitement, his mood skyrocketing. His plan was perfect, and with everything falling into place beautifully, he could not help but be giddy. He hummed one of Lou's old tunes as he drove up to the facility, pausing in the airide to prepare a kerchief and tucking it in his pocket. Then, he pulled out his Trojan pipe, using the rope to make a makeshift handle for easier carrying. To knock, he kicked the door a few times and waited for Zeke to let him into the arterial sector. Phillip smiled up at him once he did, adjusting his hold on the pipe to bring it into the silo. "Hey. Glad you're here."

"I appreciate you coming in on your day off," Ezekiel smiled himself, though it was slightly uneven. He blinked, as though surprised by something, and commented on it before turning back to the studio. "That's a sweet cologne you're wearing. Let's get to it?"

"Thanks. Let's get to it."

Zeke let Phillip guide him to the correct room, which Phillip was pleased to see had already been opened and cleared. At least Zeke understood what it would mean to change out one of the pipes; there were rags and sheets at the ready, as well as a notch valve they could add onto the gauge. Phillip nodded appreciatively of the tall man's efforts, setting down the pipe to hand Zeke the note he sent to himself. He watched as Zeke's countenance shifted with a resigned displeasure, much to his satisfaction. Taking off his dress shirt, he reached for the walkie talkie on his belt.

"Andrew? Looks like we're going to need you," Ezekiel stated quite plainly into the device, and nearly immediately received an affirmation and confirmation; unknowingly making Phillip's heart soar. Everything was going precisely to plan. He and Zeke worked to prepare the area for the exchange, and Phillip quietly pulled a monkey wrench from Chester's tool belt while Zeke was in the far end of the room, unwittingly cornering himself. In a bit of bad timing for Phillip, Zeke looked at him, likely to ask a question, and went pale – maybe he understood that his game was up; comprehending Phillip's designs too late. They both knew well enough that the tool would not be needed until much later, though Zeke probably could read Phillip's intentions well enough in his face. All six of Zeke's wings rose in trembling supplication, and in a very quiet voice said, "Phillip...?"

"Don't worry about it," Phillip falsely soothed him, smiling sharply, feeling how wide his eyes were in his own skull. Unlike Lou or Mary-Anne, this hunt had a sudden thrill – his intended target well aware of his plan. The horror in Ezekiel's expression was addictively palpable. Lightning quick, his hand shot to his walkie, but Phillip anticipated the move and lashed out, the wrench connecting to Zeke's hand with a satisfying crunch – possibly breaking his TIN at the same time. A single beep emanated from the mobile device as it clattered to the ground, and Phillip kicked it away as he stepped in with the swinging motion. Following through with his momentum, Phillip struck the cornered Zeke across the face. He crashed against the wall and sank down with an empty groan. Lights out. Hearing footsteps approach, he quickly went in their direction, coming across the groundskeeper. Stunned by Phillip's sudden appearance, he could hardly wave before Phillip cut him off. "Andrew! I need your help, quick! Zeke passed out!"

"Again?" Andrew's eyes widened with worry, darting off towards the site. Ah ha! So he was well aware of Ezekiel's inner workings. Perhaps the lanky man was prone to fainting due to his and Andrew's witchcrafts. It would connect nicely. Luckily for the pretty janitor, Phillip had no plans to knock him upside the head. He pulled out the prepared kerchief from his pocket and stole up behind the man in a run, as though hastening to help. Andrew was kneeling next to Ezekiel and gently touching under his beak. He seemed concerned and confused, and voiced as much in a murmur. "Huh, this doesn't seem like a blackout...." Phillip came closer, the moist fabric in his hand, as Andrew shook Zeke's shoulder. "Zee? Zeke, buddy, you okay?"

"He's fine," Phillip peacefully told him, smiling as he putting a hand on his shoulder. Immediately after Andrew moved to stand and face the mechanic, Phillip wrapped that arm around Andrew's neck, bringing the chloroform soaked kerchief over his nose and mouth. Instantly alarmed, Andrew valiantly struggled, but Phillip had the upper hand, the element of surprise, and the rage to hold out for the three or so minutes it took for the other to slowly flail and fall unconscious. He held the drug there for a few moments more, until Andrew had gone entirely limp. Letting out a heavy sigh, Phillip grinned. "And you'll be fine, too. You'll be just fine...."

He took the fabric and unfolded it, going over to Ezekiel and pulling it around his beak, gagging the bastard tightly by making a muzzle. Phillip despised the way that his lips seemed to curl into a smile from the strain. Pulling the rope off the pipe, Phillip bound an end around Zeke's many wrists, then tightly tied that knot to his ankles. Then he cut it, moving on to Andrew. He bound him in a much less painful way, simply tying his hands together, and a loose loop between each leg to prevent him from having a wide range of motion. Then he picked Andrew up, slinging him over his shoulder as he brought him to the treatment room. He carried him one armed down the ladder to the main output and then brought him to the chains that helped keep the device from crumpling or ripping off the floor. With the remaining rope, he bound him to the side of the machine, taking that end of the rope with him. He had knotted it in such a way that he could detach it from the pipework while leaving the bindings intact.

Then, he went back up to fetch Ezekiel, tying the end of the rope next to the control board for ease of access along the way. He was much less gentle with the tall man, debating if he would just drop him down the ladder – though he decided to use the maintenance lift instead. Zeke groaned, muffled by the kerchief's fabric, as Phillip dragged him to rest in the test area of the chemical machine rather roughly. Ezekiel's eyelids flickered, struggling to rise through the chemicals on his tongue and the pain in his body. Andrew, too, was beginning to stir. Phillip smiled. He made a loop of wire, slipping it into the mesh in the throat of the machine, unraveling it and tying the other end to the back of Zeke's gag.

Phillip walked to and then up the ladder, standing at the balcony and inspecting over his handiwork with a satisfied eye. Then, he slowly turned on the machine, taking out a matchbox from his pocket and setting it on the control dial. Soon, there was a steady drip going down the back of Zeke's neck, guided by the wire. The man shivered in his daze, eyes fluttering again for a moment. The noise and vibration seemed to rouse Andrew, the janitor giving a heavy groan, face scrunching up with discomfort. Phillip could only beam.

"Goooooooooood morning, gentlemen!" he boomed. Andrew jolted awake with a gasp, and Ezekiel's head slowly rose, full body swaying somewhat. While he seemed to have difficulty focusing, blinking rapidly and with a furrowed brow; Andrew's eyes snapped immediately to Phillip, jaw dropping open. What an amazing actor. Phillip fought a sharp smile, and lost, feeling it spread wickedly over his face. Finally, he would have his revenge. "Hello, Andrew-boo, hi there, Zeke-beak! Nice to see you're finally awake!"

"Phil? What's going on?" Andrew gawked, pretending oh-so sweetly, with such false alarm, that he had no idea what was happening. He tugged with a slight panic on the rope, trying to step forward and tripping, slung back to the machine. With the motion, he caught glimpse of Zeke, whose eyes flicked between Phillip and Andrew with terror-cold acidic water flowing down his back like the sweat of the condemned. Fear set in even more intensely as Andrew barely managed to right himself. "Phillip Putnum, answer me! What the hell is going on!?"

"Can't you tell, little spellcaster?" Phillip teased, turning the knob that sped up the flow of water. Ezekiel's white undershirt slowly turned more and more grey with the fluid, his pants soaking it as well. "I'm testing a witch and his apprentice!"

"Wha- Phillip, what the hell does that mean!?" Andrew whined, confused and afraid. "Testing for a witch? Zeke's not a witch! I'm not a- a- a spellcaster! I'm a maintenance man!"

"Well, if that's true, then you'll drown," Phillip calmly said, exponentially raising the drip to a steady stream. Ezekiel cried out in his throat with alarm, trying to yank forward and failing due to the wire. He wriggled, but the rope gave no leeway for his shifting. Phillip watched his struggles with vague amusement. His gaze drifted to the horrified groundskeeper, melting a touch at his sweetly frightened expression. "Of course, Andrew, you can apologize for what you've done, and I might have it in my heart to forgive you... all of this was for you. Andrew, you're the reason for it all."

"What do you mean!?" Andrew nearly screamed, unable to keep from yelling. Zeke yanked on the rope and wire, chemically-treated water flowing heavily over his shoulders. "Phillip, please- please stop this!"

"The only person who can stop this is you," Phillip shrugged, casually leaning on the railing and observing with approval. The liquid was pouring out of the machine at a remarkable rate, already coating the room in a few inches of the viscous liquid. Ezekiel would spasm in fits of coughing every now and again, which was quite pleasing to watch. "Just admit you did things that were bad, dear, and then it'll all go away. Wouldn't that be nice? We can finally be together, without anyone in the way, without any insidious sneaking about and lying."

"You're crazy!" Andrew shouted, yanking on the rope once again. Ezekiel made a noise of warning or demand, Phillip could not tell, but Andrew understood him perfectly and went slack. His teeth were grit together and sweat dripped down his forehead, as though he were attempting very hard to fight off Ezekiel's malicious influence. Another weak tug, and he sank against the metal. After some labored breathing, Andrew raised his head with splotched cheeks, looking up into Phillip' eyes. He had to fight a shudder and the urge to drop his gaze. "I'm not a bad person, Phillip. Never one to be a liar, either. Zeke's also not a bad guy, Phil... please, stop."

"Not a bad guy?" Phillip grinned broadly, sharp and toothy. "Don't make me laugh! That conniving witch forced Mary-Anne to almost lose her life, and Yunus and Lou to lose

287

theirs! He's the one that constructed the entire elaborate scene and pushed it to come into reality!"

"Zeke did nothing of the sort!" Andrew barked, firmly standing his ground – even as Ezekiel seemed to protest the words he spoke, admitting his guilt, no doubt, or he could have been doubling down on his innocence. Phillip, however, knew the truth all too well, and did not need to hear Ezekiel's pitiful excuses. "I know him! Zeke's more likely to cut off his own hand than even hit someone, let alone break their face with a fucking brick!"

"Lou was pushed onto you!" Phillip roared. Andrew jolted, staring with a jaw clicking quietly open, though no words came out. "Lou was never meant to be with you, and Zeke put your space right next to him! Put you both in a private little nook, he did, and said nothing about your blatant indiscretions! I'd bet that he even encouraged it, didn't he? Put you both under an enchantment, a false happiness, stealing you away from me! You're the reason this all happened, Andrew! It's all because of you!"

"Phillip, I…" Andrew stared at him, but there was something in his eye that made Phillip incredibly incensed. There was pity and loathing in his eyes, each fighting to come to the top. Neither, however, were what Phillip wanted to see. He had hoped that Andrew would suddenly understand, that the light would bless him, but no. Darkness still enveloped him. Rage and hatred against Ezekiel swelled within Phillip. "Please don't be saying what I think you mean-"

"One more thing, Andy, my dear," Phillip cut him off in a hiss, pulling out the matches from the box. Andrew and Ezekiel's eyes both widened at the exact same time (more proof of their connection) in absolute horror, and he relished in it. At long last, after many agonizing weeks and months, they would get their just deserts and burn. "I'm not crazy. You burn a witch to get rid of it."

Phillip struck the match even as Andrew screamed and begged for him to stop, making Phillip only smile. Finally, the cold throughout his body would be swept away in the sweet heat. Not that Phillip would stay and burn with the witches, no, but the action alone would unfreeze the chill from his wrists. Andrew, when he realized that his pretend pleading and false reasoning was futile, cursed at him, howled about Lou, about Yunus, and Mary-Anne. He demanded explanations, yanked wildly on the ropes, and swore up and down that Phillip would pay.

"See you in Hell, Andrew," Phillip merely smiled, preparing to toss forward the ignited match. "I'd say the same to you, Ezekiel, but I don't rightly know where you'd end up. Probably somewhere very deep and dark, so enjoy the light while it lasts."

With that, Phillip flicked away the fire. It sailed gracefully through the suddenly silent air, all three watching it spin in its inevitable downwards trajectory. It landed without a sound, nearly directly in front of Ezekiel.

The instant conflagration was impressive.

It flared up with a roaring cackle, a violent and destructive force ripping across the entire floor and lapping up the walls. Phillip jerked back, but only for a moment, leaning forward toward the heat with a triumphant laugh, even as Andrew shrieked. Ezekiel thrashed in a beautiful ball of flame and heat.

Phillip's heart and joy stopped quickly, though, as the quiet hiss of sprinklers began.

Right.

Ezekiel had upgraded the entire facility and its security.

Phillip's smile remained plastered on his face as he worked to come up with a new plan. Around them, steam rose up, the chemically treated cooling water fighting valiantly to overcome the fuming flare that fed on the other, burning water. Phillip knew, however, that it would only be a matter of time, and sure enough, soon there were only flames licking the walls in retreat. The sprinkler's shushing was soothing to the pair beneath the mechanic, Andrew sighing with relief and Ezekiel moaning with the remnants of his pain – but free of the fire that had attempted to devour him.

Witch.

Even now, he was five steps ahead of the mechanic. There was nothing he could do. He could only watch as Zeke looked towards Andrew, beseeching him with his doe eyes. Andrew seemed to hesitate as he perhaps tried to fight off Ezekiel's influence, though he dropped the gaze and sank against the machine with exhaustion. Giving in.

A fiery, futile rage poured into Phillip' heart, reigniting what was doused by the sprinklers. Yet he calmed himself with a deep inhale, and exhale. The pair was still in his power, even if they had slipped through is initial cage – the pit would only drag them in deeper.

Avoiding the quick consumption of a fiery death?

The slow suffocation of drowning would easily answer instead.

With a smile so cruel it could only be categorized as a snarl, Phillip cranked up the ink machine's output to the maximum. Ezekiel nearly buckled under the weight cascading onto his shoulders and back. Andrew screamed, furiously fighting the bindings once again. Water began to swell up around them, quickly rising past Andrew's ankles up to his knees, and swiftly climbing higher up his legs. Zeke was bent forward in his desperation to keep breathing, spasming with random fits of coughing and shuddering. As the chemical laden waters gradually reached Andy's waist, the man suddenly collapsed, with painful tears tracking down his burned face.

"Phillip, I- I'm sorry," Andy said at last – finally seeming to break free of Ezekiel's bindings. "You're right, I was, I was bad... I didn't mean to do... any of it... please, Phillip, I'm scared."

"I'll protect you, Andrew, don't worry," Phillip crooned, heart feeling much much lighter; as if all the chemicals pouring from the machine was the cold within his heart finally coming loose. "Just promise you'll never betray me again, and that you'll always be by my side...."

"I promise, I promise!" Andy begged, the ink up to his chest. "I'm sorry, I'll be good, get me out please Phillip-"

With a flick of his wrist, Phillip undid the upper knot holding Andy to the machine. Stumbling forward, Phillip guided him towards the service lift, which was still working by way of a miracle – or it was hexed to, thanks to Zeke. The frigid semi-treated water had risen up to his chest by the time he was on the platform, shivering and soaked with the heavy liquid.

"Oh, Andy...!" Phillip beamed at him, voice soft and insinuating beneath the pounding splashing of acid water. He opened his arms to him as he freed his raw wrists from the bindings. Feeling warm again; for the first time in a long time. "I'm so glad you've finally come to your senses and free from Zeke! You were the reason for everything, and I'm so happy that it's all working out now."

"Yeah, me too," Andy mumbled, leaning in to the hug. Phillip rested against the barrier, smelling Andy's shampoo through the sharp, dry scent of acid wafting around them. Everything was finally as it should be. "Me too, Phil."

The sudden force on Phillip's shoulders shocked him for a moment, and then another push sent him tumbling back over the banister. He flailed, grabbing onto one of the bars of the wooden barrier. Not that it mattered, though, as a sudden crack to his shoulder put everything in slow motion.

Phillip saw Andrew staring at him, wrench in hand, looking at him with fear, pity, and hate.

His hand, suddenly struck by the intense pain up his arm, let go of the railing.

Phillip landed with a splash into the dark, tainted water, thrashing in agony. His arm, spasming, involuntarily curled up to his stomach, and he could feel where it had been broken.

Phillip could hear Andrew working quickly, the flow of water suddenly cut, the hiss and curse of someone sliding down a ladder, the splashing run to a man's side. To Ezekiel's side.

Not his.

"Zeke, Ezekiel, buddy, are you okay?" Andrew was asking desperately as Phillip gingerly pushed himself up with his non-broken arm. The lanky bastard was gasping in air, the gag removed from his foul mouth, spluttering out the embittered waters of the Sota. Andrew gently, oh so very gently, helped the witch to his unsteady feet. "Come on, Zee, let's get you out of here...."

"Not so fast," Phillip growled, staggering to his feet. Diluted acid dripped down his body, that and the broken arm lending to an even more hellishly monstrous appearance of the crazed mechanic, like a strange, twisted swamp beast. The hate he had seen in Andrew's eyes only increased the feverous desire to have that snake crushed dead, and his need to carry out the necessary duty of beheading its charmer. "Tricked me for the last time, you did...."

Andrew's tight grip on the wrench shifted, bringing attention to the weapon. He and Ezekiel warily circled around towards the ladder, though they hesitated when they reached it. Andrew, though, shoved Ezekiel to it, holding the wrench like a bat.

"Go on up, Zeke, I'll be right behind you," Andy promised, not taking his eyes off of Phillip. After a moment more of hesitation, Zeke nodded, and painfully pulled himself up the ladder, his acid burned hands catching painfully on the bumpy ladder spokes. "Good... I'll be right there...."

The acid ridden water, even though it was steadily draining, was up to Andrew and Phillip' stomachs, and it severely hindered their movements, tingling at their skin. As Andrew's hand pressed to the ladder, Phillip charged at him with an inhuman roar. However, he did not get far, as an entire crate of testing supplies suddenly landed between himself and Phillip, the force of displacement shoving him back and stunning him, allowing the other to rush up the ladder. Phillip, recovering from the shock, grabbed at his ankles, but a well aimed kick pushed him back. Freed from Phillip's grasp Andrew scrambled up the rest of the way one handed, unwilling to let go of his defense, and Zeke pulled him up once he was close enough.

Phillip ran after them, but slammed into a metal grate.

When had Ezekiel installed this?

He yelled in rage and futile hate, clawing at the metal and driving against it. Eventually, Phillip's energy and strength gave up, sinking against the metal grating. He could hear sirens reverberating through the pipes, approaching in the distance. The draining acid appeared soothing and inviting.

Footsteps.

"Phillip?"

Andrew's voice. Andy's sweet, insidious voice.

"What?" Phillip hoarsely croaked, betrayed to his very core. "What more do you want from me?"

"I never wanted anything from you, Phillip. I can't forgive you," Andrew said quietly. "Probably won't ever. But I hope you'll get the, uh, help, that you obviously need."

Silence for a long moment. Phillip's hands clenched at the banister, face contorted with rage.

"I think about Lou every day." Andrew whispered, swallowing hard. "And Yunus. I'll never forgive you for them. Goodbye, Phillip."

Phillip listened with despair as Andy's footsteps retreated.

A scream bubbled from his throat.

Everything was for nothing;
and it was all his fault.

Mirrored Joy

7.14.2025

The mirror was like an addiction.

At least, Nora likened it to one, and her opinion on the matter was rather a strong one. She thus avoided it with the utmost care and caution - potentially because she, like her parents, was well aware at this point that most of the worlds that flicked by showed horrific circumstances and unpleasant realities. Most other individuals were fascinated by the device, though oftentimes these were the people who found that their alternate realities were just as comfortable as the one that they were in, and thus were satisfied both with their world and the ones beyond theirs.

Her spouse, Ash, however, knew that many of the worlds outside of their current one were less than ideal, yet many of them held happy ends and pleasant factors which inclined them to keep looking. When they received a notification on their phone letting them know that their father would be coming to visit at the next stop, Ash quickly wracked through their brain in an attempt to figure out what to do - the kids were going to be going out with Nora and June the next day to a water park, so Ash would have at least a full day to entertain their father outside of the usual 'seeing the kids and grandkids' event that typically occurred at the traveling oddities show.

Thus the mirror.

Their father, Richmond, was aware of it, and while most of the other worlds saddened him (much for the same reasons that they upset Nora and her family) he still would watch the hazy images of his other self flickering by with passive interest. Ash wondered if he watched out of pity for the other Richmonds in the cosmos, or because it made him feel better about his own self - a thought that Ash would always banish for its lack of kindness towards their father. They heard Nora's voice in their head scold them gently for entertaining it once more; their wife's, "sometimes people have become cold, because it is hard to slice a frozen shell" passing through their mind. In a way, the mirror certainly helped Ash understand their father more, as being able to see some of the things that their father could have lived through (and could not bear to say aloud) gave them a distinct insight.

And, of course, the other worlds could be rather entertaining to watch, some of them funnier than the best romcoms, and some more fantastical than the entire fantasy genre.

Hence why Ash and Richmond were seated now on the couch of the Waiting Room (as Nora designated it), gazing into the mirror, framed by its blood red velvet curtains. A small bowl of snacks was nestled between father and child, and it was difficult to tell which had placed it there to avoid contact with the other. The dreamlike quality of the mirror would shift every now and then and provide a glimmer into another world, though one could be summoned on demand, such as the one that Ash just pulled up, after a good bit of time simply drifting around according to the mirror's whims.

"Can we see Toyland?" Ash had asked the mirror, and smiled as it wavered and shifted scenes, now displaying a small shop. Various toys of size and shape roamed about happily, before the mirror's gaze focused on the little bat plushie that was Ash. The human Ash then smiled at Richmond, who seemed vaguely intrigued by the toyshop in which these living toys resided, watching that world play out with quiet thought and consideration. "I like this world," Ash sheepishly commented, earning their father's gaze. A trickle of embarrassment crept along their cheeks, and they cleared their throat before continuing. "I think it's a very, uh, tranquil little slice of life."

"I can see why you like it," Richmond replied, returning his eyes to the wonderful little world, and Ash could not help but feel as though it was a swipe at their personality. Even trying to summon Nora's reassurances failed them here, and they sank into the couch. They forced themself to look back at the mirror, pointedly ignoring the burning in their face and the heavy pound of their heart. They continued to watch in silence, and little did Ash know, but an intense nervousness was building into Richmond's heart. He knew his child - knew them well - and yet could never manage to break through and make a connection to them. How could he address the shame and mortification that came with knowing that his only beloved child would rather turn to a notorious, dangerous loan shark instead of their own wealthy father? How could he gently bring up their relationship with Nora, give it his blessing, when Ash had only seen Richmond's latent fears and distrust surrounding the young lender? How could he even begin to explain to his gentle, green child about the grim upbringing that he endured that brought about his own stifled personality? Ash was so... robust and open. Rich Sr. made sure that Richmond would certainly not be. He gave a start, trying to free himself of his own mind and swirling thoughts. Ash looked at him with a flicker of concern, and Richmond gave them a wry smile, trying to think of something to say. He glanced back at the mirror, a thought gently passing through his mind. "I like the world where I'm alive, and not possessed or haunted or tormented by my father, dead or alive."

"Huh," Ash, mildly stunned, said, looking back at the mirror, brow scrunching as they tried to think back to what Richmond could be referring to. After a moment, they gave up, and made themself ask. "Which world is that one?"

Richmond looked at Ash.

Ash looked at Richmond.

It clicked.

"Oh," Ash softly said, looking down at their hands. A frown tugged at the corners of their mouth, and Richmond felt like kicking himself. Why the hell did he say something so negative? Why ruin his kid's apparently happy mood for no good reason? He covered his eyes with a hand, before a glimmering movement struck him.

The mirror shifted once again.

Father and child watched with trepidation as the world changed, a quiet tink tink tink taking over the echoey, water barrel audio that emanated from the mirror's smooth surface.

They saw a flash of a car, a burst of red. A hand reaching out to a smaller one, and then another small hand reaching out and grasping. Scenes of flowers and echoing childhood laughter, two children playing in a field, joined by another pair. A blur of movement, a spike of red, a flashlight silhouetting two small figures under a blanket in a sick room, animatedly talking. A concert, and another, and the hum of machinery and flashes of fresh paper. Traps flinging away in a beautiful chain reaction, a kiss, fireworks setting off more snapping, wonderful gears. Laughter, a flash in a cloudy eye that spoke of warm friendship, a man everyone knows.

The quiet rhythm of a several piece drum kit.

Voices at last, the scene solidifying. Ash felt their heart chinch as they recognized flecks of their childhood home. The mirror took them down a corridor Ash had never saw anyone use, and entered a room that, as far as Ash knew, did not exist. Richmond, by the way he stiffened, knew it well.

"No, no," Richmond's strong tones rippled outwards towards the two otherworldly watchers. "Hold your wrist like this, Ashley. You'll make your it ache otherwise."

"Like this?" Ash's softer, brighter voice wafted through. A noise of approval, and then more beats. "This is so fun, Dad! Not as fun as coloring, but still fun."

295

One could hear the giddy smile in Ash's voice. Then they could see it, as the viewpoint of the mirror drifted into the room. Miriam sat in the corner of the room, sitting by a loom as Ash and Richmond sat before the man's piano, watching the pair with amusement. Richmond had an easygoing smile on his face, propped up by his hand under his cheek, elbow resting on the edge of the musical instrument. Richmond, on the couch, sat stock still, staring with something akin to awe and fear. Ash watched, baffled and feeling a soft tugging at the base of their heart, achingly dragging it towards their stomach. The young Ash sitting on the piano bench wore a sparkling tiara that the adult Ash vaguely recognized, and a puffy blue tutu. Richmond's nails flickered with polish as he instructed Ash carefully, a bow nestled on the top of his head moving with each nod of approval.

A watch beeped - Richmond looking down at his wrist. Ash looked up at him as he stood, disappointed that their lesson was to end.

"Don't worry," Richmond assured them. "We'll play again tonight, if you'd like to."

"I would!" Ash nodded happily, excited. "It's been such a good day. I want to learn to play for the big special time! Which means I will practice while you are at your meeting."

"Speaking of," Richmond remarked, glancing at his nails, "Can I take this polish off now, Ash? I'm not sure how appreciated it will be at said meeting."

"You gotta wear it, Dad," Ash solemnly remarked, shaking their head. "You need to wear it for my new little sister. She would want it. It's pretty."

"Ash," Miriam hesitantly said their name, her voice tinged with amusement and joy; even as Richmond stiffened on the couch, a furious, painful chill spreading down his spine. Frustrated and longing tears shone in his eyes. "The baby won't come for a good long while, dear."

"How long?" Ash asked, sounding crestfallen. "Two hours? Three?"

"Five more months, Ashley," Richmond gently corrected, his own happiness underlying his tone. Ash stared at him with shock and horror, then shifted to think about it. "So what's the plan, Ash bash?"

"Well, then we have to buy a lot of nail polish," Ash stated, assured of themself. "To make sure Dad doesn't run out until she comes."

Richmond and Miriam looked at one another, and soft laughter bubbled forward.

Ash was suddenly aware that the couch was trembling. They glanced at their father, whose eyes were glued to the scene with intense longing and pain, shaking from emotion. They could hardly recall a time where their father was so affected barring an instance or two, which their felt fade from their mind.

"Close the curtain, Ashley," Richmond whispered, his voice nothing more than a soft breath. "Cover it. Cover the mirror. Right now."

Ash, stunned, could not move, gawking at their stricken father.

Richmond, close to bursting, mouthed; "Please."

Ash snapped out of it, leaping up and yanking the sound proofing curtains to cut off the visions streaming in from that other world. A hole ached violently in their heart.

They turned around to see Richmond's heel leaving the to the main space of the trailer. Ash stood in a daze, trying to process everything they had witnessed, digesting their father's reaction. Then Ash ran after him, realizing Richmond's devastation. They suddenly felt like they knew their father far more from this singular glimpse into a wonderful world than any of the violent, horrible pasts that he had seen before.

Ash caught up to Richmond within two minutes on his way to the passenger seat, crashing into their father and hugging him tightly from behind. They felt him freeze, quaking in their grasp. A sob escaped him. Ash released him, only to gently urge him into a small side room to properly hug him. There were tears streaming down their father's face, only visible for a moment as Richmond gripped them back into a tight hug.

They rocked together for a long moment, Richmond sobbing his heart out on his child's shoulder. Ash felt immense love for their father slowly replenish their heart.

"You know, Ash," Richmond managed to choke out through his tears, a sad humor in his voice. "I like the Toyworld, too. It's a nice world."

They looked at each other, and burst into laughter tinged with tears.

Wrinkles

8.31.2025

Wrinkles oft symbolize wisdom,
Across the animal kingdom,
You will find brilliance,
In crinkles, not by chance,
Those wedges are surely not dumb.

Look at the nose of our friend hog,
Which stores scents in a catalog.
Then wrinkly elephant,
Altruist sans repent.
Their lined minds free of deep, thick fog.

Wrinkles of elders are not shy,
You will find this is not a lie.
Koalas brains unlined
They care not, you will find.
Thus we should let them go and die.

Acknowledgments

This book has been a journey. There have been those who have come and gone along the path that it has taken me to get to this point. There are, however, some individuals I personally would like to thank.

First and foremost, I would like to extend my appreciation to my family. You may not enjoy this book, or understand it, nor approve it, though I am grateful for your effort. Thank you for putting up with me, my fluctuating emotions, and my 'agendas'. A tiny thank you to my tiny dog. Prince, you may be an idiot, but you are my idiot.

I owe much to Anna – without you, this book would have taken much, much longer than two months to compile and repair. Your editing and proofreading is priceless. Not only have you assisted me with cobbling together this hodgepodge of tales, you have been here for a great deal of these stories creations, witnessing even their original forms and listened to my off-the-wall ramblings that led to their inceptions. Next one's ours! Cheers, and thank you.

Madeline, thank you for your constant encouragement and support. Your gentle commentary, keen eye for improvement, and solid critique has made this book infinitely better. I always look forward to discussing new stories and pathways with you. Your unflagging encouragement despite the black moods that consistently overtake me has made this possible. Thank you for laughing at my terrible jokes and making each day just that bit brighter. Thank you, so much.

Of course, to my readers, new and old alike! If you have come across this book and my work for the first time, thank you for giving me a chance. To my wonderful longstanding readers, thank you for your continued readership. I hope you enjoyed your time in the cosmic ocean.

Finally, baruch HaShem. It's done.

Now, can I please have the energy to do the million other things I have planned?

Thank you!